WEATHER WOMAN

a novel

Cai Emmons

 Red Hen Press | *Pasadena, CA*

Book Design by Hannah Moye and Mark E. Cull

Library of Congress Cataloging-in-Publication Data
Names: Emmons, Cai, author.
Title: Weather woman : a novel / Cai Emmons.
Description: First edition. | Pasadena, CA : Red Hen Press, [2018]
Identifiers: LCCN 2018021770 (print) | LCCN 2018023133 (ebook) | ISBN
   9781597096300 (ebook) | ISBN 159709630X (ebook) | ISBN 9781597096003
   (paperback) | ISBN 1597096008 (paperback)
Subjects: LCSH: Identity (Philosophical concept)—Fiction.
Classification: LCC PS3605.M57 (ebook) | LCC PS3605.M57 W43 2018 (print) |
   DDC 813/.6—dc23
LC record available at https://lccn.loc.gov/2018021770

The National Endowment for the Arts, the Los Angeles County Arts Commission, the Dwight Stuart Youth Fund, the Max Factor Family Foundation, the Pasadena Tournament of Roses Foundation, the Pasadena Arts & Culture Commission and the City of Pasadena Cultural Affairs Division, the City of Los Angeles Department of Cultural Affairs, the Audrey & Sydney Irmas Charitable Foundation, the Kinder Morgan Foundation, the Allergan Foundation, the Riordan Foundation, and the Amazon Literary Partnership partially support Red Hen Press.

First Edition
Published by Red Hen Press
www.redhen.org

WEATHER WOMAN

There are more things in heaven and earth, Horatio,
Than are dreamt of in your philosophy.

—*Hamlet*, Act I, Scene 5

WEATHER WOMAN

PART ONE

Discovery

1

Since she was a child she had understood the earth's oblique murmurings. Her pores, like the braille-reading fingertips of the blind, easily interpreted messages brought from the air. She had thought nothing of it, it was simply the way she was made. But then, a month after she turned thirty, just before the summer solstice, all her senses sharpened, and she and the earth, now co-equals, began to duel and dance. At the time, this appeared to happen without warning, certainly without conscious instruction. But thinking back she believes she may have hastened the change a year earlier, by deciding to move to New Hampshire.

2

Bronwyn sits in a warbling column of late-spring sunlight and tries to laugh along with her longtime mentor, Diane Fenwick. There is every reason to celebrate. Summer is barreling in and soon its milder rhythms will be firmly in place. The term is over. Grades are in. The team's various research projects are trundling along as expected. And today, Diane has declared her regular meeting with the graduate students to be a social occasion and has brought in homemade ginger cake and her signature maple-walnut scones along with a carafe of strong, dark French roast. She is talking about her husband Joe's love of kayaking, how meticulous he is with care of their boats and paddles, how much time he spends cleaning the boats *before* launching them, which seems to her like a waste of time when they're bound to collect sand and seaweed. She reports all this with fond amusement, her plump bosom and gray-flecked black hair trembling with each burst of laughter. There is nothing more joyous than laughing with Diane Fenwick. Her humor is an exuberant salve, her laughter buoyant to the point of giddiness; joining in Bronwyn feels like she's bouncing on a trampoline and recovering the freedom of childhood.

But today Bronwyn can't let go enough to laugh authentically. She knows she's a terrible heel. She has taken a job in New Hampshire as a TV meteorologist, which is far more suited to her talents than being a doctoral student in atmospheric sciences at MIT where, for the past two years, she has been researching the intricacies of cloud formation alongside Diane. She should have broken this news to Diane a month ago when she got the job, but the thought was too terrifying. They have known each other for almost a decade, since they were both at a women's college nearby, Bronwyn a know-nothing undergrad, Diane one of the most admired faculty on campus. It still mystifies Bronwyn that Diane singled her out in that large introductory science class. She was smart, yes, but so painfully shy she never raised her hand, and during rare face-to-face meetings with Diane (Dr. Fenwick to her at that time), she could not control her blushing and was always at an embarrassing loss for words. But Diane was aggressive about telling Bronwyn she was suited for science, and over the next couple of years Bronwyn took three more of her classes. She began to loosen up and Diane began to invite her for dinner at her home, initially an excruciating experience but one Bronwyn came to love—the elegant old house on Brattle Street, the gourmet meals, her easy-to-talk-to husband Joe, a novelist. It was at those dinners that Bronwyn became comfortable calling Diane by her first name. When Diane left for a job at MIT and Bronwyn graduated, it was obvious they would stay in touch, and during the five years after Bronwyn's graduation, when she was waitressing and caring for her dying mother in New Jersey, Diane was true to her word and communicated regularly. She visited Bronwyn after her mother died and helped her clean out the small house, all the while urging her to capitalize on her talent and come to graduate school. Bronwyn isn't sure what kind of strings Diane pulled to get her into MIT, but she is sure some strings must have been pulled.

So how, after all of that belief and encouragement and concrete help, do you simply say: *I'm leaving.*

What Diane doesn't seem to see is that Bronwyn never belonged in graduate school in the first place. She has no business being a scientist, certainly not a research scientist, working at an esteemed institution like MIT, among people as brainy and observant as Diane, people who daily see patterns and aberrations from patterns and make quick connections that lead to hypotheses. Bronwyn knows more about clouds and weather than your run-of-the-mill citizen, but nowhere near enough to be in this sharp-edged, Nobel-aspiring, what-do-you-have-to-say-for-yourself atmosphere. For the last two years she has felt as if she's been standing on the vertiginous edge of a precipice, bare toes clenched, liable to lose her footing at any moment and plunge to the swift, heartless river below.

It is true that Bronwyn has always been a weather lover. As a very young child she was entranced by clouds. She made her first barometer in second grade, had a sizable weather station by the time she was ten. How could you *not* love weather, extreme weather in particular, coming as it does and changing the rules, eliminating the ho-hum routines of life-as-usual, the strictures of school and parental tyranny? When she was a child and extreme weather came in, all bets were off, life became about surviving, and she could escape from her mother's hyper-vigilance for a while and do as she liked. What she liked was watching and feeling the way the wind and rain tiptoed over her skin, altered her heart rate, even changed her brain. She can't think of a single memory from her childhood that is not framed by weather. Certainly the best times she ever had with her mother were when big storms hit. During hurricanes they would go up to the attic of their small New Jersey home and watch the trees whipping back and forth like dervishes, waterfalls of rain smearing the windows so they could hardly see out. Even her mother, Maggie, always fearful, seemed excited at those times, perhaps because she knew the weather wasn't her fault.

Once, when Bronwyn was a teenager, she and her best friend Lanny drove to Atlantic City to witness the hurricane drama, defying Maggie and ignoring public warnings telling people to stay home. The waves had lost their metric regularity and they pummeled the boardwalk like club-wielding Mafiosi. Some even crossed the street and threatened to enter the casinos.

In eighth grade there was a blizzard that took down power lines and shuttered everything for a week. She and Maggie camped out in the living room with blankets and sleeping bags, candles flickering like friendly ghosts on all the surfaces around them. The stove was out so they roasted hotdogs on skewers in the fireplace and ate them, bunless, with ketchup-slathered hands. Maggie was relaxed for a change, unconcerned about the mess. In a crisis, mess was irrelevant. They were human beings making do, dependent on fire for heat and light.

It wasn't just the local emergencies that excited Bronwyn, she followed weather all over the world, checking the daily temperatures in the world's major cities, trying to imagine how arctic temperatures would feel on a face, wondering if she could endure the boiling heat of Riyadh. She thought she would be one of the bold and resilient ones, venturing outside, cracking an instantaneous sweat that would cool her and enable her to forge on as she waved at the people glassed off in air-conditioned high rises.

The twisters excited her too. No one could see them coming or explain why they followed the paths they did. They were anticipated in the Plains States at certain times of year, but once she read that a tornado had hit Wisconsin, uprooting a cheese factory and an elementary school. That was the thing about weather—it had a mind of its own, you couldn't control it, or predict it accurately, how could you help but be fascinated?

"You make me feel like a glutton, Bronwyn," Diane says. "Have some more, please. If you people don't eat, I'll have to take it home, and since Joe isn't around, I'll eat it myself and the consequences of that will not be happy." She squints at Bronwyn. "Are you alright? You're quieter than usual. Quiet is fine, but there's contented quiet and discontented quiet."

Bronwyn sees Jim and Bruce exchanging a glance. The two of them, both graduate students who also work with Diane, have played no small role in making Bronwyn feel out of place. They are younger than Bronwyn, but they've been in the doctoral program longer than she and they love to hold that over her. Conniving and ambitious, they have the tiny brutal eyes of mantis shrimp. A fission of acknowledgment passes between them now, the quick pulsing of electrons, a communication taking an infinitesimal amount of time, barely detectable. They compress away budding smiles. Diane has not seen. She has no idea what happens when she is out of the room, how many ways Bruce and Jim find to torture Bronwyn, concealing their torture in packages that might be read by a stranger as mere playfulness, as wit, as legitimate scientific debate or platonic dialogue. One of their games is coming up with words they can use as nicknames for red-headed

Bronwyn. *Hey, Cinnabar. Hey, Stammel. Hey, Rufulous.* As if, in addition to being gifted in science, they are also great linguists. Both Harvard-educated, both scions of affluent families—Jim's from California, Bruce's from New York—they never hesitate to wave their pedigrees as indisputable evidence of their brilliance. They cannot stand the fact that Diane likes Bronwyn, respects and favors her. Bronwyn could have complained about them to Diane, but she could see how that would go. Diane would chide them, and they would retaliate more covertly and fiercely. Bruce and Jim have always felt to Bronwyn like a crucible life has set for her. If she can't endure whatever mockery they serve up, how can she possibly survive what lies ahead?

Bronwyn and Diane stroll along the Charles River, both glimpsing the sky as they always do, by instinct and training. Today sun predominates delectably, only a few small cumulus clouds, high and sprocketed. Across the river the Boston skyline rules like Batman's Gotham. The day is expansive, jubilant, a gateway to the great arc of summer ahead. It is one of those days when you want to open your mouth to the sun and drink it like liquid. It's a Friday, but no one seems to be working. Sculls dart by, fleet as dragonflies, scarcely seeming to touch the water; small sailboats drift here and there in search of more wind. Runners are out in droves, the fit and the wannabe fit; starlings poke around the rafters of the boathouse.

Bronwyn has broken her news, and Diane's terrible look of dismay upon hearing it keeps flashing across her mind. Diane looked as if she'd been slapped. Though she recovered quickly, Bronwyn can still see the sense of betrayal lingering in her quickly blinking eyes.

"I think you're making a big mistake," Diane says. "What you feel is a difference in *style*, not *brain power*. Your approach may not be the same as many others around here, but that's exactly why we need you. We need people seeing things from a variety of angles."

Bronwyn shrugs. She has always allowed herself to be persuaded by Diane, and Diane has usually been right. But now is different—now she feels compelled to follow her own instincts.

If only she could describe to Diane the way Bruce and Jim laugh at her. It isn't just that they laugh, it is the *way* they laugh, a thousand harmonics of derision dressed up to be funny. It is the sound of past gym teachers and assistant principals and the sound of her own mother sometimes. *That's not realistic, Bronwyn. Face the facts.* What has fed their egos so they feel they have the right to laugh at her so openly, to pretend her ideas are trivial, her thinking lame? Is it that she came to the program from a women's college whereas they came from Harvard? Have they failed to note that Diane herself came to MIT after teaching at that same women's college? Can it be that she is a scholarship student, daughter of a single mother?

No doubt they have mothers who are too doting, too servile, too impressed with the brilliance of men, mothers who are too ready to proclaim their sons geniuses, smart women themselves, but women who readily fade to the background and resign themselves to second-class status. Can't such mothers see what a disservice they do to the plight of womanhood? To the plight of the entire nation?

The thought makes Bronwyn livid. She wishes she knew how Diane has prevailed in the company of so many men like Bruce and Jim, young and old men who look past her when they speak, who interrupt her, who are surprised by the quality of her work when they happen to notice it in the first place. Diane has clearly found a way to ignore these denigrating people, and do what she needs and wants to do. But Diane is an extrovert and has social skills Bronwyn lacks; she knows how to ignore the people who must be ignored, and she knows how to throw her weight around when necessary.

"Well, maybe you need a year off to think. I can respect that. I forget sometimes how hard it can be when you're starting out, especially for women. But I want you to promise me that we'll revisit this in a year. I hate to lose you, a good researcher and a woman to boot. I hope you don't have any of that gender-wiring drivel stuck in your brain. You must remember—scientists aren't *born*, they're *made*."

They stroll in silence, Diane's red sneakers clopping along the pavement, her billowy purple tunic and wide-legged trousers flapping. Bronwyn envies Diane for knowing herself so well, for being heedless of what others think of her, for being on the other side of so many hurdles. Diane does what she wants, says what she wants—Bronwyn has never met anyone so fearless. If only Bronwyn could talk to her mentor about how her brain really works, about how much time she really spends "in the clouds," evaporating entirely. But if she were to say these things surely Diane would lose respect for her. Diane wants her to think differently, but not *that* differently.

"Sure," Bronwyn says. "I'll keep in touch."

"What does your honey think of this plan? Reed."

Bronwyn is amazed that Diane would be thinking of Reed now. The two have only met a few times. Reed has been busy in law school, and Bronwyn has always tried to keep her worlds separate. But Diane is perceptive and she forgets little, and about Bronwyn she records and remembers things as a mother might.

"He's okay with it. He'll stay here for a year to finish law school, maybe find a job in New Hampshire when he's done."

"That won't be necessary though, will it, because you'll be moving back here by then." Diane laughs and it appears to be genuine. "I'm terribly bossy, aren't I?"

She draws Bronwyn into her capacious bosom, and Bronwyn rests there for a moment. No bridges burned. Not yet.

3

SOUTHERN NEW HAMPSHIRE
June—13 Months Later

On the day of Reed's scheduled visit, just before the summer solstice, Bronwyn wakes far too early. It's still dark, but for the first faint tinctures of dawn tonguing the river. She bolts out of bed and hurries from her tiny bedroom to the porch of the cabin, where she stands with her face pressed to the screen, listening and watching. The air is dead still, just as it has been for the last three or more days. Through the semi-darkness she senses the presence and weight of the stratus clouds that have been settled too long on the horizon, firmly fixed as struts. There is no rain, not even a sign it rained overnight, but those clouds are unusually tenacious.

She considers going back to bed. She has hours before she's due to meet Reed, who is coming up from Cambridge—11:00 a.m. at the Blue Skiff for an early lunch so she can bring him by the cabin after they eat and still get to work on time. She needs the rest, but she's far too wired for sleep. She fixes herself a pot of strong coffee and takes a mugful to the porch where she collapses on the Goodwill couch to watch the day lighten.

Since she moved a year ago from Cambridge to this little cabin on the Squamscott River in southern New Hampshire, she has spent much of her free time on this porch. She has a weather station set up in one corner, and by the couch there's a high-end Celestron reflecting telescope for clear nights, as well as a pair of 10x42 Zeiss binoculars on a tripod that can airlift her straight to the center of the river's wildlife.

The day is not developing well and, while she rarely wishes the weather were different, today is a day when she fervently hopes for sun—not cloud-filtered gray light, but the visible ball of hydrogen and helium itself, burning against a backdrop of histrionic blue. Most days any weather is just fine. She takes it as it comes, watches and monitors and speculates, appreciating its every occult aspect. But today is different. Today is Reed's visit, and he has not yet visited her here. In the year since she moved, she has been the one who has done the weekend traveling to Cambridge. Reed has been swamped in studying and has wanted to maximize his time, so she was perfectly willing to make the hour-long drive early Saturday morning, returning to New Hampshire on Monday morning in time for work.

But a couple of months ago it began to feel strange that he hasn't even seen where she lives. She began to pressure him to visit. Twice he had plans to come then canceled at the last minute, once on her birthday. Of course that hurt, though she's tried hard to take it in stride. She knows he's been stressed, busy with classes and exams—soon the bar exam—and trying to line up a job. Their last visit was three weeks ago. She went down to Cambridge, and he had just begun studying for the bar and was unavailable for most of Saturday, so she walked the rainy streets of Cambridge alone, feeling uncharacteristically nostalgic, wondering if she'd made a mistake in leaving. When she ducked into the Harvard Coop for shelter, who should she spot but Bruce. Fortunately he didn't seem to see her, and she hurried back out into the rain.

That night she and Reed went for dinner at the apartment of one of Reed's law school classmates. It was a group of eight, all lawyers but she. Reed got drunk and fell asleep as soon as they got home. On Sunday he was hungover and glum, and she left that afternoon instead of Monday morning. After that she was confused and miffed and didn't attend his graduation where she would have had to interact with his parents. Reed has said he understands, it was okay she didn't come, he isn't mad, but honestly, she wonders—*shouldn't* he be mad? Does his lack of anger mean he doesn't care enough and is pulling away? This visit, she thinks, will be a bellwether; it will show her the truth. He can't spend the night, but she'll show him as much as she can in a few hours. She wants him to love this place as much as she does, love seeing the life she's been able to make. She's hoping he'll begin to picture his own life here too, the two of them side by side. He has always made her feel so safe.

She has spruced up, bought new accent pillows and soaps, cleaned as much as she could. It's a modest cabin, a rental, but all she can afford now. The porch screens are full of holes that let in flies, several boards on the front steps are broken, and in various places pink insulation pokes through the wall-seams like tufts of cotton candy, the result of an amateur's attempt at winterizing. She took the place not for its internal charms but for its location. Its two secluded acres lie on the bank of the Squamscott River, where egrets and owls and hawks are regular visitors and the river rolls indolently by on its path to the Atlantic.

Yes, she loves this place, but she's well aware that Reed's standards are higher than hers. He grew up in an affluent suburb of Boston in a fancy house with acres of yard and meticulous landscaping. His father is a doctor and his mother works in publishing, and they're the kind of people who never shop in discount stores. While Reed makes fun of his parents' snobbery, some of their attitudes have rubbed off on him. It still makes Bronwyn wince to remember one incident early in their courtship. She bought a sexy, cherry-red taffeta lingerie outfit from Target. It was mostly a joke, though she thought Reed would like it, but when she put it on and sidled into the bedroom trying to parody a striptease artist, his face could not conceal his deep disgust. She was mortified. *It's—I don't know—vulgar,* he said, but it felt as if he was saying *she* was vulgar, and suddenly she did feel vulgar and beneath him in ways that could never be changed. In Reed's world, or at least in the world of his parents, any child of a single mother and an unknown father had to be a little suspect, and it didn't help that Bronwyn's mother, after being laid off from her job as a school secretary, spent her final working years as a house cleaner before dying of breast cancer. Bronwyn and Reed do not discuss any of this, her uncertain paternity, her mother's menial work, the lingerie incident.

Dawn is arriving slowly, impeded by the clouds, but in the reluctant gray light she sees the cabin's defects more clearly than ever. It is unlikely Reed will be charmed. He might, however, overlook the cabin's deficits if the day were to be sunny. When he announced he was coming he put in a specific request for sun—*It's no fun being at the ocean without sun*, he said—and like the rest of the world he seems to think that she, a weather forecaster, can do something about it. It doesn't matter how often she reminds people, at the station or anywhere, that she doesn't *make* the weather, she only reports it, they still seem to hold her responsible.

Bronwyn, still in her nightgown, feels the light tread of molecules along the bare skin of her arms and legs. Her pores take full measure: temperature, humidity, air pressure, dew point, wind speed. Over the years she has learned to sense these things with relative accuracy. There isn't a scintilla of wind. The air is so still it carries reports of rustling wildlife at the river: an egret preening; a Great Horned Owl, the one who's been a regular visitor of late, consuming the last of a mouse. She can feel the ocean thrumming thirteen miles in the distance, can almost smell the low tide's sulphury scent. What are the odds of sun? She should be able to guess, but after nearly a week of strangely stagnant weather, she honestly doesn't have any idea what will come next, and neither does the National Weather Service. They're *saying things*, of course, turning in their usual meteorological predictions as if everything is business as usual, but she evaluates their online data and predictions every day at the station, choosing what to say in her own broadcasts, and it's apparent to her that the National Weather Service has no better idea of what's happening than she does.

She opens the porch door and steps outside. Coffee sweat trickles behind her ears. Something grazes her face—a dangling spider. She blows, sending the spider sailing into the semi-darkness, her breath traveling past the creature, down to the river. A strigine chuckle wends to her from the poplar trees along the river bank. This owl is often here at the end of his night patrol when Bronwyn is drinking her coffee. The owl wants something, it seems to her. Or maybe he's offering advice. Bronwyn hoots back and the lonely sound traces the path of her breath, through the still air to the river and on out to sea.

It is close to 8:45 a.m. when Bronwyn awakens the second time. She has dozed on the couch without meaning to, despite the cup of rocket-fuel coffee. The owl is still nearby and hoots as if welcoming her to the day. An auspicious sign, she thinks. But, as she expected, the day is dark, its light strangely sepia-colored. She thinks of calling Reed and telling him to hold off until the weather is better. But they need to see each other, and he has only a short break before his bar review course begins.

She pops up and checks her weather station numbers. Temperature: 80 degrees. Air pressure: 1010 millibars and steady. Humidity: 63%. Wind speed: 0 knots. All the measurements are the same as they have been for three days. Actually the data aren't precisely the same— the humidity has gone up ever so slightly. There's a soggy hum in the air, and moisture clucks and stutters through the azaleas like a flock of hens.

She needs to get moving. First do a final cleaning. Then figure out what to wear. Will clothing ever cease to be an issue? The station— read: her boss, Stuart—likes her to dress in body-skimming dresses and skirts, high heels, and subtle jewelry. She spent much of her first two paychecks on new outfits. It was fun, but not altogether comfortable. She still feels unlike herself in these clothes, a poseur only acting the role of a professional. When she can inhabit these clothes unselfconsciously, she thinks, she will have truly become a responsible adult others can trust and respect. Before this job she'd been wearing the attire of a budget-conscious graduate student: jeans and T-shirts, everything from Goodwill. She usually managed to look nice no matter how skimpy her budget was. Her natural attributes helped—big green eyes, long bushy hair, waifish figure. Reed has always liked her simple dressing style, and he doesn't like her to use makeup, which isn't her habit anyway, though she's required to wear it on the air. Today he'll have to accept the "professional" Bronwyn, as she won't have time to change between lunch and work.

She feels rushed and unreasonably nervous. It's only Reed, for heaven's sake, Reed who she's known for three years now. They're buddies, old friends. He's irreverent and fun; he makes her laugh. She hopes he'll come with her to the station so she can introduce him to people. Her pals, Archie and Nicole, Stuart too, she supposes, if he's around.

Reed has certainly heard enough Stuart stories over the last year to pique his curiosity.

She cruises from living room to kitchen to bedroom, eyeballing everything with Reed in mind. In the bathroom she pulls a few hairs from the sink drain and slaps a sponge at a patch of congealed soap. *Enough already.* He'll have to accept. It's not as if he's such a paragon of cleanliness himself.

She dresses in a long-sleeved red knit dress, then thinks of the lingerie fiasco and takes it off. She stares at her closetful of other options without inspiration and finally chooses a sleeveless black sheath. Black is always safe, though it looks very formal at this hour of the day, and she'll be way overdressed at the Blue Skiff. She can't be bothered with that now. Her blood pressure is rising like a vertical shear. She needs to calm down. She covers the sheath with a short black jacket, puts on some black pumps, no stockings, and hooks some silver shell-shaped earrings into her ears. She can do her makeup at the station—Reed will appreciate seeing her face au naturel. She brushes her hair and leaves it long, which he also likes. She'll either tie it back or put it up for the evening broadcasts.

You look okay. Okay is good enough. Breathe. Relax. She sets out at 10:25 a.m. under a grimy sky, heading east to the coast in her ancient orange Volvo, twenty-eight years old, only two years younger than she.

She parks in the lot of the Blue Skiff and gets out, intending to ignore the sky. But the sky is hard to ignore by the ocean, especially with clouds pressing down as they are now, inescapable as the heedless black boot of an overhead giant. But she refuses to let the weather alter her mood—embracing all weather as she does on principle—and she enters the restaurant with newly minted optimism.

It was her suggestion to meet here because of the establishment's unusual location. It is situated on an outcropping of rock as close to the Atlantic Ocean as it is possible to build. It has suffered repeated damage from storms, but each time, due to the brevity of human memory or the force of human optimism, it is rebuilt as if such an assault will never happen again. When she suggested it, however, she neglected to think about how little the atmosphere and food are suited to Reed's tastes. It's a place for tourists, replete with the tacky décor that romanticizes coastal life—fishing nets suspended from the ceiling like hammocks, lobster pots carefully stacked to convey nonchalance, plastic starfish Krazy-glued to the walls, ceramic terns and seagulls perched on shelves to gaze eternally out to sea. And the food is unremarkable American food, carb-ridden and greasy: fried clams, lobster rolls, burgers and fries.

She pauses in the foyer and peers through a veil of plastic ferns by the hostess stand. Reed sits at a table by the window, gazing out at the ocean. He's dressed informally, but preppily, in belted khakis and a short-sleeved blue linen button-down shirt, reminding her of a golfer or a sailor, someone of the leisure class. She guesses this attire is part of preparing himself for entry into the legal profession where one must be ready at every turn to encounter potential clients and contacts. The sight of him planted there, so substantial—confident and handsome in a sandy-haired, waspy, thinking-man's way—and almost a certified lawyer, sets her blood pressure soaring again on a tide of deep affection. He has a certain languor about him, a certain immovability—if he were a wind he'd be a headwind, constant and forceful. It is a sharp contrast to her own gusty, mercurial nature. He knows who he is and what he stands for, which will make him a good lawyer, she thinks. His solidity would make any person, client or mate, feel confident in his presence.

She pushes past the hostess, pointing at Reed and navigating through the tables, most of which are still empty. He doesn't notice her until she stands beside him, and then he looks up almost sheepishly and smiles. She expects him to rise and embrace her, but when he doesn't she bends to kiss him, hand on his shoulder. How unexpectedly awkward it is to touch him after three weeks apart. She withdraws quickly and takes a seat opposite him.

"You look quite formal," he observes. "Have I ever seen you in heels that high?"

"Work clothes," she says. "Not my choice."

He nods. "Not that you don't look good. I'm just not used to it."

"Neither am I."

"When I set out from Cambridge I thought it might rain." He flicks his gaze out the window, then to her, then to the menu on the table, then back out the window.

"Sorry."

"It's not your fault."

He raises a single eyebrow. She laughs instinctively, nervously, then stops herself. He hasn't laughed yet. Usually he would have found something to laugh at by now. Something weighs him down, holds him back.

"It might get nice," she says. "You never know. New England and all—famous for its changeable weather. I keep being amazed that people don't realize that weather changes dramatically *everywhere*, not just here." She pauses. "Thanks for coming up here. I really appreciate it."

"Of course." He reaches across the table to pluck something from her hair, then drops whatever it is to the floor before she can see it.

"What?" she says. She thought she checked herself carefully and feels remiss.

"Nothing."

"I'm hoping you'll come by the station to meet some of my friends."

He frowns. "We'll see. I don't have a lot of time—"

"But at least you'll come to the house? Cabin, I should say."

He smiles. "Are you happy here? You seem happy here."

"It's good. It's not exactly where I want to end up. I'd rather be in a place with big weather events, like Florida or Oklahoma, but for now I'm learning a lot and I think I have a knack for it." She takes a quick breath. Her palms are sweating. She smiles extra broadly. Why is she addressing him as if he's a stranger?

"I don't mean this as pressure—but everything would be *so much* better if you were here. I'm sure you could find a good job in Manchester. It's really booming now. Or Portsmouth, which is smaller, but really quaint. Well, I know you've been there, but maybe not recently. There are some great new restaurants and—" What is that look in his eye? "I'm sorry. I'm talking too much, aren't I?"

"You're fine," he says. He looks down at his menu. "I guess we should order."

She could kick herself. She can almost hear him thinking, *She hasn't asked word one about me.* "How are *you*? Graduation went well?"

"Yeah, sure. But come on, you don't really care about that. If you cared you would have been there."

"So you *are* mad I didn't come—"

He shrugs. "It is what it is."

Something comes over her; his body casts a long entrapping shadow. "I guess I could point out that you didn't come up for my birthday either."

May 15. Not just any birthday, her thirtieth birthday. A totally depressing occasion. The day went by with the usual pro-forma Facebook greetings, the usual lame comments about her being over the hill. Flowers arrived from Reed with a note that said: *HB xo R.* Like Morse code, for god's sake. Only Lanny sent an actual present and card. Then, after the last broadcast, Archie came through. He brought out a bottle of champagne and a plate of nachos—her all-time favorite food—and he got the crew to sing. Then they all left, declining champagne, citing exhaustion, so she and Archie went out to his truck and ate and drank alone. She would always be grateful to him for that, but it wasn't the thirtieth birthday a girl would imagine for herself.

A membrane surrounds her, discrete but permeable as the amniotic sac. Heat lays siege to her abdomen, spreads like water. A tone pulses through her entire body, as much movement as sound. What's happening? She glances out the window to regain her equilibrium, wishing she were outside, plunging into those truculent clouds, lancing them. She blinks. Her vision telescopes. Sounds tumble away. From somewhere in Mongolia comes the tink of silverware and the murmur of voices. Her eyes are awls, forceps, piercing and gouging the clouds. Her lungs make the lewd sucking sound of a mud flat. Her retinas ache. She expels breath with explosive force.

"What's wrong? Are you alright?" Reed asks, rising from his seat and hovering. "Should I do something?"

She can't speak. She tries to wrest her gaze from the sky. Something is terribly wrong. The heat subsides a little, the tone grows fainter, and the sounds of normalcy return. "I'm fine," she finally manages to say. "I'm really fine."

He raises a single eyebrow in doubt and relaxes back down into his seat. "If you say so."

She can't shake the daze, the sense of remove from her surroundings, from Reed. She glances to the window again—the clouds are marching southward like a herd of reluctant buffalo. She drags her attention back to the table. Where to go from here? The conversation is waterlogged.

People have come into the restaurant without her noticing. They're all middle-aged or downright old, people whose skin and hair have been leached of color, people you never want to imagine being. She's quite sure she'll never get old, not like that.

The waitress has arrived. She stands by the table ready to write, looking bored, or as if they've affronted her.

"I'll have a burger with fries. And a Diet Coke," Bronwyn says quickly, wanting to be decisive and to get rid of the waitress as quickly as possible. She's been trying to eat better—less meat, more vegetables, no fried foods—but the options here are limited.

"I'll have a green salad and mint tea," Reed says. He hands the waitress his menu and she takes off before Bronwyn can change her order.

Salad? Tea? He has never been a particularly healthy eater. Why now? How can she not conclude that he's trying to show her up? It leaves her rattled, insulted, loathe to say a thing. She waits for him to take the conversational ball, wrapping her arms around her abdomen and giving herself a hug while trying to avoid the magnetic pull of the sky. She fixes her eyes on his tremulous gray ones.

"I guess I should get to the point," he says. He lays his bare hairy forearms on the table as if emptying a heavy suitcase of purpose there.

"You came here with a specific point to make?"

"Didn't you?"

"You're mad at me, obviously."

He blinks. "Not mad."

She searches his eyes, and it all seems so obvious. The metallic gray of his irises has liquefied into a viscous pity. "Are you saying—? What are you saying?"

The world falls away again, the tables full of elderly diners, the plates of fried clams and lobster rolls, the cups of coffee rattling against their saucers, the fishy smell. All of it, unperceived, ceases to exist. She is in a sac, everything around her blurred, muted, distant. Even Reed appears to be miles away, his arms gesturing, his mouth moving nonsensically. She is alone again. Five years ago her mother's death put her here. Now Reed.

". . . Can you honestly say that?"

Honestly say what? She missed it entirely. She feels her eyes bulging.

"Can you honestly say that we haven't been out of sync for a while? It's probably my fault. I know I've been too preoccupied with school. Long distance, ugh, it's so impossible."

"That's why I'm hoping you'll move here."

"But the jobs I want, the good litigation jobs, they're mostly in New York. A few in Boston, but mostly New York."

"Then you're saying you won't consider moving here?"

The waitress plunks down their plates. "Anything else?"

They both shake their heads.

Bronwyn stares at her burger, wondering if it could be plastic. She picks up a French fry and squeezes it between thumb and forefinger, watching the soft white potato inside ooze past the fried casing. So that's the long and the short of it. He won't move. No matter how beautiful it is. He's not going to move just for her.

"You've been seeing someone else?" she says.

He nods.

"You're in love?"

He nods again.

Three years they've been together and now that history vanishes in seconds. There will remain a few stories, nothing more. Possible accusations rise and recede in her mind like spring showers. *You should have . . . We should have . . .*

"Tell me about her."

"What good would that do?"

"She's better than me, I guess."

"Don't do that to yourself. You're a wonderful woman. What's happened—it's no one's fault. It's just the circumstances. The luck of the draw, you know?"

Someone's luck perhaps, but not hers. "Well, she must have something I don't have. Is she a lawyer? Is she rich?"

Reed sips his tea.

"What's her name?"

"Does that matter? You don't know her, if that's what you're asking." He pauses, reaches across the table to stroke the fingernail of her pinkie. "I'm so sorry," he whispers. "Really."

Bronwyn's breath is deep and loud as a diver's, a reminder of what it takes to stay alive. She lifts her burger, takes a bite, then another and another, barely chewing, swallowing as fast as she can.

After Reed has left she sits in her car in the parking lot for a long time trying to envision his nameless woman. She's lost in a cyclone of loneliness. She's a star without a planet, a magnet with no further ability to attract. A motherless child. There is something awry with her mind; it seems to have unseated itself from her brain, a dissatisfied guest.

She remembers Reed once likening her to a meteor, saying she burned hotter than most women. But obviously his view has changed. Either her heat no longer appeals, or she has used it up. Whatever the reason, he has now discarded her. How wrong-headed she was to think that if anyone ended the relationship it would be she. She supposes she should have seen this coming, but how? There were no signs as far as she could see. Her powers of perception have always been keen, though perhaps not in relation to people. Maybe what has happened was always destined to happen. Reed knows his worth, as one of the nice and sensitive men who women look for. (Well, he wasn't always a hundred percent nice and sensitive. Once, during his first year of law school, she came in on him with some of his buddies reviewing a list of their female classmates, playing a "game" called "Fuck, Marry, Kill.") It hasn't helped her case that his parents have never liked her—she should have taken their dislike more seriously. Her mother, it turns out, was right. A woman who expects too much gets beaten down. And Bronwyn has definitely expected too much, aspired too high, thought she was smarter and more attractive than she really is. Well, now she's been shown up, outdone by some other woman, a lawyer no doubt, who will be the recipient of Reed's attention and charm and money and protection.

She wishes she could cry, but she can't. She's never been a crier, has always responded to life's blows with a mute, blank affect that seems like better protection. Above her the clouds are now stationary, impassive as a firing squad. She slams her eyes shut. The sky and its atmosphere are doing strange things to her. She has to stop looking up for a while. There are no portents there. She's a scientist for heaven's sake, she doesn't believe in portents.

The rejection has altered her body and is affecting her brain too, her only real asset. There is still time before she must be at work. A walk on the beach could be restorative.

4

At Odiorne Point State Park the sight of the ocean is immediately tranquilizing. She loves the sand, the cool trembling water, the ranting gulls, the waves' susurrus. The ocean holds onto an untouchable wildness that the rest of the world is losing. Today, a Wednesday, the park is deserted, no doubt because of the overcast sky. No families, no hand-in-hand lovers, no tourists with maps and binoculars. She sees only a single runner, a woman, adhering to her fitness routine, face set in an expression of grim stoicism. Bronwyn always finds this a sad sight; she hates the thought of anything in her own life becoming so doggedly, cheerlessly habitual, and yet there is something in the woman's face she understands, and she worries her own face might sometimes look as cheerless.

She puts on the running shoes she always leaves in the trunk and chooses a path that leads over a lawn, then slopes gently down through tall beach grass to the shore. It's a shaggy, scraggy beach, one for walking and skipping stones, its sand coarse and multi-colored as wild rice, and strewn with pebbles and fist-sized rocks and driftwood and whorls of dry black seaweed. Unraked, unmanicured, it doesn't have the fine-grained white sand that appeals to sun-bathers and swimmers. Bronwyn likes it for that. She appreciates an unpretentious beach, a beach that still belongs more to the earth than to humans.

Whenever she comes here she thinks of childhood trips to the Jersey shore, to those wide flat beaches where swimmers and sunbathers flocked during heat waves—Long Beach Township, or Surf City, or Seaside Park, sometimes further north to Manasquan or Belmar. Maggie always had strict rules. No running, no rolling in the sand, no throwing rocks or shells, no swimming until she said it was time. But mainly Bronwyn was to always stay in Maggie's sightlines. *Dreadful things are done to girls who are found alone*, Maggie would say, though when Bronwyn would push to know what exactly was done to those girls, Maggie would never say. *Girls just never have an easy time of it; men call the shots in this world, you might as well know that from the get-go.*

Here the shoreline curves in a gentle crescent. The tide is out and timid waves nibble the sand. At the far end of the beach a woman tosses a stick for her dog. Bronwyn loves dogs, has been teased for the way she brings her face right down to a dog's to exchange sloppy kisses.

Usually she walks quickly, savoring the elasticity and power of her legs, but today her dress is restrictive, and the sky's strange antics grip her attention, keeping her in place. The clouds are cleaving in a solid impenetrable line, as they have been for several days, barring the brief movement she witnessed at the Blue Skiff. In all her years of weather watching she has never seen such prolonged and defiant stillness. It reminds her a little of how her mother's face used to look just before an outburst, battened down, so uncannily motionless it almost seemed dead, or as if she was compressing all her energy to bring additional force to her imminent explosion. There's that feeling now, of limitless energy hovering behind the gray-brown wash of clouds. The sun is clearly there, but inaccessible, a curtained wizard waiting, unwilling to reveal his next move.

Surely things are moving in other places—natural forces are never static—so why not here on this stretch of New Hampshire coastline? It's almost like being at the eye of a glacially moving storm. A catalyst is necessary, a slight change of temperature, or air pressure, or wind speed. A sword of righteous anger.

She draws a line with her gaze up from her shoes across the rough rock and sand and desiccated seaweed. It travels over the black water to the murky horizon where sea and sky are scarcely differentiated. In the path of her gaze the molecules are stuck in their dance like human veins occluded by plaque. She locks her eyes on a distant point where the clouds look most menacing. Her vision takes in a wide swath of sky. Eyes like telescopes, she zeroes in on the distant droplets. She sees molecules: hydrogen, oxygen. She hears the rise and fall of her own breathing, nothing more. Then a pulsing hum. Her body expands in steely concentration until it domes the beach, the ocean. An inferno, hot as the sun, explodes in her gut, spreads to her chest. She doesn't move, at once sunk in her body and soaring out of it. She presides here for a while, swirling in moisture and light, in a trance but more sentient than ever before.

A spear of sunlight tears the sky vertically, lightning-like, dividing it in half. She pants, grabs another breath, deeper, and holds it for a long time, releases it slowly, to a sound like a pigeon's coo. Before her, the sky is ripped and frayed by the light streak, the cloud masses on either side parting and drifting in different directions as she's never seen clouds do; the light in the middle spills out, viral, blooming, a gold limned with silver. It's like the light after drenching rain storms, prismatic, promising rainbows, light so sudden and welcome it appears more dimensional and colorful than other light.

The dog surprises her, bounding up to her legs, barking enthusiastically, demanding attention. Bronwyn pants, turns, begins to hear the world again. The light has blinded her, leaving dark floaters drifting across her vision like a flotilla of tiny boats. The day has become a circus, loud and confusing. She crouches to greet the dog. "Hey there, buddy." She looks around to find the dog's owner, but there isn't a soul in sight, and the dog takes off back down the beach.

The sky looks dappled now, like the forest floor on an exceptionally sunny day. Not quite as disturbingly dramatic as it was a minute ago, though still impressive. She thinks of Reed, wonders if he is seeing this. To whom could she describe this piercing beauty? Suddenly she panics. She's due at work in ten minutes and at best it's a forty-five-minute drive. She hikes her dress to her thighs, sprints toward the car, trips on some of the loose rocks, falls, scrambles up. She arrives at her car panting, discombobulated. Behind the wheel she studies the sky again. The light has gone from gold to white, a canvas to be filled. She gets out of the car and brushes the sand and curls of seaweed from her dress. She peers at herself in the window's reflection. Her hair jets out in all directions, but she has nothing with which to groom it except her hands.

She drives too fast, eyes on the horizon. Stuart doesn't take lateness lightly. He lectures tardy employees about professional carelessness and about their disrespect for the "team." Will she make a ploy for sympathy by telling him she's been dumped? Would it make any difference with Stuart? She's certainly not going to tell him she fears there might be something wrong with her brain.

She makes a resolution: when she arrives at work she will enter cheerfully, genuflect to Stuart, apologize, pander, tell him she's sorry and she'll never be late again. Then she will prepare for the first of four nightly broadcasts. She will download the National Weather Service data and make some sense of it all; she will prepare her remarks, create her graphics. By the end of her last broadcast it will be close to midnight.

In the rearview mirror something catches her eye. Crap, a New Hampshire State Patrol car, flashing its lights. She pulls over and watches the cruiser pull in behind her. A Paul Bunyan–sized officer gets out of his cruiser and lopes to her car with swaggering, no-nonsense, officer-of-the-law authority.

She rolls down her window to act the part of the good citizen, aware she does not *look* like a particularly good citizen now. He leans down, his chest curving over the window gap and blocking the sky like a giant umbrella.

"I don't suppose you know how fast you were going?"

"No."

"Seventy-eight. In a forty-five-mile-an-hour zone."

"Oh."

"That's all you have to say for yourself? Oh?"

"What would you like me to say?"

"I'll bet there are a lot of times you have a heck of a lot to say." He stares at her with a blank unrelenting look that is hard to interpret. Suspicion? Lasciviousness?

"I'm late for work."

"You and every other schmo. I need to see your license, registration, and proof of insurance."

She digs into her purse and the glove box, mind running triple speed, unreasonably furious. She hands him the documents, and he glances at them, slaps the top of the Volvo twice so the car's entire body shivers, and heads back to his cruiser.

Bronwyn smoothes her hair. She needs to bring this day into submission. An earring is missing. Damn. She can't go on the air with a single earring. That is something Stuart would definitely scold her for. She searches the passenger's seat. Not there. She unclips her seat belt and looks on the floor. Not there either. She's just getting out of the car to search the back seat when the officer returns.

"Get back in the car," he orders.

She does as he says. The power is all his, legal and personal. He can do whatever he wants with her—ticket her, arrest her, rape her if he chooses. He's easily twice her size. She is just a speeding, unstable girl, a possible suspect, no doubt looking for drugs on the floor of her car.

"I lost an earring," she says in self-defense.

He hands her papers through the window and leans down. He's smiling. "You're the weather gal, aren't you? I watch you every night."

She nods, noticing the hand that hangs at his side, thick as a baseball glove, broad and leathery.

"I didn't recognize you at first. You're a tiny little thing, aren't you? Even prettier in real life than on the tube."

"It's been a hard day and I'm late for work. Can you just ticket me and let me go?"

"Hold your horses, sweetness. Guess what? You're in luck. I'm giving you a warning, no ticket. But watch your speed. We don't want you in a ditch. We need you on TV."

"Thanks. I will."

"Hope you don't mind my saying . . ." He flaps his fingers in an inchoate gesture over his head. "You have stuff in your hair. You might want to fix that before you go on the air."

Her hand leaps up to finger her hair. She pulls off a piece of seaweed. She's trembling. He watches intently.

"You okay? Trouble with your boyfriend, maybe? He gives you any guff, you call me. Good-looking gal like you, no one should give you any guff." He hands her his card. Ken Donovan. He means well, she supposes.

"Good to meet you, Bronwyn. Hey, you should get yourself a new car. Being a celebrity and all." He licks his upper lip. "You got my card."

She nods and smiles weakly. By now Stuart is probably furious.

5

Bronwyn is fifty minutes late and there is no way to enter the WVOX building inconspicuously. Nicole, sitting at the front desk applying eyeliner, is unavoidable. She and Bronwyn always talk.

"Jeez, what happened to you?"

Bronwyn looks down at herself. Powdery car dust covers the bodice of her black dress; a grease spot highlights her sternum, centered like a fallen third eye. Panic flares—she can't go on the air like this.

"It's been a very bad day," she confesses.

"What?" Nicole leans forward to sculpt a cave of secrecy around them, eyeliner stick wanding the air. Her eyes are not made more beautiful by the layers of black she paints on them, but Bronwyn wouldn't dream of saying so. She likes Nicole, who is twenty-four, a high school graduate from a small town farther north, a good-times girl who has no aspirations beyond settling down with her boyfriend Mike. Their wedding is scheduled to take place in mid-July. Nicole's situation could so easily have been Bronwyn's, so Bronwyn usually feels for Nicole a unique blend of sympathy and pity, though right now Bronwyn wishes she *were* Nicole, sitting at a desk with nothing particularly pressing to do, preoccupied with dreamy thoughts of an upcoming wedding.

Bronwyn brushes her dress ineffectually. The grease is not going to disappear without a stain remover. She should have thought to leave a change of clothing here at the station for such an eventuality.

"Well—?" says Nicole, still waiting for an explanation.

Bronwyn sighs, glances around her. "My boyfriend dumped me. I didn't see it coming. Then, I was already late and I was stopped by a cop. Has Stuart noticed?"

"I don't think so. Why would he dump you? That sucks. I can't imagine anyone dumping you."

Nicole looks genuinely heartbroken, and Bronwyn feels an unexpected surge of gratitude that almost brings tears. "Apparently he found someone better."

"He didn't do anything to you, did he? Did he rough you up?"

"No."

"Then why do you look so . . . messy?"

"It's a long story. I'll tell you sometime. But I should clean up before Stuart sees me. I need to fix this stain. My jacket won't cover it."

"You can borrow my sweater."

"Really?"

"Sure. It's not exactly classy, but it'll cover the stain. I only brought it in case the AC gets too cold." Nicole forages in a bag under her desk and comes up with the sweater in question, a yellow nylon that crackles with static electricity.

"Thanks," Bronwyn says. "I owe you." Stuart will not like this makeshift outfit. He will comment about the pale yellow clashing with her auburn hair.

"No problem. I'm really sorry about your boyfriend. He's a loser." Nicole shakes her head. "Would this be the wrong time to remind you about July 14th? No rain, no clouds, no humidity. None of this shit we've been having. Just a warm, dry, sunny day?"

Bronwyn freezes, grabbed and stilled by the memory, the spectacle made by the parting clouds, the extreme light of silver and gold.

"You'll arrange that for me, right?" Nicole says. "July 14th? A perfect day?"

Bronwyn blinks, stuck in the vision. Overhead the fluorescent bulbs thrust out their ugly hissing light. Nicole is only asking what everyone asks. "Yeah," Bronwyn says. "Sure. I'll see what I can do." She winks.

"Any chance you and your boyfriend will get back together?"

Bronwyn shakes her head.

"I've got a really hot cousin who's coming to the wedding. *And* he's rich. He's a real estate developer. Shopping centers and stuff. And last

year he opened a new ski resort—Gold Mountain. He looks like Brad
Pitt, I swear to god. I would have married him in a nanosecond if he
weren't my cousin."

"Thanks, but I don't think so. I'm not ready."

"Wait and see. You might like him."

Bronwyn nods, waves vaguely, and wobbles off down the hallway,
stopping in the bathroom to fix her hair, rinse her face, and gather herself a little, though more fixing will be necessary before the broadcast.
Marginally improved, she continues down the hallway past the control booth and the newsroom and editorial. She keeps her gaze down
in *don't interrupt* mode, afraid of being snagged for a conversation.
Everyone loves to talk to her about weather, but here at the station it's
meaningless chatter. People want to tell her what they *think* of certain
weather—*too hot, too cold, too humid*—what they want to *do* in it. No
one seems to appreciate the pure marvel of it, how weather showcases
the invisible, unpredictable, powerful forces at work on the Earth. Today she'd be just as happy not to talk to anyone about anything. She's
already looking forward to going home after the last broadcast, collapsing on the couch with a glass of wine, and hooting back to her
Great Horned Owl.

Her office is situated on the set itself, a row of computers behind
the weather console. She works standing, or perched on a stool, always ready to respond to various members of the "team" coming and
going, some with questions for her, others with messages, still others
with business that doesn't involve her at all. Today Brant, one of the
two evening news anchors, is already on the set, pre-recording a news
segment about a rash of robberies for a station farther north. Bronwyn
tiptoes quietly to her post, saved from having to engage with Brant.
He's always cordial, but he's vain and insufferably self-involved.

Her first task when she arrives is to read—or reread—the feed from
the National Weather Service. That becomes the core of her report and
is the reason that people without a lick of weather knowledge can do
her job adequately (and why it sometimes embarrasses her to be here,
a mere cog, her background in atmospheric science non-essential).
Usually she embellishes the Weather Service information a little with

her own take on things, drawn from her instruments and her practiced talent of observation. Sometimes she has a "Fun Weather Fact" to share, but not today. Today, whatever the Weather Service says goes. Today, the more automatic the better. Today, the great challenge will be getting words out of her mouth in the first place.

Unlike the news anchors, Gwen and Brant, she does not read from a teleprompter. She stands in front of the green screen on which the weather map is superimposed, and she ad libs. On both sides of her are monitors with graphics she has composed beforehand, and she can take her cues from them, but the words are invented on the spot. Sure, there's a basic template that repeats from day to day—first a recap of the last twenty-four hours, then a run-down of current conditions, then the five-day forecast. She pins her words around that format, but they're her words, generated spontaneously on the air, and she has to try not to repeat herself while gesturing elegantly in front of the empty green screen and looking into the camera where she sees, of all things, her own image. All this requires extreme concentration so that she says what she means to say and acts cheerful as she says it. If her concentration lapses, everything falls apart, and she forgets certain things, or says them incomprehensibly, or fails to smile, or gestures too wildly. And meanwhile she must be cognizant of fitting everything into a very precise time slot. It's a sacrilege to go over time. Better to come in under, and amble over to the news desk, and chat insipidly for a few seconds with the anchors.

She turns her back on Brant and feels a momentary relief at being in this windowless, artificially lit space where she has no direct information about outside conditions. She logs onto the National Weather Service's digital forecast database to discover that things haven't changed since she last checked. They're calling for 60% chance of rain tonight, clearing by morning, a slight breeze at five mph, low humidity, temperatures in the high seventies, then a spate of sunny, not-too-hot, not-too-cold days to close out the month. She scrolls down, searching for some mention somewhere, perhaps from one of the trained local weather spotters, of what she witnessed on the beach before she came here. There's no mention of it. Forget it, she tells herself.

She immerses herself in the building of graphics—a weather segment won't fly without graphics—but she's short on time, short on attention, and she keeps expecting Stuart to arrive on the set and lecture her publicly. Now Brant is completing his segment.

"Bronwyn!" he calls, as if summoning a dog. "What's going on?"

She can feel the tension rippling through her trapezius muscles. "I'm behind, Brant. I've got to keep working."

But Brant is already ambling to her area. Because he is featured on several local billboards and is occasionally recognized in local establishments, he thinks he's famous, and believes everyone is delighted by his company. Old enough to be Bronwyn's father, he fancies himself king of the station. He stands behind Bronwyn.

"You got some good weather in store for us?" Schoolmarmish, he won't go away.

Bronwyn turns and makes her face a smooth, placating plate. "We're in New England, Brant, you know what they say. Wait five minutes and the weather changes. Have you ever been to the top of Mount Washington? You can start out on a summer day and meet winter at the top. There are the highest ever-recorded surface wind speeds up there."

"I'm not talking about Mount Washington. I'm talking about good weather right here in Manchester and Portsmouth. My golf swing is going to hell."

Bronwyn smiles wanly. "Sorry. I really have work to do."

Behind Brant, the cameraman Archie, a laid-back, fifty-something, unreconstructed hippie, is making faces at Bronwyn. She raises an eyebrow in acknowledgement of Archie, and Brant gives up, sensing the mockery, and exits the set without a word.

"What a piece of work," Archie says, joining Bronwyn at her bank of computers where they've been left alone. Archie is close to Brant's age, but they could not be more different. Archie wears baseball caps and sandals and Hawaiian shirts even in winter; he fastens his long gray hair in a ponytail, and his face is half masked by a coarse Brillo beard.

"So, solstice tomorrow," Archie says. "I've been wondering. I know solstice means a change in *season*, but does it have any effect on the *weather*? You know what I mean?"

"Can I take a rain check on that? I'm really under the gun."

"Ten-four. You okay?"

"Tired."

"Yeah, you look beat to shit."

Bronwyn nods. She appreciates Archie's honesty. Archie spends a lot of time looking at her from behind his camera. He has often helped her tweak her appearance, adjusting her clothing or telling her she needs more blush. He's never rude about it, just protective and paternal in a touching way. She has often felt rescued by him. But now his attention makes her feel like crying again. Not that she *would* cry.

"I'll fix myself up before air time."

Archie leaves, and she lowers her head to the console. She needs sleep. She can't imagine pulling herself together for the five o'clock broadcast. She has only an hour to compose her graphics and plan out her patter.

For the next forty-five minutes technicians and reporters wander in and out, some conducting business, others killing time. Some make their way to Bronwyn to schmooze, but she blows them off as well as she can. She chafes at the lack of personal space she has here. There's no door to close, and everyone has as much of a right to be on the set as she does. On most days she's fine with that, but today she's too addled to work this way. The director has given her a longer segment than usual, three minutes and thirty seconds, and she doesn't have nearly enough to say to fill that time. So often she wants to get into the finer points of the forecast, but today she's just as happy to do the golfer's version: Will it or won't it rain? How warm will it be? Will there be wind? End of story. If that doesn't fill her time, she'll have to think of trivia for shooting the breeze with Gwen and Brant.

Everyone gathers on the set ten to fifteen minutes before the broadcast: the two cameramen, Archie and Larry; a handful of reporters; Don, who does captioning; Jerry, the director. Gwen and Brant sit behind the news desk attaching their mics and fiddling with their ear buds through which the guys in the booth can direct them. Stuart has not yet made an appearance.

Bronwyn still scrambles. She's forgotten to get sunrise and sunset times, and though she could probably hazard a guess, a guess won't do. It is her policy to make sure the data she reports are correct and verifiable. At the last minute she dashes out to the bathroom, swabs on some makeup, and buttons Nicole's yellow sweater over her dress. It isn't right, but it's all she has.

The floor manager calls for places. Bronwyn attaches her mic. Even as she situates herself in front of the blank green screen she's uncertain about what will emerge from her mouth. Gwen eyes her with a maternal gaze. She has a twenty-year-old daughter she worries about, and she often consults Bronwyn for advice. What a joke, that Bronwyn would have advice for a twenty-year-old when her own life is so out of control.

Archie's gesturing demands her attention; he's tugging his earlobe frantically. She remembers her earring. She only has one. She yanks it off, drops it on the floor. It clatters, spins, rolls off the platform. A look of alarm passes over the floor manager's face until he sees what it is—the earring that has now settled. Archie smiles.

"Three. Two. One."

Bronwyn activates her smile like a spigot. She's gotten good at this in the last year. As low as she now feels, she can still find her smile. Her image comes back at her from the camera. She might as well be addressing her own bathroom mirror, and today she can't help seeing that Archie is right. She looks beat up. Her big eyes are too big. She's far too pale. Can others see in her face the disjuncture of mind and body?

"We're on the air folks."

At 5:03 p.m., she's on camera two for the weather teaser. Her full report won't come up for another twenty minutes or so.

"And Bronwyn Artair is here," Brant says in his booming, slick TV locution, "to tell us what to expect from the weather. Some sun in our future, Bronwyn?"

"Yes, Brant, we finally have some good weather heading our way. Clearing all over southern New Hampshire. Throughout our viewing area, inland and on the coast, we can expect some beautiful early summer days for the foreseeable future."

"Glad to hear it," Brant says. "Just what we've all been waiting for."

As soon as Bronwyn is off the air she wilts and crosses quietly to her weather console where she perches on the stool as Brant continues with a report on an infestation of blue-green algae on Lake Winnipesaukee, followed by Gwen on Summer Safety for kids, stories Bronwyn only half hears. Talking is forbidden on the set when they're live, which allows her to escape into the pleats of her brain, not sleeping, but not fully conscious either.

Since she came to New Hampshire she has felt as though she has another life, a more authentic life, happening elsewhere, moving along in tandem with the life she has been living here. In that other life there is forward momentum. She would be marrying Reed and on her way to being employed at a more important, reputation-clinching job. That life has had an intense hold on her and thinking of it motivated and ennobled her. It was the life she was entitled to and knew would eventually be hers. But as of today, she understands that this life here is her only life, a life that is circumscribed and lonely, and she is the only one to propel it forward. She has no mother or boyfriend to weigh in and cheer her on. Having abandoned Diane, she can't expect to consult with her, especially since they've scarcely spoken over the last year, sharing only a few shallow emails. There's her old friend Lanny, but Lanny still lives in New Jersey and can't be relied on daily. Her real life is turning out to be a solo journey, difficult and small, just like her mother's.

Archie pokes her. It's time!

Panicked, Bronwyn pops back to place in front of the green screen. *The smile, find the smile.* Thank god it's Pavlovian. Smile in place, the words follow, not sophisticated words, but automatic, straightforward, fill-in-the-blank sentences. She grins, a big, fat, crowd-pleasing grin, not the grin of a failed scientist, or an abject lover, but the grin of a woman in love with the world.

"So folks, as you well know we've had some gloomy weather here in southern New Hampshire for the last week or so, a stagnant front of low stratus clouds, warm temperatures, high humidity, but things are changing as they are wont to do with the weather. We can expect some rain tonight, tapering off toward morning. The skies should be clearing by nine or ten a.m., and for the solstice and into the fore-seeable future, we can expect to see some perfect summer days, as a high pressure system asserts itself and the humidity abates. So break out your bathing suits and golf clubs and fire up those barbeques. Get ready for summer."

Her arms swing over the Eastern seaboard in grandiose arcs, as if she is absolutely sure of what she's saying, as if she is coaching major league baseball, or conducting the Boston Symphony, instead of de-tailing the temperatures in Portsmouth, Manchester, Nashua.

"Let's appreciate this weather while it lasts because, let's not kid our-selves, we all know that as each year passes the weather is becoming more dire and less predictable and—"

Archie is motioning for her to close. He appears desperate.

The booth cuts to Gwen on camera one. "Thank you Bronwyn. You've made us all happy." She continues, conciliatory as ever. "My husband and I are going fishing this weekend and it will be a lot better with sun."

Archie hooks Bronwyn's arm as she steps off the set. "Sorry," he whispers. "The booth was barking at me to cut."

She shrugs, nods. *Bring it on. I don't care.* She knew the risk, even before she spoke of dire future weather, but for some reason she couldn't stop herself. It's 5:30 p.m. now. There are more broadcasts at six, then later in the evening at ten and eleven. She has to vary each one a little for the repeat viewers and as new weather information comes in. It's hard to imagine finding all that energy three more times. She heads for the break room where she keeps a supply of Red Bull. Nicole intercepts her.

"Stuart. He wants to see you now."

"Damn." Did he see the broadcast? Or is her lateness the issue?

"You did good, by the way," Nicole says. "And the sweater looks awe-some."

"Thanks."

"You were a little manic maybe, but I liked it. We could use a little more manic around here. Good luck with Stuart."

Meetings with Stuart are Bronwyn's least favorite part of this job. For one thing, they always go longer than they need to. If you ask Stuart what appears to be a simple, short-answer question, he always answers with a disquisition. But the more important problem with him is that he can't be trusted. At first she thought he was a very nice man, sympathetic, but it didn't take long to see how his *niceness* was a screen for an untrustworthy nature. He is known for telling his staff one thing, his higher-ups another. In the end he always panders to the advertisers and the board, and the concerns of a mere meteorologist mean nothing to him. In her first month or so at the station she used to try to engage with him, but now she has learned it's advisable to say little and allow his advice and lectures and attempts to be witty to simply run their course. She should have understood from his comb-over that he attempts to hide far more than his balding head.

Stuart's office has a picture window that gives out to a grassy area bordered by woods. Rain falls in translucent beads that, even through the glass, can be heard resonating softly as they hit the ground. It's a comforting sound and a peaceful, sylvan sight, and it brings to Bronwyn, despite the day, a rill of pleasure. Stuart's gaze follows hers, and they both stare out.

"It must make you feel good having your forecasts come true."

"You make me sound like a fortune teller."

"Aren't you?" He laughs, as if what he has said is terribly funny, and rolls his office chair forward into the mealworm curve of his desk. The desk is a reddish-brown and so heavily lacquered it seems to have its own light source.

"You're a great asset to the station, Bronwyn. I'm sure you know that by now. Revenues are up since your arrival. People like hearing their weather from a pretty girl like you." His brow ripples. "But we cannot, we *simply cannot* have you flying off in this speculative manner. Yes, I saw the broadcast, and I know where you were heading. First, you have no idea what the weather of the future will be like, and it is frankly irresponsible to pretend you do. Furthermore, even if you did know, our viewers *don't care*. They want to hear about *tomorrow's weather* and maybe a few days out to the weekend and *that's it*." He squints as if to make his stare pointed and hurtful, like one of those electronic fences that keeps dogs in check.

The rain seems to be coming down harder, though it may be that Bronwyn is confusing the rain with her own beating heart. Will it really clear by tomorrow morning? Today, like never before, Bronwyn feels invested in having her forecast come true.

"Bronwyn?" Stuart leans across the slick desk. "Bronwyn?"

She turns. "Yes?"

"Am I making myself clear? We've had this discussion before. I thought you understood."

"I do understand."

"You do understand, but—?"

"But nothing."

"It sounded as if there was a *but* there."

Behind Stuart's head the rain is mesmerizing. It is a singular blue-gray which shimmers with all colors, and it descends with a singular beat which houses hundreds of variations. She can't stop looking.

"There wasn't a 'but,'" she says, trying to track.

"We are here, you in particular, to be comforting, not alarmist. People want to know if they should take a jacket or an umbrella with them. You provide them with a practical tool to get them through their day."

Her attention is fully in the room now, and she stares hard at the reflections in Stuart's glasses. "I don't think it's always enough to simply tell them what the weather is going to be. I think they sometimes want to know *why* it's going to be that way. Why, for example, have the tornadoes been so bad this year? Why has it been so hot and dry in the Southwest and California? I think people are interested."

"But we don't know why. We're not scientists."

"I'm sorry, I *am* a scientist. And I think we know quite a bit. We all know the planet is warming. Are you a skeptic?"

"My personal beliefs are not on the table here. Look, Bronwyn, you're a smart woman, don't ruin things for yourself. Just do the job you were hired for and don't let your smartness turn to arrogance."

Neither one of them speaks. Stuart's breath is quick and shallow as if he's taking a break in a boxing match. "That sweater isn't right. It's too big for you."

She smiles. "I'm trying." She unbuttons the sweater like a flasher to expose the grease spot on her sternum.

The Red Bull gets her through the night, but barely. She stares into the camera imagining Stuart watching her. She delivers cheerful conventional reports and only with effort holds herself back from sticking out her tongue afterwards. She thinks fleetingly of Reed, who indicated once that he did not much like her TV persona, though he didn't say why. At eleven-thirty she's in the break room gathering her things to go home. Archie comes up behind her and puts a cold beer in her hand.

"I can't, Archie. I'm dead tired."

"One beer."

Exhausted as she is, the Red Bull still boils in her system. A beer might help. She takes it and collapses into a chair beside Archie.

"Is Stuart on your case?" he says.

She nods. "He's so paranoid about me mentioning global warming."

"That doesn't surprise me."

"How can I report the weather without at least *sometimes* mentioning why it's happening the way it is? He says people don't care. Do you think that's true?"

"Hm. They care, they just don't want to be bothered with it right now."

She nods. "I guess that's more or less what he's telling me." She sips her beer, thinking of all the things she would rather not be bothered with at the moment.

"Hey—change of subject. You ever been to Alaska?" Archie says.

"No. I've hardly been anywhere. I took a trip to Colorado once with my old mentor. And my mother and I went to Yosemite when I was, like, eleven or twelve."

"I was up in Alaska about this time ten years ago. Solstice, up in Homer. God, it was spooky. Beautiful spooky. The light changes, and you suddenly realize it's not going anywhere. To me, it almost felt like being in water. Or like I was an astronaut suspended in space. Weightless. Something."

"I'd love to see that. Did you sleep?"

"Oh, for three or four hours a night, not much more. Definitely puts you in an altered state. And I felt like I understood something about where I was on the Earth—all that shit about the Earth's axis and rotation and all, it suddenly made sense to me. But at the same time, there was like this religious or spiritual thing happening—and I'm not woo-woo like that at all, believe me—but it was like other powers were at work. I was thinking about that today. We humans, we're nothing, you know? We don't know much about anything really."

Bronwyn smiles. She can imagine Archie as a young man, tripping on acid, blabbing on about his mind-blowing insights. Bronwyn pushes her half-drunk beer toward him.

"You finish this. I've been up for too many hours. I need to go home."

6

It has been raining steadily since Bronwyn left the station almost four hours ago. She was wide awake, disconcerted by the sound of her lids scraping across her dry eyeballs. Despite her exhaustion, she hasn't slept for more than a few minutes at a time. As soon as she got home she peeled off her dress, hurled her shoes toward the bedroom, and came out to the porch couch. She's been here ever since, rattling around under a sheet. And now it's almost 4:00 a.m. and she can already hear a few waking birds. The dark is alive and porous. Dawn is clawing up the horizon, fighting with the rain like a scene-stealing actor impatient to make an appearance.

She always believed in her future with Reed. But why? There was never any hard data. It was all hunch and hope, the kind of lazy thinking Diane used to deplore. Bronwyn thought she'd cured herself of such thinking. She likes to think her opinions are fact-based, scientifically verifiable.

What exactly did she do to lose Reed? Was there a single moment where one thing sent their relationship perilously off course? Or were there innumerable miniscule things that, done differently, might have changed the outcome? How could you possibly know what those things were? Crucial, but so unknowable. The Butterfly Effect, sensitive dependence on initial conditions. Maybe she is just congenitally bad at relationships and will end up alone like her mother. Maggie slept with Bronwyn's father a couple of times and never saw him again. He was an older man, a history professor she met on a train. He was probably married. There was no point, Maggie said, in Bronwyn looking for him, as Maggie never learned his last name. Bert Somebody. Who even knew if the Bert was true.

Perhaps one initial condition was that she and Reed were never suited to each other in the first place. Who knows? Relationships seem like fractals for which Bronwyn has no equation, oddly like the weather that defies easy computing with its multitude of variables: air currents and mountain ranges and bodies of water and gravity and rotation and humidity and wind speed. On and on. Everything in flux. This is what draws Bronwyn to weather, the salmagundi of forces that are nearly impossible to parse with absolute accuracy. Maybe previously uncharted human factors are also involved. Human intention. Human will. Human desire. A measurable energy attached to thought. She knows too much to rule that out. And far too little. Sometimes the things she knows are stashed too deeply for her to even realize she knows them. Then suddenly she does know. The onion peeled, her vision clears.

Though now her vision is far from clear about anything. Snippets of yesterday have been scattered randomly in different parts of her brain. She lifts and examines them. Reed's pitying look. The celestial look of the light on the beach. The heat in her brain and the pounding singularity of her focus. Stuart saying, *We're not scientists.* So glib. So rude. She feels a footprint planted on her heart.

She can't call Lanny until at least 9:00 a.m. Lanny is off from teaching for the summer and she likes to sleep, long and hard. Her husband, Tom, takes the bus to the city to work in insurance, or some such thing, and Lanny sleeps and sleeps and sleeps. Often until ten or eleven or even noon. Once she confessed she didn't even wake until 2:00 p.m. It is not in Bronwyn's constitution to sleep that much. Perhaps her body could sleep that long, but her mind always wants to scold her body to attention.

She remembers it's the solstice. Just her luck that she has to endure the longest day of the year when she feels so low. She makes herself stay put in hopes of more dozing. At 5:00 a.m. she glides along the uppermost surface of sleep, a state still hinged to waking consciousness that disallows the pleasure of oblivion. At 7:15 a.m. she finally concedes that the day has begun. The rain has stopped but the foliage is shedding droplets noisily and sunlight illuminates everything, spreading tiny rainbows and making every water-sheathed leaf and stem precious. The world is unusually active, as if it's preparing itself for something. Her forecast was right after all, clearing by morning just as she predicted, but being correct doesn't yield much satisfaction right now.

Despite the rain, the river looks unusually indolent today, almost sluggish. From where she lies she sees a hawk out on the water swooping low, intent on some prey. She will not succumb to the terrible inadequacy Reed has made her feel. She will climb out of this chasm into which she has fallen. She will pay close attention to the faulty functioning of her brain and try to repair it. She suspects that the antibiotic she took in late May might be responsible for her odd experiences yesterday. The doctor said it was a virus that was making her so tired. Then he prescribed an antibiotic. Didn't he know antibiotics don't cure viruses? Why do some doctors insist on doing that? Of course it is her fault for taking it, despite knowing better.

At 8:30 a.m. she can't hold off calling any longer. Lanny grunts a greeting and adjusts herself in the sheets, waking reluctantly. But Bronwyn is out of the gate, already talking. As little as a grunt from Lanny can make Bronwyn feels she's back in eighth grade, or even that she's five or six years old again. She's known Lanny that long; they could be sisters. Bronwyn doesn't care how juvenile she sounds, how angry at Reed and his parents and his privilege. After ranting about Reed, she rants about Stuart, then whispers about her fear that she's losing her mind, *on the solstice no less*. She pauses, on the cusp of crying, but not crying. Lanny has not said a thing. Bronwyn stops to listen. "Are you laughing?"

"No."

"Yes, I heard you laughing."

"I didn't know who you were at first. You didn't announce yourself. I thought you were some kind of weird recording. But I'm really not laughing at you."

"Well, there's no laughing *with* me because I'm not laughing. It isn't funny." But then, suddenly, it *is* funny, and Bronwyn begins to chuckle, a low sound fizzing up from her gut, involuntary, biological, unexpectedly delicious.

Lanny is fully awake now. "Call in sick," she instructs Bronwyn. "We're going away, you and I. I'm going crazy here anyway. It's hot and everyone but me is working. I'll come up there and we'll go camping."

"What about Tom?"

"He's under a deadline. I've hardly seen him since school ended."

"It's been ages since I've camped. I have no idea if I still have any of my gear."

"I've got everything. Find a sleeping bag and pull together some food and I'll bring everything else. Junk food, comfort food, whatever you're in the mood for, I don't care. Oh—can you get us a campsite somewhere? I'll pick you up in a few hours, as long as it takes to throw together my things and drive up there. I'm fast when I'm motivated."

What a relief to have a plan and to be in the hands of someone she trusts. It was always this way in school, Lanny took the lead. She was the big brave one, the risk-taker. Bronwyn held back, formulating questions, calculating odds, not exactly the brains of their team, but certainly the thinker.

At 9:00 a.m. she calls the station and tells Nicole she expects to be out for two days. "Are you really sick?" Nicole asks. "Or is it more like mental health?"

Bronwyn clears her throat. "Of course I'm really sick."

"You want to talk to Stuart?"

"God, no. Just tell him I sound bad. Chip will probably be happy to fill in for me."

Chip, a reporter, has subbed for her a few times. He doesn't have a deep understanding of weather, and Stuart doesn't seem to like him much, but he can put together a passable report from the National Weather Service feed, and he has an acceptable, if somewhat boring, camera presence. Bronwyn likes having someone dull replace her occasionally so her contribution is more appreciated.

Once off the phone a little blip of glee comes over her, a feeling that she's given Stuart the finger. Still not dressed, she wanders around the house in her underpants, a little aimless, making a pile on the living room floor of things she will take. She loves how bracing it is to sleep outside and wishes she camped more frequently, but the demands of school and work have made it hard in the last few years. She remembers her assignment to get them a campsite, and finds a place online, just off the Kancamagus Highway in the White Mountains, not far from Mount Washington. A surge comes over her—not well-being exactly, but the possibility of well-being awaiting her in the future. Outdoor living and some nights of solid sleep—surely they'll begin to repair her bruised heart.

People often laugh upon meeting Lanny and Bronwyn together. What they see is a snapshot of an unlikely pair. Lanny, a high school gym teacher, is six feet tall and burly; she clips her hair short. Bronwyn is five-foot-two and slender, her long, wavy, dark-red hair a defining feature. Next, people notice their contrasting behavioral traits: Lanny's boisterousness and lack of a verbal filter, Bronwyn's public reserve. It is clear to everyone that theirs is a friendship born of complementarity. But what is not visible is the long history that holds the friendship together, their knowledge of each other's families and of the private pains of the past. Bronwyn was there in early high school when Lanny's parents went through an ugly divorce. Lanny knows how difficult it was for Bronwyn to grow up with a frightened and often bitter single mother. They both remember Lanny getting her first period in seventh-grade math class, blood pooling over the seat. They remember Bronwyn's broken arm from a ninth-grade bicycle accident. Bronwyn attended most of Lanny's high school basketball games, and Lanny came to Bronwyn's science fairs. After Lanny got her license she would often borrow her father's car and take Bronwyn on road trips to the shore, or the Delaware River. Sometimes they took the bus into the city and wandered around the West Village. Lanny liked shocking people. She was the first among their classmates to get a tattoo, not a delicate one, but a dragon breathing fire that spiraled around her left arm. For almost an entire year in high school she wore the same pair of neon-orange cargo pants and a red paisley shirt. But in certain arenas Bronwyn and Lanny's tastes have always been identical. They have always liked the same junk food (nachos above all else), and they are both hooked on the same old movies (*Gone with the Wind*) and old TV shows ("Seinfeld" and "The X Files"). Though tough on the outside, they are both closet romantics. Bronwyn has no idea how she would get through life without a friend like Lanny, even though they sometimes go through long periods when they're out of touch.

Now they sit in low camp chairs at their campsite overlooking the Swift River, sipping bottles of beer, mesmerized by the river's pell-mell rush over the rocks, bathing them in its negative ions. Chipmunks and nuthatches dash here and there. The light is a delicate damask; the air gloves their skin, a temperate seventy degrees. Nature could not have engineered a more perfect situation for soothing a human being.

The sun slips behind the trees, dimming the air, imparting a contemplative mood to the landscape. Lanny wants to climb Mount Washington tomorrow. Bronwyn is game as long as she gets a solid sleep. She hopes she's in good-enough shape for such a climb. They prepare a dinner of spaghetti with meat sauce and salad and are in their sleeping bags by 9:00 p.m., the tent flaps open to the last embers of light. Night critters are venturing out. A bat circles overhead. An owl hoots. Tree frogs bleat. She and Lanny breathe in unison, as if entrained.

When the birds awaken her before 5:00 a.m., Bronwyn takes measure of herself. A good sleep has swept away apprehension. She feels surprisingly rested, ready for adventure, and eager to kick the Reed chapter of her life into history. She stares at Lanny, still slack-jawed in sleep, and slathers her friend with love as if spreading her with a thick layer of honey. Lanny knows her better than anyone in the world and will always be her best friend.

It's cold—high thirties, maybe forties—and geodes of frost still linger in the patches of shade. But it's mostly clear, a few high clouds to the west that Bronwyn deems unthreatening. Once the temperature rises a little it will be a perfect day for hiking. She nudges Lanny awake, pulls on some clothes, and begins scrambling eggs. Within forty-five minutes they're packing small backpacks with sandwiches and nuts and chocolate and two full quarts of water for each of them. They have rain gear, extra clothes, a first aid kit, compass, flashlight, and map.

Though it's been a while since Bronwyn has made an expedition like this, she knows the protocol: be prepared for all eventualities, and know, above all, that the weather can change.

"I won't be able to keep up with you," Bronwyn says. "You're in much better shape than I am."

"I'm not as fit as I look."

"Last night I dreamed you were wearing those orange cargo pants and that paisley shirt."

"Oh god, what was I thinking back then? I should have kept those pants as a souvenir of my youthful stupidity."

Sunlight bristles over the picnic table and the day charges forward, calling them to action. At 6:03 a.m. they're on the road in Lanny's Subaru. The eastern sky is clear. A few stringy cirrus clouds, not of particular concern, laze high to the west. Temperatures are in the low fifties now and rising. Spectacular weather for the White Mountains, spectacular weather by any standards. Climbing a mountain seems like such a pure and uncomplicated thing to do, and it gives Bronwyn a satisfying sense of purpose.

Bronwyn squints through the windshield and holds her hand out the open window.

"What're you doing?" Lanny asks.

"Sizing up the day."

"Highly scientific, I see."

"Actually, it is scientific. Observation is where science begins. You establish norms and departures from norms. But it all begins with looking and noticing."

Lanny laughs. "Always calculating, aren't you?"

They set out on the Jewell Trail at 7:20a.m., Lanny in the lead taking long, aggressive strides. The trail, ascending along Mount Washington's western ridge, is the longest but most gradual trail to the summit. It will take them four to five hours to reach the top and another three or four hours to descend. Allowing an hour for lunch and rest breaks, they estimate they'll be done by six p.m., safely back at the campsite before nightfall.

The first part of the trail slopes gently uphill through a deciduous forest, underfoot a soft bed of leaves and earth, moist from spring rain, muddy in some places. The air is still cool, but sunlight, yellow and sweet as butterscotch, speckles the forest floor.

Lanny swings her arms and sings "I'm Happy When I'm Hiking" with child-like abandon. She has a talent for sinking into the moment and plumbing it fully. Bronwyn herself speculates too much about the future, effacing the present. When you situate your mind in the future you do not feel the soft loam giving way as each boot hits the ground. You do not hear your knees creak, or feel the sweat slithering down the back of your neck, or see the garter snake making his quick getaway. You do not hear the birdcalls or revel in the sunrise. You scarcely hear yourself breathe.

When the trail crosses a brook they stop for a break and sit on rocks, snacking on walnuts and raisins, sipping their water. They do not speak, and the silence seals their bond.

"It feels like it's going to rain." Lanny peers up through the canopy to the few chips of visible sky.

"It won't rain," Bronwyn says.

"If you say so. You'd know, I guess."

"I'm paid to know." But in fact she hasn't checked the National Weather Service. She has consulted only her own instinct today, reports from her pores.

They allow a foursome of twenty-something men to pass them, and Bronwyn feels a twinge of envy for their youth and fitness. Thirty isn't old, but it's getting there, and something about the springy, sinewy calves of those men brings this home acutely.

A series of switchbacks takes them up the side of the ridge, and by mid-morning they emerge above the tree-line. The air is noticeably cooler and windy, and though blue sky still predominates, a posse of dark-bellied nimbus clouds rolls in from the west. After so much time under the trees, the massive stretch of sky is disquieting. Light but dark. At once revealing and undisclosing. They've lost their protection. Lanny was right, rain is all but certain now. Bronwyn should have known better than to think they could reach the summit without some weather to contend with. Nevertheless, the clouds are still high enough to permit an impressive view of the Presidential Range: Mount Jefferson, Mount Adams, and Mount Madison preside like a receiving line to the north. *We're here, we're always reliably here*, they seem to be saying. Ahead, along a ridge directly in front of them, stands the peak of Mount Washington, still a fair hike away. A sudden gust of wind kicks up from the west-northwest and careens into Lanny so she teeters, almost falls.

"Jeez, that was rude!"

"You should put on your rain gear to break the wind," Bronwyn says.

"Yes, Mom."

"I know, I'm sorry—" Bronwyn can't stand this cautionary role of hers, but she plays it well, as she always has. They both take out their jackets and put them on without speaking.

"Good to go," Lanny shouts over the wind.

The trail now requires extra caution as it ascends over boulders. Ahead of them hikers dot the mountainside like a herd of colorfully jacketed goats. Bronwyn is highly alert, highly focused, shifting her attention between monitoring Lanny's uncertain progress over the rocks and scrutinizing the advancing front which is clotted with black pannus clouds, a sure sign of precipitation to come. She tries to estimate the speed of the front's approach and surmise what it will deliver. The winds are gusting at thirty to forty miles per hour, she guesses, which makes talking almost impossible. Worse, it makes the mountain unfriendly, even sinister. She hates this job of trying to forecast with incomplete data. There is so much about which she cannot be sure. Ahead of her Lanny marches on, apparently unperturbed. Is Bronwyn crazy to think they should quit? Yes, the summit is in sight, but it will take them at least another hour to get there.

"Maybe we should turn around," Bronwyn suggests, yelling over the wind.

"You've got to be kidding. I'm not giving up now. Not when we're so close to the top."

"It's farther than it looks."

Lanny makes a face. Bronwyn vacillates. It isn't clear who's in charge. But Bronwyn feels Lanny's intransigence, and it would be foolish to separate. Bronwyn gives a slight nod and they continue.

Because Bronwyn is who she is—because her body is earth-sentient and she has spent her life thinking about weather—she feels the updraft before it manifests, warm air rising, smashing into the cooler air above. She pictures the fracas of colliding molecules overhead, imagines she hears them.

"I don't like this," she says.

Lanny either doesn't hear, or chooses not to respond.

The clouds have assumed the steely look of military tanks; they knock against the sky's boundaries. The cog railway, chugging uphill, emits noxious black smoke that rises like a feisty runt to test itself against the storm clouds. Sheet lightning explodes, whitening the sky, as if to erase all memories, making a clean palette for itself. It pixelates everything, illuminating Lanny and making of her a hallucination. *One one-thousand, two one-thousand.* Thunder detonates. They both jump. Rain follows, sudden, hard, cold, slicing the air at a sharp angle, obscuring everything.

"Stay there," Bronwyn shouts to Lanny, leaning into the wind, bent at the waist, eyes slitted. She reaches Lanny, grabs her arm, tugs. Lanny, taller than Bronwyn and much heavier, resists. Then, without warning she yields, allowing herself to be guided to the nearest boulder where they both crouch under a ledge. Lanny says something made unintelligible by the tumult. She leans closer. "We're going to die," she says directly into Bronwyn's ear.

Bronwyn shakes her head, an emphatic *no*. They aren't safe here, but it's better than venturing into the open in such low visibility to make grounding rods of themselves. She thinks briefly of Reed, how he would react to hearing she had died in an electrical storm on Mount Washington. Would he feel remorse? Would he think his rejection drove her to recklessness?

Rain is everywhere, petulant, soaking her waterproof jacket, running in full-blown rivers down her torso. Lanny, famously always-warm Lanny, shivers. Bronwyn pulls her close to help them both preserve heat. What fools they are. Bronwyn should have steered them away from this mountain whose weather lore she knows so well. There are plenty of other mountains they could have climbed with far less fickle weather. They should have turned back at the first sighting of storm clouds. She shouldn't have relied on her own instinct, should have investigated the weather reports before they set out.

An aura surrounds them, cool and merciless, the beckoning arm of Death. It is so senseless to die this way, accidentally, beneath nature's fist. She is overcome with fury, with a wish for things to be different than they are, furious for all the things she cannot change, beginning with this moment and bleeding back into everything else: Reed's disinterest, Stuart's stupidity, her mother's negativity. Another flash blanches the sky, stealing all dimensions but two. Scarcely a second passes before thunder cracks.

Rain turns to hail, vitriolic and personal, each pellet big as a Barbie head. Her rage spikes. Her brain seems to pucker and roll inside her skull. Her head is on fire. Her vision wavers. She sloughs her backpack and pushes herself to standing.

"What're you doing?" Lanny shouts.

Entangled in something, Bronwyn can hardly speak. "Stay there," she croaks.

Gripped by the storm, enshrined in its clamor, she turns west to its source and folds herself into the symphonic chaos. Her chest throbs. She strains to keep her eyelids apart. Hail batters her cheeks. Red fills her vision. Clouds swirl around her, malevolent evaporating tongues. She summons all her will, heaving with the effort, with rage and need. She hurls forth the volcanic heat in her brain, her eyes like rapiers jousting with the crazed molecules. She slides through a portal and is sundered from any sense of self she has known, wholly devoted to some other entity, hearing only her own strained breath, life at its limit.

The mountaintop is still. Hailstones litter the rocks. The sun glistens. The sky is blue, the air gilded. There isn't a breath of wind. Bronwyn scans the Presidentials, etched in perfect clarity against the guileless, cloudless blue. Where exactly is she? Who is she? A warm presence at her side. A human body. A woman. Her old friend Lanny, churning out sound that could be laughter.

"My god. What just happened?"

Bronwyn pants. The laughter comes at her like a raucous Greenland piteraq. She shakes her head, sits on a rock, cradles her head, sniffs the post-rain ozone and petrichor.

"Bronwyn, talk to me. That was wild. If I didn't know better, I'd think you did something to call off that storm."

Bronwyn reaches for words, but they're sealed in a remote part of her body. Even if she could find them, they could not touch or express her experience of what has happened.

More laughter rolls from Lanny, then stops abruptly. "I *do* know better and I *still* think you did something. You made that storm go away. I watched you. I swear to god you cast some spell."

Bronwyn remains motionless, depleted, baffled.

7

Lanny has taken charge, driven them back to the campsite, made a fire and dinner, all the while exhaling amazement and attending to Bronwyn as if she's an invalid. Now night has descended fully, and they relax in their low camp chairs, drinking hot chocolate, mesmerized by the flames which swell and shrink and twirl around one another. Grottos, tabernacles, entire cities grow and tumble, like human civilization itself, rising and falling and rising yet again from embers.

Lanny has theories, lots of them. It could be telekinesis, she says, like the movie *Carrie*. "Or did you ever see that George Clooney movie, *The Men Who Stare at Goats*? They just looked at the goats and, boom, the goats keeled over. Or *Chronicle*, that was awesome. These boys get telekinetic powers, and they end up using them to do horrible things. I know you've seen *Carrie*—we saw it together."

Bronwyn laughs quietly. "Those are just movies." She remembers *Carrie* vividly, the anger and humiliation that were the underpinnings of Carrie's retaliatory acts.

"But why would people make movies about this shit if there weren't some truth to it? Do you think you can do it again?"

Bronwyn cannot weigh in. The day has decimated her. Like a mass extinction. Which of her faculties will come back first, if any? But despite her exhaustion, something glows at her core as if she has swallowed one of the fire's embers. And while her vision seems to be dimmed by a furry grating, her hearing is unusually acute. Even over the river's noisy tumbling she is quite sure she hears the scrabbling legs in a nearby ant colony, a garter snake sucking up an earthworm.

"You were kind of like doing telepathy with that storm, right?" Lanny says. "It reminds me of *A Wrinkle in Time* where they do that kything thing. Remember? Or have you heard of those people who randomly turn out streetlights just by looking at them—it was kind of like that."

Bronwyn has not heard of people putting out streetlights. Why would someone want to put out a streetlight? She lays down her hot chocolate and feeds another log onto the fire. The lower logs slump and fracture under the weight. What exactly is *it*? It felt almost involuntary and then she was in the midst of it. Why has Lanny been so quick to conclude that Bronwyn stopped the storm? Humans, by nature, look for causality and see causal connections where none exist. Think of the Greeks who attributed weather phenomena to a slew of gods, each with its own province. But wouldn't most modern people regard the storm's retreat as coincidence? Yet, Lanny is not just anyone. She knows Bronwyn exceedingly well. She observed Bronwyn today and perhaps felt vicariously Bronwyn's own sense that she was linked somehow to those clouds, the wind, that lightning.

"You think I did something, but I didn't *do* anything. Something happened. And it could have been coincidence—we were hoping the storm would stop, but it actually stopped randomly."

"Uh-uh. You caused it. You stood up there and did something—I don't know what, but something. Maybe you could do it again."

How could she possibly do again what she was never aware of doing in the first place? "Maybe I couldn't."

Lanny clucks. "Such a pessimist."

They stare into the fire, sinking into their different habits of mind. *Am I a pessimist?* Bronwyn wonders. *No, only a realist.* She isn't comfortable being scrutinized like this, even by Lanny. She has never been to a shrink and she never will. Her mind is her own affair, and it doesn't need to be pawed and probed by some pseudo-scientist.

She pulls herself together enough to find her phone and check the Mount Washington Observatory's weather report. The severe electrical storm is reported with winds that gusted up to 120 mph. The storm subsided abruptly, the report says, and a high pressure front moved in. She reads the report aloud to Lanny, shivering, unsettled.

"That's not telling us anything we don't already know," Lanny says.

Just because events are sequential does not make them causally related, Bronwyn reminds herself. Her intent to stop the storm and her sensation of enormous energy output could have had nothing to do with the weather changing dramatically. Could she repeat what happened under controlled circumstances, the gold standard for solid proof? It is nearly impossible to imagine. There is no controlled laboratory for weather.

What a relief it is to be alone in her small homely place by the river. But her mind is untethered, drifting from one thing to another, not perching on anything for long. The density of her brain feels different. Her head floats, balloon-like. She goes to her bedroom and forgets why she's there. She makes a grocery list, sets it down, then can't find it. Has she lost her ability to concentrate and think rigorously? Is this how dementia starts? One does not expect to discover new emotions at age thirty, but what she feels now is undeniably new; the incredulity and confusion, muddled with the recent rejection, have combined alchemically into a glowing feeling of newness. She has the sensation of looking at herself from a vantage point outside her own skin, ten or twenty feet away.

Maybe she and Lanny are both wrong. Maybe nothing happened and nothing will happen again. But she knows as well as she ever knows anything that something about her life is different. Questions abound. How can she learn what really happened when everyone knows that using oneself as an object of study makes objectivity impossible?

A prick of fear. A sheen of wonder. An urge to explore. Sharp images appear before her, like faces desperate for breath bursting up from under water. Amoeboid gray shapes. Flashes of light. Something shiny and red fills her vision. Memories from Mount Washington, she thinks. The shapes of the clouds, the lightning. As for the red, she cannot say. A by-product of overstimulation, perhaps.

The problem with analyzing what happened is that her memory of it is sketchy. First, she was filled with heat and feeling, facing the storm with hell-bent rage, but then what—? Then she lost track. It was as if her *self*, the self through which she sees and hears and organizes the events of the world, vanished, and she was subsumed into another entity, and for a while she was only that other thing, not Bronwyn at all. How do you remember an event if it happened to someone other than the person you currently are?

If Lanny had not been there, insisting something unusual happened, and if there had not been that earlier moment on the beach, then Bronwyn would have decided she'd imagined the impossible very deeply. But she has to concede Lanny might be right—maybe she did *do* something. There is little to be gained in denying the possibility.

A mouse has come inside the cabin through one of the holes in the porch screen, and it has settled under the couch where Bronwyn is sitting. She can hear it scratching around, finding cracker crumbs and dried-up nachos. It's probably a regular feast under there, given the number of times Bronwyn has eaten makeshift meals on this couch. She was hoping to sleep here tonight, but she won't with a mouse at large. She can't stand the thought of a rodent scurrying over her chest while she sleeps.

Her mind rolls it over and over as a tongue investigates a dental problem. There is a dual difficulty: first proving that something happened, then explaining it. Subjectively, it felt that a high volume of energy was pouring from her brain, annihilating the storm. It was as if the heat in her head could boil oceans, evaporate clouds, mollify the overexcited elements. But what happened empirically? The brain is a self-contained adiabatic system, functioning without the gain or loss of heat. She has never heard of a brain transmitting energy beyond that system. Did her brain really somehow generate a massive amount of heat on its own? If so, how? And how could such energy pass through her skull? If that is indeed what happened.

She thinks of her old college boyfriend Anish, who is now a brain surgeon. What would he have to say on this matter? They broke up because his parents wanted him to marry an Indian woman, but they stay in touch, albeit infrequently. She'd be embarrassed though, trying to explain herself to Anish.

Occam's razor, a fundamental precept: In evaluating hypotheses, the simplest explanation is usually the best. But in this case, even a simple hypothesis is hard to put forth. She thinks about the monks in the Himalayas known for being able to raise their body temperatures dramatically. But even that exertion, impressive though it is, is contained, not a transmission of energy outward.

She must monitor herself closely and keep a low profile. No one can know about this. She has sworn Lanny to secrecy. Any small breach of confidentiality could have unpleasant consequences. Things go viral so easily these days. And people are not merciful.

The absence of Reed in her life makes the weekend seem extra long and aimless. Her phone is morbidly silent, her inbox dead. It is surprising to realize how much of an organizing principle Reed gave to her life, even when he was physically absent.

She sleeps in the bedroom on Saturday night instead of on the porch, grabbing rest in short snatches, worried about the mouse. She dreams of a wind with leering eyes that morphs into Reed's new woman, a blonde, statuesque femme fatale.

At nine o'clock Sunday morning she is at the grocery store, watching the checkout clerk beep her items. Chips, cheese, salsa, refried beans, and mousetraps. She's lost her appetite and might as well eat one of the few dishes that still appeals. But even so she feels ashamed by her purchases and averts her eyes, answering the clerk's cheerful, *How's it going?* with a succinct, *Good.*

She sets traps in every room, using cubes of cheese as bait. She makes a plate of nachos and takes it out to the riverbank. The day is sunny and warm, not too hot. There's some low-lying haze to the east, but it's clearing fast, making the day one about which no one can lodge a complaint. The river is lazy; the dragonflies and flies and bees are lazy; and the sun's warmth encourages human laziness too. She releases herself to this tide of inertia. Her syncopated internal rhythms ease. She pictures her blood thickening like red mercury, slowing to a crawl. The saccades of her eyes cease. Fat flies come circling to sniff at the melted cheese. They move so slowly they are easy to bat away, but they keep returning. Eventually she gives up and lays the nachos in the grass where the flies swarm to feast on the grease.

The river's dark water is black and blue in the sunlight. It is such a benign river, but, like many rivers, it conceals complicated currents. She has not tried to swim in it though she isn't sure why, as she loves to swim. Fear of the unknown sums up her reluctance. The possibility of snapping turtles and water snakes, though she really has no idea if they exist in this water. Perhaps she doesn't swim in it because she hasn't seen anyone else swimming in it. There are two houses on the opposite bank within view, but she never sees people coming and going there.

A few years ago she took an online test whose results concluded she was a person of "thin boundaries." It defined such a person as undefended, vulnerable, flitting between fantasy and reality, often incapable of separating thoughts and feelings. Much as she had suspected this, the confirmation frightened her. Ever since, she has worked hard to conceal this shameful part of her character and armor herself more effectively against it. She is aware that her social reticence makes her appear more armored than she truly is.

She has never shared the results of this test. A scientist, she is quite sure, is hampered by having thin boundaries. Thin boundaries could make a researcher too easily seduced and persuaded by scant evidence. Nevertheless, without her supposedly thin boundaries would she sense the weather as she does, receive it so accurately, be so attuned to the nuances which signal change? Without thin boundaries would she see and hear, even smell, so much?

Back inside she dumps the remains of the nachos into the garbage and checks the traps. Not one, but three mice have been caught, an infestation. Who knows how many more are creeping around beneath the furniture. Now she must summon the bravery to dispose of the flaccid bodies. For the time being she leaves them where they are. Her phone's ringtone sounds with the melody she programmed, "Singing in the Rain."

A text from Lanny: *We have to talk. I need to know what's happening, if you're alright.*

I'm fine, Bronwyn texts back. *Let's try to forget it happened.*

I won't ever forget it! We could have died out there—you saved my ass!

Bronwyn doesn't respond. There's an email from Stuart expressing concern about her illness, hoping she's better, confirming how much he admires her work and reminding her he expects to see her on Monday. Another from Diane, who says she will soon be on her way to Maine for a two-week vacation, and she'd love to take Bronwyn out to dinner. *I have an ulterior motive,* she writes. The thought of seeing Diane is paralyzing, especially in light of recent events. For all the encouragement Diane has given Bronwyn over the years, Bronwyn is still sometimes afraid of her mentor, who is imposing and opinionated and readily divides the world into "we" and "they." Bronwyn is aware of how easy it would be to unwittingly find herself in the wrong camp. Yet Bronwyn can't say no to Diane who has been so good to her for so long. Supportive and generous with her time, Diane has always made Bronwyn feel she had a viable future. The *ulterior motive* Diane mentioned is no secret. She wants Bronwyn to return to school and be a member of her research team. Bronwyn wonders if Diane has seen any of her weather broadcasts. She sincerely hopes not. Diane made it quite clear that in taking this broadcasting job Bronwyn was demeaning herself. She tries to imagine sitting across the table from Diane, eating a meal and navigating a conversation about her career in atmospheric science, while concealing the events of the last few days. Now more than ever, she's sure she has no future in academia.

She closes her email, leaving both Stuart's and Diane's messages unanswered. She must change her ringtone. "Singing in the Rain" once seemed clever; now it's a cruel joke.

8

A memory comes in the middle of the night. It has the hazy erratic texture of a dream, though she knows it's a memory, not a dream. She was ten or eleven, and she and her mother had just had an argument. What was it about? She can't quite get to the specifics, but she remembers standing in her room upstairs, so shaky with rage and helplessness her cheeks and neck twitched. She wanted to defy her mother, but didn't dare. She gazed out the window to the small back yard. A thunderstorm hit as she stood there watching. What luck! She couldn't believe the weather could match her mood so perfectly. Each time lightning flashed she felt it trembling inside her body—she was sure it must be glowing through her skin. She counted to the next clap of thunder, throwing her anger out into the yard so it snarled and growled in unison with the elements. She spread her arms as if conducting things. She was Zeus, wronged and righteous, inflicting a storm on someone who'd rebuked her.

Her mother rushed out to the yard to bring in the outdoor furniture. Metal furniture—didn't she know better, she shouldn't be touching metal with all that electrical energy flying. Another flash of lightning illuminated the yard like a movie set. Her mother's eyes were dark tunnels of terror. She could get killed out there, Bronwyn thought, and for a moment Bronwyn hoped she would be killed. The memory chills Bronwyn, even after all these years.

Awake, alone in the dark, she misses her mother. Sleep wands back over her, gloving her in stillness and oblivion. She awakens feeling ready, sniffing the air, laughing a little to herself. A memory of power has attached to her like a palimpsest.

She drinks a quick cup of coffee, drops the dead mice into the garbage and, without even a glance at her weather station, she goes outside and down to the river's edge. A light rain falls, a mist atomizing her skin. This rain will keep up for a while, she thinks. The few days of sun she forecast last week have come and gone. She doesn't care. She sticks out her tongue, tastes the molecules that once made up a cloud. Inside her head she senses the movement of atoms.

As a child she used to wonder what would happen if all the forces of energy gave out entirely: the sun's radiation, the pull of gravity, wind, ocean currents, human metabolism. All movement, all light and heat, suddenly deactivated. All human intention and will snuffed. The Earth ceasing to orbit or spin. Insects and birds falling from the sky. Blood coagulating in vessels. Synapses fizzing to a halt. Everything inert. When she thought of this she would begin to run, to prove to herself that she, at least, could still generate energy.

Something inchoate surfaces in her. A desire to feel that power again. Not Zeus's power, but Athena's. She plants her bare feet more firmly in the scratchy crabgrass, lanky dandelion stems grazing her calves. She trains her gaze on the dark river, takes a breath and holds it, sensing the atoms inside her body as they begin to oscillate synchronously, heat filling her belly and rising to her chest. It fans out to her arms and legs. As deliberately as she can she directs the heat to her head, disciplining her consciousness to stay in the moment so she will remember later. Behind her forehead the heat ignites, a conflagration almost out of her control, though not quite. She hears a thrumming, feels the pulse. The world falls away. Her eyes soar and she thrusts the heat rhythmically, struggling to stay alert, taking aim at the river's midpoint. Her body seems to rise. She swoops, broad as a condor, over the water's surface. The current picks up speed. Small ripples appear, the ripples become whitecaps, and soon the water rushes over itself, eddying and back-splashing. Full-blown rapids flash by, a huge volume of water, quick and dangerous.

She floats back down to the riverbank, gasping for breath, gradually rejoining the known world again, her vision widening and clearing. She turns around, suddenly self-conscious. Has anyone seen? The river still rages, rambunctious and deafening in its sudden haste to join the sea. The sight of it brings her up short. What has she done? She has to stop it, but she's too spent. She sits on the muddy grass and waits, both hyper-vigilant and incapable of moving, never so alone. She can't leave the river surging hysterically like this. It could wreak havoc: floods, drownings, habitats destroyed. She tries to attach her gaze on the mid-point of the river again, but her focus is shot. Her gaze flits. She still hasn't caught her breath. Her face is hot, but the rest of her body is wracked with shivers. She needs to refuel, she thinks. She drags herself upright and lumbers inside.

The refrigerator is perilously empty, except for the nacho ingredients. The thought of nachos disgusts her right now. She takes out the peanut butter jar, and dips a spoon into it, and sucks on the spoon, still standing with the refrigerator door open, the river roaring behind her. She shouldn't be playing around with natural forces, altering them at her whim. Who does she think she is? *Who do you think you are?* The refrain of her childhood. *Don't think you're so great.* The peanut butter jar slips from her hand, shattering at her feet, a hunk of glass and shit-colored goo. She tosses the spoon into the sink and takes herself outside.

The rain still falls and the feisty river still churns dangerously. The choler gathers until she can scarcely hear herself think. She plants her feet, though her legs are quivering and barely supportive. She stares at a place where the waves leap up like truculent cowlicks. She locates the atoms that support her intention, prods them. The heat blooms again, this time like a liquid flooding her heart. She keeps it there, forces it up, up, up, to her brain which seems to snap audibly. Synapses crackle, ignite to a bonfire. There is no other sound but the slow ballooning of her lungs. She contains the blaze, shrinks it to a manageable size, and lobs it directly ahead. Tottering, she keeps her gaze on the leaping water then hurls the fireball again.

Slowly, slowly, the obstreperous current slackens, composing itself as if it's been chided. She collapses on the muddy embankment, staring out at the quiescent water with relief. Less than a minute has passed, though to her it could have been a millennium. A few skater bugs, oblivious to the rain, skim along the water's tamed surface. Laughing quietly, she vows to remember.

9

By the time Bronwyn leaves for work the misting rain has intensified; it drubs the foliage into submission and outpaces her windshield wipers. The National Weather Service has corroborated her hunch, predicting this rain may persist for close to a week. People at the station will be complaining, no doubt. They feel entitled to days of endless sun as soon as summer hits. In an effort to show them things aren't all that bad, she will tell them, as her "Fun Weather Fact," the story of *The Summer That Never Was.*

The summer of 1816 was exceptional around the world. June frost was seen at various locations in New England; fog reddened and dimmed the sunlight; snow fell in New York and Maine; in July and August ice was observed in lakes and rivers as far south as Pennsylvania. Temperatures swung from ninety-five degrees Fahrenheit to near freezing within hours. Cool temperatures and heavy rains were seen in Britain and Ireland. In China, the cold killed trees, rice crops, even water buffalo. In Hungary, there was brown snow; in Italy, it was red. Around the world widespread crop failures resulted in famine.

Two primary causes are cited for these worldwide anomalies. First, there had been an increase in volcanic eruptions, beginning in 1812 and culminating in the Mount Tambura eruption in Indonesia in 1815. The explosion ejected vast quantities of volcanic ash into the upper atmosphere and caused an overall lowering of the Earth's average land mass temperature. That, coupled with a period of unusually low solar activity, made for the extremely "bad" weather. The current rain in New England is, by comparison, a mere inconvenience.

She enters the station furtively. It feels as if she's been gone for eons. So much has happened in her days away. She is not the same Bronwyn she was last week, and as she dressed for work she could see that so clearly. Her face appeared in the mirror as a hologram, ghosted by another face, shifting between the two. She has sprouted invisible sentient whiskers all over her body. She moves through space as if the air itself is a piece of fabric that might be lifted and examined. She is in love with the Earth as never before. But words are a challenge.

The station is windowless and dimly lit, its décor an investigation of all the hues of brown. It would be a perfect place for illicit activities. The inner rooms are soundproof, but in the lobby, where Nicole sits at her desk, the rain outside sounds catastrophic.

Nicole hops up. She is a spring breeze of a girl, Bronwyn thinks. Full of hope. "I have to show you," Nicole says. She pulls a large box from beneath her desk and beckons Bronwyn to the women's room. The dress that has been under discussion for weeks billows from under its tissue paper, a summer cloud of chiffon and beaded taffeta, a young girl's Cinderella dream of a dress. Nicole lifts it as if it's fragile as eggshells, and eases it to her chest, mugging for admiration.

"Oh. Yes. Beautiful." Is it beautiful? Bronwyn honestly can't say. She has lost the framework necessary for ascribing beauty to anything man-made.

Nicole frowns. "You don't like it?"

"Of course I do. You're going to look gorgeous. What does Mike think?"

"He hasn't seen it. Not until I walk down the aisle."

"I didn't realize people still did that."

Nicole stows the dress back in the box as if tucking it in for sleep. "But what if it rains? I am so afraid it's going to rain like today. I'll die if it rains."

"I've heard that rain on a wedding day means good luck. But don't worry, it won't rain. I promise."

"I wish. Hey, you're coming aren't you? You haven't RSVP'd."

"I'm sorry. Yes, I'll be there." Until this moment she wasn't sure, dubious about her social skills, certain she'd be out of place.

"Good, because I'm setting you up with my cousin like I promised."

"Oh, Nicole. I'm not ready. It's too recent."

"You might be ready when you see him."

Bronwyn scuttles down the hallway, averting her gaze from the offices on either side. The heavy door to the sound stage thuds closed behind her. The room is empty, thank god. She hurries to her perch.

Today the weather presses on her as never before. The summer has only just begun, but it is already walloping the country with high heat and drought in the west, tornadoes rolling over the plains states like an endless cue of deadly bowling balls. Strike. Strike. Strike. She refuses to judge these events—they are the Earth's way of being itself, indifferent to human need. And yet, she's human too. And for humans, these events are dire.

She scrolls through the satellite and NEXRAD data, studies various weather maps and aerial photographs, lingers on some storm chaser footage of a tornado that passed through Oklahoma just yesterday. She thinks of Vince Carmichael, the legendary Oklahoman meteorologist, a mentor of sorts though she's never met him. She first discovered his broadcasts when she was in high school. He is lively on the air, sure of himself, physically extravagant in the way of a toreador or a gladiator, and his tornado predictions are remarkably accurate. He is more than an extreme weather voyeur—he actually saves lives. She hasn't seen one of his broadcasts in quite a while.

When the set becomes active she scarcely notices, cocooned as she is in another conversation. Her gaze is singular, and she hears only the regular pull of her own deep breathing as she tumbles through data.

At broadcast time Archie summons her with a touch on the arm. Time to go. She wrests her gaze from the computer and forces her attention to expand outward again. How fortunate she is to be able to rely on habit. She locates the muscles that smile and those that speak. Still, the image of herself in the monitor is not the usual Bronwyn. Like the bathroom's mirror image this morning, it flutters between two things, as if the sight in each of her eyes refuses to be coordinated into a single vision.

No one likes her "Fun Weather Fact" about *The Summer That Never Was*. She should have known. Archie laughs, but Larry, the other cameraman, glares at her. Gwen can't believe she's never heard this before. Brant, who doesn't like to appear uninformed, nods grimly. Bronwyn slinks back to her perch feeling like a pariah. She has not communicated well. What she meant to say was that despite the rain coming down now, it could be worse; this bleak weather is only relative.

Years ago weather forecasters were thought of as heretics. In seventeenth century England you could be burned to death if caught forecasting. In World War II American forecasts were restricted, as they might provide information to the enemy. It's very possible, Bronwyn thinks, that as dire weather increases in frequency, and mass panic ensues, similar strictures could again be imposed.

Between the 6:00 p.m. and 10:00 p.m. broadcasts, during the long stretch of evening programming, it is customary for the news staff to relax in the break room. There are snacks and coffee and soft drinks and couches and easy chairs. People chat, catch up on work, check Facebook, answer emails and texts. Tonight Bronwyn stays at her station on the set. She stares down at the blue veins streaking the insides of her forearms, wondering if they've become more prominent than usual.

"Bad night?" Archie says, sneaking up behind her.

She whirls to him. His face is close enough that she sees the acne scars beneath his beard. She used to think he was coming on to her, but now she sees him as genuinely considerate.

"Why are you so nice to me?"

"Because I remember being where you are now."

"Where is that?"

"At some juncture. Not sure what's next. Feeling like life has left you with the short end of the stick."

She blinks, wondering what she might say to him, if he would believe her. The idea of saying more suddenly seems foolish, and she closes like a touched sea anemone. Not yet. It is said that humans want to be seen, but Archie already sees her much too clearly.

"Share a spliff after the show?"

"You're always trying to get me high."

"I'm trying to help you relax."

"Thanks, but not tonight." She remembers something. "Would you go with me to Nicole's wedding? She invited you, right?"

Archie looks surprised.

"Not as a date," she adds quickly.

"I wasn't sure I'd go."

"Nether was I. But I think I should. She keeps asking. And I can't go alone."

"Why not?"

"It might rain and she'll be furious at me."

"Bron, get a grip."

"I told her it wouldn't rain. Guaranteed it."

Archie chuckles softly. "You're kind of whacked." He pauses, squints, and seems to inch his face closer to hers. "Something's up isn't it? I've been looking at your face up close for months now. You might fool some people, but not me."

She turns away, his inquiry a too-bright, potentially damaging sun. "Okay—so I've been dumped."

"Shit, sorry to hear that. I knew something must have happened. You look so pale and a little spooked or something."

"Don't worry about me. I always look pale—you know that. I'm fine. Maybe I need to be left alone for a bit."

Respectful, he leaves her alone, but minutes later the stage door opens again, and footsteps track toward her, and she knows instinctively who it is. She doesn't turn until he's directly behind her. "Archie said I could find you in here," Stuart says.

Bronwyn nods and raises a hand to her face, as if to shield herself from his fault-finding gaze.

"I think you need to redo your makeup before you go back on the air. You look a little . . ." He makes a brushing motion with one hand.

She can't believe it—he's so predictable. She nods. There's no point in resisting unless she's ready to risk being fired. She wonders if this insistence on her looking a particular way could be construed legally as sexual harassment. "Is that what you came to tell me?"

"I have an idea. What if you were to sing some songs about the weather, instead of the Fun Weather Facts? 'Here Comes the Sun' for example, or 'Rainy Day Mondays.' You know—light, funny. You wouldn't have to sing the whole song, just a line or two."

She frowns, tries to find his eyes in the watery landscape of his glasses. "My voice is terrible."

"You wouldn't have to sing *well*. Just belt out a line or two."

"Why would you want me to do that?"

"Honestly? You have a tendency to get a little over-serious with your reports. That story you told today—sure, it's interesting, but it depresses the hell out of people."

"I'm not here to make people feel better."

"That's exactly why you're here. We're all here for that. Do you know how many people turn on the TV because they're lonely? They want to see another human being and hear another human voice. We're their company and we have to smile and be upbeat to cheer them up. The people who aren't lonely are getting their weather and news online, or from their phones. We can't afford to alienate the lonely people who choose to watch us. They need us. And, coincidentally, we need them."

"God, that's depressing."

"I'm telling you how it is. A line or two of song would spice things up a bit, maybe even make a few of those lonely viewers laugh. Even on rainy days. Especially then."

He reaches into his shirt pocket and brings out a folded sheet of paper. "I've been compiling a list to get you started. I'm sure you can come up with a lot more on your own."

He examines his list and throws back his head, breaking into James Taylor's "Fire and Rain." "Love that one. Or this: 'You Are My Sunshine.' That's a crowd-pleaser. Maybe Johnny Nash's 'I Can See Clearly Now,' and the Beatles' song, 'I'll Follow the Sun.' How does that go? Gosh, there are so many good ones."

She watches his enthusiasm from afar and sees he fancies himself a singer. The humidity has frizzed his sparse hair so it has retracted from his comb-over and sizzles on both sides of his head like clusters of honey bees.

"I think you'd be better at that than I would be," she says.

"You'll do fine. It'll be fun."

"So you're saying this isn't negotiable?"

"That's right. It's non-negotiable. You don't have to do it tonight. You can begin in the next day or two."

After Stuart has departed Bronwyn looks at the list. At the top it says *Weather Songs* and it is divided into two columns, *Sun Songs* and *Rain Songs*. He has come up with fifty titles. What about blizzard songs and hurricane songs, tsunami and tornado songs? Songs of heat and cold and wind and humidity? She'll find those songs too, and then Stuart will be sorry for making her do this. She puts the list in her purse. She supposes she should be grateful that he hasn't asked her to don silly costumes and hats, or deliver her remarks alongside cutesy Chihuahuas dressed in raincoats. Now more than ever she hopes that Diane will never watch her on the air.

At home later that night there is a hiatus in the rain. The moist warm air feels good. A scythe of a moon pokes hazily through the cloud cover. She feels its magnetism tugging lightly against her chest. She casts off her work clothes, unclips her hair, and steps outside to feel the river's presence more directly. On cue her owl hoots. *Who-hoo-hoo are you?*

10

From across the street Diane—standing in front of the restaurant on the lookout for Bronwyn—appears to be a mirage, shimmering, at once there and not there, the fabric of her loose, coat-of-many-colors outfit rippling with her movements, her hair flapped over her head haphazardly as tinsel. She is short and buxom, but even at this distance she radiates a never-miss-a-trick energy that commands attention as if she were tall. In Bronwyn's view Diane alternates between the dusty hot wind of a Sirocco, straight from the Sahara, and the cold Mistral of France.

The familiar cape of shame descends over Bronwyn, the shame she has worn since last May when she finally told Diane that she wouldn't be returning to school. The day before Bronwyn's move they ran into each other at the Harvard Coop where Bronwyn was buying yet another roll of strapping tape. Bronwyn would have avoided Diane, but they were already face to face.

"Ms. Artair," Diane said. She stared down at Bronwyn's tape and raised a knowing eyebrow, smiling a little. "What do you think of this?" She held up a book called *Freedom*, a title which seemed to Bronwyn a little too encompassing for any book.

"I don't know. I haven't read it. Should I?"

"I'm getting it for Joe. It's been out for a while and he hasn't gotten around to reading it. He says it's a must-read. For novelists, that is. I don't think you and I need to read it."

She winked, an inclusive familiar gesture that made Bronwyn feel even worse about what she was doing. Diane was being unreasonably nice. Had she forgotten what an ungrateful beast Bronwyn was? Only now does Bronwyn understand how much she's missed Diane in the last year.

Diane arcs her arm back and forth, summoning Bronwyn like one of those airline workers who guide planes into their gates. Bronwyn hurries across the street and allows herself to be pulled into the squishable shelf of her mentor's bosom.

"I'm so sorry," Bronwyn says, suddenly wishing she could undo all the decisions she's made in the last year. If only she hadn't . . . if only she hadn't . . . if only she hadn't . . .

"Enough. Enough." Diane guides Bronwyn inside. "I got us a table by the window with a perfect view of the water."

The Portsmouth restaurant Diane has chosen is the kind of classy establishment Bronwyn would never consider going to on her own. Restaurants like this are so far out of her price range they're scarcely on her radar. It's the easiest way to be poor, simply ignoring the multitude of rich people's activities that are inaccessible to you. Their table overlooks the Piscataqua River which feeds into the Portsmouth Bay. Sailboats are taking advantage of the break in the rain. It is dusk, and "dead" clouds, which will not yield precipitation, cover much of the sky. What a relief it isn't raining. Rain taunts her these days. She isn't sure what will happen to her in its presence—her brain can't be trusted not to launch some project of change. She consciously averts her eyes from the sky, worried that some atmospheric detail might captivate her and, coupled with an intense feeling, she could find herself doing something to embarrass herself. To have any of these fugue states overtake her in front of Diane would be mortifying.

They sit and Diane executes an array of quick decisions, organizing the world with the same crisp efficiency with which she organizes her data. They are brought water, and warm crusty bread, and hors d'oeuvres of polenta and crab, along with a bottle of Bordeaux that Diane swears is "divine." After the waiter has poured, Diane raises her glass and Bronwyn follows suit. They clink and sip.

"So, my friend, why have you been avoiding me? What was it—three emails and four phone calls before you responded?"

"I wasn't avoiding you. I've just been busy." She hesitates, hating to make a ploy for sympathy but, sensing Diane's potential prickliness, she feels she has no choice. "My boyfriend and I broke up."

"I'm sorry to hear that. The lawyer? Reed."

"Yes." Bronwyn is surprised once again that Diane remembers Reed's name.

"You can do better. As I recall, he was a little lacking in spark. Was he in your camp?"

Bronwyn has forgotten how disarming it can feel to be in Diane's forthright presence, but she knows better than to be offended. "It's actually kind of my fault. I wasn't giving him much attention."

"Of course you weren't and rightly so. You have things to accomplish, places to go. I was the same way when I was starting out. My first husband was a molecular biologist—I've told you about him, haven't I?—and he couldn't stand that I wasn't willing to make the sacrifices he was unwilling to make. But when someone your equal comes along it'll change. You'll see."

Bronwyn holds back a smile. She wouldn't have thought that Joe the novelist was Diane's equal, but she's glad Diane seems to think so. Diane picks up one of the polenta rounds and pops it into her mouth. A dreamy look comes over her, and she closes her eyes. Bronwyn has never seen anyone give herself over to food so fully and unapologetically.

"You have to try it," Diane says.

Bronwyn takes one hesitantly. She has never been a fan of polenta but, coupled with the crab, it's perfect.

"Tell me," says Diane, leaning forward and lassoing Bronwyn's eyes with her own. "Is it really this brouhaha with your young man that has kept you out of touch?"

No, Diane, I never belonged with you in the first place. Now I understand that even more certainly. My brain is unraveling. I see electrons dancing in the clouds. My brain fills with volcanic heat and I imagine myself banishing rain. I am coming unhinged, and I don't entirely dislike it.

"I'm pretty busy at work too. I've had a lot to learn on this job."

"I don't buy that for a minute. I've watched you a few times lately. You acquit yourself quite well. But honestly, these weather reports, they're all so reductive. You could phone them in. It doesn't take a woman with a brain like yours to do this work."

Bronwyn sighs. *Please, let's not discuss my brain.* "I don't belong at MIT. I—"

"Oh, come on now. I forbid you to undersell yourself. You're the best research associate I've ever had. You have a strong head for science."

"A lot of people on the team, well Jim and Bruce in particular, would dispute that. They were always rolling their eyes when I said things."

"Of course they were. They feel a need to belittle you because they can see, as I do, that you outshine them. Do you know what makes you so good? You're a very astute observer. You don't miss details. *And* you are capable of thinking outside the box. The world is filled with silly men who begrudge the sharp brain of any woman, especially a pretty one. You can't let it affect you."

"Thank you for saying so—"

The moon has come into view, waxing and tumid, and under the cloak of clouds it seems to shimmy. Why must she see movement everywhere? Diane's silvery hair gives off an aura, but Bronwyn won't look at it. How is it that what was only recently a source of pride has now, in Diane's presence, become a source of shame? What would Diane say if she knew? She would disown Bronwyn on the spot. No one can push bad weather away. No one can summon sufficient energy to govern the elements. Even the seeding of clouds is only partially effective. *No, Bronwyn*, Diane would say. *This is not thinking outside the box—this is thinking outside the range of known human capability. It isn't rational.*

"—but I really think that I'm not—"

"You don't have to decide now, this minute. I understand I'm probably in for a lot more expensive dinners with you." She laughs. "But don't shut me out after all these years together. I understand a lot more than you think."

11

Singing changes you. It asks you to feel something. It finds what is dormant and close to your soul. Bronwyn takes to Stuart's singing mandate unexpectedly.

Singing "A Hard Rain's A-Gonna Fall," her voice is thin and not remotely like Dylan's, but it doesn't matter. Everyone on the set laughs, and even Stuart seems happy with her attempts. At home she listens to music on her computer and sings along. When she's out shopping or running, she's often humming. In only a week her voice strengthens, and Stuart begins to receive approving emails from viewers.

The singing has arrived at the perfect time, giving her a new, expanded on-air persona. At the station it provides a kind of cover, an easy topic of conversation that diverts people from seeing anything else about her that might have changed. Meanwhile, so much has changed. In private she is exploring and embracing her emergent self.

Let go of your frontal cortex. Think of yourself as a creature with sharp skills that have nothing to do with executive function. The vaunted sight of a hawk or an eagle. The keen hearing of a dolphin or bat. The sure nose of a bear that can smell as far as eighteen miles. Think of fireflies. The way they glow from the inside out, transmitting signals, looking for mates. *Come find me, I'm wonderful.* There's the dung beetle who navigates by the Milky Way; starlings and ants who navigate with the sun; bats and sea turtles and some bacteria who use a magnetic field; salmon who use scent to locate their spawning ground. Everywhere, creatures are going about their business without fanfare, receiving and transmitting signals with a high degree of precision in order to stay alive. So why limit your thinking? Give up some of your ordinary human brain function in exchange for something remarkable.

Sitting by the river she tries to give herself over to her creature nature. She closes her eyes, thinking of blind sand scorpions who sense vibrations as small as a millionth of an inch. There are worms beneath her, nests of bees perhaps, thousands of ants. Hard as she tries, she does not feel their presence. Perhaps she hasn't hit the right analogy yet. Where is the creature who sees the movement of electrons in rivers and clouds? What creature has spells that make her brain febrile with impossible heat? The meteorologist, confronted with confounding weather, says: *Too tough to call.* Is that what it is? TTTC?

She rides a flume from glee to fear. There is so much to explore, so much that exhilarates her imagination. When fall comes she might be stopping hurricanes. She pictures herself on the beach, facing down the wind and rain and waves, smashing them into submission with her own fiery brain. Blizzards, too, could she tame them? Why not? The physical forces at work are similar. Perhaps she could bring on the rain and snow as needed, a dash here and there like a master hydrologist, replenishing the water table. She has no idea how far-reaching her efforts might really be, so she entertains all possibilities.

The excitement is tempered by her experience with the river. It was scary to witness the water roiling by so raucously at her behest. She could so easily imagine disaster resulting, lives being lost. And once she got the river stirred up, it was not a simple project to stop it. Weather, she reminds herself is more than excitement. She mustn't act rashly. However, as she considers her next move, she cannot help but feel excitement.

The Saturday of Nicole's wedding, July 14th, Bastille Day, is the tenth day of rain in July. When Bronwyn went to bed after her last Friday broadcast there were patches of clear sky, a few stars, and she harbored hopes of a clear day to come, but the National Weather Service was forecasting rain and they have turned out to be right. Nicole will not be happy.

As Bronwyn lies in bed listening to the drops clatter through her gutters, foreboding spikes up her spine like a power surge. It shouldn't matter to her whether it rains or not. It's not her wedding. But on Nicole's behalf, she cares. She wishes she hadn't asked Archie to go with her. Would it be exceedingly rude of her to bow out? Nicole will have enough on her mind, maybe she won't notice Bronwyn's absence, and Archie didn't seem all that driven to go.

In the distance, far away, thunder rumbles. The rain drones on. How cocky of her to assure Nicole the weather would be good today. Faced with a specific task, she doubts her ability. And calling off the rain for such a frivolous reason as a wedding seems somehow wrong. *If* she could even do it.

Archie arrives early. "I got the day right, didn't I?" he says, seeing she isn't dressed. He wears an orange and purple Jerry Garcia tie over a lavender shirt. His dark gray suit is too tight. He demonstrates that the jacket won't button over his gut.

"I've had this suit for twenty-five years. At least I can still get into it."

Bronwyn retires to the bedroom to change while Archie wanders to the porch to inspect her weather station. She stares at the ridiculous array of dresses in her closet. She doesn't feel like herself in any of them. Though what can she honestly say is "herself" these days? Selfhood is turning out to be a far more fluid notion than she ever imagined. She selects a sleeveless navy blue dress with a matching jacket that is snug and short. It isn't customary attire for a summer wedding, but given the rain it seems appropriate. She puts on the usual black pumps and assesses herself in the mirror. She might almost be going to work. Her hair, however, she leaves long so it rustles down her back and over her chest and makes her feel loose and free. No makeup except for a slash of bright red lipstick which makes her mouth unruly. Her divided self is perfectly encoded in her appearance: the demure navy clothing of someone with restraint; the hair and mouth of a renegade.

Archie sizes her up. "If I were twenty years younger . . ." He shakes his head. "Hey, I had no idea what a geek you are."

She smiles. "Former geek maybe."

"All that equipment."

"I'm not looking at it now, don't make me look. It's my day off."

Archie eyes her strangely. "It's fine. Relax. I'm not making you do anything."

They take his truck. The wedding and the reception are scheduled to take place at the elegant Shady Hill Country Club, an unexpected choice for working class kids like Nicole and Mike. Bronwyn suspects this is one of those foolhardy weddings where the couple is taking out loans to make it happen. One unforgettable, magical day and hefty payments for years after. Is that what love makes you do? What a cynic she's becoming.

The wide driveway that leads to the clubhouse is lined with sentry-like old growth firs and maples with boughs stretching to the road like the servile arms of butlers. Acres of irrigated emerald grounds fan out in all directions. The rain is still coming down, not hard but steadily, so women are being dropped off under a green-and-white-striped awning that leads to the front door. The men, heads bent, rush back from the parking lot through the downpour, arriving at the door with plastered hair, shaking like dogs, trying to recover their composure. Bronwyn and Archie don't recognize a soul.

"Shall I drop you off?" he asks.

She agrees.

"We could share a joint first, if you want. We might need it."

Today she is tempted. Maybe getting stoned would alleviate her anxiety. But then again, it might exacerbate it too. She declines, and he lets her out by the awning and takes off to park. Surrounded by dressed-up strangers, Bronwyn gives in to an urge and veers onto a path edging the first fairway. The golfers have been chased away by the rain, so she is alone with the squirrels. It's a stunning location. The well-tended grass and the grandeur of the trees make it feel manorial. She drinks in the view, not minding the light rain, until she realizes Archie will be looking for her.

"Where did you go?" he asks. He's waiting in the foyer, looking dismayed.

"I was checking out the grounds. They're pretty impressive. Now I have to use the ladies'. Why don't you get us some seats—I'll find you in there."

Before he can answer, she turns down a long carpeted hallway, passes through swinging double doors, and finds herself in a large sitting room with chintz-covered easy chairs, a fireplace, landscape paintings on the walls, windows giving out to views of the golf course.

There, standing at the window gazing out, is Nicole, clad in her Cinderella gown with the beaded bodice and train, sobbing. She is flanked by a black-haired bridesmaid in pink who holds a box of tissues and comforts Nicole, stroking her arm almost aggressively. Both women turn toward Bronwyn. Nicole's mascara has smeared her round cheeks so she resembles a child-like, jilted-at-the-altar bride, but Bronwyn knows better.

"Excuse me?" says the pink bridesmaid, her tone conveying *get out*.

"No, she's fine," says Nicole, rushing to Bronwyn and hugging her spontaneously. "You *said* it wouldn't rain. You promised."

Nicole's sadness penetrates Bronwyn's chest. She feels like a mother, flattened by her daughter's distress. "I told you if it rained you'd have a great day anyway. Didn't I say that?"

"Well, I'm not having a great day. I'm horribly superstitious."

"Where's Mike?" Bronwyn looks around. He must be somewhere close at hand. This is his problem, not hers.

"We aren't supposed to see each other until we get to the altar."

"Oh. Right."

"It's *time*, Nic," says the pink bridesmaid. "*Beyond* time. You have to clean up." She inserts herself between Bronwyn and Nicole, but Nicole reaches around the bridesmaid and grasps Bronwyn's hand.

"Oh, Bronwyn, I want *sun*. Sun means everything will be *good*. A good future. A family. A good life."

Bronwyn does not make a decision, her body's empathy decides for her. A vessel, she floods with potential energy. "Can I talk to you for a minute, Nicole?"

"Yeah?"

"Privately," Bronwyn says.

"Look," says the bridesmaid sharply to Nicole. "You are walking down the aisle in thirteen minutes. You don't have time for private conversations right now." To Bronwyn, "Whoever you are, your timing sucks."

"She's Bronwyn," Nicole says. "The weather woman and my friend. Don't be mean to her." She rubs her eyes with the back of her hand, making a worse mess of her face. "Is it important?"

"I think you would think so, yes."

"Kathy, I've got to talk to her. Get lost for a minute."

"I don't believe this," Kathy says, stomping out, her high heels and floor-length dress huffing objections.

By the time the door is closed Bronwyn's heart is chugging so fast she isn't sure she can speak. "I think I—if you're really upset—I—"

"What're you saying?"

"This rain is really upsetting you? I mean *really, really*?"

"Duh."

"Okay, that's all I need to know." She turns to leave, already overcome by vertigo.

"Wait, where're you going?" Nicole rushes after Bronwyn, follows her through the swinging door and down the hallway. She catches up outside the front door under the awning.

"What're you doing? You have to tell me."

Bronwyn stares at her and shrugs. Words are out of reach. The pink bridesmaid is standing in the doorway behind Nicole, yelling. "Nicole, are you fucking crazy?! No one is supposed to see you yet."

Bronwyn gives a quick nod and steps out from under the awning into the rain. She stumbles toward the fairway, high heels piercing the soggy grass and soil. She must work quickly, but first she must get out of view. Someone calls after her, Nicole maybe, but the sound is muffled and indistinct. She travels on legs only partially under her control. The rain makes snaky strings of her hair. Every ounce of her energy is caught in an updraft, electrons doing double, triple, quadruple duty, resolving together in molecular euphony.

She comes to a triumvirate of majestic fir trees and steps off the path into the lap of their shelter. She sees the red flag of the first hole and centers her gaze past the veil of rain to the perfect circle that is the green. The heat has vanquished her chest by now. She coaxes it further up, to her head and brain, until her frontal cortex seems to contain flammable gas. It ignites, and she struggles to condense the flame into a ball. Her gaze lengthens, spirals. A bitterness floods her tongue. The world falls away and with it all sound but breath. She thrusts the heat forward, finds a rhythm. Rising over the fairway, she sees it undulating beneath her, a verdant ocean of grass. Time has vaporized. She is alone, surrounded by a vast emptiness, a profound silence. Gradually, the rain turns in on itself, contracting to a mist, then taking leave altogether.

Sometime later, Bronwyn finds herself leaning against the trunk of a maple tree, soaked, so weak she can scarcely stand. The fairway, still saturated, glistens in the afternoon sunlight. The air smells fresh. She has no idea how much time has elapsed.

She sinks into the sodden grass, utterly still, all her kinetic energy dissipated. She is neither happy nor sad, neither proud nor disappointed. She is in suspension, dormant. She could exist here forever until the Earth received her back, cell by cell, molecule by molecule, atom by atom. The sunlight is yolk-yellow. It fills her eyes and blinds her. To live in this day is to be at the bottom of an immense gold bowl, museum-worthy, hand-wrought by the ancients.

A golf cart stops on the path in front of her. She was scarcely aware of its approach. Nicole and Archie step off, Nicole gathering her train.

"Oh my god, Bronwyn, I'm so glad I found you. What did you do? I saw you out here, at least for a few minutes until they dragged me inside." She rushes to Bronwyn, oblivious of her elegant dress trawling the wet grass.

Archie follows. "Are you okay? What happened?"

She blinks up at Archie and Nicole as if she's emerging from surgery. Nicole's face is polished with joy. She crouches.

"What time is it?" Bronwyn asks.

"Time for the reception. I'm all married up. And it's sunny. You made it sunny, didn't you?" Nicole's face, inches away, smells like flowers. "You did something. I know you did something. What did you do?" Behind Nicole, Archie, in his too-small suit, looks stricken.

Bronwyn shakes her head. No words emerge. Then, "Not really." She reaches for breath.

Nicole keeps her face very close to Bronwyn's, the fabric of her gown billowing around her hips, filling Bronwyn's view like a cloud. Nicole remains there for some time, pondering something.

"Your dress—" Bronwyn says.

"Fuck the dress. You're like—there's no word for it—it's, like, super-natural. You're blowing my mind. I honestly can't believe it. Can you walk? We have to get you inside. Get you something to eat."

The men and women who greet them at the door—Mike and seven or eight other people who Bronwyn doesn't know—are aghast. Nicole's gown carries a fringe of grass around the hem and, on the front where she knelt, there's a fecal-looking splotch of dirt. Bronwyn looks as if she's been swimming. Is she drugged? Drunk? Having a psychotic episode? She can see them wondering and disapproving.

"She's fine," Nicole says. "She had a dizzy spell. She'll be alright. I'm fine too. It's just a stupid dress."

The group finally disperses, and Archie and Nicole escort Bronwyn to a small room to recover. They bring her a plate of finger food and a glass of champagne. Nicole is summoned back to the party, but Archie stays with Bronwyn. She sits in an easy chair looking out at the reworked day. It is undeniably beautiful. Peaceful even. And her workmanship. She should feel proud, and privately she does. But she also feels raw and exposed.

"Are you going to tell me what happened?" Archie says. "Nicole is saying crazy things." His hovering presence tells her he is not only worried about her, he pities her.

She can't look at his face. Pity is something she has no use for.

"You just took off," he says.

She sips the champagne and it goes straight to her head. She floats. She thought Archie, of all people, might understand, but now she thinks differently. Despite his apparent openness and curiosity about the world, there are places his imagination will not take him.

"I'm really tired now," she says. "And it's hard to explain." She closes her eyes, overwhelmed by the day's piercing beauty. "Maybe someday."

12

Sunday is quiet and sunny, and Bronwyn lolls around in a daze, straightening her cabin, sitting by the river, speculating about everything, ignoring the plethora of texts and emails coming in. Can this sunny day be her workmanship, or has the effect of yesterday's effort already faded? How far afield does her range of influence extend exactly? Did it clear up in Boston? In Rhode Island? In Caribou, Maine?

Curiosity sends her to her computer. The weather in Boston yesterday began with rain, but sun took over in the late afternoon. In Rhode Island and Connecticut the rain also stopped in the afternoon. Caribou, Maine, almost four hundred miles north, cleared too, but not until the early evening. Her work, or not her work? Impossible to say.

Excitement perforates her exhaustion. She emails Lanny. *You won't believe* . . . And Lanny emails back. *You're going to be famous! But Tom thinks we're both crazy.* What is it, Bronwyn wonders, that makes a believer of someone? Lanny and Nicole were so quick to conclude she had done something, but Archie was clearly skeptical. If she were on the other side of this experience wouldn't she, too, be skeptical? This thought takes her immediately, uncomfortably, to Diane.

She must choose a song for Monday's broadcasts. According to the National Weather Service more rain is on the way. "Rainy Day Mondays" is an almost irresistible option. Or the Doors' song "Waiting for the Sun."

She steps outside. The night could not be more perfect. Seventy-five degrees and cloudless, 20% humidity. It has been a long time since she's seen so many stars. Even the gossamer swath of the Milky Way is clear. Is it really possible that rain is on the way? She moves closer to the river and closes her eyes. There is no wind, but the air swaddles her in sensuous Brownian motion. No, if her body is the accurate receptor it has always been, she is quite sure tomorrow will be clear.

She is borne away by a long, solid current of sleep and awakens with a start. It *is* indeed sunny. In fact it is a day meteorologists call *severe clear*. Not a smidgen of a cloud. The entire troposphere is visible. She was right. She knew it. She leaps from bed, happier than she's been for days, since the breakup with Reed and even before. She drives to the beach for a walk and treats herself to a late breakfast at the Blue Skiff, eradicating thoughts of Reed as she devours a cheese omelet and home fries with hot sauce. She decides Diane was right about Reed having no spark. She pushes through the WVOX doors humming a sunny Sheryl Crow tune.

An exceedingly young and nervous-looking temp with a nametag saying *Hi, I'm Chelsea* sits behind the front desk. A sub for Nicole during her honeymoon. Bronwyn greets the girl warmly, but sees no need to linger for chat.

"Excuse me?" Chelsea says. "Are you the weather lady?"

Bronwyn pauses, nods.

"Mr. Snyder wants to see you."

"Stuart?"

Chelsea nods and glances back toward Stuart's office. "He said to go back right away. As soon as you get in. And so, I guess—" She looks as if she might cry.

Stuart hasn't even laid eyes on her and he wants to talk. She stands defiantly in his office doorway for close to a full minute before he decides to look up.

"You wanted me?" she says. Harsh light ricochets off his lacquered desk, forcing her to squint. My workmanship, she thinks.

Stuart returns her steady gaze. He has the same mood-dousing glower of a low pressure front. He reaches into a drawer and pulls out a newspaper folded in half. He slaps it on the edge of his desk. It's the *Portsmouth Reporter*, a crappy local rag, full of ads and pseudo news.

"Well—?" he says.

She takes a step closer to see what he wants her to see, but she fails to glean whatever it is. "What?"

He taps a small box at the bottom of the page. Her eyes focus.

BRIDE CLAIMS LOCAL METEOROLOGIST
STOPPED RAIN AT WEDDING

A local bride, Nicole Simms, was disappointed that it was raining on her wedding day this past Saturday, but when one of the guests, local meteorologist Bronwyn Artair, parted the clouds and stopped the rain, the bride was ecstatic. "It was totally supernatural," the bride said. She plans to honeymoon in Bermuda.

"Fuck." The word escapes before she can stop it. What was Nicole thinking? What was the reporter thinking? What a stupid, uninformed article.

"Is that all you have to say?"

"It's ridiculous."

"Meaning?"

"It was raining and the rain stopped. Right? It has been known to happen."

"Don't be snide. You understand how damaging it is to employ a weather reporter who makes a claim like this."

"I'm not making that claim. That's Nicole's wishful thinking. Or something."

"Or something," Stuart says.

"No one pays attention to that paper."

"Plenty of local people read this paper. And they happen to be our viewers."

Bronwyn looks past Stuart's head to the lawn and trees behind the station, a patch of beauty and sanity. What a coward she is. If only she dared to embrace who she is publicly, show Stuart what she can do, regardless of how he'd respond.

"We may have to do some damage control. An on-air disclaimer."

She shrugs. "Why is this my problem when Nicole made the claim? No one interviewed me."

"Because your reputation is at stake."

She shrugs. "I'll say whatever you want me to say."

"I've said this before and I'll say it again—you're a great asset to the station. Everyone loves your songs." He pauses, as if he has handed her a sought-after compliment that is supposed to make her smile and genuflect. She doesn't need to be a station asset or a feather in Stuart's cap. So why has she been letting him, a drab nothing-burger, define her identity all these months? It is, of course, so much easier to think these things than it is to say them. *Goodbye Stuart. I am sailing to the edge of the heliosphere on the solar winds.*

"So, we're on the same page then?" he says when he sees her attention has fled. "You're not making any crazy claims?"

"Sure."

"What's your song today?"

"We'll see."

"There's no need to be adversarial, Bronwyn. I'm only trying to protect you."

When she arrives on the set Archie and Larry are both there dusting their cameras. She feels their lurch toward silence and is quite sure they were discussing her.

"It's me," she announces. "The Sorceress. Miss Weather-changer. Don't pretend you weren't gossiping." She doesn't look at them, strides to her bank of computers and logs on, fuming. Why does she allow everyone to make her feel so ridiculous, so feeble and female? She's quite sure she knows things they have no idea about.

Neither of the men disputes her claim. For a while all three of them stay intent on their activities, though Bronwyn can't focus. Gwen comes in to record with Larry a brief segment for later airing. When she and Larry leave, Archie ambles over as he usually does.

"You okay?"

She shrugs.

"You've got to admit, Saturday was pretty weird," he says. "You saw the article, I guess."

"Stuart showed me. No one ever interviewed *me* for that article."

"Why are you angry at me? What did I do?"

She thinks. Why is she so sure he wouldn't believe her if she explained the truth? Maybe he isn't a skeptic. She hasn't given him a chance. Still, she has an intuition about how he'd react.

"Stuart is furious because he thinks the article destroys my credibility even though it's really more about Nicole than me. Her credibility should be in question, not mine."

"You need to lighten up a little. Try to let it go." He cocks his head and raises his eyebrows imploringly. Maybe he's right—maybe she should lighten up.

She does not tie up her hair for the 5:00 broadcast. She leaves it loose, unfettered.

"Your hair?" Archie says two minutes before they're on the air. He makes an occult preening gesture with one hand.

She shakes her head, no.

"Okay. Just thinking of Stuart, that's all."

"I'm trying as hard as possible *not* to think of Stuart."

She delivers her report with as much neutrality as possible, thinking of the people who might be watching her and questioning her sanity. She smiles more than usual. A few days of sun and moderate temperatures, she tells the viewers, will be followed by a heat wave moving in from the Midwest and Gulf of Mexico. Temperatures are likely to rise above a hundred degrees Fahrenheit. Her closing gambit is the Sheryl Crow song stuck in her brain—about soaking up sun and lighening up.

She knows Stuart will try to read too much into those lyrics, but so what, she's only doing what he told her to do.

"Did you make up that song?" Archie asks later.

She smiles. "Sheryl Crow. I can do a lot of things, but making up songs isn't one of them."

13

In taking action she has opened herself to ridicule, and the experience has brought back memories of sitting in those terrible team meetings with Bruce and Jim, her every sentence being met with a hail of silent mockery. She made herself speak, however. She couldn't stand to let them think they could shut her up. She would bolster herself before each meeting with a specific image of one of the many heretics of science who held fast to theories that were widely reviled. A particular figure of bravery for her was the meteorologist Alfred Wegener who first put forth the idea of continental drift. He froze to death in Greenland after delivering emergency supplies to a meteorological station, and never saw the widespread acceptance of his theory. Perhaps all scientists doing truly original work are heretics. Not that she qualifies as a scientist anymore.

She wishes she didn't care what anyone thinks, but she hates to be regarded as ridiculous. She must school herself (again) to ignore her detractors—Stuart, Archie, whoever read that newspaper article and scoffed. She would give anything for even a fraction of Diane's steeliness.

There are things to be done that aren't trivial. She immerses herself in weather data. This summer it is particularly easy to be fascinated with the weather. Records are being broken across the country. A high pressure system from the Gulf of Mexico has settled twenty-thousand feet over the Atlantic, creating a dome that traps the hot, humid air. A classic Bermuda high with unusual staying power, affecting people from Maine to Florida. Temperatures over 100 Fahrenheit coupled with humidity of 80-85% has made for a heat index often surpassing

130. In the West and Southwest there has been negligible precipitation for months, and the drought is beginning to have severe consequences: extreme fire danger, scarce water for home and agricultural use.

Bronwyn's attention, however, has settled on the Midwest where the frequency of tornadoes is startling, even to veteran meteorologist Vince Carmichael. Tornado season is usually most severe in the spring, tapering off as summer deepens, but now it is late July and there has been no sign of tapering. Every few days a new twister passes through, and these are serious tornadoes, F3 or F4 on the Fujita scale, with cycling winds reaching past 250 mph, many over a mile in breadth, advancing with reckless intention, uprooting trees, leveling houses, flinging cars with the strength of Godzilla.

She rehearses in her mind. Heading out across the plains in an armored storm chaser vehicle, someone else at the wheel. Eyeballing the horizon, opening her window to sniff the air, sensing the spinning winds, sussing out the location of the dry line where the supercell builds. She orders the car to stop. Now! And she goes to work. Saving lives in her own way, just like Vince.

Vince Carmichael has noticeably changed since she last watched him regularly. He has aged dramatically. His droopy lower lids mirror the arc of his eyebrows. His forehead is stamped with an orderly row of deep divots. His back and shoulders hunch unhealthily. And yet he still hops around the sound stage with near-Olympian athleticism, leaning into multiple weather maps and radar displays, explaining the Doppler, sometimes lunging forward so quickly he goes out of focus, arms spreading majestically in both directions.

In Bronwyn's book he is still a weather god, one who appreciates the power of the Earth's forces as much as she. She used to imagine herself taking over for him when he retired. She would become the female version of Vince, as tireless and energetic as he, surviving on adrenalin and the resultant windfall of feel-good hormones, using her elfin physique as an advantage, not a liability. She would leap from map to map, gesturing flamboyantly, exciting her viewers about the natural forces at large, while reassuring them with the necessary advisories. She still holds this fantasy, though Vince Carmichael has no idea who she is.

But maybe . . . If she . . .

She composes an email. It can't hurt. They're kindred spirits, after all, both obsessed in a similar way. She has always admired him, she writes. She would love to meet him. Could she visit his set, see him in the flesh, in action? The rest—the confidences—she thinks, can come later, first a relationship must be built. What a team the two of them could be! Her hand trembles as she hits *send*.

Kissed by a sudden streak of defiance she chooses "Tornado" for her evening song. She loves its incendiary lyrics about starting a storm, relishes the thought of Stuart's reaction.

She dresses in pimento-orange, a color she almost never wears as it clashes with her hair and blanches her face to the pallor of a scallop, but hanging in her closet, the sassy color of fire, it demands to be chosen. At work she sits idly at her bank of computers thinking about Vince, wondering how quickly he'll respond—*if* he'll respond at all. Everyone is bellyaching about the heat, but the soundstage is air-conditioned so their complaints seem a bit ridiculous.

Stuart pops in and glances in her direction. The mere sight of him dampens her boldness. Best not be mutinous now. She can't afford to lose her job. Not yet. In place of "Tornado" she chooses one of her heat songs. Good heat songs haven't been easy to find because so many of them are ardent love songs, which isn't right for the evening weather. But when she culls a few lines it sometimes works out.

She belts out "Ring of Fire," picturing herself descending willingly into spires of flame, going down, down into their devouring circle.

She's no Johnny Cash, but still her effort earns her a light round of applause. She retires to her post for the rest of the first broadcast. Usually she spends this time checking for updates since Gwen and Brant are reporting the news and she must be quiet. But now she sits idle, fidgeting. She can't stop thinking of what it might be like to work with Vince, their skills so complementary.

She floats into a reverie. She wonders: Are there others out there who quietly, secretly are doing what she does? Perhaps. Maybe human beings are evolving in such a way that someday her skill will be commonplace. She may simply be one of the first, an anomaly for the time being, but not forever.

She's been tearing at her cuticle unconsciously. Now she sees it's bleeding. She digs into her purse for a tissue, doesn't find one. She'll have to wait 'til the broadcast is over. She licks the blood, tastes the lusty strength of her own iron, and is suddenly aware of being watched. On the far side of the sound stage, a man stands near the door, staring at her unabashedly. His thick dark hair tops his head like a beret. His eyebrows are unusually thick too. He doesn't look away. Embarrassed, she smiles, and he returns a smile that illuminates the entire corner where he stands.

They sometimes have visitors, it's not unusual, but who is he? She needs to know. She looks away, afraid of revealing her interest, and fists her hand to staunch the blood flow. She allows a few moments to pass before looking up again. He's still there, still staring. His smile waxes more slowly this time, its radiance undiminished. It is one of those smiles that seems to carry with it a sound. She turns to her computers in a sudden bout of thermal disequilibrium, despite the air conditioning. For the rest of the broadcast she does not allow herself to turn. When it's over, and she's free to move again, he's already gone.

Oh well, she thinks. It's too soon for that kind of monkey business anyway. And what can you tell of a person from only a charming smile and your own thrumming response? It isn't enough. Reed comes to mind and she pushes the nebulously unpleasant thought of him away, her mind too crowded.

Nicole comes to the set for relief from the heat. It is cooler in here than at her desk in the foyer. She returned from her honeymoon with her hair shagged and dyed a boot-polish black.

"Can't you do something about this heat?" she begs Bronwyn, whispering melodramatically.

"Shhh. You promised." Bronwyn looks around. Larry, the only person present, is cleaning his viewing system. He appears not to hear. Still, it's bad practice to discuss this publicly, and she has sworn Nicole to secrecy.

"I'm dying. And Mike is dying too. Working construction in this heat is the worst."

"You're uncomfortable," Bronwyn says. "You're not *dying*."

"You *could* die in heat like this. People do."

"Sure. Elderly people. Not people like you and Mike. Who was the visitor?"

"Some reporter who wants to go into broadcast journalism. He wanted to have a look. Stuart gave him a pass."

"He didn't stay very long."

Nicole shrugs. "Don't ask me." She inspects Bronwyn and chuckles. "Oh, I get it."

Bronwyn arrives home to find a dead raccoon lying in the grass not far from her front steps. Its mouth hangs open to reveal pink gums and tiny pointy teeth. Why did it die here? There is no blood, no visible injury. Could it be the heat? She knows she should remove the body before decay sets in, but she isn't sure how, and she's too hot and tired to figure it out now. She pushes inside. The cabin's air is thick and hot. She needs to get hold of a fan. She strips off her ridiculous orange dress, and steps into the shower.

In bed she checks her email. No response from Vince Carmichael. Now that she has an idea in mind, a plan of sorts, she feels a terrible impatience for the rest of the world to comply.

She lies in the dark thinking of the man across the studio, the surprising allure and comfort in a human smile. Perhaps a smile's advertisement is false, but it seems to say: *You are who you are and I see what that is.*

14

She's awakened by loud knocking. The clock shouts 9:15. She has slept long, hard, dreamlessly. It must be the heat. The knocking persists. In her year here no one has ever come to the door. Well, once a UPS driver, but that's it. She leaps from bed, exchanges her boxers for a pair of shorts. From the kitchen window she spots a red Ford Escort parked in the driveway next to her orange Volvo. The person at the front door is blocked from view.

She goes to the porch facing the river and slips out through the screen door. She rounds the side of the cabin and peers at the visitor from behind the azalea bushes. It's the guy from yesterday, the reporter with the electric smile. She sees him more clearly now: dressed informally, he is short and lean, with the sinewy bow legs of a soccer player. He turns to leave, spots her, laughs. "You're ambushing me," he says.

She feels silly. "Aren't you ambushing me?"

"It's my specialty."

An awkward silence drapes the lawn between them.

"I saw you yesterday on the set," she says.

"Yes, you did."

"I'm Bronwyn. Bronwyn Artair."

"I know who you are. I'm Matt Vassily."

She nods.

"Do you have a minute?"

She hesitates. "I'm sorry, I'm not awake yet. I'm not much good until I've had coffee. Come in while I make it."

Inside she excuses herself to wash her face and brush her teeth. She takes off her sleep camisole and replaces it with a fresh tank top. She swipes her armpits with deodorant. Marginally better. When she re-emerges he's in her kitchen making the coffee himself. She watches him from the living room. His movements are economical, as if he's used to being here, but what hutzpah to appropriate someone's kitchen and make coffee without being invited to do so. She could use more of such forwardness.

"You don't have to do that," she says.

"I don't mind."

She joins him in the cramped space and takes out mugs, aware of the pallor of her bare arms reaching up to the cupboard. She sets out milk and sugar and spoons. They move around one another as if they've been doing this for years.

"Your place is beautiful," he says.

"I wouldn't call it beautiful inside, but outside I love it. Shall we take our coffee out to the river?"

They sit on the riverbank, silenced by the purr of the coursing river. Occasionally its surface is breached by what might be a fish. An invisible warbler sings from a nearby tree. Beneath them the grass has gone brown from the heat. The coffee is dark and strong, just as she likes it. Later today the sun will be monstrous, but now its temperate heat, striking one side of her face, is exquisite. Matt's eyes dart about, taking it all in. A bird swoops low over the water, maybe a petrel. She has no idea why he's here, but she doesn't care; his presence lifts and suspends her as a good vacation does.

"So—" she finally says, "why are you here?"

"I heard about you. I came to find out."

"Find out what?"

He hesitates. "The true story."

A tremor runs through her. "You mean—"

"Yes. I read that paper. The bride saying you changed the weather."

"You're not here to write another article are you? I was told you wanted to learn to be a broadcast reporter."

"I lied."

She feels punched.

"I know. I'm sorry," he says. "I didn't expect—"

"Nobody talked to me before they wrote that story. It was unprofessional."

"You don't want to set the record straight?"

"No." She is suddenly unpleasantly hot and sweaty and discontented. She gets up and goes inside. She pours more coffee. She checks her phone for messages. There's a brief one from Vince Carmichael. He's happy to have her visit, next week would be fine. She stands at the screen door, sipping her coffee and staring out at Matt who still sits in the grass, back to her. It's not the lying that bothers her. It's the fact that he used his smile to get to her.

"There's nothing to write. You can go home now," she says loudly enough for him to hear.

He gets up and comes to her, standing close, but separated by the screen so his face is altered. "Can we start again? Please?"

She looks away. She needs to disengage, stay on task, make plans for her trip to Oklahoma.

"Okay. Sorry. I'm leaving," he says. "This was a bad call."

He lays his mug by the door and takes off, rounding the corner of the house, brushing the azaleas with his shins so they shiver after he's gone. She stays where she is, deflated by his swift departure, poked by regret. Does she misunderstand other people more than most people do? Recently it seems so. She showers for a long time, asking the water to rinse her anger, annoyed at herself for allowing attraction to derail her. It is just as well the guy left. How could she explain herself to him honestly? How can she explain herself to anyone? Anyone except Vince. She emails Vince—*I'll be there on Monday*—and books a flight from Boston to Wichita (flights to Oklahoma City are full). She has a sister in the hospital, she'll tell Stuart. She must visit this sick sister for at least a week.

A sheen of accomplishment comes over her, along with a newly broken sheen of sweat. The sun is already exerting its muscle, and the heat and light that were gentle earlier have swollen into forces that will soon be diabolical. She takes a towel and strides down to the river under the glare, suddenly bold, seeing the water's rippled surface moving from blue to black as she approaches. She peels off her shorts, tank top, underwear, moves quickly enough so her fear shrinks to a mere belly-flutter. She balances on two small rocks then steps in, her foot sinking into the cool soft silt. A few steps then she plunges, strokes out to the river's midpoint. The water is surprisingly warm, its current palpable but not intrusive. She rolls onto her back and floats. A trio of swallows passes silently overhead. From the willow tree a brash crow calls out. She thinks of what might be swimming beneath her and decides it's fine, whatever is down there probably prefers to keep to itself. Closing her eyes, she loses herself in the water's melodic lapping, the solid rhythmic bass of the muddy riverbed, the sun's whir. All the timbres and rhythms side by side compose an encompassing silence, and she dissolves into it, trading molecules with the water until she and it are indistinguishable. Never again will she apologize for who she is.

She opens her eyes and is surprised to see how far downstream she has drifted. She strokes hard, across the current, back to the bank where she towels dry, her skin alive with cool gratitude. She cinches the towel at her chest, turns to go inside, and sees the red car, still in the driveway. The sun whitens the windshield so she can't tell if anyone's inside. The car door opens. Matt steps out and saunters down the river bank toward her. He must have seen her swimming.

"You're still here?" she says. "Or you came back?"

"I won't write about you, I promise."

"Thank you."

"You're right that I did come here to do that, but when I saw you yesterday—" He shrugs. "I knew I couldn't."

"Okay—"

His face runs a relay of sudden movement interrupted by radical stillness—it's obvious he's trying to say more.

"Thing is. I write for a crappy Florida paper called *The Meteor*. I'm not proud of it, believe me. It's kind of like the *National Enquirer*. My boss spotted that article about you—he's always on the lookout for unusual things—and he sent me up here. And I came expecting you would be—well, honestly, a little wacko. But now I see there's no story here. And even if there were, I wouldn't subject you to that."

"Wacko?"

"Well, that article—"

"Why would you work for that kind of paper? I hate those papers. Magazines. Whatever they are."

"I do too, believe me. But if you've got student loans to pay off . . . I looked for a real journalism job, but they're hard to come by. I'm always looking."

"You don't have to explain. I'm not particularly proud of my job either."

"How was the water?" He smiles.

"Cooling." She blushes. "In case you're interested, I'm not *wacko*."

"I know. I see that."

The caesura returns, the sensation of drift, the air itself altered by the collision of so many silent messages. She looks toward the house, wonders what time it is, if she should ask him in again. Something thrums up from the prickly grass through the soles of her bare feet. She is acutely aware of wearing only a towel. She is acutely aware of the length of the fraught silence. She senses if she walks to the house he will follow and he does. She hears him wandering around the living room and porch while she dresses. She wishes she didn't have to leave for work so soon.

"Wow," he says, looking up from her binoculars. "You clean up well."

"Thanks."

"Your hair is impressive."

"Thanks—"

"All these instruments you've got—" He gestures over them, shaking his head.

"I'm weather-obsessed."

He chuckles, cracks his knuckles, turns to look at a white-tailed rabbit hopping by close to the house. She is pleased that he seems more nervous than she. The filaments between them are galvanized by the silence. They list toward one another, plants to light, a natural imperative.

"I spend most of my life asking people questions, but now I'm kind of tongue-tied."

She nods. "I'm always tongue-tied."

"So why did that woman, the bride, say what she said about you changing the weather?"

She is the touched anemone again, her edges retracting. The situation calls for honesty, but she is not ready to divulge the truth.

"You've got to admit it sounds crazy. Magical thinking. I mean, really—"

Crazy. The word burns. "You'll have to ask her."

"I guess I've offended you."

She shakes her head. Not offended, wary. *Crazy. Wacko.* This is how the world is bound to see her if she speaks out. Why would he be any different?

"So you're heading back to Florida now?" she says, eager to divert the conversation.

"No, Rhode Island. Where my parents live. Two birds, you know?"

"I'm a bird?"

"I don't mean—" He sighs. "Hey, that raccoon out there—you want me to take care of it?"

"It's okay."

"If you have a shovel I can heave it into the woods."

She has to think. A terrible city slicker until this last year, she has no tools of her own, but there might be some in the landlord's shed. Leaving Matt to investigate the raccoon, she goes to the shed. There are bags of soil, two hay bales, an old hand-powered lawn mower, and two shovels, a narrow one for digging holes, the other one wider, for snow. She carries them around to the front of the house and hands them over, along with some yellow rubber kitchen gloves.

He gets to work immediately, bending over and wedging the snow shovel beneath the decaying raccoon without any evident disgust, using the smaller shovel to manipulate the inert body. She watches from the front door, admiring his ease with the task. Once the animal is centered on the wide shovel blade, he looks around for a dumping site, and heads to the woods that mark the edge of the property, maybe fifty yards from the house. When he's done, he leans the two shovels against the front of the house, removes the gloves, and lays them on the bottom step. She expects him to come back inside, but he doesn't, he heads to his car.

She calls out. "Don't you want to wash your hands?"

He shakes his head, raises his arm in a wave, and drives off.

She stands at the open door after he's gone, staring at the patch of ground where his car was parked. Why did he leave so quickly? Did he not feel the same as she, the interest, the possibility, the animal attraction? Wasn't that why he was tongue-tied? She may never see him again. He didn't even leave his contact information, and she has no idea how to spell his last name. He was a momentary gift, offered by fate, then rescinded. Things come and depart, isn't that nature's lesson? This heat wave will end too, without any help from her.

15

He'd chosen his words badly. *Wacko. Crazy.* He never meant to apply those words to her—he should have known better. Now he can't stop thinking about her as he drives to Rhode Island to visit his parents. She is the kind of woman you can't help but notice. Partly because she is pretty, yes, and because of the voluminous red hair, but mostly because of her quiet radiant intensity, a little frightening honestly, as if there is light coming off her, or heat, or something. And when she sang "Ring of Fire" on camera he felt as if he was falling into the fire right alongside her. He'll tell Josh there's no story here. If he wrote the story she'd never speak to him again.

He replays their conversation again and again, reviewing the way her cheeks and forehead and chin periodically quivered, as if each of her thoughts activated a very specific muscle, so he felt he was witnessing a complicated dance being staged in miniature. Part of his job— the part no one addresses directly in journalism, but which he believes is his forte—is to read people in order to find a way to induce them to speak. But today he botched it. She proved to be a bigger challenge than most of his interviewees. He thinks about the strangeness of that raccoon being right there at the bottom of her front steps, abhorrent with decay. The heat had made the stench intolerable. Why had she left it there? He didn't have to move it, but it wouldn't have been very gentlemanly not to offer.

He's glad he's got some time off. He'll stay with his parents for a week before heading back to Florida. Actually he likes visiting his parents, finds them mostly good company, despite his father Ivan's mockery. *What is this crap you write? Who reads it? You would have been better off as a plumber. Everyone needs a good plumber.* Matt is the youngest of the Vassily children, his five older siblings are all settled in honorable professions—law, accounting, teaching—and have houses and families. They rarely visit, so Matt, unmarried and unsettled at twenty-eight, is the lone happy recipient of the nurturing his parents still have to give. This summer they have taken a cottage at the shore, and Matt cannot imagine a better place to take a break from the heat. Heat in New England can be bad, but Florida heat is something else again, a condition that settles in like an unwanted house guest, stalking you relentlessly, even in air-conditioned buildings, robbing you of appetite, interrupting your sleep. Since the heat wave began Matt has had the feeling there's an annoying phantom hair on his arm that he can never find and remove.

He is well aware of the perks of living in Florida. There's the water and the welcome winter sun. The job, too, embarrassing as it is, has some benefits. He can usually wear shorts to work and they pay him a living wage. Sure, the publication is not known for its journalistic excellence, but he's getting his school loans paid off. And what other job would allow him to peer into the human psyche as this job does? He has written three stories about people who claimed to have seen aliens, one about a woman who owned a plant that "sighed," another about a teleporting monk. Some stories come from calls they get, many come from the brain of his editor, Josh Blackburn, who combs small local papers across the country. Matt is fascinated by the eccentric people he meets, and he likes the travel. He also likes to think he gives something back to the people he writes about: a listening ear, a chance to shine.

Maybe crazy *is* the right word for her. But what does it matter—he's already blown it.

16

She skulks through Logan Airport, buoyant as a dust kitty. Having lied to Stuart she expects to run into someone who will say, *You don't even have a sister!* Her paranoia may be due to what happened last night. After the last broadcast she gave in and smoked a joint with Archie. He drove his pickup to the far side of the parking lot and stopped in the shadows. For the first time in days there was no haze cloaking the stars. He lit a joint, took a toke, and handed it to her. She has smoked only a few times in her life, and beside Archie, she felt like a neophyte. With the first inhalation her entire body seemed to vaporize. She floated and listened to Archie prattling. He was more loquacious than usual, discussing his drug experiences when he was in Eugene, Oregon in the 1970s. He and his friends ate the psychedelic mushrooms they found under cow patties. Sometimes they got sick.

"But it was worth it," Archie said. "Those babies made everything so intense. You'd eat a banana real slow and you'd understand what it was like to *be* a banana."

Bronwyn laughed.

"Why did you change your mind about smoking with me?" he said.

She shrugged. She couldn't explain. Nothing she might say would make any sense. "A need to be a banana?"

He laughed out the smoke he had just ingested. "So—are you going to tell me what happened at the wedding? You said you'd tell me sometime."

Overhead the Big Dipper and Orion's Belt were close enough to touch. There was immense heat out there and immense cold. "You have known what it's like to be a banana. I'm an amoeboid cloud of synchronously oscillating electrons."

Archie regarded her curiously. She kept her gaze on the sky, finding the Pleiades.

"O-kay." He waited. "You want to say more?"

"I think that's enough. I'm not really going to see my sister tomorrow. I don't even have a sister. Don't tell Stuart."

That night—last night—she dreamed she was Mr. Potato Head, her face bulbous and uneven, all her parts removable and made of stiff plastic. Her mouth was on her forehead, an ear was attached where her nose should be, a single eye clung to either side of her head. She woke up laughing maniacally. She has become a divided self: the powerful, private Bronwyn constantly thinking about how she might deploy her energy, and the secretive public stand-in.

The flight takes off into a clear sky with good visibility. The unobstructed view of the Boston skyline tightens her throat. So much has happened to her in the Boston area, the place she came of age. After half an hour, over New York State perhaps, or Pennsylvania, pale gray clouds begin scudding past the window. Moisture from the Gulf of Mexico is wending its way east. It is the same front that is converging with cooler Canadian air and spawning all those twisters in Tornado Alley.

Her thoughts swerve between Matt and Vince. She hasn't lost Matt—you can't lose something you've never had in the first place. Still, she feels loss. How quickly the heart leaps to its own conclusions. She thought she'd learned better from her experience with Reed. But Vince will distract her, is distracting her already.

Bronwyn's seatmate is an older woman named Doris. She doesn't like flying and sits in the middle seat with her eyes clamped shut well after takeoff. She reminds Bronwyn of what happened three summers ago, just before she started graduate school. She accompanied Diane, by special invitation, on a data gathering trip to Colorado where Diane was part of a long-term study of aerosol composition over the polluted cities east of the Rockies, Denver in particular. They went up in a mid-sized Piper aircraft equipped for data gathering, with instruments mounted on its wings measuring such things as cloud density and particulate concentration. Inside the plane a small team of researchers monitored the data. In addition to Diane and Bronwyn and the pilot, there was a man from the National Center for Atmospheric Research, and a professor from UCLA with his graduate assistant. Bronwyn was the only one without a specific task to perform so she was free to watch.

Diane, sitting up front, directed the pilot. They began high, maybe twenty thousand feet up. For five or ten minutes they flew in one direction, then they reversed direction and revisited the same stretch of the troposphere at a lower altitude. All the while they were gathering data and samples. Diane leaned close to the pilot so she wouldn't have to yell. Her tunic, wet with sweat, clung to her back. Every once in a while she turned around and glanced at Bronwyn, her smile twitching. Bronwyn wanted to help, but wasn't sure what to do. When they came in for a landing Diane closed her eyes and sat eerily still. Later she admitted to Bronwyn that she was still scared of flying. She had tried to desensitize herself, but it hadn't worked. A therapist said her fear of flying spoke to her fear of losing control. "Could you be more obvious?" Diane said. "Of course I fear losing control! It wouldn't be smart not to fear that." Her physician offered her anti-anxiety medication, but Diane refused to take anything that might blunt her cognition. "There's always someone who's trying to normalize you," Diane said. "They want to tell you your experience is wrong or bad or untrue, when all it really is is your honest report of what happened and how you feel about it." But the fear never seemed to hold her back. She was always flying off to one place or another for business or pleasure.

Later, on that same trip, Bronwyn saw her first lenticular cloud. The sun was setting over the mountains when the cloud appeared, an indigo lozenge with a spindle of lighter blue beneath. This was the kind of cloud frequently and famously mistaken for a UFO, and it was not hard to see why. The symmetry of its design was what struck Bronwyn, a symmetry commonly associated with manmade objects. Certainly nature, too, produces abundant symmetry—honeycombs, peacock tails, spider webs, crystals—but not usually in the form of clouds. She and Diane gazed up without speaking, then looked at each other and shook their heads in wonder.

Twenty minutes shy of landing, the flight becomes more turbulent. The plane dips and rises suddenly. Outside the clouds, hematite-gray, speed in the opposite direction like full-sailed pirate galleons. Doris, Bronwyn's seatmate, seizes Bronwyn's hand, clutching it to her belly like a valuable purse. She looks out with such panicky eyes that Bronwyn doesn't have the heart to withdraw her hand.

A thin wire of lightning draws Bronwyn's gaze back to the window. This storm system wasn't supposed to come in for another twenty-four hours or more. The runway is slick. The plane shimmies and skids. Doris emits a rodent-like squeal. After assisting Doris in getting organized, Bronwyn, unmoored, wends her way up the jetway and through the Wichita airport, eyes wedded to the banks of floor-to-ceiling windows that showcase the tenebrous sky, quietly at work building clouds. How can so many around her be so nonchalant? Isn't the probability of death as great here as it is in certain war zones? Is it possible to become inured? Will her newly sensitized skin function the same way in this unfamiliar landscape?

Because she was unable to find a convenient flight to Oklahoma City, she chose Wichita instead, and now she must drive 160 miles south. Her rental car, a late-model Ford SUV, is far too big for her needs, but it does make her feel safely armored. The landscape on either side of the road is a lesson in geometry, with its squared-off fields, its round hay bales, its ruler-straight roads. Evidence of devastation appears unexpectedly, road signs crashed and crumpled, uprooted trees with tumorous root balls exposed, barns sheared to half their height. In one place, just past a town named Hope, she spots a mound of sheetrock and shingles, pipes and wires, a pink toilet turned on its side as if napping.

The mid-level altocumulus clouds are a metallic blue, with defining crenellated castellanus tops, announcing unsettled weather ahead. The sun glows through them, turning the yellow fields beneath them gold. It's Dorothy's Kansas, before the tornado arrived to sweep her off to Oz. Bronwyn scans the horizon for a wall cloud, a tornado's precursor, but so far she sees nothing.

At a rest stop she pulls over, gets out, sniffs the air. The pavement is dark with recent rain and humidity clings to her face and arms with the tenacity of burrs. Beyond the restroom, fields stretch clear to the horizon. The sky here is huge, full of bravado, gulping everything and dwarfing the land below. A bout of loneliness engulfs her. Blood whirs in her cheeks and neck. Is she imagining it, or is that really thunder growling in the distance? She doesn't trust any of the reports she's read from the National Weather Service, but Vince will set her straight.

Movement in the middle distance snags her attention. A prairie dog? Having never seen one, she can't be sure. But she has read about prairie dogs. They have a sophisticated system of vocal communication, and one member of the colony will sometimes sacrifice his life to warn the other group members of danger. An altruistic suicide.

Oklahoma City rises suddenly from the flat plain, its skyscrapers glinting in the setting sun, almost blinding. The word skyscraper has always amused her. Buildings rarely reach as high as most clouds, so naming them skyscrapers is certainly hyperbole—yet humans love to think of their achievements in grandiose terms.

The Holiday Inn is as she expected, generic and reasonably comfortable. She doesn't, however, have high hopes for sleeping, despite her exhaustion. She's too nervous about tomorrow's late morning meeting with Vince. She should have talked to him on the phone rather than making all the arrangements through email. She would have liked to hear the timbre of his conversational voice before interacting face-to-face. It's too late now. She turns the TV to Vince's station and gets into bed at 8:00 p.m., reading a magazine to kill time until Vince comes on at 10:00.

She has the feeling she's seeing him for the first time, or seeing things about him she's never noticed before. His eyes are slightly asymmetrical, a soft gray, and they seem to follow her every movement. His report matches that of the National Weather Service—a storm front will be coming through in forty-eight hours. He appears exhausted and is hopping around less than usual, perhaps saving himself for the upcoming crisis. Still, he speaks with gravitas, as if standing in a pulpit with the dominion of an entire religion behind him. Who wouldn't be ready to follow such an impressive man? Reassured, she switches off the TV before he's done.

17

Matt has never been much of a sunbather, but he accompanies his parents, Ivan and Marie, to the beach, ferrying their folding chairs, and the umbrella and picnic basket, and the bag with towels and water shoes, to the place in the sand they deem suitable. They're in their early seventies and reasonably fit, but they appreciate the help. Sometimes when Matt is around they act a little more helpless than they really are, and he realizes they're all preparing for that unpredictable moment when parents cease to become the caregivers and become the cared-for.

Ivan was a plumber all his working life, and he can still wriggle into small dark spaces to diagnose a plumbing problem even if his hands are too arthritic to fix what's wrong. Marie, too, is still strong, but she's put on weight and doesn't move as quickly as she once did. They relax into the low beach chairs, sighing with satisfaction. Matt is touched by them, by the brambly gray hairs that fur Ivan's chest, by his mother's columnar, age-spotted shanks. They don't care how they look—they have too much to be proud of.

It's a popular public beach, crowded all summer, especially on hot days like this. They sit in their chairs, feet immersed in the hot sand, silent for the moment, drugged by the heat and the sun ball and the murmuring Atlantic. There is a serenity about the day, an illusion of permanence. It seems as if there will always be this brilliant sun, this hot sand, this whispering water. There will always be these human beings taking pleasure at the shore. Matt feels frozen in time even as he sees the illusion of it, the invisible racing of other turbulent forces beneath the repose.

"I never dare ask," Ivan says, "what crazy thing you got going."

"Can we not use the word crazy?" Matt says.

"Don't kid yourself, son. I read your paper now and then. Bunk, all of it. You went to college for this?"

"If there were another job out there, I'd take it, believe me. It's hard these days."

"Don't bother him about it," Marie says, fingers grazing Ivan's forearm. "He'll find something else soon. Won't you, honey?"

"Sure, Mom. I'm working on it."

It's the ritual conversation. It doesn't bother Matt, not any more. Ivan gets his digs in and moves on without belaboring the point. He has other children to brag about—he can afford to leave Matt alone. Matt and Ivan have an understanding, a bond that doesn't depend on how either one of them functions in the world. They are similar in certain ways; both brazen but gentle, they see themselves mirrored in the other. Matt is quite sure he'll be the one to preside over his father's passing when the times comes. Not that anyone talks about this, but Matt knows.

He lies in the hot sand without a towel, closes his eyes, and buries his toes. His job has bothered him before, but never as much as it bothers him now. How humiliating it was to see how Bronwyn responded to hearing about it, her face cruising from dismay, to disappointment, to disgust. How does one come back from a starting point of such humiliation? The thing is, she's right, writing about her *is* a reprehensible thing to do. The need for money is no excuse.

When Matt told his boss Josh there was no story, Josh balked. "Hey, man, can't you make something up?" But long ago when Matt was hired, he made it clear to Josh he wouldn't make things up. He certainly isn't going to start now. How depressing to realize that so many people assume that's what he does routinely. What other work could he do? His father would be more than happy to teach him plumbing, but Matt is sure he wouldn't be happy meddling with clogged drains and overflowing toilets. The world of work seems to offer so few good choices for a humanities guy like him, a lover of people, a lover of travel, a man wedded to his own curiosity, too interested in everything to allow him to stay focused for long.

More pressing than the work dilemma is the meteorologist herself. Bronwyn. Bronwyn Artair. He thinks he might be smitten. No, he *is* smitten. He's had plenty of girlfriends over the years. There were three in high school, maybe four depending on how you count them, and in the ten years since he graduated from high school there have been more girlfriends than he can count on two hands. The longest relationship lasted just over a year—a girl named Darcy who became anorexic after they split up—but more usual has been four to six months. He slides into relationships with relative ease, but he has a tendency to get bored just as easily. He goes berserk being hemmed in, and many of his girlfriends got clingy, which made him want to flee immediately. He doesn't think of himself as a Lothario—when he's in a relationship he's very present and attentive and entirely monogamous—but he hasn't conquered the longevity issue and he can't begin to imagine '*Til death do you part.*

He has always told himself *someday.* What if this is that day? Of course you can't tell at the outset, during the infatuation period, but when he thinks back to how he felt on meeting girls in the past, this feels different. He's never felt so urgent, so clear that time must not be wasted. For so long he felt he had years and years before he'd have to settle down and begin to build a life with a mate. But now he seems to have careened into adulthood. Is it only because she's so resistant to him? He doesn't think so. He thinks of the moment when they sat drinking coffee by the river. The world bustled around them—birds swooping overhead, rabbits hopping by, the river on its merry unstoppable way to the sea—but they sat in a nimbus of hush and stillness. It was dream-like, almost sacred. He is not usually so appreciative of the natural world; he tends not to notice it; he couldn't tell anyone a single thing about the flora and fauna of Florida. Yeah, flamingos, sure.

He doubts she wants anything more to do with him now. If he wants to see her again he'll have to work at it. He's sought out girls before, but he's never had to chase them. The thought of actually chasing someone is a little frightening, to be honest, but he can't simply let her go. He's been horribly restless since he left her, stuck in the clutch of longing's penumbra.

He is suddenly aware that his parents are no longer beside him. He lifts his head and sees their square, lumpish bodies wading into the water, hand-in-hand, his mother squealing a little as each small wave rides higher up her legs. They've been lucky with each other, he thinks. His siblings have been lucky with their mates too. He hopes such luck will be his.

A cluster of girls—early twenties, young women really—are hanging out around the lifeguard station, swatting each other with towels and laughing. They're all wearing skimpy bikinis—parts of breasts and fannies hanging out as if they're in Rio—and trying to grab and hold the attention of the poker-faced lifeguard with the six-pack and the absurd tan and the too-cool shades. The lifeguard is the guy Matt, for a brief period in high school, wanted to be. He's glad he's done with that phase of his life. Not so long ago those girls would have prompted him to rise and saunter over for a chat. But today they hold no draw for him; they only remind him of Bronwyn's incandescence.

18

Vince Carmichael's TV station is far bigger and splashier than Bronwyn's New Hampshire station. The receptionist's desk is fit for a CEO, and the receptionist herself, blonde hair slashing eye and cheek just so, wears a tight white dress that reveals more cleavage than seems appropriate in a place of business. Bronwyn feels prim in her black skirt and black cotton sweater; she ought to have worn something flashier, but she thought flashy might cast doubt on her credibility.

The Weather Center is busy as a Hollywood set and infused with, if not a sense of alarm, at least a sense of focused attention and high purpose. Vince, his back to Bronwyn, sits at the center of a semicircle of screens displaying maps, radar, Doppler, reports on the weather all over the country, into Canada and Mexico and across the Pacific. His minions work at stations in an outer ring, some on the phone, some gazing so fixedly at their screens they appear catatonic. Raised monitors throughout the room play a daytime drama currently being broadcast from another part of the station. To one side of all this activity is a stage from which Vince delivers his reports.

The receptionist instructs Bronwyn to wait on the periphery and approaches Vince, leaning down to whisper in his ear. He nods. "He'll be with you shortly," the receptionist tells Bronwyn before gliding off.

Ground zero, the center of all things. The din makes it hard to focus. People whiz by. On the daytime drama a woman sobs. A guy on the phone is ordering lunch. "No mustard, I said. *No mustard!*" On the far side of the room, someone yells. "Typhoon in the South China Sea!"

She waits, watching Vince. After several minutes he turns to assess her, squinting a little and making a single culvert of his two exhausted eyes. Bronwyn smiles. A man on the daytime drama gasps, he's just been shot. Vince turns away, raising a single finger in her direction. "Fire in Yosemite!" someone shouts.

After another ten minutes, Vince rises, cardboard coffee cup in hand, and walks past her, nodding. Assuming this is her cue, she follows. Down a hallway they march, into a large brown office, walls covered with framed photographs of tornado-damaged landscapes, photos of supercells taken from space, award certificates, citations of excellence. Man cave. Brag chamber.

Vince sits behind his desk into a chair that dwarfs him. He leans back, regarding her with curiosity. She stands still, letting herself be scrutinized while scrutinizing him back, trying to match the intensity of his gaze, her spine lifting and straightening with purpose. He is so much smaller and craggier in person, his face textured as a dry riverbed.

"Well—?" he says.

"I'm Bronwyn," she says. "Bronwyn Artair?"

"Yes, of course. Have a seat."

"As I said in my email, I've been watching you since I was in high school. You're the reason I wanted to become a meteorologist."

Vince's face relaxes and he laughs. "You're not the first. But thank you. What can I do for you?"

She probes his irises, tests the air. Yesterday's sky fills her vision, the metallic clouds, the rain-perfumed air, the immensity of it all. "I felt I had to see you in person," she says, slowly reaching for a rhythm. "I know I have a lot to learn from you."

"You said you're from—?"

It is suddenly clear, he doesn't remember her email. He has no idea who she is though they supposedly have an appointment. "Originally New Jersey. But now I'm in New Hampshire. I do weather at WVOX out of Manchester."

He chuckles. "Ah, tame weather! You don't have weather like ours back there, do you."

"We have plenty of hurricanes and blizzards."

"The difference is you can see that weather coming for days. You know exactly what it's going to do."

"Sometimes."

"I'm guessing you're here to ask for a job?"

The question itself does not surprise her, but she wasn't prepared for it to arrive so soon. She wanted to compare notes first, tell him how she used to watch clouds as a child, lying in the backyard and staring up, imagining herself drifting among them. If only his face were a cloud she might rearrange, but it is immutable and deflecting; he is bolted in his seat like a heavy child on the see-saw holding her up at his whim. She must shift the conversation's terms.

"Not a job exactly. Or at least not in the way you're thinking."

He raises a single eyebrow, tips back his chair so it squeaks, and the sound releases something in her, and she takes the plunge, overriding doubt, looking first at him, then into the refuge of her lap, then at him again. She's here, after all, she came here for this.

"It's hard to explain exactly, but something has happened to me that—I don't know how exactly, or why—but I seem to be able to—" clearing her throat, smiling to please then consciously eradicating the smile "—alter the weather."

Vince frowns. The capillaries in the tips of her fingers twitch. Vince leans forward.

"Excuse me?"

She has piqued his interest. She smiles, this time intent on pleasing. "Yes, I know it sounds unusual, but I have a way—I generate an enormous—I've done this a number of times now and—"

"Yes?"

She rides the wave of his encouragement. "I stopped an electrical storm on Mount Washington. I have witnesses. I've also—"

"Hold on, hon. Back up a minute. I'm trying to understand." Vince leans further forward, his rutted chin in the lead. "Did you really just tell me you can change the weather?"

"Well—" She grins, sheepish and proud. His eyes spark, two little fireflies. "Yes." She has never said this aloud, and it feels strange and boastful, but if she's going to confess this so straightforwardly to anyone Vince Carmichael is that person.

"Let's get our terms straight here. Weather—you're talking wind and rain, thunder and lightning, hail and snow, humidity and temperature. Are we on the same page here?"

"Yes."

"This isn't a metaphor?"

"No."

He nods, a long slow up and down that resembles bowing. "You said you stopped an electrical storm? What's your technique?"

"It's hard to explain exactly. It's a matter of concentration . . ." His attention on her is avid, unswerving; she is the force of the moment, the tornado passing over his radar screen. Enlivened by his focus, she gestures, spreading arms and hands. "I corral a lot of energy and then it's almost as if I leave my body and become the weather myself—"

He holds up a palm. "Wait a sec. I want some other people to hear this." He pokes his intercom. "Cathy, can you send Rob and Earl in here. Thanks, hon." He sits back, shaking his head. "Astounding."

Finally she is talking to the right person, someone who understands these forces, someone who watches them daily as she does. She wants to tell him about the river, the wedding, about her sense of attunement and power, but this is all so personal and private, she'd really rather explain without anyone else present.

"Can't I just tell you?"

"But it's so damn interesting."

A young guy is already standing in the doorway, someone Bronwyn saw on the set. His eyebrows are stuck in the raised arc of a genuflector. "You wanted me?" he says.

"Yeah, yeah, Rob, have a seat."

Next a bulbous head appears around the door frame. It floats, seemingly unattached to a body, sporting thick rimless glasses and a lazy, glistening lower lip.

Vince beckons flamboyantly, impatiently. "Hey, Earl. Come in. You gotta hear this."

Earl's full body comes into view and fills the door frame. He stands well over six feet, and he wears a clerical collar, baseball cap, and green Converse sneakers.

"I'll get another chair," Vince says.

"No, no. I'm good," Earl says. He occupies a position against a bookshelf behind Rob.

Vince lays both palms on his desk. "Okay. Earl, Rob—this woman here, Ms.—what did you say your name was?"

"Artair. Bronwyn Artair."

"Guys, this is something big here. Ms. Artair says—well, go ahead sweetheart, you tell them."

Bronwyn winces at *sweetheart*, but decides not to make a point of it now. Vince sits back, keeping his gaze on her as if she is his prized student. Bronwyn hesitates. "Go on," Vince urges. She recrosses her legs and clears her throat.

"I've always been really interested in weather—since I was a kid. I used to study atmospheric sciences at MIT, but now I'm a meteorologist at a station in New Hampshire. And recently I've come to realize that I have the capacity to, well, alter the weather—you know, stop storms and so forth." She pauses to let them absorb what she's said, examining their faces but finding no visible reaction other than a slight widening of Rob's eyes.

"She stopped a thunder storm on Mount Washington. Isn't that something, Rob?" Vince says.

Rob's gaze flicks from Vince to Bronwyn to Vince again. "Yeah, I guess it is."

"You *guess*? You *guess?!* Come on, Rob, grow some balls. This is big news, right Earl?"

Earl's placid lake of a face remains untouched, and Vince does not press his point.

"We had something like this happen once before," Vince says. "Remember that Native American gal? Real short and wrinkled. White hair. From the Kiowa tribe—or the Kickapoo, I don't remember. She was one of the elders anyway. She said she could get her spirits to call off the tornadoes if we agreed to stop using our cell phones. Not just here at the station, but all over Oklahoma." He rolls his eyes. "Yeah right, that was really going to happen. But this is different, right Ms. Artair? No strings attached here."

Bronwyn nods. Vince seems to want her to speak, but only so much.

"You and I could be a terrific team," he continues. "I spot the tornadoes developing and you zap them. The old one-two punch. What do you think, Earl?"

Earl pulls in his lower lip, but holds to his poker face. Perhaps her efforts offend his religion.

"You know what I think?" Vince says. "I think this is big enough that we should get on the horn to the President. You think so, Rob?"

"Sure."

"We need to let him know we have a huge resource at the station here. A national resource."

"Wait," Bronwyn says. Things are happening way too fast. What president does he mean exactly—surely not the U.S. President? She came here thinking this meeting would be private and under the radar, but she's lost ownership somewhere along the way. "I don't really want—"

Vince is already on the intercom, this time speaking through the receiver. "Cathy, can you get the President on the line for me? . . . Of course the President of the United States. Who did you think? The President of Estonia?" He returns the receiver to its cradle.

Bronwyn, panicked, looks at the other two men for help. Rob is staring into his lap where his interlaced hands form a fist. Earl wears an expression of ambiguous consternation. Vince relaxes back in his chair again. How long does it take to get the President on the phone? Maybe the call won't go through. Vince catches Earl's eye and winks. He turns back to Bronwyn with a smile that does not look exactly team-building. Bronwyn has rarely felt so uncomfortable. If only she could control social situations as she controls the weather.

"Do you talk to the President often?" Bronwyn asks. What a lame question, possibly even insulting.

Vince's smile beams on.

"Vince," Earl says.

"Shut up, Earl. See, I can say that to Earl because we go way back. High school buddies, Earl and me. Right, Earl?"

"Vince," Earl says again.

"Ms. Artair, every time I see a supercell building on that radar screen I think how great it would be if I could stop that sucker. I have that wish at least once a week during tornado season. No—more, much more. Hell, almost every day I wish I could control the weather. Who wouldn't want that? A perfect day for the beach—bingo! Snow for skiing, bring it on! Everyone wants that kind of power. If I could order up the right weather I'd be raking in the bucks. Heck, I'd rule the world."

He pauses, reveling in his contemplation of world power. "But guess what?" He leans forward again so his chest is almost lying on the desk. "I can't do that, and that Native American gal couldn't do it with her spirits, and you, Ms. Artair, you sure as hell can't do it either . . . Oh, wait, let's not assume anything. Surely you know we're going to be slammed by another bad storm system in twenty-four hours, give or take. Why don't you call off that system right now?"

He sits back in his chair again, chuckling a little, sure he's called her bluff. "Come on—we all know you can't do this stuff, so stop wasting my time." He reaches for the intercom again, not bothering with the receiver. "Cathy, it's time to escort Ms. Artair out." He shakes his head dolefully at Earl and consults his cell phone. "Nut job," he mutters.

Wind whooshes in her eardrums. He never put in a call to the President. Why was she so slow to see he was mocking her? Earl saw, and probably Rob did too. All these years she's admired this terrible, mean-spirited, close-minded man. The swanky, white-clad receptionist has materialized beside her. "Okay. Time to go." As if Bronwyn would resist.

For a cloud to form, particles must exist on which vapor can condense. Soot, salt, bacteria, a variety of particles encourage condensation. Anger, too, needs a surface on which to perch and grow, its own version of hygroscopic particles. She exits the station quietly swearing, anger at Vince curling around the residue of her former worship. She was stupid to have pinned her hopes on him. They have nothing in common. And he is not a nice man. He isn't even polite.

She takes a few anger-fueled steps and stops. The Oklahoma City skyline wavers in the heat, as if the buildings feel the earth speaking. Cumulonimbus clouds are beginning to group, curdling like sour milk, but so surreptitiously it is possible no one else sees. What now? She should have considered this possibility, but she was so taken with her own grandiose plan she acted impulsively. Why would Vince believe her? Why would anyone? Assume disbelief unless there's a solid reason for thinking otherwise. She is a victim now of her own poor judgment and planning. Her failed imagination. She does not read people as well as she reads the Earth.

She resumes walking, humiliation congealed into anger. It's one thing to have Stuart thinking she's a little off, but to have Vince Carmichael call her a nut job is completely different. The anger deliquesces into the indignation of a scolded child. She tries not to cry. She needs to get inside, out of the excoriating heat.

The coffee shop she enters is only a few doors down from Vince's station. The place is pleasantly cool and mobbed with a lunchtime crowd eating burgers and sandwiches, surprisingly animated given the outside heat. She pushes her way to the back to a single empty stool at the counter where she orders coffee and watches the cream making serpentine spirals as it sinks into the black liquid. How could she have misread Vince so profoundly? She pictures herself bringing on a terrible storm in his presence, for no other reason than spite—she wouldn't work with him now for anything. He didn't even ask her why she made such a claim. He is one of those people who possesses not a single mote of curiosity or imagination—and she is beginning to think there are probably far more people like him in the world than she ever would have guessed. The ready believers like Nicole and Lanny, they're the rare exceptions, not the rule.

Maybe she should change her flight and go home. Forget fighting tornadoes, find other venues in which to make her mark. It might have been overreaching to think she could do such a thing in the first place. But if she gives up, she'll arrive home chiding herself for failure. She came here to use her gift for something worthwhile, to help out, to save lives. She still could, though the logistics are unclear. Where should she position herself? Does she know enough about the propensities of tornadoes to intercede in a meaningful way? Or is she like those people who try to 'save' ghetto-dwellers and third world people, and proceed so shortsightedly they only catalyze more problems?

The coffee is acrid; it must have been made hours ago. After a few sips she puts it down, pushes it away. Why has this burden landed on her? She never asked for this, never wanted it, never sought to be exceptional. Well, of course she's always wanted to be *good* at what she does, maybe even *very good*, but no more than most people. Melancholy carps in her throat and nasal passages, threatens to emerge as tears. She squeezes her nostrils with one hand, brushes some crumbs—not hers—from the counter, wishing she were home where she wouldn't have to be making decisions. "Miss, you ready to order?" She shakes her head without looking up. If the waitress wants her gone, she'll have to say so directly.

She is dimly aware of a large man two stools down rising and changing places with the person beside her. After a few seconds she sees it's Earl. She looks away, wondering if she's been recognized. Of course she has been. The problem with red hair is that people tend to remember you.

He casts a long shadow. They sit in silence, he perusing his menu, she pretending to find interest in the linoleum countertop. Several minutes transpire this way, and the more time that passes, the more they become an island of two. When she asks for her check he speaks.

"I should have stopped him earlier, I'm sorry. He was terribly rude. But he was gobsmacked by you, too, in case you didn't know. You got under his skin."

She turns, finds him grinning.

"I haven't often seen him undone like that. Maybe never. And I've known him a long time." He laughs. "Not too many people get Vince as riled as you did. Consider it an accomplishment."

She nods, unsure where he's taking the conversation.

"He's an unusual man, Vince is. When it comes to weather, he's a hundred percent reliable, but about other things he can be a bit of a loose cannon."

She nods. "I saw that."

Facing forward, they speak as if riding in adjacent seats on a train. "Ham and cheese," he tells the waitress. "You sure you won't have something?" he asks Bronwyn. "It's on me." His eyebrows rise over the thick bifocal lenses of his rimless glasses.

"Ice cream," she says suddenly. "A scoop of coffee ice cream. But you don't have to pay."

"I do though, because I'm keeping you here. And I want your company."

"Did Vince tell you to follow me?"

"Oh dear me, no. Happy accident to find you here."

His coffee arrives and he floods it to near whiteness with cream.

"You know Vince is not religious at all, but he has a very superstitious streak. During tornado season he gets pretty riled and he calls me in to bless him. It's funny—I don't really do a thing, but he seems to need it."

"That's why you were here?"

Earl nods. "He's worried about what's going to happen when the next front comes through. It's been such a bad year, you know." He inserts his fat lower lip under the cup's rim so the cup seems to perch there, then slurps with concentration, as if trying hard not to spill. He is massive, and he makes her feel smaller than usual, and he emanates a great moist heat. Sometimes large men have scared her—Reed had a law school friend who threw his body around so recklessly she was always careful to stay out of his path—but this Earl does not scare her that way. Perhaps his size is mitigated by his clerical collar. She tries to imagine him blessing Vince—is a blessing actions or words, she isn't sure. She feels gleeful to think Vince needs a blessing. Even Vince knows that Vince is not invincible.

Earl swivels on his tiny seat to look at her, twisting shoulders and waist, slow as a dirigible. She stills herself in the shade of his regard. What does he see? The waitress has laid her ice cream on the counter. The creamy brown mound is shape-shifting, oblivious to the café's air-conditioning. She waits, communing with the ice cream.

"To have a little thing like you challenging him . . ."

"I didn't mean to be challenging him. I was just telling him the truth. And he was trying to make me look like a nut, but I'm not."

"I'm sure you're not. Vince just likes to be in control. He doesn't want anyone else sharing his limelight." Earl takes a handkerchief from his jacket pocket, removes his glasses and mops his face. "This heat. If I weren't so gosh darn big. You probably don't feel it so much, tiny as you are."

Earl's sandwich has arrived, oozing cheese and grease, and he dives into it with singular focus. She spoons up the soup of her ice cream, curling her tongue to cradle it. Beyond the café windows the day has dimmed noticeably. There is no sky available for inspection, but the charged atmosphere trembles. Earl notices too. He lays down his sandwich and his gaze follows hers to the window.

"The nasty light of evil," he says.

"Evil? I don't ascribe intent to natural forces."

"Oh my, if you lived here you would. Once you've seen a tornado like the ones we've been having here. It's been a terrible year. In our little town alone, just over the border in Kansas, we lost seventy people—and our whole population is only twelve hundred. Just terrible." He shakes his head. "They're not random, believe me."

"I'm not religious."

"What I'm saying has nothing to do with religion. It's about people having ill will. All that negative energy has to go someplace." He turns back to his sandwich. "If I could do something I would."

As they eat they become an island of silence again in the café's clamor. Earl could ask questions, but he doesn't, and she is puzzled by this. She's used to being pummeled with questions, not just recently, but all her life, all through school, question after question, each one a quill. But Earl seems to navigate not knowing by holding back and waiting for things to disclose themselves.

A bumper sticker on Earl's black Ford Explorer says: *It's Not Religion, It's a Relationship.* It gives her pause, but only momentarily. He wants to show her the tornado damage in his town, and why not—though it's almost a two-hour drive, she has no other claims on her time. They speed north, back along the same stretch of road Bronwyn drove yesterday. Earl grew up just outside Oklahoma City, he says. He loves this countryside, its flat fields of wheat, sorghum, soy beans; its gentle hills; its beneficent skies; its modest people. *Vince, modest?*

"We may fry in the heat here someday, but I'll still be here. A big old sweaty, greasy Earl-burger."

Minister of what he calls a "come-hither-come-all" church, Earl holds services in his own home. He refuses to name his church. "In my experience names don't do people much good. In fact, they often get people fighting. So I don't like to get hung up that way."

The air conditioner in the Explorer is broken and they both sweat copiously despite the rush of wind through the open windows. The day is unsettled. Thunder grumbles in the distance. The sky *does* appear bedeviled.

Earl's town, Jobsville, a few miles off the highway, is a snapshot of tragedy straight from the evening news. Hardware store, grocery store, beauty parlor, café—everything demolished. They park and get out. Mountainous piles of rubble spill across the road in such random disarray that Earl has trouble remembering how things used to be. The air is acrid with the smell of rubber and gasoline, with ruin and despair, with the mephitic smell of death.

They get back in the car. Bronwyn can't relax. The clouds are long arms striating the sky, churning and bilious, black beneath and flocked with icy white on top. The fields that yesterday looked golden are now a dull brown. Earl lives a few miles away. He has invited her to his house before they head back to Oklahoma City. She should have brought her rental car to save him all this driving.

There is a feeling haunting her all the time now: that she should be elsewhere, doing something other than what she is presently doing. But she can never identify what that other thing is. "Don't you feel lonely here?" she asks. "So few houses and people and all this sky and grassland?"

"Lonely is an inside thing. A state of mind. You think there aren't lonely people in New York City? Thousands, believe you me." He turns from the wheel. "You are either a very young soul or a very old one, I can't tell which."

Earl's way of seeing is bleeding into her a little. She is acutely aware of her own porousness. Something is fomenting, the day hankering for a fight, not just with anyone, but with her specifically, vengefully, as if Vince's will is behind it. Lightning streaks down from aloft, a thin zipper. Thunder snaps, then morphs to a long low groaning. Earl echoes the groan. Bronwyn drifts. Her skin begins to hum, her vessels dilate, the heat coalesces and slides through her blood. Her gaze ticks over the cloud directly in front of them. A classic wall cloud.

The skies hemorrhage. Hail pounds the windshield. Ahead of them a tornado swaggers into view, shimmering like a hologram, snaking east, an animated column, skinny at its base, splayed wider at it its top, its edges indistinct but still a discrete thing. It twists and bends like a human with a waist, supple as a hoola-hooper, mocking in its gyrations, prowling laterally across the horizon. As they watch, it swerves, reverses directions, advances straight toward them as if the two of them are its intended prey. She thinks of Vince. Earl pulls to the side of the road, shuts off the ignition. He bows his head. "Blessed Father, hold us safe . . ."

Bronwyn tumbles from the car into a granular rain and steadies herself on the road's shoulder. The funnel is closer now and it swivels and taunts, advancing quickly one moment, then taking its time, continuously spewing digested debris. She stares it down as the heat rises to her head and sounds of the ordinary world—the battering rain, Earl's muttered prayers—slide away.

She ascends into the spinning wind, the whizzing electrons, the immense charge, meeting it all with her own immense charge. Then begins the rhythmic hurling, her brain seethes and pops, and she falls into blackness.

19

She lies under a quilt on a couch in a dim shabby living room. An image swoops into her mind like an eagle coming to perch: the tornado swaggering toward them, darkly malevolent. She squashed it, but she herself is not squashed. She is whole, awake, present.

Earl sits a few feet away in a straight-backed wooden chair, cap and glasses removed, bald pink head bent toward her, hands in a teepee, muttering syllables of prayer. He senses her wakefulness, opens his eyes and fixes them on her. They are large and faceted, robin's egg blue.

"Praise God! How're you feeling?" he asks.

"Fine," she says, discovering that she is. She's carved out and a little dazed, but essentially fine, even elated. She did what she planned to do.

"I was so worried. You were out there in the storm and the tornado disappeared, real sudden, and a second after that you went down. Boom! You've been out for two hours now. I'm so happy you've joined us again." Earl stands abruptly. "Can I get you something? Tea? Soup? A sandwich?"

"Water would be nice."

She props herself up while Earl fetches water. The room is a product of decades past, the mid-twentieth century perhaps, with fading floral wallpaper, chairs upholstered in fraying chintz, lace curtains without utility. One section of the room is defined by an upright piano with chairs grouped in a semicircle around a braided rug, as if a small choir is expected any minute. The other half of the room features the couch on which she is lying and four easy chairs oriented toward a fireplace and a TV. A stack of folding chairs in one corner makes it clear the room is accustomed to hosting large groups. Despite the need of upkeep, the place exudes a sense of safety with its lagoon of deep silence and the soft early evening light sifting through the dusty window panes.

Earl rattles around in the kitchen. She tries to review what happened. Why wasn't she scared? For a while, driving along with Earl, watching the storm approaching, the wall cloud foreshadowing exactly what was to come, she *was* terrified, but then a moment came when the fear dissolved, and she swooned into the storm, spilling herself beyond her usual edges, becoming part of it as if her body had undergone some alchemical change. She was folded into the trumpeting thunder, the strands of lightning, the concealed moraines of the clouds. She gave herself over to the spiraling winds. It *was* malevolent and yet she withstood the malevolence. Now she understands firsthand what Earl said about tornadoes harboring evil intent. But her own intent—where does that fit in? She thinks of Vince again with a flash of hatred.

Earl carries a tray into the living room. A glass of water, a bowl of tomato soup, and saltines. She laughs. "My mother always gave me the same thing when I was sick. I'm not sick."

"But I'm sure you're tired. You don't have to eat this, but if you want it, help yourself."

He draws a small folding table up to the edge of the couch, lays down the tray, hands Bronwyn her water, and takes his seat again, intent on her, his face a tablet of concern. Sweat makes eels of his broad hands. He must have lifted her to get her here. He is a mouth breather, and he has trouble controlling his lower lip, and she can smell the coffee on his breath, possibly the plaque on his teeth. In other situations she knows he's someone she might avoid.

"It's cozy here," she says. "Do you have a family?"

"I have a boy, Luke. He's fifteen. He lives with his mom across town."

"So you're here alone?" She studies his eyes again, drawn by some mystery they seem to evince even through his thick bifocals.

"Oh, I live alone, but I'm not really alone much." He laughs. "I'm a people person. You can see that, can't you?"

She sips her water, trying to repel his expectant gaze, concentrating on the way the water's molecules fill her mouth but do not impinge on her teeth. She finally turns to him and finds his eyes awash in tears.

"I've seen some amazing things in my time. But never, ever have I seen the like of what I saw today. I would have to call it a miracle. 'He rebuked the winds and the sea and there was a great calm.' Matthew 8."

"Oh, please don't. Please. That makes me terribly uncomfortable."

"But you turned that tornado to dirt. I watched that sucker tumble like a slain soldier. Honestly, I've never seen anything like it. If only Vince had been there to see. I have half a mind to call him."

"Please . . . I don't . . ."

Earl nods, frowns. "He means well."

She disagrees. "It isn't a miracle," she says. "I don't know what it is exactly, but it's something else."

"We don't need to name things," Earl says. "You call it what you want to call it. I've told you what I think of names—they usually get in the way. Don't worry, I'm not going to ask you how you did what you did, that's your concern." He pauses, frowns. "I don't want to tire you out, but when you're feeling up to it, I got a favor to ask you."

What a relief to not be questioned. What a surprise. She likes this Earl. "What would that be?"

"Some folks want to see you. They want to thank you."

"You told people?"

"Only good people, people who understand—" He leaps up from his chair, kneels by the couch and takes her hand in his sweaty one so they slime together. His tears are flowing now. "Oh, dear me." He drops her hand to find a handkerchief in his pocket. "I'm embarrassing myself." He blows his nose and stashes his handkerchief and stands. "Pull yourself together, Earl." He walks to the window and gazes out. "It's going to be a beautiful sunset. What do you think about those folks coming over?"

Warmed by Earl's kindness, she can't say no. There is something too sad and loveable about him to refuse his request. He leaves her to rest for a while. She eats some soup and dozes. She hears Earl showering. She would like to shower too, but all her things are at the Holiday Inn in Oklahoma City, along with her rental car. Earl comes bustling back.

"I thought you'd want to hear this." He goes to the TV and turns up the volume. It's Vince Carmichael.

"It was a stroke of incredible luck. Today's supercells, which were sporting high winds and had already spawned several serious tornadoes, crashed very suddenly. The winds were powerhouses one moment, and then they simply lost all their momentum in a matter of minutes. In all my years of broadcasting weather in Oklahoma, I have never witnessed anything like it . . ."

Earl lowers the volume as Vince, gesturing wildly in his trademark way, details the storm's path, its divergence into two supercells, and its subsequent demise.

"That's *you!*" Earl is as animated as Vince. "*You* did that! You wowed even Vince." She can't keep her eyes off Vince's windmilling arms. She's not in the habit of watching him without sound, but it does seem as if he's more active and excited than usual. "I might not have become a meteorologist if it weren't for him."

"You won't let me call him?"

She vacillates. It would be satisfying to have Vince know what she did, but would Earl's testimony sway him? "Please don't," she says.

The visitors let themselves in, coming through the kitchen door and parading into the living room in single file. Earl has laid out plates of Oreos and Dixie cups and a large pitcher of pink juice. He sits at the piano pounding out "This Little Light of Mine" and singing along, nodding at his visitors, nodding at Bronwyn. They come right up to where Bronwyn sits, and one by one they introduce themselves. She shakes their hands. Patty Birch. Dixon Mason. Winona Burns. Glen Otway. She loses track of their names as the living room fills. Eventually the room is crowded with twenty people, maybe more. They seat themselves, keeping her, their object of study, in view. Some of them begin to sing quietly along with Earl. The women are all large, with pillowy bosoms, dressed in pull-on pants and loose tunics, their hair gray, their faces smooth and rosy-cheeked and pleasantly placid. The men, somewhat leaner though not a lot, are also gray-haired, middle-aged, casually dressed. What is it about this group that makes them appear so devoid of meanness? Perhaps it's their curiosity that tinges them so, or the fact of Earl's singing which casts an all-is-right-with-the-world religious tone over the gathering. Are these his parishioners or friends? Probably both in a town of twelve hundred.

They gaze at her unabashedly and, though she first feels herself recoiling and wanting to hide, she tries to be polite and sit still and think of their regard as nothing more than a certain kind of rain that will not last. She is quite sure she would want to study someone like herself as closely as she could. Perhaps they gaze at her with the same open-eyed wonder she brings to the clouds.

Finally Earl stops playing and draws up a folding metal chair to the circle that has formed around Bronwyn. "Evening all," he says.

He is greeted with a chorus of *Evening, Pastor* and *Hey, Earl.*

"Help yourselves to refreshments. So glad you came by. We can chat for just a bit, but you understand that Ms. Artair needs to rest and doesn't want to talk too much."

Bronwyn wishes Earl would keep playing. She would really rather not chat at all. These visitors will want her to explain herself, and she has no inclination, ability, or stomach for that. They are used to being at Earl's place, and they help themselves to punch and cookies without needing encouragement. One woman fills a plate and cup for Bronwyn, and Bronwyn accepts them gratefully. It occurs to her that she has eaten very little today—some toast before her meeting with Vince, the melted ice cream, a little soup.

Night has colonized the windows and seals them in hermetically. Earl's lamps shed warm yellow light. He sits beside her, patting her knee with proprietary pride, then removes his glasses and rubs his eyes. He must be tired too. Without glasses his voluminous head, pink and rubbery, looks naked, and his blue eyes stand out even more. She has the feeling she's seeing something very personal about him, a certain sadness he usually, as a public person, keeps hidden.

"Did you all see Vince Carmichael tonight?" Earl says. "I've never seen him more flabbergasted."

"Oh, yes," says one of the men, chuckling. "He was struggling for words. You don't see Vince Carmichael struggling for words very often."

"He said more storms are on the way, later this week," says a man with a gold front tooth.

Patty Birch, one of the women whose name Bronwyn remembers, looks stricken by this information. "I didn't see that. I don't watch the news anymore. It scares me. My sister wants me to move out to California with her, but I can't do that. What would I do in California? Honestly, I couldn't leave everyone here. Besides, they have earthquakes there. And fires." She sobs quietly. The woman beside her squeezes her shoulder.

"She lost her husband back in May," another woman explains to Bronwyn. "That tornado just lifted his truck and that was that." She shakes her head. "We have needed someone like you so badly. Are you here to stay?"

Since the meeting with Vince the future has vanished. There is only now. "I live in New Hampshire. I work at a TV station back there."

"Tornado season should be over soon," says the man wearing a jacket, curiously overdressed on this hot night. "Should have been over a long time ago, but if we can make it through this next round we might be okay. Can you do anything to help us out?"

The dolor of Patty's quiet weeping seeps through the room and hushes them. Bronwyn regards the assembled faces, all listing in her direction, all painted with hope as if she has wisdom or power to sprinkle like seeds. No one is saying: *What the heck? We don't believe you. We need to see to believe.* Or: *We need to understand to believe.* It almost feels as if she's at a terrorists' cell meeting where certain articles of belief need no further clarification. She is not accustomed to being regarded as a source of power. She *does* happen to have a kind of power, but why do they accept it so readily? Would they take on faith anything Earl said? Their gullibility unnerves her, almost as much as Vince's kneejerk skepticism.

Patty Birch has stopped sobbing and is now gulping deep audible breaths.

"I have to get back to my job," Bronwyn says.

Earl senses her discomfort. "I think we need to call it a night. This gal needs some sleep. Let's take a minute to give thanks."

Everyone bows their heads and shifts their attention to Earl.

"Almighty God, we thank you for your divine gift to us in our hour of need. You have brought this brave and talented and holy woman to us. Bless her and guide her and keep her from harm. And hear our thanks for all you have given us. Amen."

Amens ripple throughout the room and people stand. They face Bronwyn, bowing a little. How embarrassing! She is not holy, not remotely so. But she nods back at them nonetheless. Patty and another woman are standing in front of her, obviously wanting something.

"Is it alright if we touch you?" Patty says. "We could use some good luck. And from what Earl says you seem to be very good luck."

Bronwyn smiles, shrugs. Patty reaches out and slides her palm down the side of Bronwyn's head, fondling the tips of her loose hair. The other woman does the same.

"You don't see hair like this every day. This dark red color. So beautiful. Magical really," says the woman who is not Patty.

"Thank you for indulging us," Patty says. "Who would think our little town would be blessed with a miracle worker."

"Please, I can't do miracles."

"Call it what you want. In my book, it's a miracle. Thank you from the bottom of my heart."

20

Joe has gone out for the Sunday papers. Diane awaits his return, sipping her coffee, nibbling her toast. Maybe later she'll make some eggs, but now she is happy to simply sit here, reveling in this moment of summer at its ripest. The tide is out and long strands of morning sunlight illuminate the salt flats, bringing a sheen to their fetid gray. Sometimes she likes to walk out there in her knee-high rubber boots, inhaling the sulfurous smell that most people revile, checking for clam bubbles and collecting pearlescent shells for the mosaics she imagines making but never has time for.

She would love to live in perpetual summer with its languid rhythms and loose routines that leave room for surprises. Winter is the season of hard tasks: grants are written, squabbles mediated, blizzards endured. Back in the city Joe gets moody, and worried about his work, certain he's lost his talent, sure he has written the last good thing he'll ever write. She tries to reassure him, but there is only so much she, a non-writer, can say. So, when they both survive those grueling dark winter months, and summer arrives on schedule, and they return to savor the Maine summer, it always seems at least one part miracle.

The house is modest, built in the early twentieth century, with creaky floorboards and a leaky roof and rot that needs to be fixed, but it is beautifully situated on a private, semi-wooded promontory above a tidal cove. They purchased it fifteen years ago, mainly as a summer retreat for Joe, but now she is as attached to it as he is. Occasionally Joe returns for a few days in the winter months, but Maine is lonely then and, although he loves solitude, he never lasts here more than a week in the off-season. He likes the knowledge that people are nearby, even when he isn't actively engaging with them.

Beyond the glistening mud flats the ocean is calm. The pacific Atlantic. She loves this ocean, this patch of land, this needy house.

She hears Joe pull into the gravel driveway and shuffle up the outdoor steps to the deck. He likes going for the paper at Cushing's, the mom-and-pop store that has been owned by the same family for over a century. It sells newspapers and magazines, ice cream, various canned foods, souvenirs, local crafts, penny candy, such an odd assortment of items she's amazed it's still in business. Joe likes talking to Mr. Cushing, a taciturn down-easter who only speaks to a few select individuals, one of whom happens to be Joe. He doesn't engage with Diane, a summer person only, and in Mr. Cushing's view one of the despised invaders who is ruining the state by crowding the streets and making real estate unaffordable for the locals, but Joe, who is around more often, has developed a rapport with Cushing. He always comes home with new stories about Cushing and his family members, usually dismal stories about n'er-do-well sons-in-law, and women who have eschewed family and fallen prey to the bad values in Massachusetts and New York.

Joe plunks down two papers, *The Boston Globe* and *The New York Times*, keeps another one stashed under his armpit. He grins and leans down to kiss her. He is firmly rooted in summer, unshaven, blond hair tousled, wearing shorts and flip-flops.

"News from the front," he says, only half-suppressing a grin that tells her he's got something up his sleeve. "Cushing is going for medical tests in Portland. He's been having some abdominal pain." He pours himself coffee and sits.

"That doesn't sound good."

"He's seventy-four. But the more important news is this." He pulls the other newspaper from under his arm, flattens it on the table with his palm and angles it toward her. *The Meteor*, one of those tabloids.

"Why did you get that?"

"Look. That's Bronwyn, isn't it?"

She stares down at the pixelated newsprint picture. It's a blurry closeup, but unmistakably Bronwyn, clearly identifiable by the mane of russet hair and the planet-sized green eyes. She stands in front of a weather map, gesturing, looking different than she did a few weeks ago when Diane took her for dinner. A little thinner maybe. It is the largest photo of three on the cover, even larger than the unflattering shot of Angelina Jolie. WEATHER WOMAN INFLUENCES WEATHER HERSELF, says the caption under Bronwyn.

"Oh, for god's sake, what *is* this? Did you read the article?"

Joe shrugs. "The usual tabloid fare."

She flips through the pages, past weight loss ads and ads for penile enlargement, until she arrives at the page with yet another photo of Bronwyn, the same one maybe, but this one showing her full body. Diane reads aloud over Joe's intermittent chuckling.

"'Robots are making our purchases and doing our taxes these days, so why couldn't a meteorologist change the weather? It turns out this is exactly what meteorologist and former MIT student Bronwyn Artair says she can do . . .'" Diane glances up at Joe. "This is ridiculous." He shrugs; she resumes reading. "'At a recent wedding in Southern New Hampshire, the bride, Nicole Simms, reported that Ms. Artair stopped the rain. *It was awesome. It was supernatural,* said Nicole. *She did it because she knew I was desperate for sun.*'"

"Imagine writing for a paper like that," Joe says. "I wouldn't mind having that job."

"Please, this isn't funny. I don't understand how this happened."

"Pure and simple. They needed a story, they made it up. It's great copy for a hungry readership."

"But what would prompt it? It must be based on *something*. They wouldn't make it up out of the blue. And why did they have to mention MIT?"

"They probably wanted to say something that would make it seem credible."

"I wish I could find this as funny as you do. I wonder if she's seen it."

"Don't bother getting worked up. It's only entertainment. Nobody believes this stuff and it's not hurting anyone."

"Easy for you to say—it's not your reputation."

"This has no bearing on you."

"Oh, I think it does."

Joe reins in his amusement and turns to separating the sections of *The Times* and *The Globe*, laying out the news sections for her—she likes to read those first—the sports and book reviews for himself. It still surprises her to see how meticulous he can be in isolated activities, when in most areas of his life he's such a slob. At night he abandons his clothes wherever he takes them off. At least she's trained him to pick them up later—she's made it clear she's not his mother.

A seagull comes in for a blustery landing on the deck's banister. She looks down at the picture again as if to wring from it an answer. Is this something someone did to Bronwyn, or something Bronwyn brought upon herself? When they had dinner in Portsmouth it was clear she was a little abstracted, and more nervous than usual. She'd been dumped by her boyfriend, so that was upsetting her, but Diane remembers thinking there might have been something else. Bronwyn can't really have said these things the paper says she has said, can she?

Joe isn't reading, he's eyeing her across the sports section. "Will you get in touch with her?"

"Of course. I have to find out how this happened."

"Would you want her back at school after this?"

"I'm certainly not going to hold against her what someone else has said or done. There has to be some credible explanation."

Joe lifts his face to the sun and closes his eyes, and in mock-rote fashion he quotes what she has so often said to him: "Intuition, imagination, chance, and anomalies also play a role in the scientific method."

Sweet Joe. No matter how rattled she is, he can always make her laugh. How lucky she is to have found this rumpled younger man. She loves that Joe's brain works so differently from hers and encourages her to see things from other angles. Joe the Gem. She laughs, then grows silent, pushes the paper aside, and turns back to the bubbling mud flats to pick at her worry.

21

She spends the night at Earl's because, kind man that he is, he suggests it, and it seems cruel to ask him to drive her two hours south to the Holiday Inn and then two hours back again. Lying in the single bed of his small guest room, every flat surface covered with a collection of ceramic pigs, she is too agitated to sleep well. She dreams she's pressing though a crowd of many women of different ages, all reaching out to stroke her hair. When the crowd parts, she spots the white-haired Native American woman Vince spoke of. She beckons to Bronwyn and winks. Bronwyn jerks awake and Vince fills her mind. She remembers him mocking the Native American woman, laughing at her communion with spirits. What a despicable human being he has turned out to be, and how strange that he and kind Earl are friends. She thinks of Earl's flock, Patty Birch and the others, taking her skill for granted and thinking it means she is good. They only think that because, after all the destruction they've been through, all the death they've witnessed, they need to believe *something* is good. But just having this skill does not make her a good person. She isn't bad either, she hopes, but she doesn't like people boxing her in, telling her who she is. Perhaps this is the same reason Earl dislikes naming things. Tomorrow Earl will drive her back to Oklahoma City and she will collect her things at the Holiday Inn and book a flight out. This trip has not turned out as she thought it would, and she can't figure out how to reshape it to make it feel right.

She gets up and stares out the guest room window. It is hazy, but a slim crescent moon sheds more light through the vapor than it seems such a scant moon should, illuminating the fields around Earl's house. Such an incorrigibly lonely landscape.

She takes the quilt from the bed and tiptoes downstairs and outside where she settles in the grass, insects trumpeting, the stillness deceptive. She lies on the quilt pressing her ear to the earth. Across the plains in Western Kansas and Oklahoma fronts are converging, winds have begun to spin. The haze drifts lazily over the moon. Even the earth likes to hold onto secrets, she thinks. Everything throbs with imminent mayhem.

Much later, the first light of dawn serenades her awake. She rises, light-headed but settled in her body again and clarified, knowing what she knows, happy to be going home. Inside she dresses, and when she comes downstairs Earl is in the kitchen making them breakfast. Scrambled eggs, toast, bacon. She eats so ravenously Earl laughs. He wants her to stay, not only for the week, but permanently. Of course she can't do that. If she were working with Vince that would have been one thing, but what does Earl have in mind? Simply waiting for tornadoes to materialize would not make for a full life.

"But you have a mission here," he says. He is straightforward and guileless. Is that what makes him likable?

"I'll think about it," she says. But her mind is made up.

"You miss people at home? A boyfriend maybe?"

By the time they finish breakfast the sky has darkened again, sooner than she expected, and she goes back outside and wanders the perimeter of the lawn. Earl knows to leave her alone, let her think. He probably hopes she'll change her mind about leaving. Dour mammatus clouds march by overhead, turning the daylight to dusk as if night will arrive early. This place, she has to admit, is a cloud-lover's paradise. Through the open window she can hear Earl moving quickly about like a terrier in a thunderstorm.

A car pulls into the driveway and someone gets out and goes inside, she doesn't see who. Perhaps someone is here for pastoral counseling. The TV goes on and through the open window she hears Vince's stentorian pronouncements. All over Kansas and Oklahoma people are tuning in to his station; every ten or fifteen minutes his advisories will be updated. She tries to block it out. The earth and its atmosphere have more important things to say to her, but their language is more nuanced and subtle, and understanding it requires her full attention.

A few more cars pull in. Why didn't Earl mention he would be having visitors? Or are these visits unplanned? She recognizes some of the faces from last night but, resisting the distraction, she ambles farther away from the house and looks southwest, her uplifted face devoted to the sky and the parcels of undulating air which take her into their tutelage. She visualizes the advance, feels the summons, hears the hum, low and intermittent at first, then gaining in strength and volume. Her limbs tingle. The foreground dims. Earl's yard, the alfalfa fields beyond, the copses of cottonwoods, all vanish from view, and the TV's clamor, the passing cars, all dial back to silence. The hum rules. The wall cloud advances. Rain comes down in a sudden wash like a plummeting drop cloth.

She is aloft now, near the dry line, an electromagnetic and thermodynamic force, anger and intention and hope turned to heat, an element in the chaos, disembodied, abstracted, pure will set against wind shear, spin, lift.

After the bombast has receded and given way to a quiescent day, mild and clear, she goes back inside where Earl's guests, ten or twelve people, greet her, clapping, bowing, shaking their heads in amazement. They make room for her to lie on the couch, bring pillows and quilts. The TV is still on, but muted now. For a moment she thinks Vince himself is in the room, but it's only because of the virulence of his stare which pierces the fourth wall angrily: *You, you, you—this is my domain. Get out of here.*

Before the guests leave they press gifts upon her: a plate of oatmeal cookies, an amber amulet hung on a leather thong, a black velvet hair ribbon.

"We wish you wouldn't leave," Patty Birch says. "My husband would have loved to meet you." Tears pool on her lower lids, making flood plains of her eyes. She pats Bronwyn's arm with her bloated hand. "I hope you'll think of us."

Bronwyn and Earl drive in silence back down the now-familiar road to Oklahoma City. She stares at his green Converse on the gas pedal and a great fondness blooms in her for the existence of Earl, who she has known for less than forty-eight hours. She feels guilty for leaving. In the lobby of the Holiday Inn an instrumental rendition of "Here Comes the Sun" plays over the sound system. She and Earl hug. What is there to say? He wants her to stay and she is not going to stay. She watches him traverse the lobby to the front door where he turns and takes off his cap. Grinning, he bows.

22

She arrives home after dark, sniffing the river's brackish scent and the faint lingering smell of the dead raccoon, feeling her way into the cabin by the river without turning on lights, as if to exist for a while unseen will delay her return and its inevitable medley of decisions. The cabin smells musty. She makes her way to the screened-in porch and lets her skin imbibe the air. A slight breeze from the river carries the perfume of wet wood and decay.

It's good to be home seeing the sash of the river, the silhouettes of the bowing willows. *Who am I?* she keeps asking. In answer she says her name over and over, "Bronwyn Artair, Bronwyn Artair." The sound of her name echoes through the cabin without any meaning attached, making her wonder if she has cast off too many atoms during the episodes, dismantling and rebuilding herself too many times.

In three days away so many messages have piled up, three emails from Diane alone. She doesn't open them. She was another person with an entirely different genome when she worked alongside Diane. She unpacks slowly, forgetting for seconds at a time where each item belongs, then retrofitting herself to remember. Time seems to bounce around like lobbed tennis balls. She misses Earl, feels guilty again about having left him. He has proven to be the perfect counterbalance to Vince.

Before retiring she turns on the TV to watch her replacement, Chip. He has a square face, eyebrows that hunker too close to his eyes, and a serious mouth he purses and re-purses. She can see why Stuart is eager to have her back. She emails Stuart to tell him she has returned early and will be at work tomorrow.

After turning off the TV and turning out the light, she lies in bed for a long time, wide awake, thinking of Earl and Vince, and of Patty Birch's husband being lifted in his truck. Maybe he felt weightless for a moment before he was gone, pleasantly stripped of mortality and responsibility. She sees the apocalyptic wall cloud turning day into night as it lowered. New Hampshire seems tame after Kansas, quiet and deceptively safe. She is only able to relax and find sleep when she hears the hooting owl that she has come to think of as hers.

She dresses carefully for work, assessing the proper feminine-to-professional ratio and choosing, with Stuart in mind, the outfit with the higher feminine quotient, a purple skirt and a formfitting pink sweater with a lower neckline than she usually favors. She needs to regain her footing with Stuart, needs to appear contrite and compliant, at least until she decides to be otherwise. So continues her double life: the steely thermodynamic Bronwyn clad deceptively in pumps and pink, the brave and fiery woman playing the timid one, the remorseless woman feigning contrition.

The station sucks her back into its cavernous claustrophobic dimness then explodes over her in the form of Nicole who jumps up from her desk in a tempest of anxious whispering, eyebrows rising and falling with encrypted messages.

"Bathroom," she says.

"Now?"

Nicole seizes a bag from under her desk and takes off. Bronwyn follows, ducking a little, as if a storm system is besieging them and the roof is unreliable. The bathroom is empty, but Nicole still feels a need to whisper.

"It's been so weird since you've been gone. Stuart hated what Chip was doing. He's a real loser on air." She leans so close her words become wind on Bronwyn's cheek. "But here's the thing—I was at CVS yesterday and I saw this." She yanks a folded newspaper from her bag and lays it on the sink. *The Meteor.* "Quick," she says.

Bronwyn looks down at a grainy photograph of herself giving a weather report, the map of New England a backdrop. Her organs cluster and surge, as if governed tidally. WEATHER WOMAN INFLUENCES WEATHER HERSELF, says the caption. She grabs the paper from Nicole. "Ugh. I can't believe this. He promised he wouldn't write anything."

Nicole shrugs, her eyes mournful. "I'm so sorry. It's my fault, I know. I mean if I hadn't said anything—"

"It's not your fault. It's *men*. It's always *men*." As soon as she says this she thinks guiltily of Earl. "Has Stuart seen it?"

"He hasn't said anything. I doubt if he buys papers like this."

"Yeah, but someone will tell him. One of those lonely viewers he's always talking about." Bronwyn opens the paper and leafs quickly through it to find another unflattering broadcast photo of herself. She skims the copy. Entirely fabricated.

"You can keep that. I saved it for you."

"Thanks. I should get to work." Bronwyn pauses to assess herself in the mirror. Her skin has the look of a frosted window pane with patches of translucence through which underlying blotchiness shows. "Hey, Nicole, do I look like—like I'm—leaking?"

"How do you mean? Leaking what? Like pee?"

"No. My face? Does it look regular?"

"Okay to me." Nicole laughs nervously.

Bronwyn navigates down the hallway, across the set, and to her console in a daze, waving greetings without pausing to talk. What a stupid article. Why would anyone write such drivel? For what—to sell papers and pander to people's schadenfreude? Once again she has misread another human being completely. To think that she was, for a moment at least, attracted to the guy.

She logs onto the National Weather Service feed. There's a tropical depression in the Caribbean that could possibly affect New England weather next week, though it doesn't appear to be gaining much strength. But there's worse news. The fires in Southern California have mushroomed out of control to become worse than any on record. And Tornado Alley is in for another bad spell. Global warming aside, there's no denying that this is an exceptionally bad weather year. God, she feels terrible for Earl.

Her own report for today is straightforward. A high pressure system will keep things sunny for a couple of days, but then some of the rain from the Midwest will be coming in. It's such a standard report she could phone it in. She stares at the screen, doing nothing, chips of conversation floating around her, bubbly as phosphorescence. Gwen and Brant are discussing their Labor Day plans, and weighing the value and danger of pit bulls. She will leave a message for Matt Vassily telling him what a dick he is.

She scrolls and clicks around her computer and arrives at some news footage of one of the LA fires. It is mesmerizing in its hunger, its insatiability, its elusiveness. It seems to retreat for a while as if going to sleep, then it rears up again without apparent provocation. It gallivants through the trees, a Siren confident she'll never be punished. *Come, come, I will warm you.* It takes what it wants on its own terms, oblivious to human needs.

Fire entrances humans, she thinks, because, like water and wind, it cannot be held, cannot be known tactilely, haptically. What can't be touched and held cannot be controlled. She thinks of how she herself has sometimes resisted the touch of a man. Men are always bigger than she, and usually stronger, and to be touched by them has meant relinquishing something.

23

Matt would not have returned early to Florida if he hadn't been so livid at Josh, but he needed to see Josh face-to-face to tell him what a serious asshole he is. Now, however, there's little satisfaction standing in front of Josh's absurdly messy desk, papers skating off its edges, three giant computer monitors placed fatuously at the desk's center, surrounded by a graveyard of Styrofoam take out containers and cardboard coffee cups, the office air foul with musty air and fibrillating dust, Josh's acrid body odor made worse by the heat, and, worst of all, Josh's pretty-boy, curl-framed face smeared with an aggressive and gleeful imperviousness: *Whatever you say won't get to me.*

"From what I could see she had it coming," Josh says.

"You have no idea. You didn't go there. You didn't see her. You didn't talk to her. What you wrote is all hearsay."

"Do you not understand what kind of an operation we are? Did I not make that clear when you started?"

"She could sue you. I hope she will."

"I've got myself covered."

"Honestly, how do you live with yourself?"

Josh rolls his chair around the edge of his desk. He's a lazy son-of-a-bitch. He hates to move, hates to even stand, and he's begun paying for his lethargy with an incipient paunch that is soon going to render his pretty-boy face not so pretty. Matt hops back to avoid being run over by the chair's casters, and Josh brings himself to an abrupt stop at Matt's toes.

"I get it," Josh says. "You have the hots for her, don't you? You're trying to get laid."

Matt says nothing.

"Not a professional way to go, buddy." He winks. "I might have to fire you."

"Go ahead, fire me."

"Why—you don't have the balls to quit?"

"Of course I do. I quit."

"You can't quit—I've already assigned you to a story in Alabama. A hoarder in Huntsville with a couple of houses full of stuff. The third cousin of some Hollywood mogul. Could be good."

"You'll have to find someone else. You heard me—I quit."

Matt immerses himself in the perpetual carnival of South Beach. Its atmosphere coordinates perfectly with the bucking inside his brain. He feels good, he feels bad, he feels crazed, almost desperate. He's been wanting to do this for ages, but was afraid of not being able to find another job, afraid of those monthly payments, afraid of having to choose a real life. Now, god, he can get through the summer, but after that? Maybe he'll ask his parents for a loan. Maybe he'll ask his *mother*, though he knows she would never give him money without telling Ivan. But his first order of business, before finding another job, before obsessing about the future, is to apologize to Bronwyn. His chances with her are all but ruined, but at least he can clean things up and clarify that he was true to his word—he did *not* write that article.

He studies the pedestrians coming toward him, wonders how many of them are unemployed, recently fired, recently spurned in love. So many of them are laughing and apparently carefree. He's pretty sure he does not look carefree, yet he does feel something positive. He's a man with more integrity now than he had an hour ago. The thought brings a lightness to his step. He's done with the likes of paunchy, odiferous, pretty-boy Josh who has no belief in human dignity.

24

Tornadoes rise and take possession of the plains, lumbering across them like prehistoric beasts, furious, shape-shifting, coming to redress old insults, bent on annihilation. Each is a mile wide or more. Town after town goes down, a random game of Russian roulette. Transfixed, Bronwyn cannot turn off her computer, which streams Vince's Oklahoma City station. She perches on the edge of the couch, computer in her lap, afraid of moving, as if the barrel of a chilly gun rests at her throat. Vince is performing as usual, but she sees it differently now. He seems to smile as if he is finally enjoying himself, can only enjoy himself in the midst of mortal mayhem, people being crushed, electrocuted, trapped under the familiar walls of their collapsed houses to perish slowly and quietly, beyond anyone's view. He struts in front of his maps and screens like a four-star general, puffed-up, believing his mastery makes him desirable, his craggy face a detailed history of archived disasters. "It's nuclear, folks," he says, shaking his head.

"People are dying out there!" she yells into the neutral silence of her living room.

Earl is not answering his phone. He is out offering aid, no doubt, in a cellar somewhere with his flock, consoling them, singing hymns and leading them in prayer. Bronwyn can picture Patty Birch by his side, her soft body leaning into Earl, grateful for his leadership. It occurs to her that the two might become a couple, and she is touched by the thought.

The tornadoes keep coming without a lick of remorse. The largest one backtracks suddenly and heads northwest, highly unusual, playing chicken with Vince, defying his predictions, then it whips in the other direction, outwitting him again and heading northeast. It is a taunting, sociopathic, most-wanted felon.

For an instant the camera captures Vince's shock at being wrong. She sees his lips forming an 'F' before the camera cuts away and the sound snaps to silence, and the station broadcasts, for a brief but disturbing moment, the absence of all sound and image, showing only a black screen, as if to say the world has ended.

It is early afternoon. The death toll is over four hundred. The demolished town names ring out from the computer like an incantation. Is it possible that her intervention has made things worse? That unanswerable question haunts her. In an hour she must go to work. She steps outside. The sun persists. It doesn't feel right. There are at least a thousand miles between New Hampshire and the plains of Oklahoma and Kansas. They are subject to different forces out there. Sometimes the weather systems of the plains work their way to the east coast, but by the time they arrive they have always changed.

She descends to the river's edge and stares at the turbid green water. A few weeks ago a kayaker drowned not far from here. The incident was blamed on the current which can be strong when the tide is shifting. But from where she stands now it is hard to imagine a strong current. The day is given over to summer's torpor, not yet infused with the kinetic energy of fall. A water snake breaches the surface then disappears. She closes her eyes, pictures Earl's back yard and its view out to the alfalfa fields beyond. Could she wield any influence over the tornadoes from this distance? Her brain is stuck in a waltz rhythm: one-two-three, one-two-three, one-two-three. She seeks a rhythm, but not that one. She needs a rhythm that is less common, repeating itself only after very long phrases, arching throughout her body and dismantling its norms, effacing the usual, letting her electrons organize themselves in new ways.

She elongates her breathing, imagines herself levitating over the miles. She exists for a while in hope, but every once in a while a flag of disgust for Vince steals her concentration. She bats those thoughts away, tries to refocus, waiting, eyes still closed. What is the problem? Is it the distance that's impeding her? Is it a faltering ability to concentrate? Or is she merely running up against the limits of her capability. She stares at the water wondering if she should go back to the Midwest to help out. Earl would think she should.

She returns inside to a ringing phone. She rarely answers her phone these days, mostly it doesn't ring and when it does it jars her, its arrogant presumption that she is always available and wanting to talk. She would rather communicate voicelessly on her own terms, through email and text. She peeks at the number without answering. It's Stuart. She'll be at the station in a couple of hours, can't he wait? The ringing stops. She supposes she should call back. It rings again. Not Stuart this time, but a number she doesn't recognize, a different area code. Curious, she picks it up, says hello.

"Is this the weather lady?" says a quiet female voice.

"Who am I speaking to?"

"This is Patty Birch, remember me? Earl's friend."

Bronwyn takes an audible breath, surprised and suddenly suffused with dread, wanting to hear what Patty Birch has to say, but wanting nothing to do with it too. She steps outside again, phone pressed to her ear, her body seeming to vanish on its own journey to Kansas. Patty Birch calling can mean only one thing.

"Yes," she says. "Of course I remember you."

She listens numbly and gets off the phone as quickly and graciously as she can, promising to call back soon. She sits on the porch couch. Earl. Earl who didn't believe in naming things. Earl who wanted her to stay. No one else would hold her responsible, but the underlying truth is—she could have done something.

She remembers the day her mother died. She had been recently released from the hospital with a bleak prognosis. The doctor didn't say so directly, but it was obvious from the way he avoided Bronwyn's gaze that he expected Maggie to die soon. For a day she lay at home in terrible pain, despite the morphine, eyes closed, moaning a little, her cheeks so sunken she no longer resembled herself, but like some cartoonish version of a corpse. She could eke out only a few words in a row and recognized Bronwyn only intermittently. Sometimes she was racked with shivering, other times she burned with heat. Bronwyn fed her sips of water which dribbled down her chin; she mopped her brow with cool cloths. Near the end of that day she called Hospice and a wonderful nurse arrived almost immediately and, speaking with the soothing voice of a saint, told Bronwyn what to expect. She administered a shot of morphine and together they eased Maggie into a new position. The nurse left promising to return the next day. Alone, Bronwyn did not dare leave the bedside. Maggie hovered in some liminal state, neither dead nor alive, not breathing in any audible or visible way, her heartbeats faint and slow and randomly spaced. Then suddenly, unexpectedly, she was dead. Bronwyn sensed the exact moment. She didn't take Maggie's pulse, but she immediately recognized the presence of death in the room with her. Why did it feel so unexpected when it was the very thing they'd both been waiting for? She sat there for a while as Maggie's face slackened. Bronwyn knew what she needed to do, but it took a long time to find the will to do it. She could not have saved her mother, but Earl she might have saved.

In a state of high alert she answers the next phone call thinking it might be Patty with news that she was mistaken, Earl is not dead but still very much alive. But it's Stuart again and once she's picked up she can't bring herself to hang up. His voice is taut.

"Do you know a man named Vince Carmichael?"

What can she possibly say? She says nothing.

"I had a call from him this morning. He told me you visited his station earlier this week. I don't know what you think you're doing but—"

She holds the phone far away from her ear so his voice weakens until it is no louder than a mosquito's whine. Then it is so much easier to cut the connection. Why give Stuart the opportunity to lambaste her this way? She feels her firing coming, almost welcomes it. She must hold herself together in any way she can. For the moment anger is good glue.

25

Diane tries to reach Bronwyn three times on the drive from Maine back down to Cambridge. Away from Joe, her worry is unbridled, it sweeps through her brain stirring up nightmarish scenarios, and culling long-forgotten memories. Is it possible that Bronwyn has had a breakdown of some kind? That is one possibility, but not likely, she thinks. As anxious as Bronwyn has been at times, Diane has never seen evidence of psychosis. At the other end of the spectrum, and equally disturbing, is the possibility that Bronwyn has some enemy who is attempting to discredit her. Diane certainly remembers the way Bruce and Jim conspired to humiliate Bronwyn. They didn't want her around showing them up. Now, in retrospect Diane wishes she had put a more definitive stop to that—she could have, she held the power.

Diane has half a mind to stop in New Hampshire and find Bronwyn, but she has no address. Who would know? She can't think of anyone. There are several Portsmouth exits. She drives past the first one then reconsiders and takes the next. Once off the highway, she heads west toward Manchester. Which river is it that Bronwyn lives on? The Piscataqua? The Squamscott? She should have listened more closely. She drives slowly as if Bronwyn might materialize by the roadside, then she realizes it's a fool's errand she's on—she could drive forever without results. Maybe she should go to the TV station which shouldn't be hard to find. But if Bronwyn is working it might be hard to talk. She turns around and goes back to the highway, heading south toward Boston again, exceeding the speed limit, wishing she'd stayed put in Maine with Joe. She has things to get done at work, but they can wait, and she won't be fully focused at work until she knows what's really happened with Bronwyn.

Perhaps she should not be so invested in Bronwyn, but how does one disengage? She has held Bronwyn under her wing for a long time now, since she first taught her in an earth science class years ago. It was Bronwyn's freshman year and Diane was also new to Wellesley. Diane was lucky to have the job after having been asked to resign from UCLA's atmospheric sciences department following the Fiorini debacle. This is a period of her life she still prefers not to think about, but meeting Bronwyn helped her get through that dark time.

Bronwyn drifted into the classroom, tentative as milkweed. She sat in the front row, off to one side, and did not take her eyes off Diane the entire time, scribbling a little but mostly watching, entranced or terrified, Diane couldn't tell, but definitely different from the other students who dug in their backpacks and immersed themselves in their phones and occupied their chairs as if trying to establish dominion over tiny republics.

Another memory of Bronwyn comes to mind. In the weeks following Bronwyn's mother's death, Diane went to visit her in New Jersey in the place she grew up. Bronwyn had finished with the immediate post-mortem tasks—disposing of the body, notifying friends and family, holding a small memorial service—and she had just begun the work of clearing out the tiny house in preparation for selling it.

Maggie Artair had been living in the house for more than twenty years; Bronwyn had lived there for the eighteen years before she left for college. It was a depressing little dwelling—small and dark and cluttered and situated in one of those armpit towns that seems not like a place unto itself, but like a place en route to more important places. It was hard to imagine such a forlorn house as having played a prominent role in Bronwyn's past.

Bronwyn was unexpectedly gracious and happy to see Diane. It might have been the first time Bronwyn was the one to initiate a hug before Diane did. She showed Diane around and wanted to talk about the death: what it was like to recognize the terminal prognosis in the doctor's evasive demeanor, the excruciating pain Maggie had suffered after being released from the hospital, how watching that pain made Bronwyn feel helpless and made her contemplate the fragility of human life and the futility of human effort, and how she recognized immediately the moment when her mother's death arrived. She did not report these things as if the depressing thoughts still inhabited her, but as if they had passed through her and moved on into part of her history, replaced by relief.

Then Bronwyn led Diane outside to a small area bordered by a high chain-link fence where they sat on folding metal chairs on a rectangle of concrete next to another rectangle of bald lawn. There were no plantings, just the yellowish grass that had yet to show any signs of newly arrived spring. "One of my favorite places in the world," Bronwyn said, laughing, knowing how this would strike Diane.

She used to lie out on this tiny plot of grass, she said, and gaze up at the clouds. It was there where she first fell in love with weather. Diane would have been embarrassed by this last admission, and by everything, had she not been riveted by seeing fully, for the first time, the distance Bronwyn had traveled. Who wouldn't want to escape this place? Who wouldn't, living here, need to reach for the clouds? It was that visit that made Diane determined to help Bronwyn get her PhD.

She picks up the phone and tries the number again. She's leaving a fourth message when a highway patrol car swoops up behind her, lights whirling a hue-and-cry, arriving as they always do out of nowhere.

PART TWO

Now What?

26

The once-known is now strange. Bronwyn has been on this New Jersey beach dozens of times in her childhood and adolescence, but cycles of storm damage and rebuilding over fifteen or twenty years have made things nearly unrecognizable. New food concessions have sprung up, gaudy and neon-lit; the amusement park has replaced all the old rides; the boardwalk is so jammed with people it's hard to navigate without bumping shoulders and elbows.

She and Lanny have bought hot dogs for old time's sake, and now, as they eat, they light out across the beach to escape the pandemonium. The hot sand sears the soles of their feet. Didn't it used to be whiter sand, not nearly as coarse? Bronwyn doesn't remember seeing so many raisin-sized bits of black tar in the past. Much as she is a student of flux and flow, devoted to understanding time and nature as sculptors ceaselessly at work, she still wishes this beach were the same as it used to be, charming her as it once did.

Lanny, however, has not changed, or not appreciably. When Bronwyn left for college she found other confidantes to take Lanny's place, boyfriends and roommates mostly; none of those people have remained close and none of them ever knew Bronwyn as well as Lanny does. Now Lanny has resumed her old role. She knows about Earl and Vince and Stuart and Matt. Bronwyn has told her everything.

It is a moody summer day, hot and hazy, the kind of day that makes it hard to get much done. Most of the kids are in the water, the adults recline in low chairs under umbrellas, or splay themselves on their towels, faces flopped down like depleted seals. The lifeguards drowse on their high perches, hypertrophied muscles slack.

"You could move back here, couldn't you?" says Lanny. "There's nothing holding you there anymore."

Bronwyn has considered this, has wondered if she might find a job in New York or New Jersey. It's unlikely that most people here would have read that stupid article. But frankly, New York and New Jersey seem ugly to her now, too much concrete, too many exhaust-spewing cars, so much affronting the natural world. Even Cambridge feels too urban. No egrets and owls. No nearby beach.

"I love my place by the river. It's all I have now."

"It's pretty sweet. But here you'd have *me*. Someone in your camp. I could be your agent and make you famous. There everyone's against you."

"Only Stuart really. The other people who are against me, like Vince, are elsewhere. Anyway, I'm not looking for fame. That article shows where fame would lead. Nothing but humiliation."

"Still, moving would be a great reset."

Moving holds only the illusion of improvement, she thinks, only the false promise of change. It wouldn't alter anything fundamental. It wouldn't restore Earl. She shakes her head.

"You can't crawl into a hole. You can't pretend this isn't happening to you. I won't let you."

The hole to crawl into doesn't exist. The task of forgetting is thankless. Impossible. Reminders lurk everywhere. Back at Lanny's quaint craftsman house they watch *Gone with the Wind*, holding off on dinner until Lanny's husband comes home. They want to cry over the movie and use their tears to slide back into their adolescent selves, but the movie seems a bit stupid now—Vivien Leigh and Clark Gable both overacting—and Bronwyn and Lanny don't cry. After the movie the weather report comes on the TV, unavoidable. It silences them. They could turn it off, but they don't. What strikes Bronwyn is the phrases the man uses, the same phrases she herself has spoken so many times. And his report is only a tiny fragment of the full weather picture. The next few days will be hot, he says, and there is the possibility of thunderstorms. Sure, sure. But he doesn't mention—perhaps he doesn't know, how could he really?—that the temperature will be higher next week, significantly higher, and it will stay that way for close to a week. This man is jovial and reassuring, exactly as Stuart always wanted her to be. Lanny raises an eyebrow at the mention of thunderstorms, but says nothing.

Bronwyn has entered a new phase. Every so often, unpredictably, a rush of sound comes over her, swarming in her ears and subverting all her ordinary senses. It's the Earth speaking, inchoate, but demanding her full attention. Her limbs tremble, her hands flutter. She hears nothing but full-throttle whispering that rises to a roar. She excuses herself to the guest room to wait it out. It takes a minute or two for the roar and trembling to subside. When everything is quiet again meaning takes root. She can say then, with remarkable accuracy, as she did in Kansas, what is soon to arrive.

Lanny finds her after one of these episodes. "What's happening? You have to tell me."

"I don't know exactly."

"What are you going to do? You have to do something. Learn about this. See a doctor. Anything. But *something.*"

"You think I don't know that?"

Lanny gives her a look and leaves the room.

A thunderstorm does arrive one evening, just after they've come home from their day's jaunt. Bronwyn stands at the living room window looking out to the back yard. Heat lightning flashes, thunder cracks directly overhead. The rain's jaunty rhythm brings calypso to mind. She is overwhelmed with nostalgia. Home is out there, swaying in the trees.

"Well?" says Lanny, coming up behind her. "Aren't you going to do anything?"

Bronwyn continues to stare out, smiling now. "No. We're perfectly safe."

Each day arrives bearing a host of new questions. Some of them she buries, or tries to. She brings her coffee to the back yard where Lanny's morning ritual includes lifting weights. Lanny, the queen of late sleeping, has been getting up early to get a workout in before the heat gets serious. She has always been impressively muscular, even back in high school, but when she went to college she began to work on her body more concertedly with weight training, running, protein drinks. The results are visible. She is strikingly symmetrical now, and her long leg and arm muscles are chiseled as those of a fit man. She lays down her weights, does a quick set of push-ups, comes to sit with Bronwyn, and goes to work kneading one of her quadriceps.

"When I woke up this morning I thought of something—you should go talk to your teacher."

"Diane?"

"Yeah, her. She's always been good to you, hasn't she? She might be able to help you figure this thing out."

"I can't do that. She wouldn't get it. She's a completely rational logical person. She has no room in her head for this kind of thing. She'd probably disown me."

"She doesn't *own* you in the first place."

"I know. But she, of all the people I know, is the least likely to be able to understand that what I do would ever be possible."

"What if she saw you in action?"

"Even then. And I couldn't do anything in front of her. I'd be way too nervous."

"I think you're underestimating her. She'd have to take you seriously—she's practically your mother." Lanny sighs, stands, raises her arms overhead in a stretch. "I have to tell you, girlfriend, these seizures you've been having, or whatever they are, they're making me nervous. What if you're dying?"

"I'm not dying."

"But you don't know. You might be."

Day after day of impossible heat, but nevertheless they stay on the move, visiting their old haunts. At Cape May they stroll on the beach. At the Delaware River they hike in the woods. They take the bus to New York and walk from Soho to Central Park. The scissoring of their legs helps them remap their youth, walking as memory and walking as medicine. But nothing is the same.

On a fire hydrant someone has scrawled: *Ain't nothin scares me.*

On 34th and Broadway: a snake with the girth of a fire hose drapes a man's neck. A crowd has gathered, titillated, nervous. A cop, keeping his distance, tells the man to put the snake back in its cage, but the man refuses, laughing.

At Columbus Circle the feeling comes over her, the roar and the trembling. She sits on a low wall by the fountain, waiting it out as traffic tears by.

Lanny speaks of her husband, how different they are in so many ways. He despises exercise, would rather read, and he doesn't require much talking. They like each other a lot, but will these differences undermine them over time, Lanny wonders aloud.

Bronwyn listens, preoccupied, restless. She's being summoned, it seems, but to what exactly? How does one find a purpose when there are no models that have gone before? Who can she emulate? Vince's Native American woman perhaps? Maybe that woman, inspired by ancestral spirits, was doing exactly what Bronwyn does. If only Bronwyn could find her, but to do so she'd have to contact Vince who didn't even seem to remember the woman's name. She wants to embrace this talent of hers, but it has turned out to be so fraught. How lonely she's become inside this skin of hers, even around Lanny.

"Can you break this heat?" Lanny asks. "We'd all love you for it."

She might be able to, but it doesn't feel right, changing the weather for reasons of discomfort, altering who knows what else in the process.

She awakens on the eighth day knowing it's time to leave. She can't wait any longer. This isn't her home anymore. Lanny protests. "I've loved having you here."

"You don't need me," Bronwyn says. "You were doing fine without me."

"But you need me."

27

She travels north through New York, Connecticut, Massachusetts, on roads she has traveled countless times during breaks from college and when her mother was sick. She knows all the landmarks, road signs, mileages. She knows where the ocean will come into view and when it will no longer be visible. She can drive these roads without giving a thought to the task of driving, scarcely realizing she is driving, the car regulating itself. She passes the exit that would take her north to New Hampshire and instead continues east toward Boston, as has been her habit for so many years. Oversight or intention, she honestly can't say. Route 2 takes her past Fresh Pond to Memorial Drive along the glistening Charles. She turns into the residential streets, and as her vehicle slows her heart speeds. She looks for a legal parking place, hard to come by on these narrow leafy streets of Cambridge's most patrician neighborhood.

Once parked, she walks a few blocks to Diane's house, amazed by her own boldness. How is it that she, always a judicious and cautious young woman, is now running on impulse and instinct? It is perfectly possible that Diane is not here on a summer Saturday afternoon. She might be in Maine with Joe, or at work, or out doing errands, or on a business trip. Bronwyn stands on the sidewalk staring at the front door, Chinese red with a brass knocker in the shape of a lion's head.

This is the pelvic floor of summer, heat throbbing through every organic and inanimate object with the intensity of a bad fever. All up and down the street the prized, shade-giving maple leaves droop and curl into themselves, as if giving up on photosynthesis. Bronwyn pushes through the wrought-iron gate, up the walkway and front steps. She knocks with her knuckle and waits in an epic hush. Ear to the door, she listens for remote interior movement. Nothing. This time she uses the knocker and its thunk echoes stridently down the quiet street. Still nothing. Obviously no one is home. She collapses on the concrete step as if she has endured some extreme exertion. She's a little relieved. She hasn't prepared properly. With a person like Diane, a meeting should be scheduled in advance. Her time should not be wasted.

The door opens. "I can't believe you're here! I thought I heard something. Come in, come in!"

Diane looks as Bronwyn has never seen her, bleary-eyed and truly startled. She pats her uncombed hair, apparently reading Bronwyn's assessment. "Oh, I look terrible, don't I? I was napping, sorry to say. This heat just ruins me."

"I can come back . . ."

"Certainly not. I've been *dying* to talk."

They go inside and stand in the foyer while Diane gets her bearings, peering into the dim living room strangely, as if she isn't entirely sure where she is. Bronwyn is a bit embarrassed for her, though Diane doesn't appear the least bit embarrassed for herself.

"We can't stay inside. It's too stuffy in here. I've never wanted air conditioning, but recently I've been rethinking my position—let me pull myself together and I'll bring some iced coffee to the back yard. I'll meet you out there."

She disappears before Bronwyn can offer to make the coffee. But she would feel flummoxed making coffee in Diane's kitchen with its marble countertops and top-of-the-line appliances. She wouldn't know what cups to lay out, or where to find a tray, or how much ice to use. So many decisions required in such a simple offering.

She passes through the dining room to one of the doors that leads outside. The deck, a relatively recent addition, runs the full length of the house. Stairs descend to the yard which, though not large, is Bronwyn's idea of a perfect outdoor urban space. At the far end is a venerable maple with a massive trunk and unusually symmetrical branches. From one of the lower limbs a swing hangs. Along the periphery of the wooden fence are fruit trees—pear, apple, cherry—that bloom in the spring, and bear fruit in the fall, and offer a modicum of privacy from neighbors. Along the side of the deck are hydrangeas in various shades of blue and purple, and a small vegetable and flower garden occupies the yard's sunniest corner close to the house.

The yard, Diane once told her, was supposed to feel like a "secret garden." "You know the book?" she said. Bronwyn was not familiar with *The Secret Garden* then, a fact which shocked Diane, so Bronwyn immediately found the book and read it and loved it, and she agreed that Diane's garden recreates the secluded feeling of the garden in the book. She likes that Diane and Joe aren't overly fussy about this outside area. It has clearly been designed, but it's not forbiddingly tidy, and therefore it's a perfect place to relax.

Relax is the last thing Bronwyn can do now. How can she deliver her news and solicit advice in language Diane will find palatable? The language of science has become such an anathema to Bronwyn. In that language facts are only worthwhile if they rest on the steadfast pillar of airtight experimental proof.

She heads to a triangle of shade at the back of the yard and sits in the maple tree's swing, heart sprinting despite her deep breathing. Her brain is hostage to the heat, slow and sodden and listless—how can she possibly find a coherent way to explain herself. She gazes up through the maple's canopy. She associates this tree with the Founding Fathers, men who would disapprove of the primitive, unsocialized woman she has become. Kernels of sky interspersed with the leaves form a matrix that looks two-dimensional. Here she is in Diane's back yard, and all the bravado that has brought her here seems to have drained away. A terrible thought occurs. What if she has lost her ability, just now, at the very moment she intends to face Diane?

The weight of the sky and the heat iron her chest, and she clings to the swing's ropes and lies back, feet outstretched like a child. The world spins and blurs. The hum surrounds her, enters her. She rises through the canopy, evaporating into it, stirring the molecules of stagnant air out of their inertia. Wind, at last.

Abruptly, mindful of where she is, she sits back up. She shouldn't be doing this. She didn't mean to. Or maybe she did. At least she *can*.

Regardless, the air has begun to move again deliciously, the leaves warbling against one another like waking siblings. Goosebumps spring up along her forearms.

And there is Diane scuttling down the stairs of the deck, looking revived in fresh clothing, and carrying a tray which she sets on a small wooden table next to a pair of Adirondack chairs.

"It's so good to see someone using that swing," she calls. "Joe put it up with the romantic notion that he'd use it to nurse his ideas, but he never uses it for that purpose, or any other." She sighs and lifts her chin. "Oh my, doesn't that breeze feel good. What a surprise."

Bronwyn slides off the swing wondering if claiming the breeze would be a good way to begin. Perhaps not, she thinks. Diane pours iced coffee from a pitcher and the tinkling ice reminds Bronwyn of shooting stars, ephemeral and delicate, here and gone. There is food, of course—there's always food with Diane—this time a plate of tiny blueberry and custard tarts. "I'm sorry to say I didn't make them. I couldn't turn on the oven in this heat."

"Is Joe here?"

"He's in Maine. He never comes down here in the summer if he can help it."

They sip their coffee under an illusory membrane of ease. Bronwyn feels the aeolian rustling of the hydrangea leaves. How does one introduce two foreign worlds, two world views that have no use for each other, that have always been estranged?

"So, that ghastly article—I'm assuming you've seen it?" Diane says.

Bronwyn nods. So Diane *has* seen it. It seemed unlikely that she would find an article in *The Meteor*, a publication Bronwyn is sure Diane reviles as much as she does, but the urgency of Diane's recent calls made Bronwyn consider the possibility.

"What's at the bottom of all this foolishness? Joe just happened to see it at the little Mom-and-Pop store we go to in Maine."

Bronwyn sighs, stalling, wishing for a different conversational tone.

"How terribly humiliating," says Diane. "Who wrote the thing? Was someone trying to harm you?"

"They just want to sell their papers, those people. They'll say anything, even make things up."

"But why would they—I mean what prompted an article about you in the first place?"

Bronwyn takes a blueberry tart and shoves it into her mouth, tries to swallow without chewing and almost chokes. She coughs, spewing crumbs. Diane hands her a napkin. Bronwyn wipes her mouth, head bent to her lap to mollify her embarrassment, and to resist the open invitation from trees and sky to evaporate back into them.

Recovered a little, she slides forward in her Adirondack chair. "I have to tell you—I'm not who you've always thought I was. I've never really been that person."

Diane watches her with a mute, impassive gaze which often passes for objectivity. It is not objectivity, Bronwyn thinks. There is no such thing as objectivity.

"What do you mean exactly?"

"That article was humiliating, but not for the reason you think. It mocked me, as if I'm a fool. But I'm not a fool—"

"Of course you aren't."

"—I can do those things."

Diane frowns. "What things? Be specific."

"Changing the elements. Stopping storms and tornadoes. Working with the Earth's energy."

Diane impassive face tumbles into laughter that rocks and shivers her whole body. "Oh, you're priceless. Truly priceless. Tell me you're pulling my leg."

"I'm not. That's the thing. That's why I'm here."

The laughter is gone without a trace. Diane turns to the fence and rubs her chin hard, as if to file away a divot.

Bronwyn floats. She knew this would be hard; she can't back down now. Strangely, she isn't tempted. Seeing her difference from Diane is like gazing into a mirror in which she sees the new Bronwyn Artair coalescing more clearly.

"I came here for advice. Not to have to prove myself."

Diane's forefinger traces figure eights around and between her lips. She isn't usually given to nervous gestures. "We've known each other for a long time, Bronwyn. I've watched you mature, as a woman and as a scientist and I—I cannot understand why you would make a claim like this. Something you couldn't possibly prove. You've studied atmospheric science, you know all the forces at play to form a storm system or a tornado. Each element can't be isolated easily. How could you possibly think that, in the midst of such forces, you could personally have an impact? I'm sorry, but it isn't possible. You know that too. Any scientist would agree."

"I'm not a scientist anymore, don't you see that? I probably never was one."

"Oh, you were. You certainly were. And I'm quite sure you still are."

"I may not have research proof, but I have experiential proof. I've done these things many times."

Diane rattles her head, emitting a low guffaw. "Honestly. What do you expect me to say? Did you come here thinking I would take this on faith? You know me well enough to know that's not possible." She sighs and a moment of silence ensues. "How long have you believed this—that you can do these things?"

"Only this summer. Since June or so."

"Why then? What happened?"

"Nothing specific I know of. I had a virus back in May. For a while I thought that might be it, the drugs I took. But I have no idea. No, actually I do know something—maybe I was always destined to be this way. I look back at myself as a child and I think I already had a sense of clouds and weather that was different from other people."

She can't stand to look at Diane's face, her look of defeat. She didn't come here to vanquish Diane, only to solicit her help. "Haven't you ever known something for sure that didn't require research and proof?"

"I can't say I have. It's not in my nature. I've never been religious in the least. And I've never believed in a thing if I didn't understand *why* it was."

The anger is unmistakable, falling from Diane like dried scabs and, while Bronwyn is usually set back by anger, it now gives her license, a

ballast against which to push back. Her gaze remains steady—Diane is
the one who keeps looking away.

"I'm not saying that trying to prove things is wrong, but sometimes
it isn't necessary and it's a waste of time." A stronger gust of wind pushes the swing back and forth, as if an invisible child is listening. "By the
way, the breeze that kicked up a little earlier, I did that. I brought it on."

"Oh, for god's sake, how am I supposed to respond to a statement
like that?" Diane gets up and paces the short distance to the fence and
back. "I'm not getting the full story here. There has to be more—a larger context, please."

"It might be outside your experience, but that doesn't mean it isn't
true."

"Bronwyn, please, just tell me everything." Diane angles her chair
and sits, now facing Bronwyn. "It seems to me there must be something you're not saying. Have you had some kind of accident? Have
you joined a cult? Has something happened to you that I haven't heard
about?"

"I'm telling you the truth as I know it. But you're not hearing me."

"I'm trying to be reasonable."

Bronwyn shrugs, rises.

"Don't go, please. We can get to the bottom of this."

"I don't think we can."

Bronwyn covers the fifty feet of back yard in a swift walk-run. She
can barely breathe. She might as well be taking flight from the troposphere. On the deck she turns to see Diane watching her, standing
rock-still next to her Adirondack chair. The breeze still waltzes in the
treetops—one-two-three, one-two-three, its pattern mocking. *See that
breeze. That's my breeze. You love that breeze, don't you?*

Bronwyn inhales the deep breath of a yogi, allows herself to be
lifted and absorbed, and in the hum and heat she tamps the breeze
to stillness again. Later, after a period of time infinitesimally short or
incalculably long, she returns to the deck. The day has become silent
and hot and glum again. Diane, sitting now, has craned her neck back
so her face is skyward. Resigned? Imploring?

Bronwyn turns away and passes into the house and exits through the brass-knockered front door. Only when she reaches her car several blocks away does she notice she's trembling.

28

The porch door slammed shut in anger, and Bronwyn has vanished, leaving Diane sucker-punched in a day that is improbably hot, improbably still. No questions at all have been laid to rest, and the anxiety of the past week has been replaced by a gumbo of worse emotion.

Indignation. Bronwyn has apparently been moving in this strange direction—whatever it is—without feeling any need at all to include or alert Diane, even after all Diane has done for her, even after Diane has beseeched her to return to grad school and rejoin the ranks of working research scientists and would do anything to make that happen. Of course it's possible, or even quite likely, that this "strain of thinking" that has beset Bronwyn played a role in her leaving the graduate program in the first place.

Fear. Generalized and nonspecific. Bronwyn did not appear to be "cracking up" in any of the usual ways Diane has seen people go— social withdrawal, bad hygiene, dissociation—but who knows how she's been behaving when Diane isn't around? And surely psychosis can emerge in any number of ways. She hates to think of Bronwyn presenting herself in public as she did today, subjecting herself to more and more ridicule, scarring her reputation as a researcher and making a return to academic science unlikely.

Shame. Though she has championed Bronwyn and helped her out, she has not prevented this from happening, or seen it coming. It calls her judgment into question at the most fundamental level. She hates to think of all the times she has defended Bronwyn in the presence of people who have found her a bit odd. Have those other people seen Bronwyn more clearly than Diane herself has?

Sadness. Terrible sadness, cohabiting with her in this chair, taking up too much space. Bronwyn. *Her* Bronwyn. Her project for so many years. Her protégé. Almost her daughter. She has loved Bronwyn as much as she has loved her husbands.

She is scheduled to have dinner with some dear old friends, two couples, not a scientist among them. A museum curator and a sculptor; an attorney and a librarian. She doesn't mind being the only uncoupled person at the table, she likes that she and Joe are independent enough and confident enough with one another that they do not find such arrangements threatening—she could never be married again to anyone who felt otherwise—but being the fifth person with two couples often means the conversational focus turns to her, fine on most occasions, but not tonight. How could she discuss with them what has happened today? She wouldn't know how to position the narrative. Would she describe Bronwyn from a safe distance, thereby ridiculing her? Or would she try to take Bronwyn's perspective, standing by her, and thereby subjecting herself to ridicule? Not that her old friends would ridicule her openly—they'd only get to that later, shaking their heads ruefully in the privacy of their bedrooms—but they would be embarrassed for her. She can picture them looking away, dabbing their mouths, excusing themselves to the restroom.

Yet how can she get together this evening with anyone and *not* discuss what has happened today? She'll have to cancel. She'll go back to Maine, crawl into bed with Joe, and take solace from his caresses. They'll talk it over. He'll have thoughts on how to proceed from here though they won't necessarily match hers.

The air is still smothering and stagnant, and the heat has brought on a migraine. She stares at the tray of iced coffee and tries to convince herself to get up and go inside and take some ibuprofen and get on with things. Every tissue in her body feels bloated and almost moribund; her wrists and ankles have stiffened as if she's about to be enshrined, turned into a specimen for people of the future to examine, a person who was suddenly frozen in the stream of life due to extreme heat and a shock to the system, like the people of Pompeii. Oh, for god's sake, what lurid thoughts. I'm becoming as crazy as Bronwyn.

She tries to imagine staging an intervention with Bronwyn, as people do with their drug-addicted children. But Bronwyn, of course, is not her child. There is nothing legal between them. And even if there were, Bronwyn is not a minor. Diane shudders again, remembering the tide of anger that spirited the girl away. How quickly anger spreads from person to person. She feels shades of it herself, but will not succumb. She goads herself up and, once standing, teeters in a moment of vertigo. When it passes, she empties the pitcher of coffee into the grass. The ice is already demolished by heat. The tray is heavier now and she carries it back to the house with mincing steps, bowed by heat and headache.

She isn't easily shocked, never has been, but there have been times, oh yes indeed, when life has surprised her, when she came to understand that the appearance of what was happening concealed a deeper truth.

There was the time her sister Reena, ten years Diane's senior, told Diane that their father was not actually Diane's father. Diane, the youngest of the nine siblings, was six when Reena, the oldest, told her this. Because she and Reena were arguing when Reena said what she said, and Diane understood, even at that young age, how Reena might have said anything to hurt, Diane rejected the statement. But she filed it away and thought of it often. Two years later Diane asked her mother about it. Her mother scoffed, and denied the allegation, and made it clear she would not discuss it further. So Diane went back to Reena, and demanded to know more, and Reena, who'd been dying to say more all along, came forth with convincing evidence, delivered without a mote of anger.

Once, during a grownup party when the kids had been banished to the basement, Reena came upstairs and saw their mother kissing another man, a man with very black hair and tan skin, the husband in a couple who visited the house regularly. After that Reena, on the lookout, saw all sorts of kissing incidents between their mother and the dark-haired man, and once, when Reena was home from school sick she heard, through the wall of the bathroom, her mother and the man making love. Then, most tellingly, their mother swore Reena to secrecy, knowing Reena had seen and heard things she ought not to have. Diane herself had no recollection of this man. Reena said he stopped coming to the house by the time Diane was born. It didn't take long for Diane's conviction to catch up with Reena's. Of course she was not her father's child. They were nothing alike. Their father was smart enough, but his habits of mind were sloppy. He was often illogical and he contradicted himself. He did not value intellectual rigor. He was a man who valued social success over all else. On his job as a construction foreman he wanted to be liked as well as obeyed. In the neighborhood and in the family he wanted people to come to him for advice. Then there was the issue of Diane's appearance. The rest of the siblings had long, freckled faces and sandy hair, but Diane's face was round and olive-skinned, and her hair was a glossy blackish-brown. Gradually, she began to separate herself from the others. *This is what I am; this is what I am not.*

So, that was a big life surprise, though not shocking exactly, because she was a child then and still finding out what was true and not true, her views of the world still in flux. The "incident" at UCLA, where she had her first academic job—what she and Joe refer to as The Fiasco—was far more shocking to her, because she was an adult then and she thought of herself as discerning and not easily duped, and she believed most people were honorable. She and John Fiorini had been friendly colleagues, or so she thought. They had been on data-gathering expeditions together in the Arctic and, while they were working on different projects, they used some of the same data and often discussed their findings. So when she saw that he'd tweaked the data for a publication in *The American Journal of Atmospheric and Climate Science* (a long-term study on the permafrost), she was horrified. She went to him right away. *What's up here?* she asked him. *I know this data, I've used it myself.* He didn't look nervous; in fact his expression was almost smug. *It was peer-reviewed,* he said, *and it passed muster.* As if that were exculpating. *Of course we all want to sound the climate change alarm, but not this way, for god's sake! Don't you see where this leads?* How did he think he could get away with this? Didn't he realize he'd eventually be discovered? You couldn't just lie about data and get away with it. But she could see that he wasn't about to confess any wrongdoing, not to her, not to anyone.

After some soul-searching she went to the department chair and divulged what she knew. He appeared alarmed and promised to investigate. Then, unable to stop herself she went to the journal editor, who reiterated that the peer review had not revealed any problems. *But there are problems*, she insisted, *I know this data*. Finally, grudgingly he said he would look into it. Why was no one else as outraged as she was? It sickened her. Then she began to uncover who knew whom, a disgusting chain of cronyism. One of the peer reviewers was an old classmate of Fiorini's. Someone on the board of the journal was a relative of his. Another guy at the journal was a good friend of the department chair's. The blatant lying and cover-up in a field that required transparency and objectivity—all of it repulsed her. Three months later she was asked to resign. She would be highly recommended, she was reassured. Her research, everyone said, was impeccable.

It was during that same nightmarish period that she and her ex-husband parted ways. He had been urging her to drop her mission to expose the truth and instead face the facts about how the world worked. She couldn't believe he would take such a position when he was also a scientist. She wasn't remotely tempted to accept that such deceit was the norm. Her respect for him plummeted, and the whole incident served as an awakening that strengthened her commitment to scientific truth and accuracy.

Now this—Bronwyn's absurd claim. This is the third big shock of her life.

She has been standing at the kitchen counter for altogether too long, staring down into the flecked black granite, mesmerized, as if gazing into a hole tunneling straight to the Earth's core. An image is stuck in her head that she can't dislodge: Bronwyn on the deck staring back out over the lawn in a wide-legged stance of defiance. She felt no need to work out their differences. Her entire body announced that she no longer needs what Diane has to offer. Diane aches, already missing her.

29

The city of LA is draped in a raiment of saffron smoke and the panic is palpable. Two fires are burning out of control, one in the Verdugo Mountains just east of Glendale and Burbank, working its way west to the San Fernando Valley, the other in the Topanga wilderness. The two move in concert like loosely coordinated gangs, determined to obliterate the city.

As Bronwyn drives the streets her pores dilate with the press of the fires' distant kinetic energy. She has come here with purpose, fueled by the disastrous meeting with Diane, determined to put her skill to use in bringing these fires under control. Having a goal has enlivened her as never before, and she feels her power as a muscle, strong as the calves of a marathon runner. In the days before coming here she dreamed her head was sprouting flames like Medusa's skirmishing snakes, snakes with bellicose voices, hectoring, unbridled, reaching high enough to lick the sky. During the daylight hours she conducted a series of tests and discovered she had some skill with fire too.

In her motel room at the Sunlight Inn off Sunset Boulevard she studies LA's topography, its mountains, its cuneal canyons, its expanses of flatland. What a vast project this city is with its circuitry of freeways. Wherever she goes, she sees only fuel. The bungalows, the fire-friendly eucalyptus, the once-irrigated vegetation now gone dry. She is trying to be methodical and resist the impulsiveness that has ruled her of late, but even through the motel room walls she feels the fire's pull, Svengali-like and irresistible. She reads the Cal Fire reports but they only tell her what her body already knows.

The question is, where to position herself to best advantage? She needs to find her way close to the blaze so she can stare into the flames and learn them intimately before attempting to knock them back. Her lawn experiments have shown her she can have impact here, but she also fully expects this is an operation that will take sustained effort and time, unlike her shorter efforts with wind and rain and tornados. Each of the fires covers a huge number of acres; each will require a separate attack.

She prepares as systematically as she can, Diane's voice still an irksome, doubting chitter in her head. Maintaining her energy is paramount. She has purchased a stash of protein bars, and she makes herself eat one every two hours. She goes out again in her tinny rental car, bold and cautious. The air is smoky and she can almost feel its particulates abrading her lungs but, needing direct contact with the air, she will not wear a mask.

For two full days she does nothing but drive, keeping the window open, sniffing the exhaust and sulphur and briny salt, observing the neighborhoods, getting a feel for the place. Inland first, past the La Brea Tar Pits, to Huntington Park, Florence, Walnut Park, Inglewood, Culver City. From there to the coast, Marina del Rey and Santa Monica, taking the Pacific Coast Highway north past the Getty. People around her drive like caged rats, erratic, mad, honking without provocation. Their eyes are constantly on the move, scoping out danger in all its forms. Danger might be a wisp of smoke, a spindle of flame; it might be the person in the next car, an arsonist, or someone cracking under the pressure. Some people wear white medical masks to avoid inhaling the soot so the city appears plague-ridden. It is a kind of plague. Like viruses, fire replicates itself quickly and defies human control.

She notices so much eating! People devour food as they walk, as they drive. Is this the norm here? LA is certainly known as a place of large appetites, but this, this is extreme. And then she understands. You've cut back your brush, you've soaked your roof, you've packed a bag should you have to evacuate—what else can you do? The fire will call the shots. There is only hope and a prayer. You exert control where you can. Some go to the gym, others indulge their appetites. Crisis brings out an insatiability, an extreme need for more of everything. Big Macs, ice cream, no doubt sex. She tries to find tenderness for these beleaguered residents, though the city itself—its miles of concrete and overabundance of cars—repels her.

As for herself, she feels like a fugitive—from the East, from Diane, from academia and science. She feels liable to be mistaken for something she is not. She might even look like an arsonist herself, with her dark glasses and her volcanic, fire-colored hair stashed under a baseball cap.

The road snakes up Topanga Canyon, past houses camouflaged among thirsty sycamores and live oaks. Everything wears a patina of dust and exhaustion. There are too many stands of eucalyptus trees, their leaves like castanets in the wind, cracking audibly with dehydration. She has read that fire explodes these trees, sending their seeds in all directions. She looks for wildlife but spots only an occasional looping hawk.

Around every bend she expects to be stopped by fire crews, but no one stops her. The firefighting so far is mostly aerial—helicopters dropping blankets of flame retardant—so she continues winding slowly up, up, up, the ghost of Diane poking at the edges of her consciousness, calling up needles of guilt for the hasty way she left, breaking things off, refusing to engage in more conversation. But along with the guilt there is still anger—Diane was so damn dismissive, almost mocking. The upside is that Bronwyn now is beholden to no one, shackled by nothing, belongs only to herself. Her colloquy with the fire is all that matters. She thinks of Earl and his idea that tornadoes coalesce evil forces. Surely fire must be the same.

She pulls over at a turnout and drinks some water. Her bare arms are slimy with sweat. The phone rings. It's Matt, who has been calling incessantly, and who she has been studiously avoiding. She gulps more water and watches a squirrel scrabbling in the underbrush as the phone rings and rings.

30

The first thing Matt's eyes take in is the absence of her decrepit orange Volvo; then he sees the charred lawn, not just singed brown by the long heat wave, but truly black. Aggrieved, burned black. The cabin, however, bears no visible signs of damage. He steps cautiously from his car, a black Chevy he got cheap from a friend. ("The psoriasis machine" Josh used to call it for its numerous amoeboid spots lacking paint.) The driveway's hot gravel presses against his tender bare soles. His feet have been bare for the entire drive up from Florida—too hot for shoes.

He knocks on the front door for protocol's sake, just to make sure, though the absence of the car makes him pretty sure she isn't there. When she doesn't respond to his third knock he rounds the side of the cabin on a swath of unburned grass. What has allowed fire to come so close without devouring the entire cabin? The rest of the trapezoid lawn, from river to driveway across to the trees that border the edge of the property, is totally black. The trees have also escaped burning. It's as if a fire retardant has been sprayed in certain places. If there were a neighbor nearby he would ask what has happened, but there isn't a single house in view on her side of the river, and he isn't sure how to get to the two houses on the other side. Does she know about this fire? Now there is all the more reason to get in touch.

The river drifts by, oblivious and undisclosing, and the drone of insects crescendos around him. Underfoot the fried grass has shrunk and separated to reveal the bald earth beneath. Now what? He wonders about himself, where this sudden fissure in his life will take him. In the past he never would have traveled all this distance merely to apologize and clear his name. He dials her number for the umpteenth time and for the umpteenth time he gets no answer. The simple truth: he has to see her.

He returns to the house and presses his face against the screen of the porch. The door is locked with a weak latch and it would be easy to push inside, collapse on the couch and wait for her there. But, much as he wants to snoop, he can't quite bring himself to go in—finding him inside would only provide more fodder for her view of him as dishonorable. Still, he can't leave either. It has taken him three long days of driving from Florida to get here, sleeping in his car at rest stops along the way, cleaning only his armpits and face and teeth, changing his shirt a couple of times. He rehearsed his speech to her as he drove, and he decided that, no matter how she reacts—whether or not she accepts the fact that he didn't write the article—he won't outstay his welcome. Finding her gone is such an anticlimax. He could seek her out at work though he knows that is no place for talking. He tells himself to go away, find a motel room, clean up and get some solid sleep, then come back the next day, looking and feeling better.

He can't peel himself away. Any minute she might come home and it feels like his last chance to connect with her. When he leaves New Hampshire he will return to Rhode Island again, Providence this time, where he plans to set out on a month-long trip with his old friend Buzz. Buzz went to college in Montana and is going back there to visit some old buds. Buzz's head is screwed on right and driving west with him will be a good way for Matt to reclaim his sanity and make some decisions. He hopes a road trip will cure him of this sudden and hopeless infatuation.

He idles under the shade of the low eaves, waiting for something to happen: for Bronwyn to drive up, for a local to arrive and explain about the fire, for fate to collar him and take him by the hand, but the only thing that happens is some kind of hawk—or is it an eagle—swoops low and hungrily over the water. He calls again, futile as it is.

She does answer. Her voice is distant, distracted, electric as ever. He fears she's about to hang up. Feeling the ball briefly in his court, he blurts forth.

"It's Matt. Something odd has happened at your place. The grass here is all burned up."

Clutching the elusive thread of her, he waits for her response, and when it comes it isn't what he expects. "You're *where?*"

31

The canyon's summit is deserted, but for a coiled rattle snake basking in wan sunlight. Smoke—livid, dun-colored—foams up from the woods to the east. Every once in a while a spire of flame leaps into view. In one place flames form a thin line like a row of sharp eye teeth. Looking south, the ocean is pale blue and flat.

A Cal Fire helicopter sputters by, disgorging red retardant from its belly, a dust that doesn't fall but hangs in indecision amidst dueling currents of air. Over two weeks this fire has been burning. Twice it was contained, twice it has reasserted itself. Surrounding homeowners are furious, demanding a more aggressive approach. Conservation groups are advocating a let-it-burn strategy. Cal Fire is attempting to achieve a compromise: a certain amount of judicious burning while assuring the public that human lives will not be put at risk and property damage will be kept to a minimum. No one is happy.

She stands at the canyon's summit, speculating, planning. What if she were to bring on rain—would that douse the fire? It would have to be heavy rain to kill the fire entirely, and heavy rain could cause a slew of other problems. The landscape whines around her, teaching her about itself, the scent of burn passes through her like a veil of coarse sandpaper. There are paths here, but no path will deliver her straight to the flames. She'll have to bushwhack to get there, through sedge and poison oak, over boulders and through dry creek beds. She could encounter more rattlesnakes, coyotes. She will have to remain alert. Long pants, lots of water.

Each time a new spike of flame comes into view she pictures an arsonist, a young man damaged by his past and embittered by his limited life options, invested in nothing and ready for the world to end.

The wind comes in gusts, an arid desert wind, filled with dust and organic debris, threaded together with heat. She floats like a chrysalis waiting to open.

The reconnaissance is over. It's time. She rises from bed at first light, steps out to the motel parking lot and sniffs. She senses the fires on both sides of town becoming restive after a night of relative calm. In the smoky dawn light everything looks ethereal. The bougainvillea and jacaranda blooms are tinged with deceptive pallor. By noon their electric color will be strong enough to sear retinas.

She fills a small backpack with water and protein bars, and sets out into the somnolent morning. The day is slow to rouse itself. She drives down Sunset to the Pacific Coast Highway. The ocean whispers, but she hears it only through one ear. The other ear is tuned to the fires. She takes the turn for Topanga Canyon. This time the road is closed a mile or so shy of the summit. Two guards in helmets and Cal Fire vests are stationed at the roadblock, letting only residents through. She turns around and drives back down a stretch of road until it curves and takes her beyond the guards' sight. There she pulls off to the shoulder and parks.

Into the brush she dives, concealed under her hoodie. Long pants. Running shoes. A modicum of protection against thorns, poison oak, snake bite. The fire's hiss in her blood. A beckon. A dare.

She has been walking for five minutes or so when a house appears, tiered and nestled into the landscape, treehouse-like. A wilderness hideaway made entirely of wood. A fire's dream. She wonders if its inhabitants have evacuated. Just as she is wondering this, a door opens and a woman in a salmon bathrobe steps onto the deck. Bronwyn tries to conceal herself behind the slender trunk of a willow-like tree. The woman turns on a faucet at the side of the house, uncoils a hose, and sets about spraying the deck, the roof, and the surrounding vegetation within the water's reach. Bronwyn darts forward, trying to move quietly, but the woman spots her.

"Hey!"

Bronwyn continues, faster now, but the woman's voice lassos and stops her. They face each other through a hundred feet of branches and scrub. Bronwyn feels feral and whiskered. She understands how she appears, a little frightening to be honest, a little off kilter. A moment of silence passes, but for the hiss of water splashing onto the deck.

"What are you doing here?" the woman calls. "This is private property."

The tug of the fire. The tug of human decency. Caught between, Bronwyn stalls. The woman moves closer to the deck's banister, squinting. "Come here for a sec?" Her tone is imploring. "I won't do anything."

Bronwyn has not forgotten the give-and-take of human interaction at its best. She has not fallen entirely to the side of the unsocialized. She approaches the house, twigs and branches cracking as she brazens through, the fire's sibilance alive in her blood. She stands below the deck and pushes off her hood to give the woman a moment to inspect her fully, see her harmlessness.

"What're you doing here?" the woman demands. She is lean and tall and blonde, and close to Bronwyn's age. "You're trespassing, you know."

"I'm on a walk," Bronwyn says. "I'm sorry. I didn't realize this was private property."

"Are you *crazy?* The fire is right out there and it's moving fast. Can't you smell it? Don't you follow the news? They want us all to get ready to evacuate and they're dropping a bunch of dangerous chemicals and it's bad—it's like Armageddon."

Bronwyn nods.

"Why would you even—? Hey, you're not the person who started this fire, are you?"

Bronwyn feels like a creature at gunpoint. Fight or flight? She didn't plan for this. She expected creatures to be in her path, not humans. She holds the woman's gaze, concentrates her breath, and pictures herself leaping high as a deer and disappearing into the brush, but then she thinks of the woman calling for help and sending authorities in pursuit. The woman's eyes, the same greenish color as her own, leak terror.

"I didn't start the fire. I wouldn't do that. You'll have to believe me." Bronwyn hesitates, trying to signal good will through the rain of the woman's distaste.

Sighing, the woman drops her hose and goes to the side of the house to turn off the water. The fire summons Bronwyn more urgently and she thinks of leaving, but the woman is already coming back. Her reedy legs, her floating gait, the drift of her long hair—recognition hits. Bronwyn can't bring up a name, but the woman acts in movies.

"You don't look like an arsonist." Her voice is deep and patrician, with a hint of an English accent. "As if I know what an arsonist looks like."

"I just realized who you are," Bronwyn says. "But you'll have to excuse me, I don't remember your name."

The woman smiles with a touch of condescension. Perhaps everyone knows her name. "Lyndon Roos."

"Yes. Now, I remember." A series of vampire movies Bronwyn hasn't seen, but they've been publicized everywhere.

"And you are—?"

"Nancy Fenwick."

"So, tell me, Nancy—should I call the police? I could have them here in an instant you know, especially if I mention my suspicion of arson."

"Have a look." Bronwyn sloughs her backpack and empties its contents onto the ground. Two bottles of water, the protein bars, some nuts, a bandana. She peels back the pockets of her jeans and hoodie. "There's nothing here."

Lyndon flutters her hand, embarrassed, not the least bit interested in pawing through Bronwyn's things. She cinches her salmon robe tighter. Bronwyn kneels and repacks her backpack. Clouds of suspicion and smaller pockets of trust hang in the smoky air between them. A chime at the end of the deck is plucked by a gust of wind. The fire's whine surges. The instinct to flee is nearly impossible to resist. Concentrating hard, Bronwyn turns to the woman and holds the woman's probing eyes gently in her own green-eyed gaze. She excavates for the woman's heart, the open heart of an actress, accustomed to inhabiting different personas and feeling strong emotions. She takes the plunge.

"I'm going to tell you something a little strange."

Lyndon listens, her face placid, betraying nothing. When Bronwyn is done speaking, Lyndon's expression has not changed. "I'm a Buddhist, I've heard some odd things in my life, but—are you for real?"

Bronwyn blinks, her thoughts coagulating before they can morph into words.

"Your plan is to go out there and—put the fire out yourself? You really believe you can do that?"

Bronwyn, nearing her edge, manages a nod. The rising volume of the blaze is all she can hear. "I have—to—go. Now." She turns and, half running, hurries into the underbrush, refusing to worry further about Lyndon Roos and the police.

She travels quickly, gauging the miles to the fire. It is just past eight. She should have started earlier, before dawn, to reach and confront the fire before it is fully enlivened again by the day's developing heat. Her mind is a jumble. The rocks and trees cough up shapes of rabbits and deer. A dark blotch on the hillside above her appears to be a bear, but it is too distant to see for sure. She didn't think there were bears in these woods. Mostly she keeps her gaze on her feet, placing them down with deliberation, steering them over and around the rocks, sidestepping to avoid sudden patches of poison oak.

After an hour or so she stops in a clearing and sits on a rock and drinks some lukewarm water. The sky is murky with smoke, the air electrified. She's getting close. There is a singular line of connection between her and the fire, and though she cannot see it yet, she feels it tunneling into the dusty ravines, over the caked earth, fractious and full of reproach. The fire's anger infects her.

She gets up and soldiers on. The day has come into its own, bringing a deafening volume to every sound, her footfalls, the branches brushing across her torso, a lone squawking crow, a trio of clacking helicopters spilling more of their toxic snow, the braying of the fire itself. Heat spools around her, a visible current. She pulls the neck of her hoodie over her nose, wishing she'd brought a mask.

There it is, just below her, across the ravine. An entirely different beast than the fires she made on her lawn in New Hampshire. This is a colossus. Terrifying. Apocalyptic. Balls of flame launch into the air like grenades. Smoke balloons are borne overhead on the prevailing wind, becoming part of an Olympian pyrocumulus cloud. Blackened trees jut up from the moil like skeletons. Such hutzpah in those flames leaping and pirouetting and backbending like seasoned performers. The sound is unlike anything she's ever heard, animalistic, open-mouthed and mean. Everywhere branches, entire trees, splinter and crash. Earl was right—like the tornados, this fire seems to embody evil. She is paralyzed by the sheer magnitude of it all. It is far bigger than her meager talent can handle.

The dry air snaps. Derisive laughter cackles up from the heat. Gremlin-like faces resembling Bruce and Jim peer out from the flames, grinning, taunting. She feels targeted. Her head swims, her brain is in danger of melting, her will falters. Dizzy, she sits on the ground. What overreaching has brought her here to the brink of her own demise? She needs to go, return to the actress's house though that is now hours away on foot. She needs help from someone. But all the usual sources of rescue are well beyond reach. Rescue has always been an illusion.

She grabs one toxic lungful of breath after another, incapable of wrenching her eyes away from the blaze which lolls and loiters one moment then lashes forth again. For all its fickleness the fire is devouring the woods with the steady determination of termites. Demonic as it appears, it is transfixing, too—beautiful.

She stands, removes her hoodie, wipes sweat from her face, and confronts the blaze. Something levitates her, a crescendo within, a thought or a feeling unleashed, an intuition; it swoops through her chest and her entire body, overruling all else. Images swarm past her retina. Her long-dead mother, the river behind her house, the owl that visits, Archie and his banana, dear dead Earl, the Buddhist actress, the smoke, the flame. All the electrons of these things are integers, part of a whole.

The tone arrives on her next intake of breath and she sails into the chaos, transmuting herself, becoming part of the fire's viscera until she pulses at its core, dispersing the oxygen, squeezing the fire's life, willing its death. She is a swashbuckling toddler on newly-found legs, buffeted yet bold.

32

The fire's sudden retreat dominates the news. Matt sprawls on the futon in his friend Metcalf's bare apartment a block from Venice Beach, watching TV, flipping from station to station. They all say the same thing. *Sudden. Unprecedented.* Fox News uses the word *miraculous.* They all show the same short Cal Fire clip, taken from a helicopter, in which a monumental wall of fire shrinks, as if someone has pressed rewind. Matt is mesmerized, as is all of LA.

The wind has died down and the humidity has risen. That has helped. But no one can explain the speed with which the Topanga fire has abated. The fire on the eastern side of the city has not been affected the same way; it still rages. What if she really did do something? It's outrageous, he knows, but *what if?* What if her charred lawn in New Hampshire is somehow part of this? She was certainly evasive about it on the phone. He has to talk to someone, but Metcalf, his old high school buddy, left before dawn to work as a production assistant on some rom-com. He won't be back until late tonight.

Matt paces around Metcalf's two-room apartment tidying up. Metcalf's a slob. He always was in high school, and ten years out he hasn't improved much. His apartment is a classic bachelor pad: hardly any furniture, a mattress on the bedroom floor where Metcalf sleeps, the futon in the living room where Matt has been crashing with no sheets only a single blanket, in the kitchen a few mismatched dishes and mugs, plastic cups. The bathroom mirror is covered with toothpaste art, and the sink, gelled with old soap, is on its way to becoming a petri dish. Matt is no paragon of cleanliness and tidiness himself, but he's nowhere near as bad as Metcalf.

After Bronwyn told him on the phone that she was here, he booked a flight impulsively. She barely heard his explanation about the article—he needs to see her face-to-face. Why not, since no job is keeping him in place. But now that he's here, the task of finding her seems insane. Locating anyone in this sprawling city is like finding the proverbial needle in the haystack. He honestly has no idea how to go about it. She said LA, but she didn't say *where* in LA.

Metcalf's refrigerator is empty but for Sriracha and beer. He doesn't even have milk for coffee. The guy lives on take-out and whatever he gets on the sets of movies. He's so heavily immersed in Hollywood he's aware of little else. He reads the trade papers, works on his screenplay, and dreams of becoming a mogul. It seems pretty unrealistic to Matt, but at least Metcalf has a passion and Matt, given his own employment history, has no right to be critical.

Needing a fresh perspective, he heads outside for a walk and groceries. The Venice boardwalk is mobbed with extroverts. The quarreling rhythms of boom boxes, marimbas, the whooping of people serious about their play. Everyone vamps, wanting to be noticed. Everyone but Matt, who is stuck in his own mind. Over and over he sees the clip of the fire in retreat.

A skateboard blares up behind him and veers past, the guy's arm grazing Matt's elbow, making him sidestep like a skittish horse. Why is everyone so damn frenetic? Despite the ocean's proximity, the air is still rancid with smoke and the breeze is negligible. The scrawny palms, their high foliage like tiny heads surveying the mayhem, look as if they're as deeply skeptical and dislocated as he is.

He visited here about three or four years ago, not long after Metcalf moved in. He remembers it being laid back then, a place he could imagine living, but now it doesn't feel the least bit relaxing. He passes an area where six male Atlas-style body builders—three white, three black—strike poses, their muscles gleaming with sweat and sunlight. Their bodies are still as museum pieces, their faces solemn, as if engaged in an activity of high purpose. Every thirty seconds or so someone shouts and the poses change. This city is notorious for its population of exhibitionists, but does crisis call forth an extra urge toward exhibitionism, he wonders. If he were still at *The Meteor* he'd see this place as a treasure trove of stories, but since he's quit his yen for the next weird story has expired. The oddity of human beings is no longer news to him, and the humor he used to find in human strangeness has dried up.

An eddy of moving air brings the acrid smoky smell to his nostrils again. Everyone else appears to have become inured to this smell, but to him, newly arrived, it's sickening. He thought he was hungry, but in this bad air he can't imagine eating.

Back at Metcalf's Matt reconsiders his presence here. It's futile. He sees the embarrassing underpinnings of false hope. He emails Buzz, saying he'll fly to New York the next day, and if Buzz will pick him up there they can resume their original plan of driving to Montana together.

His Twitter feed has gone crazy with more fire news. Lyndon Roos, the actress from those vampire movies, has said some woman came into the woods near her house claiming she intended to put the fire out herself. Roos talked to the woman and has no idea what to believe, but she suggests that human beings are probably capable of more than we know. The responses to her tweets are vehement.

You've been in the movies too long.

Movies are not life, Lyndon Roos.

People are not gods! Get real!

Back off and listen to the woman. Don't judge before you know the whole story.

Matt scrolls through, reading everything, his breath catching, adrenaline shooting through all his appendages. *Can it be?* Maybe, maybe not, but he has to find out.

He dashes off a text to Buzz. *Change of plans. Sorry to be so fickle. Will be in touch.*

33

They sit outside in late summer twilight, sunset's scarves of rosy or-ange light in slow-twirling flux; seagulls yawping over the cove; a mourning dove regaling them with thoughtful poetry from the eaves; the silhouette of a lone schooner, all its sails trimmed, scudding to-ward harbor to beat the onset of night. One of her favorite meals is laid on the table before them: crab cakes, minty tabouli, arugula salad, a crusty baguette, along with her favorite chardonnay. Joe has even brought out cloth napkins and citronella candles and a fleece throw for her lap in case a chill comes up after dark. Not a single external ele-ment could be tweaked to make this occasion more perfect, but Diane can only see beneath the veneer of perfection, to the shambles her life has recently become.

It began with Bronwyn's ludicrous pronouncement and since then Bronwyn has not gotten back in touch, not tried to excuse or explain herself, offered no apology for her angry departure. On one level Diane would like to say Bronwyn has "gone off the deep end," or "had a ner-vous breakdown." But Bronwyn's behavior spoke otherwise. She was not acting like a person who was breaking down. In fact, she seemed unusually sure of herself, more confident than Diane has ever seen her. That does not diminish Diane's feeling that she has been rejected and discarded and is very possibly past her prime.

Joe keeps saying it's not the end of the story. He believes Bronwyn will return to the academic, scientific fold and eventually make good on the things Diane has taught her. To Diane that is wishful thinking. Joe wasn't there to witness Bronwyn's defiant, ungrateful exit, an exit that spoke loudly of a deep rift and a permanent departure.

So Bronwyn's aberrant behavior and sudden rejection is one reason Diane has been losing sleep, but there's something else that was set in motion that day of Bronwyn's visit, something just as worrisome, maybe more so. Diane has not been able to focus at all. Past and present are occasionally indistinguishable. Her brain feels soggy as a mushroom on the verge of decay. She tests herself by reciting various facts that have always been reliably stored in her memory bank—the periodic table, for example—and she can't get through it. She pictures the mosaic of her brain, which she has always seen as a satisfying arrangement of tessellated, neuron-rich pleats and cavities, and she now sees only a wasteland of dead cells, entire lagoons of hard-won knowledge lost forever.

Joe has been insistent—her condition is a psychological one, not an organic one. She has been worrying too much and worry is well-known for interfering with memory. The meeting with Bronwyn has destabilized her temporarily, but she'll recover. She should get a brain scan, he says, which will confirm nothing is wrong.

Diane is much too terrified to get a brain scan. What if something did turn out to be wrong? She has always drawn her identity from having a reliable, even superior, problem-solving brain, and if some test were to diagnose an anomaly—early onset dementia, for example—everything about her life and work and self would be called into question.

Diane gulps her wine and rips into a piece of crusty baguette, homemade by Joe. "I'm too vain, I guess. I'm the first to admit I wanted her to go and do something that would reflect well on me."

"Of course. Who wouldn't want that?"

"So many times when she was in the program I defended her when others wondered what kind of a scientist she would be. Now—well . . ." She floats an idea she hopes Joe will refute, "Maybe they were right and I was wrong."

Joe pours her more wine. He isn't refuting her. Maybe he's fed up with her belly-aching. His sun-burned nose looks fiery in the angled light.

"You're trying to get me drunk," she says.

"You need to relax."

They fall silent. Diane eats out of habit, but fails to taste. "It's good," she says.

"I've been thinking about her too, you know," Joe says. "And I keep thinking—what if she's *right?* What if she was telling you the truth?"

"You mean what if she really can stop storms, or whatever?"

"Yes. *What if?*"

"Go write a novel about that. It's not real life, Joe, and you know it."

"But what if it *is* real life?" he insists.

The sun drops below the horizon and the entire landscape loses its red-spectrum tint and takes on the quieter hues of blue and gray. A few mosquitoes whine up as if they've just been hatched. One lands on Diane's bare forearm and instead of brushing it away she watches it settle in for a long suck. *Suck on,* she thinks, *make way for new blood.* Across the cove a gong sounds, a mother rounding up her kids. Joe's features soften in the twilight. Diane feels unexpectedly calmer than she's felt for a few days.

"There was a guy who used to teach at Princeton, he's retired now. He was an engineer, a specialist in rocketry. But at some point he became interested in the effect that the thinking of researchers, their actual thought, had on their experiments. I'm not sure what got him started on that, but he founded an institute, PEAR, it was called—Princeton Engineering Anomalies Research. They were researching psychokinesis, right there at Princeton." She shakes her head.

"What did they learn?"

"They didn't come up with much, as far as I know, although they published some books and articles. But he, this guy Robert Jahn, was an embarrassment to a lot of the scientists there. He eventually resigned as Dean of Engineering and they closed the institute. But he wasn't fired. He kept on teaching."

"And—?"

"And what?"

"Why are you telling me this? What's your point?"

"I have no point. I was just thinking about how there are a lot of people with strange ideas out there. It's just kind of shocking when scientists turn that way."

"Diane—" Joe stops himself.

"What?"

He shakes his head, obviously irritated, and begins loading the dirty plates and glasses onto the tray which he carries inside. She's been relying too heavily on his good nature of late, shared too much of her addled state of mind and pushed him past his limit. It's probably time for her to act as if her brain is perfectly normal, and head back to Cambridge to try to get some work done, leave Joe alone to finish his novel without distraction. A little time apart.

The blue dusk presses in against her. On the slope leading down to the water the pine trees have become still dark silhouettes, measuring the slow march of the tide as it moves into the cove. The tide will be high at 2:00 a.m. and when she wakes tomorrow it will be low again. How comforting and reliable these ancient rhythms are, though she knows they won't always be this way, knows they're in continual flux, infinitesimal but measurable. A day will come, long after human extinction, when the sun will expand to a red giant and will engulf the Earth. But how impossible it is to sit here in the beauty of now and fully imagine a time when Earth won't exist.

The memory comes to her now, wafting in on the evening's indigo light. It is always evening when this memory arrives. It isn't something she talks about—she hasn't even told Joe, she wouldn't have the words—but now and then she turns it over in the privacy of her own mind.

She and her ex-husband Chuck, the molecular biologist, were on a rare vacation in Mexico. It was late afternoon and they had just had coffee, sitting in an outdoor café, stroked by the golden light which made art of the narrow cobblestone streets. As they ambled back to their hotel Diane kept darting into small shops to admire the silver jewelry and the colorful woven rebozos. Invariably that led to enthusiastic chatting with the shopkeepers, Diane shaving the rust off her under-used Spanish. She could feel Chuck chafing. He was hot and wanted to get back to the hotel to shower and change before their dinner date with another American couple.

"You go," she kept telling him. "I'll meet you there. We're on vacation and I'm having fun."

But he wouldn't leave, claiming she wouldn't be safe alone. Eventually his glowering and eye-rolling ruined her enjoyment, and she consented to return with him to the hotel. They emerged from the side street onto a main thoroughfare, a noisy wilderness of scooters and taxis and haranguing street vendors, everyone's intransigence and ire on display. Despite the clamor, the scene—with its long-angled, dust-filtered light; the polyphony of Spanish; and a chaos that was uniquely Mexican—felt picturesque, even as she understood the flaw in that perception.

They rounded the corner and wove around a thick knot of pedestrians. As they arrived at the intersection where they were to turn onto a side street that would take them to their hotel, a child darted into the street, a small boy not more than two years old, sturdy but not entirely in command of his legs. He had a thatch of black hair that caught the sunlight and glistened whitely. She sees it all so clearly even now, though it happened so long ago and so quickly she cannot help but question her memory. The high-pitched screams. The vehicle brakes slamming like angry curses. A battered white van swerving and toppling onto its side, landing on the child.

Then. This is the part she strains to remember better, the actions of that man, the father, the presumed father, who arrived on the scene almost magically. He began working his heft beneath the van's wheel well, face bulging and reddening under the strain, arms, thick and bare, laboring like fork lifts, raising the van—could it be?—and tilting it upright. Upright. Fully upright! He dove for his son, cradled him for a moment against his shoulder, and bolted to the far side of the street, disappearing down an alley.

The stupefied hush lasted a millisecond, no more. Then the drivers who had spilled from their cars returned to their vehicles and sped off, the diners and shoppers who had gathered to rubberneck turned back to their dining and shopping. Chuck, too, began walking again, as if this incident they'd just witnessed was commonplace.

Diane hurried to catch up. "Did you see that?"

Chuck didn't respond. Perhaps her question was lost in the street's chaos.

"Chuck! Did you see what that man did?"

Again, no reaction.

"He lifted that van. I can't believe he lifted that van!"

"He didn't lift the van," Chuck said.

"Then you tell me what happened—you saw."

"I have no idea. I wasn't close enough. You know as well as I do that the testimony of eye witnesses is notoriously inaccurate."

Back at the hotel he stonewalled her. He wouldn't discuss the incident further. And when she tried to describe it to their friends at dinner, Chuck's laughter dismissed her. She silenced herself. She knew what she'd seen. Or she thought she knew what she'd seen: a man, terrified for his son, had brought the entire force of his being to the task of lifting a vehicle, a vehicle that had to weigh at least a ton, possibly much more. The man had been so intent on saving his child, so ready to give every dram of energy to the effort, that he had accomplished the impossible—he lifted an absurdly heavy van. She saw that. She thinks she saw that. She's quite sure she saw that. It's history now, impossible to know, and yet her mind holds the imprint of the boy's glistening hair, the father's brawny arms and back, the tender impassioned way the father cradled the boy afterwards, soldering him to his shoulder. And she remembers the way he fled, as if he was being pursued. So often she has wondered where he went. Did the child survive? She likes to think so.

Joe is clattering around in the kitchen. She should go in and help him, apologize for being such a whiner of late. But he's already coming back out, carrying a smaller tray with mugs of tea, and a plate of figs and dark chocolate. The sight of him shames her.

"Here's the thing," he says as he sets down the tray. "You're always investigating things to find out if something is true or not. So why aren't you interested in investigating *this* thing? You're letting something get in the way of your natural curiosity."

She nibbles a square of chocolate. He's half right. She *is* an investigator. But it is also true that she has been a human being for over fifty years and in those years she has learned, empirically, what human beings can and can't do. No other human being has ever done what Bronwyn claims she can do. There is no precedent here, nothing that warrants investigation.

"You could study her, couldn't you? I mean ask to see what she does and go from there?"

Diane grunts, sips her tea, wonders if Bronwyn would consent to further contact. "She stalked out in a fury. I doubt if she'd let me study her."

"Where's your curiosity?"

"Are you mad at me?" Diane asks. "I could hear you were rattling the dishes in there."

"No. Not exactly. But I'm confounded. You adore this girl and now, just when things, for my money, are getting interesting, you seem to be dropping her."

"She dropped me!"

"Well, you have to go to the next level."

"But what *is* the next level?"

"I guess you have to figure that out."

34

She hears music, a single oneiric tone flowing over the dry landscape like water. Like blood. She wonders if she might be dead, then thinks not. A wash of pale light paints her vision. A blade of brittle brown grass, the dusty crust beneath her shoulder, the gritty air itself. Each spur of thought is fleeting, it can't be grasped or coaxed to stay. Then, the aperture of her vision sharpens to reveal a squamous slab of tan rock and the eyes of a blinking creature, encircled by fur. She sees nothing else of the creature, just the curious brown eyes set in stillness. Investigating. She isn't afraid. *Take your time. Look all you want.*

How heavy her body is. Stuck to the ground, sessile, she'll never rise again. But how light she is too, pure energy capable of rising and finding a thermal on which to travel. The tone she hears, she now realizes, is the sound of her own breathing, the music that keeps her alive. She counts its rise and fall, until she swoons back into sleep.

35

A gate and fence block the entrance to the driveway so Matt parks by the side of the road and inspects the fence in both directions looking for a way around. When he fails to find one, he scales the eight-foot gate at some peril, the pointed tip of one of the iron spikes catching his pants and ripping the crotch. On the ground on the other side of the fence, he brushes himself off and assesses the damage; the tear is pretty obvious, but nothing can be done now. He takes the packed dirt driveway through the smoke-scented woods on foot. This rustic approach surprises him. Except for the gate nothing would indicate that this is the home of a movie star. But Metcalf said she wasn't the typical star. *Woo-woo,* is how Metcalf described her. Beautiful, but a little too dedicated to strange ritual for Metcalf's taste. Metcalf worked on one of her movies and before production began, when she was still considering the role, he was asked to bring her a script, so he drove up here and drank hibiscus tea with her. It was exciting to sit in a movie star's elegant home and drink tea as if she was your friend, but it wasn't relaxing. Metcalf wanted something to come of it, some career advantage, but he knew he was stupid to hope for that. He was just a PA, a grunt, and in the end, something about her—the way she spoke with a pseudo-English accent one minute, the next minute with a tinge of a Southern drawl, and the way she stared at him in the long silences—made him so uncomfortable he was happy to leave.

Matt is at least fifty yards from the house when the front door opens and a woman he presumes to be Lyndon steps out. Even at this distance it's clear she's furious.

"Stop!" she shouts. "Don't come any closer."

He raises his hands instinctively. He really hoped this wouldn't happen, hopes she doesn't pack a gun. "Hi!" He smiles aggressively, showing his teeth as a sign of good will.

"Who are you? You're trespassing. Get out now!"

"I'm Matt Vassily. A journalist." Stupid to admit—stars always despise the paparazzi. "I wanted to talk to you about your tweets. That woman you saw who said she would put out the fire—I think I know her." He feels ridiculous yelling over such distance, his arms raised as if he's a felon.

Her stance shifts a little, but not in any way he can interpret. "I've told the world everything I know. There's nothing more."

"I need to find her, and I thought you—"

"How did you know I live here? How did you get through the gate?"

He tries to make light of it, making a face and pointing down at his torn pants. "My friend Metcalf brought you a script once. He's a PA. He told me where you live."

She descends the front steps to the driveway, stately, accustomed to being watched. In form-fitting black exercise pants and filmy turquoise blouse that flutters with her every movement, she is sexy and leggy and, except for her pony-tailed hair, she looks remarkably similar to the way she looked in the movie he saw. He is unexpectedly star-struck.

"You can put your hands down," she says when she's about ten feet from him.

He lowers his arms and they size each other up. Matt feels acutely aware of his short stature and the hole in his crotch.

"So you know Nancy?" she says.

"Nancy?"

"The woman who said she was going to put out the fire."

"Are you talking about a small woman with red hair?"

Lyndon nods. "Very intense."

He nods. "Her name is Bronwyn."

"How do we know we're discussing the same woman?"

"Are there lots of small, intense, red-haired women passing through here claiming to be able to put out fires?" Matt says.

Lyndon laughs, much to Matt's relief. "You've got a point there. Why do you need to locate her?"

"It's complicated. Kind of a long story."

"I've got time," Lyndon drawls.

36

Thirst drives her. She senses her cells wizening, slowing, failing to remember their specific tasks. Fighting vertigo, she forces herself to stand. The water in both her bottles is long gone, she should have known to bring more. Her head throbs. The sun bears down with greedy animosity. She turns her back on the depressing expanse of scorched landscape and begins to walk in the other direction where trees and bushes are still intact. A slow deliberate plodding, drawn by the promise of water. She should be trying to retrace her steps, but there are no visible steps to retrace, no signs of her passage through this scrubby forest.

Her body aches and itches everywhere, but she tries to ignore it. She imagines rain, lifting her head to it, mouth spread wide as a cistern to receive the drops in the gradual way of the earth. But it won't rain, not now—she is far too exhausted to bring it on—and if it did, it would wash away the entire hillside, taking her with it. She plods on, remembering the cascading water of the Swift River where she and Lanny camped at the beginning of summer, not so long ago, but eons ago.

She walks with her eyes closed, weaving, aimless, forgetting who she is and why she is here, wondering how far she might be from dying. Her body is numb and yet it moves, slowly, compulsively, bent on preserving itself. Through the empty cauldron of her mind vagabond thoughts keep trundling. Wind soughing; someone hula hooping; Karla Dickman, a college friend who once was mugged. She hasn't thought of Karla Dickman in years, why would she come to mind now? Arpeggios of laughter float by, Diane's laughter, close then receding. Diane can't possibly be out here. She opens her eyes to check. No Diane.

She thinks of the creature staring at her. That thoughtful gaze. She remembers opening her eyes on darkness, closing them quickly, refusing to acknowledge the presence of night.

Her knees buckle. She lies on her side on the ground, yielding to exhaustion. Where is her phone? Would it work here? The thought passes. Her vision sputters, makes dots and sequins of the sere landscape.

The voices of the birds sound human, rising and falling, considering things in the way of humans, ruminating, stopping and starting, sometimes solo, sometimes contrapuntal. She always imagined death would be silent.

Bronwyn, the birds say. *Bronwyn*. They speak quietly, reciting her name like a mantra. So touching really.

She opens her eyes. A person crouches over her, shading her from the sun. Two people. A man and a woman.

She blinks. Their faces press down, ponderous, querying, carrying signifiers she can't read. She may be mute, but her mind is alive. She must find a voice and let them know she is present.

37

She lies on her back on Metcalf's futon in death-like sleep, unnaturally still, her face smooth and pale as wax, arms at her sides, palms up. Every once in a while she mutters something incomprehensible.

Matt can't relax. After they found her they got her back to Lyndon's house, and she drank glass after glass of cold water and slept for two hours, and then Lyndon helped her shower. She was returning to normal, though she still wasn't saying much, and both he and Lyndon thought she should be checked by a doctor. Bronwyn was downright fierce in her refusal. *I just need to sleep a little more,* she insisted, which is exactly what she's been doing since they got back to Metcalf's.

He has the feeling he has custody of a rare bird, some endangered species of great importance to the world, entrusted to him. It is his charge to keep her safe. He needs to make sure she's still breathing. He can't leave her side or take his eyes off her. And he has an odd feeling that her skin is emitting something, rays of light or energy or— it's a crazy thought but he wishes he had something like a Geiger counter to test his hunch.

A text comes in from Lyndon—*How's she doing?*—A movie star! Who would think?!—*Still sleeping,* he texts back. He's glad Metcalf won't be back until almost midnight. It is shortly after noon now.

He takes a leak, staring into the foamy stream of his urine, wondering what he should do next and trying to remember when he last ate. His entire life has changed in a matter of days, and now a new agenda is taking shape in this unfamiliar city without his consciously willing it. He must stand by, see how things play out, hope for the best—what else can he do? He brought this on himself. Hearing movement in the living room, he zips up and hurries out. She's crouching by the side of the futon, pawing for something in her backpack. She looks up at him, eyes engorged with such alarm he stops where he is.

"You're awake," he says quietly.

The medley of sounds, distant and near, must be parsed. The fire's gnashing. The ocean's murmur. A hawk's caviling cry as it comes in for its prey. Closer, in this room, a man's breathing, incomprehensible words that match the percussion of his heart.

How can he be here, this man with the unusual beret of hair, in this place so far from where she first saw him? She squints, a substitute for the questions she might pose. Words still evade her.

"Are you alright?" he says. He's keeping his distance, as if she might bite, as if he, too, sees her as the creature she feels herself to be. He isn't unkind though, only curious.

"I won't bite," she says, finding a voice, laughing a little. "My phone. I think I might have lost it." She resumes her search. There isn't time to waste, not with the other fire still on the loose.

"Can I do something to help?"

She hears, but can't respond. The rhythm of conversation is alien and stilted. The fire's rasp dominates her again, its seduction magnetic and tyrannical. *Ah-ha.* She palms the phone and holds it up for him to see. They both smile. His smile is boosting. It singles her out and carries conspiracy.

"Could you drive me to my car?"

"Now?"

"Yes."

"Why?"

She hesitates. Then, what the hell. "There's another fire out there, still burning."

"Shouldn't you rest some more?"

"There isn't time."

She watches his face play with resistance. She isn't sure what he knows, what he has seen. She shuffles memories of events that have no

obvious linear order. No one was there with her at the fire. But later—
he was one of the ones who found her.

"What do you know?" she asks, a question that enfolds a multitude
of questions like the bundled strands of DNA. How did you come to be
here in this city? Where are we? Do you understand what I do?

She is suddenly lively, fluttering with nervous energy, apparently recovered. What a relief. When they first found her unconscious on the
ground, on the edge of the charred woods, he thought she might be
dead. It took several minutes before her eyes opened, and she couldn't
speak. Now she stands in apparent health and brushes herself off, a
clean floral scent wafting from her loose hair. Her expression is unmistakable. *Can I trust you?* it asks. He has not formally explained himself,
which was a primary reason for coming here, but all of what he would
try to explain happened in a past that holds little relevance now.

"Well?" she says.

"All I know is that something unusual is happening here." He smiles
faintly. "That's about it."

"Are you with me?"

"I guess so. Yes. Sure."

38

It is not the cylindrical white scanning machine itself that resembles a casket, but the position that Diane must assume inside it, arms and legs straight, head centered, everything cadaver-still. She can almost hear lugubrious funeral music and see mourners filing by, whispering and peering down to see how she's faring in death, some gloating a bit, glad her life's tenure is finally done. It's cold in here and she can't suppress a shiver. The high, saccharine voice of the young female technician comes over the intercom.

"How're we doing?"

"We're fine," Diane says, trying not to be curt, but not succeeding. The woman failed to appreciate Diane's earlier comments about cryogenics so there's no reason to assume her sense of humor has improved now.

The scanner has begun rotating slowly. Its movement is disturbingly quiet, covert as the moon managing the earth's tides. Diane closes her eyes, trying to will her neurotransmitters into firing robustly. Joe is convinced nothing is wrong, and she has tried to convince herself too, telling herself this is merely a procedure to confirm nothing is wrong, but the fillip of uncertainty inflated as soon as she entered the building. Everyone has been treating her as if she's already an invalid, as if they know something about her she doesn't know herself. Joe never tries to make her do things, but he insisted on this scan, which makes her wonder if he was seeing something he wasn't admitting.

What Diane would really like is to get Bronwyn in here to have her brain looked at. A tumor might be the root cause of her strange thinking. Diane has not been able to unlink speculation about her own brain from speculation about Bronwyn's. That, too, is disturbing. They have known one another for years, yes, but there is no biological connection between them, and Diane has known plenty of people for years without feeling disturbed by the vagaries of their brains.

Aware of holding her breath, she releases it slowly to avoid excessive movement. Her chest deflates; her arm jerks. If you're not dead complete stillness is unattainable, for god's sake, not to mention ill-advised. They injected her with radionuclides and she can almost feel the gleaming positrons cavorting about in her brain, seeking the areas of high cortical activity and, god forbid, cortical atrophy. The very words are terrifying. The technician hasn't said anything for some time. Perhaps they've forgotten about her and she will be alone in this room forever, radioactive, stuck inside this machine. This is the claustrophobia they warned her of—she insisted it wouldn't be a problem. She should have taken the sedative they offered.

She can't get the word *eternal* out of her mind. It's a word from her childhood, from the years in elementary school when she was made to attend church. All the hymns mentioned eternal tides, eternal earth, eternal life. She didn't like the idea of forever. It wasn't comforting. The school day seemed to last forever and so did church services and dental appointments. Now she regards the notion as an outright lie. Nothing is forever. Not the oceans or the tides or the earth or the sun. And most definitely not the human brain.

The image of the Mexican man comes to her again. She sees him clutching his child for a moment, stilled by relief and love. She sees the next moment clearly too, how he bolted into a side street, to a fate she'll never know.

39

Matt has agreed to take her to her car in Topanga. As they drive, she and the second fire, the one still burning, exchange silent messages over miles. Like an enthralled lover she begins to shape herself once again to the fire's will. The blaze is a torrent now. She senses its progress as it breaches the mountain's summit and heads down toward civilization. Her life has never been simpler, boiled down to a single intention.

"Do you know what I'm going to do?" she asks, wrenching herself from the swill of her dialogue with the fire.

Matt regards her intently, curiously. "I think so. You're going to try to put out the fire."

"You're not going to stop me?"

"How could I?"

"You believe I can do it?"

"I don't know. Maybe."

For now that must be enough.

Her car sits exactly where she left it, unfazed by her absence. The landscape around it is desiccated and weary, trying to find a new stasis now that the immediate crisis has passed. They drive in tandem, she in the lead, up over the summit and down into the valley, then east to the base of the mountains. Her pores sense the lure of charged ions. The sky, volatile with smoke, streaked yellow and purple, appears to be in anaphylactoid shock.

At the ATV rental they are the only customers, and she gratefully yields the negotiation to Matt. The voluble clerk keeps stealing suspicious glances at her. In her long pants she is inappropriately dressed for the hot day. She would rather not subject herself to the clerk's questions, anyone's questions. Her social skills are inaccessible, bent as she is to the fire's rhapsody.

Matt signs the rental papers, and they are given helmets, and warned where not to go. Avoid the fire, the clerk stresses. Right? Right. He escorts them to their vehicle. Matt's attention is trained on her, his body bearing the questions he isn't voicing. They mount the vehicle, he in the driver's seat, she behind. The clerk won't leave. He is telling lame jokes and spilling last minute instructions. The only one on duty, he seems desperate for company, reminding her of a sick rooster, dashing across the barnyard, shedding feathers.

The motor clatters to life. "Hold on!" Matt shouts, and she clings to his wiry waist. She would prefer to be driving, but does not want to draw attention to herself by appearing to be the one in charge.

They head up the mountain on a wide dirt road which has been heavily traveled by ATVs though it's empty of traffic now. A series of switchbacks winds through a barren brown landscape of grass and low sedge. Behind a cluster of bushes Matt stops and turns off the motor and they exchange seats without discussion. At the helm now, she starts the motor, and he clings to her waist this time, the girth of his arms anchoring. As they head uphill the motor quivers in her crotch, the wind grazes her face. She hopes there will be a view at the summit, south to the blaze.

She feels the call for a plan. She hasn't felt that before. First suppress the wind, then bring on the humidity, maybe rain. A strand of doubt has blown in, perhaps because of Matt's watchful presence. He is a relative stranger, not an old friend like Lanny. Could she drop him off somewhere? Ask him to wait?

The path narrows and rises more steeply. Earth and sky seem to merge, both jaundiced and draped with a smoky haze. *We're fucked*, he thinks. *This is insane.*

She barrels past a sign that bears a warning of some kind, but they're moving too quickly for him to read it. He imagines he hears, beyond the motor's roar, a rumbling that might be the fire. He has no idea how far away it is, but it bears down everywhere, imbuing land and sky with its eerie glow. Dread tunnels through his gut. He said he wouldn't try to stop her, but maybe he should.

Under his fingertips her ribs are unbearably fragile, reminiscent of whorled shells, but she's surprisingly strong, maintaining the vehicle's speed over ground studded with divots and rocks. He came on this expedition thinking he would protect her, and yet he is well aware she doesn't want protection. His back and shoulders ache as if he's been welded here for days.

He thinks briefly of Lyndon Roos who has been hounding him with texts since they parted. She's been asking what Bronwyn plans to do; she wants to be a witness, notify the press, and with the self-importance of a star she assumes she's welcome. Bronwyn put her foot down. *No press. Absolutely not. I don't care if she's a movie star.* He's in full agreement. What a disaster a press corps would be now, following them up here to god knows what.

Balloons of smoke rise like dozens of hyperactive parachutes, inflating and withering, swirling on the wind. The worm of dread in his gut has become flat-out fear. They're close to the top now, not a mountain exactly, but a huge mound of inert brown earth draped before them like a reclining elephant. Without a single tree in sight the place is desolate and ugly, a landscape that has no use for humans.

She turns to him, her expression blank, then guns the last several hundred feet to the top where she turns off the ignition on a patch of flat dirt. They gaze south to where the fire has bridged the mountain's saddle and begun to descend into a steep ravine. At the base of that ravine are thousands of endangered homes which are obscured by a wall of dark grayish-brown smoke. The view is stupefying: acres of unbridled chaos, lashing arterial flames, whorls of smoke, oily-looking currents of hot air, everything jitterbugging and pulsating in unstoppable motion. The sound is the thundering of an enraged universe. The entire spectacle makes him feel utterly helpless. He grabs stunted breaths. His eyes are smarting. The smell is worse than burning rubber.

Bronwyn dismounts and walks to where the hillside begins to slope down. Hair stashed under her baseball cap, pants slightly baggy, she looks very young and boyish. He doesn't approach her, not yet, but he'll need to make sure she doesn't go closer. Whatever capabilities she has, she is still human and this is dangerous.

"Stay here," she says, her voice low and hoarse, almost a growl. She skitters, bug-like, down toward the ravine, slipping and sliding on the gravel, covering distance far too quickly.

"Wait!" he calls. "That's too close!"

She hears him and stops, turns. "I came for this," she shouts back.

"Don't be crazy—it's not safe!"

"Go! Disappear for a while, please. I have to do this alone!"

"Are you kidding? I can't leave you here."

"*Please*," she begs. Her body is bent into the hillside like a scimitar. Her pale face seethes, luminous, bent on its course.

"Shit," he mutters.

She makes a gesture, pushing him away, and waits until he begins to trudge reluctantly back toward the ATV.

"Out of sight!" she calls.

He does as she says, taking a few more paces until he can't see her. He kneels in the dirt coughing, sweating, shivering. *One, one thousand, two, one thousand.* He clenches his jaw against nausea. They're both fucked.

He has never believed in imposing his will on others. As the youngest child in his family he was always being told what to do. The legacy of this is he believes in letting people alone, never presuming he knows best. But how the hell is he supposed to honor that credo now? She could die, for god's sake. They both could. Even experienced firefighters die in circumstances like this. He stands and stumbles back to the lip of the hill where bursts of heat boil into his face. The sounds from the fire are erratic explosions, battle sounds. The smell is sickening.

She stands on a rocky promontory, legs spread, chest lifted, back straight, arms thrust out from the sides of her body as if she might take flight. Tiny and elfin, yet firmly planted there. He starts toward her, stepping cautiously but slipping nonetheless. A pair of helicopters passes overhead, distracting him, shooting jets of water that are blown laterally by the wind. He continues clumsily downhill, his attention fixed on Bronwyn who maintains her stance with the immobility of a statue.

He slips, falls hard on his coccyx, and sits for a second, stunned. As he tries to gather himself, something in her stance changes. She looks lighter, almost transparent, as if she might blow away. In the coming days he will review this image again and again, wondering if he saw it correctly, questioning whether he remembers it right. But this is what he will swear he has seen. It can't be, but it is.

The flames are losing their bellicose swagger. Only minutes ago they were devouring everything in sight, but now they are almost asthmatic, desperate for oxygen and fuel, eviscerated as Custer's troops at Little Bighorn, or Sherman's troops at the end of their march. It might be an optical illusion, a hallucination, a dream.

He reaches for his phone and holds it up in movie mode, panning slowly from west to east, hoping the camera sees what he sees, this titanic inferno in sudden retreat. The spires of flame shrink to the ground; the front line recedes; the plumes of smoke that were taking over the sky now deflate and sink; the snarl abates to a whisper.

When his battery dies, the mountains both near and far look like a smoldering battleground, plundered, only a few small skirmishing flames remaining, all listless and about to expire. He coughs, erupts in a bout of sweating, shudders, spits, forces himself to standing, and runs downhill, stumbling and falling, toward Bronwyn.

Her cap has fallen off, releasing her braid which makes a bright tail against her back. When he arrives next to her she is wiping her face, spreading soot everywhere. She stares at him without apparent recognition, her eyes glassy.

"Oh my god," he says. "Oh my god." He sounds stupid. He feels stupid. "Let's go," he says.

She shakes her head, emits a guttural croak. "Not yet."

"God, look—it's out. You—"

"Not done. Go. I'll get back on my own."

Staring out at the blackened branches poking up from the scorched hillside like the grasping limbs of buried skeletons, he feels as if she and he are the last two alive. Civilization is gone. There's nothing left to save. "I'm not leaving you here alone."

She turns away from him, done with discussion, and slowly traverses the shank of the hillside, maintaining her altitude. After a moment he follows, careful to keep his distance. She makes her way uphill where she pauses at a crest that provides another view down over the ravaged wilderness. Smokes drifts overhead in long spiraling bands, confused about its allegiances.

What now? He waits, watches, wishes his camera were still working. She assumes the wide-legged stance again, staring out. A light rain begins to fall. Scarcely visible, it makes no sound, but it mists his face, pleasantly cool.

40

Her cottage sits beyond the reach of streetlights so as soon as her headlights go off it is sucked into darkness. Her eyes adjust slowly, picking out the edge of the driveway, the front steps. She stands on the stoop and sniffs the fecundity, the moist air, the pulsing of the river, traces of iron and sulphur and salt, and the decay of late summer. She has missed these smells without knowing it.

Inside, the lights in the living room and kitchen have burned out. She drops her bag by the bedroom door and feels her way to the screened-in porch where she collapses on the couch, spent, hoping the sanctuary of home and the river's current will work to restore her.

When her flight took off from Los Angeles this morning the rain was a mere whisper, as it had been all night, more mist than rain, but by the time she landed in Boston it had been pouring in LA for hours and every monitor she passed displayed images of flooded streets, people swimming from cars, piles of mud that had slumped down hillsides with houses in tow. Was this her fault? If so, she doesn't know what went awry. She'd only meant for the rain to be light and brief, enough to rinse the atmosphere and restore the air's freshness. But something went wildly out of control. All the water vapor that had been accumulating for days in the warm atmosphere above the city converged, and has come down not lightly as she intended, but with punishing force. It is more rain than the city has ever seen in one day, and the parched earth cannot absorb such a sudden overload of moisture. It has pooled and gushed and carved new riverbeds. It has barreled down hillsides, destabilizing the dirt, uprooting bushes and small trees, undermining houses. It has knocked out power stations and taken control of the surface streets and many of the freeways. Suddenly water, with its murderous power, is calling the shots.

At Logan Airport Bronwyn turned away from the monitors and hurried out to the parking lot to find her car. It was after dark and Boston was hot too, with smothering humidity, though not as hot as LA had been. She drove north fast. Maybe it wasn't her fault. But maybe it was.

Matt has texted her several times. No doubt he's been seeing the same reports. They left LA at the same time, he on a flight to New York where he plans to meet his old friend for a road trip. But he was reluctant to depart, wanted to discuss what had happened, wanted her to review the footage he'd taken with his camera, wanted to coax her to explain herself. She was too exhausted. Besides, she couldn't explain herself even if she'd wanted to.

She goes inside and turns on the TV to watch her replacement, a buxom blonde named Ceci Bontemps—can that really be her name?—giving the day's final weather report. Ceci confines herself mostly to the local weather, but shows a quick clip of LA's plight, gloating a little in her commentary, as if the relatively benign weather of the east coast reflects the moral superiority of its inhabitants. It's prurient really, Bronwyn thinks, this kind of disaster weather voyeurism. She hopes she hasn't been guilty of it, though she suspects she has.

One person in LA has drowned, an elderly woman who was walking near a burst storm drain. There was a water surge and she didn't know how to swim. No footage of the event was shown, thank god, but Bronwyn can picture it well enough—a frail woman stunned by the sudden gush of brown water—the thought is devastating. Maybe it isn't her fault and maybe it is, but the fact is she now has no idea what she can and can't do. Under these circumstances she shouldn't be trying to do anything at all. Not if it leads to this. At best she's no more effective than the boy who put his thumb in the dike. Okay, yes, she squelched the fires, but who's to say more fires won't start soon in some other part of that dry city or state, just like the tornado that took down Earl. In fact, it can most certainly be said that more fires *will* return.

She flips off the TV and goes outside and down the slope of charred grass, shuddering a little at the lingering sooty scent. Stars wink off the river's flat black surface. The night is still and the moon has not yet risen. She wishes she'd never left this riverside home, this sheltering private piece of land that is, at least temporarily, hers. She hopes she never has to leave again. Minutes pass. How shockingly silent it is here. Where have the night creatures gone? Why is the river's lapping current completely inaudible?

It's the rush of her own blood that's obscuring her hearing. *Hush.* Gradually her blood receives her instruction and subdues itself, ceding to the other sounds, bats rustling under the eaves, field mice stirring, chanting crickets, the river purling toward the sea. The volume of the polyphony amplifies, as if the landscape is reassuring her that it's happy to have her home.

41

At first Diane thought she would go alone to get the results—she has never before gone to a doctor's appointment accompanied by anyone, not as an adult—but when she imagines driving across the river, no doubt in heavy traffic, and parking in the dank hospital garage, then finding her way to the right building and the right elevator and the right corridor, everything institutionally drab and anonymous, all the doctors and nurses and technicians striding past her imperiously, pressed for time, blank-faced or stamped with patronizing smiles, trained to read people as always evincing some pathology, then arriving at her doctor's waiting room where she would wait surrounded by people who would look perfectly ordinary, but whose brains would all be carrying invisible damage—tumors, or dementia, or some neurological condition that was about to impair their functioning and make them invalids and maybe usher in their premature demise— well, she couldn't face it, the thought overwhelmed her, and she asked Joe, very quietly, if he would accompany her.

Of course he said yes. Dear Joe. He recast himself for service, came down from Maine, and put on the coat of command. He took the driver's seat—she usually drives—and drove her along Memorial Drive in the early afternoon. They crossed over the Longfellow Bridge, and the traffic was not bad, and the river was a ribbon of sunlit gems and full of boat traffic, and things might be right with the world if you looked at them in a certain way. They were both quietly ruminative. In this attenuated moment of transit she told him about the Mexican man and his son, and Joe listened and nodded, and she was glad he felt no call to comment.

Dr. Sadaranghani is an elegant and lively woman who has retained the lilting, lightly English-inflected accent of her native India though she earned her medical degree here and has been practicing in Boston for fifteen years. Diane chose her not primarily because she was on several of the "top doctors" lists, though that was important, but because she took Diane's request for a test seriously and did not make her feel the least bit ashamed.

The waiting room, which serves two other neurologists as well as Dr. S, is full, and Diane is surprised to see that the other patients are mostly middle-aged, or downright young. There's a man of indeterminate middle-age with a turban, a fifty-something black couple clutching one another, an elderly white woman accompanied by her prim middle-aged daughter, a boy of not more than four or five with his parents, and a teenaged girl with her mother. Viewed from the outside everyone appears disease-free.

The turbaned man moves to allow Diane and Joe to sit side by side. They nod their thanks and seat themselves, and Joe takes her hand and, though the gesture embarrasses Diane, she doesn't withdraw. He squeezes and she squeezes back. He scans the room, trying to be subtle, and she knows that when they emerge from here he will have made up a story about each grouping, their family circumstances, the problems that have brought them to this waiting room. He will have named and nicknamed them all, and assigned them ages and professions and obsessions. Some of what he'll come up with will seem right to her, some of it will seem fantastical. It's simply the way his brain works, he maintains, or how he has trained it to work. You mold your brain around science, he tells her, and this is my way.

If a single room can exude joy, Dr. S's office is that room. It is a tarantella of color with a Persian carpet in shades of deep red and indigo, plump carmine arm chairs with saffron accent pillows, and adorning the walls are children's drawings in the neon primary colors of PET scans. Also on the walls are various framed photographs of Dr. S's two children and her doctor husband. Diane has never seen a physician's office with such a joyous personal stamp and, though she has been here once before, it still takes her by surprise.

Dr. S wears her name badge on a stylish, pale blue linen suit. Her white coat hangs on a hook on the door. Preoccupied as she was on the first visit, Diane missed how stunning this woman is, a slim forty-something woman with the glossy hair and burnished satin skin of a teenager, and perfectly symmetrical features, a perfection that isn't precious and static, but active and playful. She shakes their hands and expresses delight at meeting Joe and they sit in the arm chairs, a slim monitor on the table to one side.

"Well, Dr. Fenwick," says Dr. S, "I won't keep you in suspense. Your brain is perfectly fine. There is no evidence of pathology at all." She pauses and smiles almost teasingly. Perhaps it is rare for her to deliver good news.

Diane hears the words, but is slow to absorb them.

Joe pats her arm. "I told you! Didn't I tell you?"

Dr. S laughs. "We all worry. It's normal to worry sometimes, especially in times of stress. I consented to test you because it seemed to me you were more worried than most."

"Oh, she was," Joe says. "For no reason at all. Her brain is ten times as good as most people's. Certainly better than mine."

"Don't be ridiculous," Diane says. "Your brain is top notch." She holds her breath, a recent tendency. There's something more coming, a "but" hovering behind what's been said that will change the story. "But that's not all?"

"Your frontal lobe is larger than most, as is your inferior parietal region. That's certainly no cause for worry—in fact it has been associated with a higher level of intelligence."

Joe is raining laughter. He can't seem to stop. "See, I told you!" Yes, he has been more worried than he let on.

"But what about the things I've been forgetting? What about the feeling that my brain is leaking knowledge at a terrible rate?"

"We all forget things. Even younger people, like the medical students I teach, have lapses in memory. Think of how often computers freeze up. You're fine, really, Dr. Fenwick. Would you like to see your brain scans?"

Diane nods, not sure at all. She is unable to receive this good news that flies in the face of her recent experience. It does not feel like the whole story. It isn't the whole story really, because she has not been honest. She is here for information about her own brain, yes, but she is also here about Bronwyn's brain too—and there is certainly no way Dr. S can weigh in on Bronwyn's brain without having seen it. And something else too—she is here to investigate something even beyond Bronwyn's brain, something about the human brain in general. What she really wants to know is perhaps unanswerable: What is the possible reach of the human brain? What are its limits?

Dr. S has turned on her computer and the monitor has come alive with bright blobs of primary color. Diane tries to recognize something of herself in those color blocks, tries to recall what she was thinking as she lay like a corpse in the circling scanner.

Dr. S uses the laser pointer. "You see these areas here—this is where there is high activity, rapid glucose metabolism. You see how healthy it all looks? It is very much alive, very active."

Diane squints, trying to see what Dr. S sees, trying to make sense of the colors and match them with particular thoughts she was having that day.

"What made you become interested in the brain?" Joe asks, ever curious, thinking perhaps about a character for his next book.

"Oh my," she says. "It's always a wonder to me that everyone doesn't want to explore the brain. It's capable of so much. And yet we're just beginning to understand it. You're a writer, are you not? I imagine you have always been interested in stories and language."

"Oh, yes. Since I was very young."

"This is true for me also. I have been curious about the brain since I was a small child back in India. I had a friend who was a spelling champion. He knew how to spell so many words, words from many languages even, words whose meaning he did not know. I wanted, even back then, to see how his brain was working from the inside."

Diane floats, hearing them at some remove, thinking of Bronwyn, wishing she could get Bronwyn to come here and have her brain examined. What would Dr. S see?

"And you, Dr. Fenwick, I imagine you, too, have always been focused on natural phenomena?"

Diane stares at the colorful simulacrum of her brain and smiles
weakly. She is not like Joe and Dr. S. She has worn and shed many
skins since she was a child.

42

When Matt arrives at the apartment in Greenpoint, Buzz and Ramona, Buzz's ex-girlfriend, are sitting next to each other on the low couch, flipping through take-out menus, a few empty beer bottles on the floor by their feet.

"Señor! Señor!" Buzz says rising to embrace Matt and get him a beer. "My chaperone has arrived at last."

"He's toasted," Ramona says.

"Like you're not," Buzz says.

It's the second act of something and Matt has missed Act I.

"Pizza or sushi?" Ramona asks Matt. "Your call."

"Give him a break. Let him chill."

Matt has met Ramona a few times when she and Buzz were still together. She wasn't exactly a bad-news girlfriend, but she wasn't good news either. She's one of those women who talks four inches from your face, and she's always asking people what they're thinking, especially men.

Matt drops his bag and excuses himself to the bathroom, no bigger than a broom closet with only a toilet and sink. The door, bulged with humidity, won't close. He doesn't pee, just sits on the closed toilet with his head in his hands. Bronwyn must have seen what he saw, water filling the streets, storm drains overflowing, hillsides collapsing, houses being dismantled like brittle Lego creations. It all happened in the time it took them to fly east. He's been calling and texting her since he landed, but she's not responding. She must have seen—it's all over the news, reporters gloating over the disaster as if it's a Super Bowl upset. No one is mentioning the fires that preceded the rain and the sudden way they expired. Human memory is stupidly short. He wishes Ramona wasn't here and that Buzz wasn't drunk. He has to talk to someone, but there's no way he's discussing any of this with Ramona around. He rinses his face and goes back out.

Ramona, tittering, turns to Matt. "Did you ever hear about the time I threw a head of iceberg lettuce at Buzz? He was busy being an asshole about something and I was furious so I just let it fly and it hit his cheek and he had a nasty bruise for, like, a week. I've got a picture of it somewhere."

Buzz dismisses her with a wave. "He doesn't need a picture. I'm sure he can imagine it. So, Señor, how was L.A.?"

Ramona stands and swishes off behind a Japanese screen that defines the bedroom. Buzz rolls his eyes. Matt understands his arrival has rescued Buzz—who is soon to be married—from relapse into a night with Ramona he might have regretted.

A day and a half later, Matt and Buzz are halfway over the George Washington Bridge, locked in traffic and heading west. He's told Buzz everything and Buzz has listened in his calm, equivocal way. Matt has even shown Buzz the footage from his phone. Still, Buzz has only smiled and shrugged and shaken his shiny bald head and told Matt to chill.

But the fact is, Matt cannot relax, not after what he's seen, first the fire receding, then those floods. He's been trying to tell Buzz how his entire frame of reference has changed, his entire belief system, but Buzz remains unmoved. *Look*, Matt keeps saying. *You've seen the footage, how would you explain that?* Buzz shrugs, apparently happy to live with the cognitive dissonance. Matt cannot comprehend the lack of curiosity in his friend, the lack of a need to understand and explain things. How slow some people are to absorb what their senses tell them.

Traffic has brought the car to a standstill. Matt stares out the window past the bridge's steel girders down to the iron-gray Hudson River. The water is moving down there, he knows, but from up here it appears to be fixed in place. Even the transport vessel smack in the middle of the river appears stationary. About this particular view he knows better than to trust what he sees. He knows how the appearance of movement is always influenced by the position and movement of the observer. All his life he has been doing what everyone learns to do, balancing what his senses tell him with what he has learned about how the universe works. When he was a child he took great pleasure in holding his hand up to obliterate the moon entirely. *Moon's gone*, he would say triumphantly, knowing full well it was an optical illusion. But none of his accrued understanding helps him now. There is only what his camera recorded, shaky and inconclusive but definitely startling, and his own internal sense that something mysterious has happened, wrought by Bronwyn.

The traffic is finally moving again and Buzz's Honda rumbles off the bridge into Fort Lee.

"Hey look, man," Matt says, "I can't do this. I'm too preoccupied. Just drop me off here. I'll get myself back."

"Oh shit, you're bailing on me again?"

"I gotta follow up on this thing."

"I hope you know what you're doing. If you ask me, this woman sounds psychotic."

Matt shrugs. No, he absolutely does not know what he's doing. That's the whole point. He isn't sure of a damn thing. Christ, by his late twenties he was supposed to have things figured out. All his friends are getting their lives together. Metcalf with his film stuff. Buzz has taken a job in a brokerage firm and in a few months he'll be getting married. No more road trips for him. Matt thought that would be his fate soon too, but now life has started to seem like one long road trip, stops here and there, but none of them lasting very long.

Buzz pulls to the curb amidst a hail of fractious honking. They part with a stiff, over-the-gearshift man hug, and Matt gets out into the blitzkrieg of Fort Lee, hoping he doesn't think back to this moment regretfully someday. Right now there is no other choice he can make.

43

Why must she struggle so hard to learn how to act in the world? She longs for a simpler time when she found comfort so easily in studying the shapes of clouds before she learned to classify them. When she was a child she used to lie on her back on the strip of grass behind the back steps and stare up for hours, as if she was attending an old-fashioned drive-in movie. She watched the vapors assembling, becoming the shapes of things she wished for—unicorns, bicycles, ice cream cones—then disassembling. It was as if they were sending her secret messages that only lasted briefly, so she had to be always attentive, always aware. If she flicked her eyes away even briefly, she might miss the news. Sometimes the clouds moved lickety-split, becoming one thing then another and another in a matter of seconds (like being dragged too quickly down the aisle of a toy store), but other days—those long hot summer days when everything was still but for the drone of insects—they hardly seemed to move at all. They hung in the sky, motionless as sleeping cats, boring to some, but not to her.

She used to need proof of everything like Diane, but now she knows certain things beyond the reach and necessity of proof. She can be a destructive force. She knows this. She feels this. She has to watch herself.

She sleeps lightly, wakes in the grip of dread. In LA the rain has stopped, but water is still camped in places it shouldn't be. So much is ruined, beyond reclamation. She calls Lanny and whispers into the phone.

"Have you seen what happened in LA?"

"Bronwyn, is that you?"

"Have you seen? I think I did it."

"Don't be ridiculous."

"I didn't mean to."

"I've been watching it—it's impossible to miss. You stopped the fires, didn't you?"

"But I started the rain too. Light rain. Then something happened."

"Talk louder, I can hardly hear you. Is someone there?"

"No one's here. I'm losing my voice. I'll call you back."

She lays the phone back in its cradle to experiment with her voice in the cabin's silence. "Hello? Hello!" The sound, transported through her jawbone is a reedy whir, nothing like a normal human voice. *Normal*, the thought is laughable. How long it has been since she's been acquainted with normal. Is she losing her ability to speak, one capability exchanged for another? She never asked for this. If only she could expunge this talent of hers, revert to who she once was. But how? She longs for the freedom and innocence of childhood.

Lying still on the couch she has no idea what the date is, but her body, unbidden, does its work, informing her that fall is coalescing. The Earth's axis tips and hedgehogs gorge on fruit before curling themselves into tight balls, deer rut aggressively, bats desperate for mates send out frequencies of love, wasps die off, the fur of the arctic fox whitens.

Bronwyn pictures herself among these animals, fattening herself and finding a hole in a tree, curling herself into it, allowing her heartbeat to slow to the bare minimum. She would like to leave this life for a while, awaken in spring after a long reorganizing sleep.

The radio plays jazz, the kind that slides over a person without making demands. A car drives up. She goes to the kitchen window and looks out. The car is old and black and covered with light splotches in the shape of large amoebas. Matt steps out. A surprise and not a surprise. Given the way they parted at LAX, she might have surmised he would come. There is so much unfinished business between them. She opens the front door. Coming across the lawn he sees her, and the light behind his face turns on. It takes her a moment to realize she's happy he's here. Someone who knows. At the bottom of the front steps he hesitates, his eagerness leashed, his smile timid.

"I thought you were on your way to Montana," she says, sotto voce, the best she can do.

"I changed my mind. Again. My friend is ready to kill me."

She nods and steps inside and he follows. She switches off the radio and they go to the porch where she's been living for the last couple of days. It is early afternoon, mild and hazy. An offshore breeze brings the ocean close, imbuing the air with salt and humidity. They sit on opposite ends of the couch. He is familiar and unfamiliar, like a brother returned from a long trip to a foreign land. He thrums with questions.

"You've seen the news, right?"

She nods.

"What are you going to do?"

She shrugs. "Hibernate."

"Lyndon Roos is all over me."

"Why? What does she want?"

"I don't know. To control shit, I guess. She wants you to go public."

"Ugh."

"Definitely."

"She believed in me. I appreciate that."

"Unlike me."

She smiles. "People should be skeptical. I would be if it weren't me."

"It's different now. I have tons of questions, but I am a 'believer,' if you want to call it that."

"Well, there's no call to believe in anything now. It's all over. I'm looking for an exorcism. Or something."

"Really? But you can't just—I mean I saw what you did. It was—it was awesome and you—"

"A woman died in those floods. Did you know that?"

"You think that's your fault? It's not your fault."

"It could be. Something went wrong. I didn't mean for it to rain like that—so hard and for so long. I don't know for sure. And if I don't know I—" She growls and rises and pushes outside where she catapults herself down in the grass.

His hand moves lightly through her hair. A reassuring gesture like the petting of an animal. He lies above her, his knobby brown knee and taut calf within reach of her fingertips. Her nerves are lit, thousands of dormant capillaries flooded. The world telescopes down to the exhortations of skin and blood. She doesn't move.

On the next breath she lifts her hand and places it on his knee. His kneecap twitches. She cannot see his face, but his conspiratorial smile is already firmly etched in her mind. Can a moment like this last forever? How she wishes it could. After this there is so much predictable awkwardness, so much working out. But this moment, here, now, in the grass by the river, his hand in her hair, her hand on his knee, the mist of anticipation scenting the air between them, this is pure and as perfect as it gets.

Her edges dissolve, she loses the boundaries of her own body as she imagines she's him, replete with sinewy limbs and penis. Like migrating birds equipped with internal compasses, they slide their bodies across the prickly grass simultaneously, neither of them moving first, the messages between them coordinated, synchronous, parsed quickly without words or facial expressions.

They face each other. He draws lines on her cheeks with his finger, circles her nose. She touches his hair, separating the locks, which are coiled and springy as sphagnum moss. This is the forgetfulness she sought, the oblivion, all thought transmuted into body sensations. He manipulates her lips into a smile that her muscles take over. He smiles back.

Nothing they do here will hurt anyone. They disrobe each other slowly, silently, his shirt first, then hers. His chest is lightly flocked with dark hairs, hers with a constellation of tawny freckles. She wears no bra. He cups her small breasts and closes his eyes, sighs. Next their shorts, her underpants.

They lie back down, exposed to the breeze, the sun. They entwine their legs and arms, singular in their focus, hushed, oblivious to the pokey spears of charred grass. Around them everything rustles and murmurs. Branches crack, wings flap the air, something splashes up from the river. They hear it all, they hear nothing, their senses at once sharpened and dulled. A heron lands in the shallows by the bank and folds in the broad scaffolding of its wings. It watches, missing nothing, judging nothing, but they sense only the slightest whisper of a breeze that could be anything.

For three days they live in near solitude, often mute for long stretches. Even in the supermarket it is just the two of them. Even as they walk on a busy beach, a planet of two. They are apprentices of each other's bodies, he exploring her bird-like shoulders, her pronounced clavicle, the blue veins of her inner arms. What abundant and colorful hair she has! She marvels at the heat of him and delights in the curiosity he showers on everything: The birds on the river, the variety and sheen of her shoes, the now-boxed instruments of her former weather station.

He takes her kitchen by storm, a cyclone of energy, singing Italian arias in his high tenor as he makes pasta sauce. They eat by candlelight, both voracious, feeding each other, swooning over the garlicky sauce, the crusty baguette, the piquant salad greens. She laughs at her own appetite. She laughs at the way humidity has fertilized his hair so it springs from his head in all directions. What a gift he is—accepting, attentive, kind.

She will not discuss her skill, but he doesn't forget it for a second. This is a woman like no other woman. They spread a quilt in the grass and laze naked in the midday heat. He presses his thumb into her supra sternal notch.

"It must be here," he says.

She smiles with her eyes.

He touches her forehead, feeling for her third eye. "Or here?"

A half-smile, but not an answer.

His finger descends along the midline of her body, grazing her ribs, arriving at her belly with its pleated button. "Then here?"

"Shh. I don't know."

"You must have guesses."

"I can't explain. Don't make me."

So he hushes, but he doesn't stop searching and speculating. The source is somewhere in this small pale body. Her heart? Her lungs? Her gray matter? Is it coming from one of those chakras people talk about? Is it qigong? He embraces her carefully, worried about hurting her, feeling beneath her skin the architecture of sternum and ribs and pelvic bone. He kisses her fingertips. He eschews thoughts of the future which scarcely seems to exist.

He is a ventriloquist with her body parts, her feet are whiny ten-year-old boys, her knees leather-jacketed bikers, her hair a lounge singer with a smoky voice. He doesn't care about making a fool of himself because every once in a while her smile cracks wide, joyous and beyond her control.

They speak a little of their families. His father, Ivan, the plumber, is a Russian immigrant. His older siblings are married with kids and successfully employed. *I'm the loser*, he says, grinning.

On her side: She is the only child of a single mother, her paternity unknown. Her parents met on a train, saw each other a couple of times, but by the time she was born her father was long gone. He said his name was Bert, his last name he never revealed. He was a professor somewhere. Of history supposedly. A big blank. For many years this was a pressing question to be researched and answered, but now it is no longer a topic that interests her.

He listens closely, his body taut, full of the limber readiness of young boys. She wonders how, at twenty-eight, he has stayed so young. She basks in the rotunda of his attention, sinking into him, becoming him. Both are porous, without boundaries, seeing through each other's eyes, subsumed in the novelty of Other.

The weather has taken on the bracing clarity of autumn, but still the afternoons are hot. Early one morning they rent kayaks at Pierce Island. There is no wind, the blue-black water is smooth as Vaseline. The still air transports every sound and scent, salt and seaweed and wet pilings and gasoline from the power boats, mingling with the gunning of motors, the screeching of gulls, the clanking of hydraulic lifts raising boats from the water and wheeling them away to winter shelter.

They glide effortlessly over the glassine water into the Portsmouth Bay. Everything recedes behind them, there is only the measured splash of their paddles entering and exiting the water. There is only the silhouette of the other set against the flat dark water and cerulean sky. There is only the tent of love and lust that shelters two souls who have found one another.

Watching her alone in her boat skimming east, his longing becomes a deep trough through which something viscous flows. Women have come to him easily and just as easily he's let them go. Never has he felt such longing, and it makes him wonder if she will always be a little beyond reach, always drifting away.

On the morning of the fourth day she awakens before he does. She lies still on her back and watches him sleep, his full lips parted, his cheeks slack. The anesthetic of love can no longer support her denial. Memories are crashing around her again. She slithers out of bed, shivering against the fall chill, the fallen illusion. She huddles under a blanket on the living room couch, thinking of the fires, the floods, the tornadoes. The old woman. Earl. So much can go wrong.

An hour later he finds her there, weeping quietly. She looks tiny, as if overnight she has shrunk. He sits beside her, rubs her back, but she won't look at him and recoils from his touch. He makes coffee, brings her a sweater to put over her night clothes, coaxes her outside into the chilly morning for a change of scene. She's too restless to sit. She stands a few feet from him, separate, tunneled inside herself. Never has a woman made him feel so helpless. He walks to the water's edge, needing to preserve himself.

As if pricked, she explodes behind him. "I have to stop this."

So she's done with him, he felt it coming. Perhaps it was too good to be real, or true, or long-lasting, or whatever he thought it was, but the trough of longing still asserts itself, strong as ever, stronger. It fills with ache now, a channel, already dug, labeled, remembered, that will hereafter fill too easily with feeling.

"I have no idea what I'm doing," she says.

"Neither do I. But that doesn't mean we should stop."

"I'm hurting people."

"You're not hurting me. I'm fine."

"Killing them."

He hesitates. She isn't talking about him, about them. She means LA, the dead woman. "I don't think that's true," he says quietly. He has no idea what really happened in LA, what she did or didn't do. Even what he saw is hard to recall clearly. He waits for her to speak again.

She has laid her mug in the grass and comes down to stand near him, still a few feet away. She stares at the brindled current, surrendered to thought, the sunlight a match to her hair, lighting it to a fiery orange-gold.

"Can I point out the obvious," he says. "You have a gift no one else has—you have to use it."

"You're saying I owe the world?"

"Don't you owe yourself? Just to understand more. Experiment."

She shrugs.

"You don't wish you'd let those fires keep burning, do you?"

She shrugs again. "It's all stop-gap. Like a doctor treating symptoms. There will be more fires there, and in other places, more devastating tornadoes and storms all over the country. All over the world, for that matter. And I can't be in more than one place at a time."

"Since you can't do everything, you shouldn't do anything?"

"If I'm harming people I shouldn't."

After a moment of quiet something emboldens him, a sudden certainty. She is a *phenomenon*, a worker of miracles, a possible saver of the world, and he is one of the few who knows. He could be her guide now. He mustn't misstep. "Wait, just think about it. Let's say that woman did die because of you—purely hypothetical—but what about all those others who *didn't* die because you stopped the fires, all the houses that *didn't* burn?"

"What are you—a cheerleader? You sound like my former mentor, Diane. She was always telling me I could do things I knew I couldn't do."

"She knows about this too? I thought—?"

"Oh god no, not this. I'm talking about research she wanted me to do. Science. But this stuff—heck no. She wouldn't ever be able to wrap her mind around this. I tried to tell her, but she ridiculed me, more or less. We had a falling out. She's the opposite of Lyndon Roos."

Shivering, she draws the sleeves of her sweater down over her bony hands and crosses her arms over her belly. Her hands remind him of starfish. "I guess she's got an academic reputation to protect. I don't care anymore."

"When did you tell her?"

"Before I went to California. Why? It doesn't matter. She and I are done with each other."

He's dying to hold her, warm her, inhale the sleep-infused scents of her hair and skin, tell her he'll help her figure it out. "So what then? You'll just go back to being a meteorologist? Keep all of this a big secret?"

"Maybe. I guess." She shrugs. "Sorry I'm such a downer. I think you should . . . go."

The trough fills again, widening to take on this new flood of feeling. Go? Now? "What did I do? I must have done something."

"You didn't do anything. But—I don't know. There's too much going on. I'm not good company right now."

"I like your company, and I'm happy to help you figure things out."

"I have to figure this out by myself. Besides, you want me to do things—and I don't like being pressured."

I could withdraw the pressure and be a good sounding board, he wants to say, but it would sound disingenuous. Maybe it is disingenuous. The fickleness of words betrays him. They wander so easily into perjury. They conceal a multiplicity of truths under a single false banner. Still, what about the last few days? Do they mean nothing to her? Are his own senses so far shot that he's misinterpreted what was happening?

"'Then this—" He gestures over the lawn. "These last few days have been—what?"

"I don't know." She won't look at him.

He goes inside and gathers his things. From the screened porch he sees her still at the river's edge. She hasn't moved. Should he go down there and say goodbye? Her entire body is so coiled in on itself he can't imagine words would touch her. He heads to his car.

A silver BMW drives up and parks beside his Chevy just as he is getting into it. The man who gets out looks business-like in his pressed khakis and crisp madras shirt, dark shades. "Hello there," he says, regarding Matt—the cargo shorts, the T-shirt, the psoriasis mobile—with vague disapproval.

"I'm just leaving," Matt says, wondering if he should give his name and offer a hand. "Bronwyn is down by the river, if that's who you're looking for."

The man nods and strides to the edge of the lawn where he pauses, scanning the black grass. "What happened here?" he calls to Matt.

"I don't know."

The man steps distastefully onto the burned lawn and heads toward Bronwyn as if crossing a minefield. Now Matt can't possibly leave. Who is this man? What does he want with Bronwyn? Matt ambles in their direction, keeping his distance, stopping twenty feet from them.

Bronwyn smiles at the man and shakes his hand, remarkably poised, especially given that she's still wearing night clothes. She's an entirely different woman in this moment from the distraught, remote woman he was just talking to, or the sensual one he so recently held.

"I honestly don't know," she says. "I was away for a while and when I got back it was like this."

"No one contacted me. You'd think the fire department would have let me know. It's a matter of record who owns the place. My god, look at this—it's a miracle the cabin didn't burn."

They disappear inside, Bronwyn avoiding Matt's gaze. Matt is fairly sure there's no cause for jealousy—he's her landlord, for god's sake, and not the least bit sexy—but he *is* jealous just the same, of the attention Bronwyn has turned on the man so readily, and of the smile he was able to raise from her.

Matt hesitates by his car again, one leg in, one leg out, not wanting to be the first to leave. His car's dermal problem looks worse next to this man's spiffy silver vehicle. He waits five minutes, ten. Then he gives up and gets in his car and drives off, though he has no idea where he's going.

44

Matt, sequestered in the office/apartment above his parents' garage, stares out past the driveway to the familiar street of his childhood, mired in memory. It used to be a respectable, solidly middle-class neighborhood of small, sturdy, colonial-style homes, but in the last decade it has gone into decline. Some of the homeowners have allowed their rooves and siding to rot, others have tried to fight entropy with cheap plastic siding or slapdash paint jobs in garish colors more suitable to Florida than Rhode Island, but the worst change to Matt's eye is the missing shade trees, oaks and maples that used to line the street, sacrificed to a bad infestation of gypsy moths a few years back. It was a good place to grow up, a happy place with a gang of children who played together, roaming from house to house, and adults who got along and babysat for each other, and attended each other's parties, and knew about each other's family dramas. Not anymore. Ivan and Marie keep to themselves because everyone else does.

The ragged state of the neighborhood piggybacks itself on Matt's state of dislocation. No one expects him to be anywhere or do anything, and while that might once have seemed a desirable state to achieve, it now feels like an indictment. He is rootless and jobless and rejected in love, and the length of his longing seems to increase with every intake of breath. It dilutes the gravitational pull on him so he hovers above the rest of the world. Across the street, kids are jumping on a backyard trampoline and, though he can't see them, their shrieks are shrill, piercing enough to break glass.

When he was a kid Ivan used to seize his arm playfully. *We check out your properties. You malleable?* And Ivan would test Matt's arm, bending and pulling it like a pipe cleaner. *Little malleable. Not so conductive, not so ductile. Durable, yes, and tenacious. Remember, the harder something be, the less tough. The more tough it be, the less hard.* Ivan hoped Matt would follow him into the plumbing business, but Matt knew from a young age that that wasn't going to happen. He wanted to see more of the world than the underbellies of bathrooms and kitchens. But maybe his curiosity is precisely his problem. Maybe if he'd become a plumber he wouldn't be here in this garage, staring at dust motes, feeling so unsure of his identity. The skills he has depended upon for survival, his charm and ease, his success with women, the very pillars of his personality, all of that has evaporated along with his understanding about how the world works. What will replace these skills to carry him forward?

His parents are out somewhere—he was awakened by the garage door groaning beneath him as if the sound was generated by the pillow itself—and for the past couple of hours he's been sitting at his computer, half-dressed, trying to compose an email to Bronwyn. He can't get the tone right. He keeps rearranging words, but every version sounds either too abject, or too formal. Even if he were to get the words right, it would be a bad idea to send it. She's obviously scared—scared of the sudden intimacy they shared, scared of her own power. He has to wait for her to make peace with herself, then maybe she'll get back in touch. Until then, he's doomed to turn corners and find her green eyes staring at him from the depths of his own brain.

He splays his fingers and the slight movement brings back the feel of her cheek, her hair, the satisfying curvature of her firm buttocks. He feels for a moment as if he can palm her entire body. He hits delete.

He arrived here yesterday afternoon and stayed up late last night, listening to the neighborhood noises, a dog barking at the end of the block, the clatter of a garbage can felled by a raccoon, an occasional car passing on a main thoroughfare several blocks away. The relative silence of suburban paradise, some would think, but to him it was almost sinister.

Moonlight filled the room, a silver liquid, too bright for sleep. He could have pulled the blinds, but the moonlight compelled him as if it was a direct conduit to Bronwyn. This same moonlight was spilling down in New Hampshire. She, too, might have been awake and mesmerized by it, thinking of him. He browsed the internet, reading about joules, teslas, matters of energy he knows nothing about. A cubic foot of air, he read, holds enough potential energy to boil all the oceans of the Earth.

It is almost noon when his parents' black Suburban pulls into the driveway and parks. He can see it is stuffed with purchases. He should go out there and make himself useful. Halfway down the steep outdoor steps, a dream comes to him. He and Bronwyn were dolphins whirling around each other, silently, synchronously, never losing touch. There was a transparent membrane over the belly of the Bronwyn dolphin, an aperture through which he could see to her core where a blue flame burned like a pilot light.

"You just wake up?" Ivan says, spotting Matt's tousled hair and bare chest.

"More or less."

"You are sleeping champion. Your mother and I, we shoot from the bed with birds. Very early—too early. But you—too late." He laughs and ruffles Matt's hair as if he is still ten years old.

The car is packed to near bursting with cartons of canned goods, super-sized bags of chips, tubs of mixed nuts, a ten-pound bag of whey protein powder, entire wheels of Cheddar and Jarlsberg each almost a foot in diameter, enough toilet paper to supply several platoons for six months. They are shopping for giants, or for a family far bigger than the one they raised. Most of these things will sit for months—or years—on the garage shelves. Is it Matt's arrival that has prompted this excessive shopping, or have they become hoarders since he last visited? He doesn't ask, it's not his problem. He humps several loads to the kitchen only to find, behind the groceries, two fifty-pound bags of potting soil and several flats of flowers whose bright blooms beam out at him like eager children.

"One bag of soil to the front, one to the back," Marie instructs.

"Isn't it a little late in the season to be planting things?" Matt says.

"Heck no," Ivan says. "The good weather, it go on. October, still sunny, still hot."

Matt hefts a bag of soil to his shoulder and follows his mother to the front yard. He drops it by the steps.

"The asters will go in pots along the steps. The sedum and sunflowers will go along the side of the walkway."

"Uh-huh," Matt says.

"The turtleheads and crocuses will go over there on the side. Or do you think it should be the other way round?"

"Either is good." He has no idea what sedum is. He could barely name an aster.

She peers at him curiously. "You okay, Matt honey?"

"Fine."

"You haven't told us your plans."

"When I have one you'll be the first to know."

"Okay," she says, apparently unperturbed by the uncertainty that perturbs him so deeply. She reaches down to clear some dry twigs off the pavers that lead to the street. From the sleeve of her housedress the flesh of her upper arm hangs like an empty pillowcase. He feels alternately sorry for his parents and envious of them. On the one hand their lives are so insular, their concerns—gardening, home improvements, cooking—so repetitive and trivial; on the other hand, they seem so content, so devoid of doubt, so unconcerned about how and when death will take them. Such a stark contrast to Matt who is saddled with more doubt than ever.

He and his father transport the flowers to the places Marie wants them, and then Ivan goes inside to make tea. Matt sits at the outdoor table in the back yard, squinting into the hazy sunlight while his mother gathers her trowels and spades and gardening gloves from the shed. The kettle whistles inside. Marie joins him, knocking her gloves against the side of the table to dislodge the dirt.

"Is it a girl that's making you unhappy?"

Matt says nothing. He could deny his distress, but knows it must be obvious.

"I just hope you've made your feelings known to her. She might think you don't care."

Matt grunts. He has never made it his practice to discuss his love life with his mother, and even with Ivan discussions about women have always been confined to jokes.

"You know about your father, don't you?"

"What?"

"I'm sure I've told you this, haven't I? After we met we went on some dates to the movies and dinner. I liked him, but I wasn't sure. He was rough around the edges and his English wasn't very good back then—he'd only been in this country for a year or so. I told him it wouldn't work and I started dating other boys. And then I got a letter in the mail from your father. It was a very passionate letter. Very soulful." She shakes her head, smiling a little. "He said he was very sad without me. He described how good I made him feel and how he saw our future together, all sorts of things I would never have imagined him thinking about. I still remember some things he wrote: *I look at ocean, I feel your heart beat. I look at sun and moon, I feel your heart beat.*" She laughs. "So romantic. After that I knew he was the one. I never dated another man after that and I never regretted it."

Matt grunts.

"I'm just saying that it never hurts to tell a woman your true feelings. Are you listening?"

"Yeah, Mom. I'll take it under advisement."

Marie sighs and stands and stares down at him for a moment. Her face is shaded, but he sees chips of white sky through the lace of her flyaway hair. "I know you're too old for me to be giving you advice. I understand that." Her hand grazes Matt's bare back as she heads to the house.

Moments later Ivan comes out with a rattling tray of tea and sandwiches. Matt rises to help. "Sit, son! I'm not so old I can't carry tray. Ham with horse radish. You mother brings pickles." He lays down the tray, beaming at Matt. "We spoil you so you come back."

Marie arrives with a second tray of condiments and pickles and carrot sticks and wedges of sliced pear and oatmeal cookies. "He forgot the napkins. He never remembers the napkins."

"Meh," Ivan says. "Picnic."

Marie removes items from the trays and serves them each a plate with a sandwich and a mug of tea, and Marie and Ivan eat contentedly, chatting about what to plant where. Marie wants a pink dogwood. Ivan wants to expand his herb garden. They act as if their tenure in this house, on this plot of land, will last forever. Matt listens to them from a great distance, as if he's been shot into space and is orbiting the Earth, seeing things simultaneously from aloft and from ground level, on the other side of a portal from which he can't return. He loves his parents and has never felt so separate from them. If he and Bronwyn were ever to couple and marry, he can't imagine their life together would be as circumscribed as Marie and Ivan's life.

Elasticity, plasticity, ductility. Durability, fusibility, malleability. Temper, tenacity, thermal expansion. These were the things Ivan thought of—maybe he still thinks of these things. He used to extol the virtues of copper pipes. For all the cost savings, he hated using PVC. *What am I?* young Matt would ask Ivan. *Fusible? Durable? Elastic? Plastic?*

Whatever he once was, it's different now.

45

Bronwyn arrives at work at 11:00 a.m., just before they open for lunch, and works until closing at 10:00 p.m. She needs to pay her rent, but more importantly she needs to keep herself busy, focused on something beyond the scent of the air, the cloud masses, the pressure gradients, the fronts gathering out to sea, and those further west or north or south.

The hostess job is easy as jobs go: taking reservations, greeting customers and ushering them to their tables, handing them menus, wishing them a good meal. It is almost entirely social, and once again, her appearance matters far too much. Devon, the manager, stressed this in her interview. She is the first thing customers see of the restaurant, an important first impression. He inspected her shamelessly with his eyes, like a TSA employee, or a dermatologist evaluating moles. Face, hair, breasts, belly, legs. A full frontal inspection. He asked her to get a manicure, told her of the owner's preference for high heels and dark dresses with low necklines—though not too low—makeup—but not too much. No red lipstick. She must look sexy in an understated way. He asked her to role-play, pretend she was greeting customers. *Good evening. Do you have a reservation? Come this way.* He wanted to hear her vocal register, make sure she had no unusual accent or embarrassing tics. For god's sake, this isn't NPR, she wanted to say.

Devon concluded she would be fine, despite her lack of experience. Bronwyn did not mention her stint at WVOX on her resume, said she was taking a break from graduate school. Fortunately Devon didn't recognize her. Perhaps he doesn't watch TV, or not that station. At any rate, he seems to like her reasonably well, though he still watches her a little too relentlessly, as if expecting her to slip up. She's a quick study, she knows how he wants her to be, and she stays on top of things. It isn't the first time things haven't gone her way and she's had to buck up. Her mission now is to firm up her boundaries, and to that end she wears panty hose that cinches her legs and belly, and an underwire bra that clamps her upper torso in place. *Begin with the body*, she thinks.

A pitfall presents itself in the form of the three commandeering picture windows that line one side of the restaurant, displaying a view out to the harbor where a wide canvas of ocean and sky delivers moment-to-moment reports on the changing weather. Most of the patrons request tables adjacent to the windows though every table offers some kind of view. Bronwyn has schooled herself to avert her gaze when guiding customers to their tables. Once there, pulling out chairs and distributing menus, she keeps her back to the ocean. Still, sometimes she lets down her guard, and her eyes slide inadvertently to the glass, and even the sight of a slight rippling on the water, the sun angled and gold and engendering prisms, makes her pores open and widen, and she must retreat as quickly as possible to her podium in the windowless foyer.

Tonight a mother and daughter come in. They walk through the front door arm in arm, the daughter resting her head against her mother's shoulder. The sight stirs an unexpected moment of yearning in Bronwyn. She thinks of Diane. Then, as the duo approaches the podium, the daughter jerks away from the mother, unhooking her arm.

"I *know*. I *will*," the daughter says. "You've said that a million times."

"Whitmore for two," the mother says, her smile brittle. "A table by the window."

Bronwyn checks her seating chart, aware of the daughter's eyes on her. The girl, in her mid teens perhaps, is dressed in jeans and a sassy red blouse that shows off the parrots tattooed on both shoulders. She is halfway between girlhood and womanhood and still feels the call to be truculent. It is so long ago that Bronwyn had a mother to resist. How much simpler those days were. Though now, of course, there is Diane.

Bronwyn leads the two to their table. Her gaze is averted from the window, but still she apprehends the sudden change in the light, the dusk darkening more quickly than usual, like a sudden eclipse. She can't resist a glance. Boats speed into the harbor like insects. The sky is alarmed, almost greenish, and lanced by a shaft of copper light. Her pores dilate. She blinks hard. The colors are so improbable.

"Hey," says the girl. "I've seen you on TV. You're that weather woman, aren't you?"

Bronwyn forces her gaze away from the harbor, ekes out a smile. "I was," she says, handing them menus. "Enjoy your dinner."

She returns to her station, reeling. No one else is reacting to the sky's strange colors. A storm is definitely coming in and, though she never listens to weather reports these days, it's surprising that no one at the restaurant has mentioned it. Is it possible she was imagining the sky's strange color? No, she feels it—the molecules out there organizing for something. She needs to get home, slide into bed, cover her head, and cauterize such messages. She'll ask Devon if she can leave work early.

A lull in the activity. She idles at her podium, can't defend herself against the assault, the too-familiar loop of sight and sound. The spectral image of Earl's face, his droopy lip, his aquamarine eyes. Ganglial lightning. A monumental funnel cloud coughing up cars, trees, tiny babies. Grottos of fire opening and closing like mouths. The sizzling, growling clamor of it all.

Customers push through the front door. She steadies herself with both hands on the podium. She pastes on a smile. *Good evening. Do you have a reservation? Your name please?* This can't continue forever. Maybe time will deliver her back to normalcy. Perhaps drugs would help. She tells Devon she isn't feeling well and reluctantly he releases her. It is full-on night now, black and starless.

About to start her car, she suddenly freezes, sensing someone in there with her. She hears him breathing, a sound that amplifies until it fills the car with a giant huffing. She almost calls out. The breath is on her neck now, quieter. Light and warm. Stroking. Her fear melts. His fingertips rake her loose hair. The warmth of his torso rises from the back seat to cowl her bare shoulders. She basks in these sensations without turning to look at him. When she finally turns, there is no one, only the intangible ambushing phantom of yearning.

46

When school begins again in September Diane is not ready. The summer has been too short, too hot, too fraught with worry that hasn't been alleviated by the brain scan. The unpleasant weather has been compounded, says her friend Harvey Baumgarten, by local air pollution with high levels of ozone.

There is no news of Bronwyn, and Diane is hungry for news. What is Bronwyn doing? How is she faring? Who else thinks of her? Diane has sent multiple emails without getting any response. She called once or twice. Professional concerns aside, the girl could be going mad, and Diane can't help feeling responsible. She was too harsh. She should have been more inquiring, more open-minded as Joe would have been. Ever since she told Joe about her experience in Mexico he has made it his business to find examples of amazing feats of supernatural human achievement. The monks in the high Himalayas who can raise their body temperatures. Stories about successful mind readers and prophesiers. He is determined to pry open the slight crack he's found in Diane's certainty about the world. He wants her to admit to her ignorance. And she does admit to ignorance—she is sadly ignorant about so many things—but still, she has to draw the line somewhere. It's lucky Joe is who he is because anyone else would drive her crazy with this project of his. As for Bronwyn, none of Joe's cockamamie ideas sheds any light on her situation. It's the silence from Bronwyn that tortures Diane—an invisible wall erected between them that is the strongest rebuke.

Diane's curmudgeonly frame of mind is not helped by her busy fall schedule. She has two big grant applications due in the next month and shortly after that she will be going to Siberia to investigate a serious problem with the Arctic Cloud Project—Dmitry Retivov, the new Russian director of the Tiksi weather station, has been withholding data, and no one knows why. He has not responded to her emails, or anyone else's, so her colleagues on the project have nominated her to find out what's happening in person. She has never met Retivov, but she knows he has a reputation for being surly. She is not looking forward to the trip at all. After that she has business trips booked straight through the spring of next year. She has always loved traveling, seeing new sights and meeting people, exercising her language skills, but recently she finds herself becoming, like Joe, a terrible homebody. She hopes it's just a phase.

Making matters worse is the fact that, despite the heat, she's been eating too much and too frequently, like a bear on the verge of hibernation made ravenous by scarcity. *Oh, suck it up, Diane,* she tells herself, *things could be worse. You could have dementia.*

Today she has cleared her afternoon for the young man, Matt Vassily, a reporter who claims to be a friend of Bronwyn's. He didn't reveal what kind of friend he is to her—perhaps lover, perhaps not—and he didn't want to state his purpose over the phone, but that was fine. He was direct, efficient, said he was a journalist, though he wants to meet for personal not professional reasons. They made a plan to lunch in Harvard Square.

The prospect of this meeting has buoyed Diane, and so she has arrived at the Harvest Restaurant early and is sorry to see, sitting in the corner, a former colleague from Wellesley, a historian named Tom Geronimo, who she will eventually have to acknowledge. Not surprisingly he's with a young woman, a creamy-skinned twenty-something, his student no doubt. It's still remarkable that Tom hasn't been terminated for one of his indiscretions with students, but he is a gifted self-promoter, always hyper-impressed with his own steady stream of publications. He writes mainstream historical biographies that he publishes with trade publishers and they always sell quite well, a fact he advertises shamelessly. As for the sexual dalliances, he seems to feel they are part of his tenure agreement. The administration has always overlooked his improprieties, believing his recognizable name attracts students to the institution. Diane has no use or respect for him, but she has never made her opinions known to him, a fact for which she reproves herself.

She spots the young man in the foyer, scanning the tables. He wears jeans and a sports jacket, and it occurs to her that she rarely sees young people dressed this way, not the students she teaches certainly, who tend to favor a slovenly-cum-cool look. Perhaps the sports jacket is de rigueur for a journalist. He speaks to the hostess now, sure of himself, but a little anxious-looking too. Oh my, how these young people move her unexpectedly.

At the table he extends his hand—"Matt Vassily, you're Dr. Fenwick, I assume"—smiling as if they are old friends meeting after months apart. The smile is spontaneous and winning.

"Diane, please."

He nods and grins again. Whatever's bothering him, it has not hijacked his ability to grin.

"Shall we get the ordering out of the way? I'm having the salmon. But everything here is good."

He studies the menu and she studies him. His hair is amusingly prominent—dark and slumped on his head like a felted handbag. Most men would cut it shorter, but he has left it alone, and offshoots have followed gnarled, kudzu-like paths behind his ears. He is on the short side, and sinewy. His eyes stand out too; set in a swarthy face, they are a dark chocolate brown. The fact that he is not conventionally attractive makes him more likeable, Diane thinks, and even if he were downright ugly that smile would be more than adequate compensation.

They dispense with the ordering quickly. He is decisive, burger and salad, simple tastes, he says. The waiter disappears and Matt looks around.

"This is a nice place." His head snaps back to her. "Do you know why I'm here?"

"Not exactly, no. Something to do with Bronwyn, I'm assuming. But you're going to tell me. She's not in any trouble is she?"

"Not that I know of."

Diane leans forward, feeling the movement marking her as a co-conspirator. "So she's alright?"

"Yes and no." He draws in his lips and fingers his utensils and stares down at the red table cloth. "I know she told you about her—*thing.* Right?"

"Her ability to fend off bad weather? You don't believe she can do that, do you?" The impossibility of this conversation, the improbability of it.

"Well, that's why I'm here—"

"Did she send you?"

"God no. She told me you two had a falling out?"

"I wouldn't call it that. A difference of opinion, certainly. I hope you're not here to try to convince me of anything."

He hesitates, sizing her up. "I was trained as a journalist and good journalists are always skeptical. It's the kiss of death to be too gullible."

"Okay."

"Let me backtrack. I used to work for *The Meteor.* A tabloid. I don't know if you've heard of it—"

"You're the one who wrote that terrible article?"

"No, I definitely did not. My boss wrote that. I don't work there anymore. I quit. It's a crappy paper." He shakes his head and draws a deep breath and forges on. "My boss had read about Bronwyn and sent me to interview her. He thought she was, you know, another interesting, farfetched story. I've done my share of interviews with people who claim to have seen aliens and flying saucers. People who talk to their plants and channel ancestors through a cup of coffee. Yada, yada. So I went to interview Bronwyn expecting—well, that she'd be another one of those weirdos. And I saw right away that she was someone I had to take seriously."

Diane laughs. "Oh, yes. She's definitely a person one must take seriously."

He upends his water glass and drinks the entire thing without stopping. When he lays it down again he's breathing heavily, and his face is curiously labile, as if all his emotions have converged there and are cohabiting restlessly. Something pained at the center of his bafflement tells her he's in love. The restaurant's din rises around them and seals them in the unexpected quietude of loud noise.

"So, when I found out my boss wrote that stupid story without even meeting Bronwyn, I quit. But I knew she'd think I wrote it. I tried to apologize to her and set the record straight, but she wouldn't respond to any of my messages."

"Sounds familiar."

"I guess you'd say I got a little obsessed. I couldn't stand that she was thinking I'd write something like that. So finally I went to her house to find her and her lawn was all black. Burned. It was strange because the house itself was fine, but there'd obviously been a fire outside. So while I was there for some reason she *did* answer my call and by then she was in California. I realized—or I surmised—that she was there to stop those fires."

"That's a rather radical conclusion to come to."

"I could tell from the outset she was really convinced she could do this stuff. So—"

"Did *you* think she could do these things?"

"Of course not." He frowns and removes his jacket and hangs it on the back of his chair. Dark circles of sweat yawn up from his armpits, belying his eroding composure.

"Okay," she says, "we're on the same page then. But for some reason, you took her seriously anyway."

"Wait—it gets more complicated. I knew I had to go to LA, just to see. I was—okay, am—maybe a little obsessed. When I arrived it was all over the news about how this one fire had gone out, really suddenly for no apparent reason. No one could explain it. Did you hear about that?"

She nods. Anyone alert to the news had heard about those fires. But it hadn't occurred to her that Bronwyn was involved. Diane had no idea Bronwyn had gone to the west coast, though Bronwyn wouldn't have told her, estranged as they've been.

"So this actress Lyndon Roos—she was in those vampire movies—"

Diane shrugs. "Sorry, I'm not a moviegoer."

"Well, she was saying on Twitter that some woman had walked by her house in Topanga Canyon saying she was on her way to put out the fire near there. I knew it had to be Bronwyn. For some reason this actress believed Bronwyn. I'm not sure why, but you know actors—they're pretty suggestible. Whatever."

Diane winks. "Unlike you and me."

"I tracked down Lyndon Roos and we went looking for Bronwyn."

"A tall order perhaps?"

"We found her collapsed in the wilderness near where the fire had been. She was really dehydrated, almost hallucinating." He wipes his brow with the back of his hand, his suave veneer fully evaporated. She can't believe she's known nothing of this until now.

"Go on."

"We got her hydrated and I took her back to my friend's place in Venice where I was staying. She slept for a long time but as soon as she woke up she was on the move again, determined to do something about the other fire, farther east, which was still burning out of control. She wanted my help driving her to her car and renting an ATV. I was happy to help her. I mean, I had no idea what was going on at all, but I was pretty darn curious by then.

"So we ended up going up this mountain on the ATV to where we could see that other fire. Then she told me to leave her alone—basically she ordered me to get lost. But of course I couldn't. I don't know if you've ever seen a huge fire like that, but it was the scariest thing I've ever seen in my life. Ferocious and loud. Horribly hot and really un-predictable. There was no way I was going to leave her there alone. So I made like I was disappearing, but I actually came back and watched her. And, okay—"

He leans forward and his eyes distend and his lowered voice seems to emerge from the end of a long pipe. "I saw her do this thing—she faced the fire and it was like she was *yelling* at it, but she didn't actually make a sound. At least I don't think she did. And I swear to god, the fire began to go out. And okay, a fire might go out for various reasons, but this one went out *quickly*, like in a few minutes, just like the other one had. There was no reason, no other explanation, but *her* . . . oh Christ, I can't tell you how—"

He blinks quickly. His eyes are moist. "She's, I don't even know how to say it—" He composes himself and peers up at her. "Do you believe me?"

Diane can't look at him. All the tissues at the back of her nose and throat are inflamed, and she feels the same terrible shock and ache she felt in her back yard after Bronwyn left in a fury. She generates a dry laugh. *"Believe*—that would be stretching it."

"Maybe this will help." He pulls his phone from his jacket pocket and fiddles with it for a moment then extends it to her. A jerky video plays on the tiny screen. A fire spreads like orange water across the mountainous landscape of rocks and trees.

Matt gets up and comes around behind her. "Wait, it's coming up in a sec. Okay. Yeah. Look closely." He points to the bottom of the tiny screen. "That's her. That dot."

Diane reaches for her reading glasses. The dot does not resemble a person exactly, though it could be.

"Okay—*now*," he says.

The fire begins to reverse direction as if someone has hit a rewind button.

For four or five minutes they watch as the fire continues to retreat. Then the screen goes black. The image returns from another angle, featuring the skeletons of blackened trees encased in thick smoke. After another minute or so the video stops altogether and they stare at an icon-filled home screen.

"That's it. Isn't it radical?" he says. "See? Proof." He takes his seat, smiling hopefully.

Diane does not smile. Devices—why do people trust their devices so much, investing them with magical power. "Matt, this isn't proof. Not in my book. Hollywood is doctoring moving images every day of the week."

"I haven't done a thing to that, I swear."

"I can't even be sure that's Bronwyn."

"On a larger screen you can zoom in and see her clearly. I can email it to you. If only you could've been there. It was—" He is too overcome to continue.

"It still says nothing about what really happened there." She pauses. "So you did come here to convince me of something." She has to keep talking; as long as she talks she feels somewhat in charge.

He stares down at the table cloth. Their meal, she suddenly thinks, is taking a long time to come. "Maybe I did, yes," he says.

"Okay, let's get this straight. You think you saw Bronwyn put out a massive fire with the sheer force of her will?"

"I know it sound crazy. But that's what I saw."

"I'm a hard sell. Even if I did believe you—which I don't—what would you want me to do?"

"Well, the thing is, she's upset now because after she put out that second fire there was a terrible rain storm that she says she started and it caused a lot of flooding and a woman died. She thinks she's responsible and that she should stop, you know, meddling. But if she really can do these things—stop storms and tornadoes and fires and bring on rain and who knows what else—shouldn't she be out there helping the world—you know, the whole planet?"

"That's a pretty big if."

"You've known her so long—aren't you the least bit curious?" Matt gazes across the restaurant. His youthful face appears battered. "She needs some encouragement and she admires you a lot. You have a lot of influence."

Aren't you curious? The same accusation Joe has been leveling. Of course she's curious. Her whole life has been organized around her curiosity. "Look, if I had any influence over Bronwyn she'd be back in graduate school finishing her PhD. I've known her since she was eighteen. She's a very independent woman."

"Couldn't you talk to her?"

"And tell her what?"

Tom Geronimo's timing is unimaginably bad. He appears without warning, standing over their table with the pretense of good cheer, oblivious to what he's interrupting. The young woman is not with him.

At least he has a mote of discretion. Matt, too, is a young person, but no one ever expects a woman of Diane's age would be committing indiscretions with young men. It's insulting really.

"It's been ages," Tom says. "How's MIT treating you?"

Oh, how he irritates her. The supercilious swerve of his hips. His compulsive habit of rolling his shoulders. "Good. All good," she says. "How's the history business?"

"Not bad. I've got a new book coming out next month. Aaron Burr."

She nods. Figures. "I'll look for it. This is my friend Matt Vassily. Tom Geronimo. Matt's a journalist. Tom's a historian."

Matt doesn't flinch under Tom's assessing gaze.

"You've really scored with a Diane Fenwick interview. You couldn't have a better subject. They don't make them any more brilliant than she. Where shall I look for this?"

Matt's face configures a question.

"What publication?" Tom clarifies.

Diane jumps in. "Leave him alone."

"Well," Tom says, "make sure you include all her trade secrets. Oh— you'll have to excuse me. Let me know when that article is out."

The young woman has resurfaced by the front door. "Insufferable," Diane says when Tom has disappeared. "Sorry to subject you to that. He specializes, by the way, in traitors and villains. And young women. Where were we?"

"You talking to Bronwyn."

"I'd like her to have a brain scan. To see if there are any abnormalities."

"You want to *study* her? She'd hate to be studied."

"If she's making such claims—"

"Ask her to *show* you what she can do. Then you'll see."

The waiter sets down their plates, lidding their conversation again. The salmon is fleshy and pink and it parts easily under her fork. She has forgotten how famished she is. She revels for a moment in the escape of eating. Of course she's curious.

"I can't think of a single precedent for this. Or a single hypothesis that might explain it."

"Haven't you ever seen anything that you couldn't explain? Something that's just a mystery?"

What is it about him that seems to call her out and challenge her at some vulnerable core? She swallows hard. A chill spreads through her gut. The pearlescent twilight. The cobblestone street. The desperate father using every ounce of his brawn and will to rearrange fate.

"I don't know a damn thing about science," Matt is saying. "But I do know what I saw. And it was amazing. Truly amazing. But now Bronwyn is suffering. She has no idea what to do. Someone has to do *something* to help her. You know?" He sighs. He has taken only a single bite of his burger. The anorexia of love. Bronwyn is suffering, he says, but clearly he is suffering too.

His hand rests on the table beside his plate. She reaches out and touches it, then withdraws quickly before he takes the gesture as any sign of commitment.

47

They abandon their meal, half-eaten, and she walks him back to his car. The streets of Cambridge are packed with students back at the business of school, filling the sidewalks with their speed and palpable ambition, forcing Diane and Matt to walk single file. It's fine with Diane—she's no longer in the mood for talking, and Matt, having made his case without convincing her of anything, has withdrawn. How has she come to this—debating science fiction with people who believe it's real.

Matt has parked on a side street off Brattle, a nearly impossible feat in this city. His car is ridiculous, the mottled black jalopy of a teenager, not a professional. "I know, I know," he says, sensing her judgment. He pulls out a business card, crosses something off it and writes on the back. "Here's my info. Maybe you'll change your mind about things."

It's one of his old cards from the tabloid. Vassily, a Russian surname. He is nervous again, apparently eager to leave. "You know," she says, "changing weather is a losing proposition. If someone could change the *climate*, now *that* would really be something."

He doesn't respond though his eyes seem to jig a little. They shake hands. Then, on a sudden impulse, and because he looks so forlorn, she pulls him in for a hug. "Tell Bronwyn I'd love to hear from her. Tell her I'm not mad, even though I still think what I've always thought."

He nods and she heads away briskly because the meeting has ended and not auspiciously, and the situation has nowhere else to go. How will she represent this meeting to Joe? Joe will want to know the blow by blow, but she needs some time to sort things out before she shares it with anyone, even Joe. At the end of the block footsteps clatter up behind her and, following urban protocol, she pastes herself against the glass façade of a kitchenware store. Matt stops in front of her.

"Sorry to bother you again, but my car won't start and I thought you might be able to recommend a garage."

"You don't have a Triple A card?"

"Sadly no."

It mystifies her how so many young people manage to survive with no innate sense of self-preservation. They have cell phones but no Triple A cards. She tries to think where she and Joe have their cars serviced, but no place comes to mind immediately. Car maintenance is Joe's purview (the result of a long discussion they had years ago about the pros and cons of sexual dimorphism). She invites Matt back to the house—Joe is there, he'll know what to tell Matt.

Matt's disappointment about the lunch discussion is compounded by embarrassment. He got too emotional, revealed too much about his feelings for Bronwyn, lost his dignity. Furthermore, he isn't in the habit of interviewing people with big professional reputations like Dr. Fenwick and she, while warm, still made him feel small and unconvincing. He hated to admit that he'd worked for *The Meteor*. It's not that she said anything that was directly disparaging, but she didn't— or couldn't—conceal her disdain. Now, seeing her house—old and stately on the outside, opulent inside—he realizes he never would have contacted her if he'd known her full story.

The husband, Joe, is there and Dr. Fenwick—Diane—is only too happy to pawn Matt off on him. She disappears upstairs, and Joe takes Matt to the kitchen where they perch on stools at a granite countertop. Joe—friendly and unpretentious, even shabby, not at all the kind of husband he would have expected Dr. Fenwick to have—gives Matt the lowdown on his options, and they make arrangements to meet a tow truck back at Matt's car.

The two men set out walking back along the same streets Matt walked with Diane. Gusting wind brings down a confetti of dry leaves. Matt can't tell if the commotion he feels is coming from the traffic and wind, or from his own brain.

"She's your girlfriend?" Joe asks.

"Well—" Matt hesitates. He isn't used to being around someone else who asks questions as freely and directly as he does. "I thought she was, for a nanosecond."

"Forget it. I didn't mean to pry."

"It's okay. Are you a scientist too?"

"Heck no. I'm a novelist. And no, you've probably never heard of me or my books."

Matt laughs.

"I was lying. I *do* mean to pry. What happened at lunch? Diane seemed upset."

"You know about Bronwyn?"

"I don't know her as well as Diane does, but I do know her, and Diane tells me a lot."

"The stuff she does—you know about that?"

Joe laughs. "It's all we talk about these days. I'm trying to get Diane to open her mind a little, exercise her curiosity."

"Really?" Matt turns to Joe and finds an expression like a cone, wide open, ready to funnel anything. "That's exactly what I said to her. To Bronwyn, too. She doesn't want to use this talent of hers any more—or even think of it. She just wants to retire, or hibernate, or whatever. But I went to LA and I saw her in action. I actually saw her stopping a fire. I even filmed it. It's on my phone. I'll show you."

The two men stop right there in the street and bend over Matt's phone, bodies angled to block the light, oblivious to the traffic's din and the fretful wind and the waiting tow truck. They are relative strangers, almost twenty years apart in age, but they recognize in each other a kindred spirit. Watching the retreating wall of orange on the tiny screen, they allow themselves to be engulfed in the mystery.

48

Diane, cadaver-stiff, lies on top of their king-size bed. The men, gone for a couple of hours, are back, and she hears them moving around the kitchen, opening and closing the refrigerator, then going out to the backyard. If she looked through the bedroom window she would no doubt see them lounging in the Adirondack chairs, beers in hand, chatting up a storm, but frankly, she's afraid to confirm what she imagines. Matt and Joe are two of a kind, Joe the perfect audience for Matt's preposterous tale, Joe the gullible listener, ready to be awed, dying to find a legitimate reason for believing the impossible. He has built his entire professional life around a vivid imagination, a belief in things that aren't real. She has understood the necessity for that, and up until now it hasn't impinged on her, but now this proclivity of his thinking seems as dangerous as that of a religious fanatic who believes in some fabricated god dispensing arbitrary dictums on how to live. If Joe has always spurned religion and maintained that the existence of any god cannot be proven, as she does, why is he so eager to jump on board with Matt and Bronwyn?

Can't Joe and Matt see the absurdity of it all? They're both bright, so why aren't they skeptical? She yearns to discuss the situation with someone who thinks as she does. Once that person would have been Bronwyn, or at least she was training Bronwyn to be that person, though she knows, as all her friends with children have always told her, that you cannot control how a young person develops, or the choices she might make, even if she shares your DNA.

A charley horse seizes her calf, forcing her to sit up. She kneads the muscle and stands tentatively and, once standing, cannot resist a glimpse out the window. She was right about the beers, right about the men getting along too well. Matt is cartwheeling diagonally across the lawn and Joe, his audience, laughs and claps.

It is certainly not the first time that Diane has felt outside the camaraderie of men. The feeling has characterized much of her professional life. Men always seem to find such physical ways to bond, roughhousing, hurling or hitting balls, showing off the various achievements of their muscles. So many of her male colleagues who were skinny and geeky in high school and college have become serious runners or rock climbers or cyclists, and once they become those things they can't resist crowing about it. She herself has always been a non-athlete; she can't remember ever having attempted a cartwheel.

Now Joe tries. He isn't much of an athlete either, and can't muster the speed, his body refusing to spin in a single plane, so he thunks to the grass on his buttocks. A second attempt yields the same result, and he gives up, laughing, not easily humiliated. She supposes she should go out and join them, find out about the status of Matt's car, offer him dinner if need be, possibly a bed for the night.

She heads downstairs, aware of the rise in humidity since this morning. A storm is forecast and its cleansing rain will be welcome. But the wind that flutters through the house is not really wind—it is the wake of a person passing through the dining room. She stops at the bottom of the stairs just as the bright flag of Bronwyn's hair disappears through the French doors to the patio.

"Bronwyn!" She hurries to the door, heart vaulting. "Bronwyn?"

She presses her face to one of the door's glass panes. The men are still out there, relaxing back in their chairs, assessing the swift black clouds overhead. The rest of the yard appears empty until the spray of red hair comes into view again.

49

They visit Walden Pond on a bracing fall day, the temperature in the mid-forties, the sky pristine, cloudless and azure. A slight breeze flutes the water. Matt proposed this activity to alleviate the anxiety that has been bouncing among the four of them since Bronwyn's unexpected arrival yesterday. Or perhaps it's only three who are anxious—Joe seems immune.

The wide path follows the pond's perimeter through woods of mostly deciduous trees, a few pines. The leaves—red, green, orange, yellow—are brightened by the sun so they appear almost fake. It is a salesman's toothy smile of a day. The conversation, mostly powered by Diane, is intermittent chit-chat; the crunching and cracking of twigs and leaves underfoot exposes and amplifies the silences. Bronwyn remembers learning in elementary school about Native Americans traversing such landscapes silently, leaving no imprint, their presence invisible. Invisibility, she thinks, is a lost art, a skill she should cultivate.

It already feels as if she shouldn't have come here. She didn't think it through. She came because Joe called and invited her. "Your friend Matt is here," he said, and then he went on to explain how Matt had lunched with Diane, and his car had broken down, and he was waiting for an ordered part to come in. "So why don't you join us. It's been much too long since Diane and I have seen you." His voice was almost begging, bolstering, flattering, just what her bruised ego needed. She was curious about Matt and Diane, of course, but most of all she came because she was lonely. Then, as soon as she arrived, it became clear she would be the focus of this gathering and would be pressured in ways she cannot bear.

So here they are, hiking to the remains of Thoreau's famous cabin, and no one is discussing anything of personal significance, which is only a partial relief, because while they're feigning interest in Thoreau and transcendentalism and the history of Concord, they're all being overly solicitous to her, waiting for her to explain herself and speak of the future.

They walk single file through the winking sunlight—Diane in the lead, then Matt, then Joe, Bronwyn bringing up the rear. Diane has not said word one about their last encounter. Is it Diane who wanted her here? Of course it must be. It suddenly seems so obvious. Diane has heard about what Matt observed, and now she wants to be an eye witness herself. Diane is never going to believe someone else's observations, she always needs to witness and judge herself.

The thought makes Bronwyn shudder. She has sworn off tampering with natural forces. She will not be coerced. She needs to talk to Matt privately about what he said to Diane. She'll take him aside later, when they can find some time alone, although things with him have been pretty strange too. All evening he was unusually quiet and awkward, and he has kept out of her way, avoiding eye contact. Diane gave them a choice of rooms, together or separate, acting as if she didn't care at all, and Matt made it quickly known he wished to sleep alone. He's been hurt, she knows, and now she is hurt too.

Her attention drifts from the company to the world around her, the eye-popping leaves and the dark pond ruffled by wind. A turtle slides from a rock to the water, disappearing with a quiet splash, reminding her of all the creatures who inhabit this pond, some living in the mud beneath, frogs and turtles, eels and worms; it's a chamber of seething activity, concealed by the water's pocked surface. The pond is stream-fed, reputedly clean and very cold.

"I have to pee," she says when Joe notices her lagging. "Go ahead."

"Carry on!" he calls out to the others. "Nature calls. She'll catch up."

She waits for the bend in the path to take them out of view then she makes her way to the water's edge and takes off her shoes and socks and lays them on a rock. She wades in. Beneath the frigid water mud covers her feet. Squeamish, she hops back out. Then, wanting more, she wades in again and allows her feet to sink into the mud a few inches until they settle. This time it feels good, soft and friendly. It's only mud, silt and water, cold but harmless.

She closes her eyes, feels the mud's chill travel up her legs. Far below, beneath the mud and water, the Earth's crust shrugs, though no one notices but she. All the discipline she has mustered in recent days evaporates. She cannot help herself. She sifts the molecules of air overhead, envisions a parcel of air. Her pores dilate, heat sparks in her gut and travels a steady path to her head before exploding.

She reels, hears a tone, passes beyond her own epidermis, and rises as pure intention, corralling moisture, directing the heat. The vapor molecules supercool and aggregate as hexagonal crystals with dendritic branches. The sky bulges with snow, sags toward the earth like a soaked diaper. She exists in the spinning maelstrom, her boundaries dissolved into the nimbus cloud, into the whirling snowflakes, reworked to pure consciousness, unbound by the flesh that bears her name.

When she returns to herself the sky is white. Her consciousness ratchets slowly back into place. Walden Pond. Concord, Massachusetts. She steps out of the water, her feet stiff and red. Snow no longer falls. An inch has come down, maybe less, enough to powder the forest floor, but not completely cover it. The pond is not frozen.

They materialize on the path before her, gaping. "There you are," Joe says. "You—" He smiles oddly.

Matt leaps toward her. "Your feet must be freezing." He takes off his hooded gray sweatshirt and hands it to her. "Dry them with this." He brings his face to hers, lowers his voice. "That was your doing, right?"

She doesn't answer, watches Diane, whose broad face is stern, the familiar expression of consternation she wears when problem-solving. Years ago Bronwyn used to think it meant Diane was angry, and it made Bronwyn doubt herself. And now, again, she doubts herself. She shouldn't have done this so spontaneously and haphazardly. What a dope she is. She was overcome, yes, but it doesn't prove a thing to anyone. And she doesn't seek to prove herself anyway—at least she didn't think she did. But here is Diane before her, not saying a word and look-

ing at her with that furious stare. How can Bronwyn let this moment
pass without taking up the challenge? Purely a matter of self-respect.

She drops the sweatshirt, steps back from Matt, and looks up. The
sky has returned to blue again. She wiggles her frozen, still-bare toes,
situates them firmly in the dirt, and directs her pores to do their work.
Out in center of the pond snapping turtles burrow into the mud; deeper, the mantle throbs; at the Earth's core, fire burns. She borrows the
diverse pulses of these things and corrals the communal energy into
a single song.

Snow falls. The world grows silent and white. Each flake is a tiny
miracle of symmetry, and she whirls among them, a dance she has
come to know. When she returns this time, heaving a little, shivering,
slowly recognizing the faces before her, their stunned silence tells her
she has passed a point of no return.

"We have to talk," Diane says.

50

Diane is surprised by herself. Not in a good way. She has always confronted things head on and asked the questions that demanded to be asked. It isn't her habit to shy away from difficult things. But now, as they turn onto Route 2, heading from Concord back to Cambridge, Diane remains silent at the wheel, feigning immersion in the act of driving. Everyone else, taking her lead, is silent too. Ordinarily Joe would take up the conversational slack, but even he, sitting next to Bronwyn, in the back seat, has been stunned into speechlessness.

Diane hasn't stopped working the problem. Questions whip through her mind. *What* is Bronwyn's skill exactly? *How* does it work? What are the conditions under which she can do what she does? Where does a human being locate the energy to rearrange natural forces at the molecular level? What is the rule here upon which future predictions can be made? What might be the practical application of such a skill? Can others learn to do what Bronwyn does? How could an experimental situation possibly be structured?

A tsunami of feeling washed through her watching Bronwyn's tiny body "performing." Legs spread, gaze fixed skyward, her expression was neutral though there was no mistaking her iron-clad concentration. You could almost see her transforming herself into an instrument, receiving and transmitting. Watching, Diane teared up. Her own body tensed in sympathy and anticipation and worry, and at the same time she felt so close to the girl, closer than she has ever felt over the years, as if they were both engaged in the activity together, both invested in the outcome. And then—this is the strange part—when it started to snow (the second time that day), Diane did not doubt for a second that it was Bronwyn's doing. She knew, she simply felt it, just as she knew, a long time ago, that the Mexican man had lifted that van.

Afterwards, not knowing what else to do, they all made their way to Thoreau's cabin and stared at the rock remains, hardly seeing a thing. Dutifully Joe read the plaque aloud: "I went to the woods to live deliberately, to front only the essential facts of life, and see if I could not learn what it had to teach, and not, when I came to die, discover I had not lived." Beyond a few stones that marked the cabin's former footprint, there wasn't much to see. A replica of the cabin had been built elsewhere, across the road, leaving the original location untouched, as Thoreau would have wished. Diane supposes this historic place was a fitting location for Bronwyn's startling demonstration to take place, though Thoreau himself might have been dismayed.

A few other tourists were pacing the perimeter of the clearing, an American couple, apparently local, with guests who were Japanese and spoke only rudimentary English. The American woman wanted to chat. "Can you believe the weird weather today?" she said to Diane. "Snow in September!"

Diane smiled and shrugged, hoping the woman might think she was also not a native English speaker. The sun was out again and most of the snow had melted. Diane's group hurried away, back along the path through the woods to the car. Bronwyn and Matt walked together, arm in arm. Diane didn't hear them talking, and she and Joe didn't talk either, though they were going to have a lollapalooza of a conversation once they got time alone.

Back at the house Matt gets a call from the repair shop so he and Joe go out together.

"You said you wanted to talk?" Bronwyn says when the boys have left. Her attitude has changed since this morning. She appears calm and available, no longer nervous and distant. Her statement has been made. Strongly.

They take seats in the living room, Diane trembling a little, wishing she'd written her questions down, wanting to take notes, but realizing that might feel too formal. As soon as they sit Diane realizes she can't possibly stay still. She suggests a walk and they head out to the river which used to be their ritual and which she always finds soothing.

"You must be tired?" Diane says.

"Not too tired. Just a little cold."

Only then does Diane notice that Bronwyn is wearing two sweaters, a jacket, a skull cap, and she's keeping her hands jammed in her pockets. "You're okay being outside?"

"Fine."

The wind has come up since this morning, and sailboats have gathered at the boathouse for a regatta. They loll on the riverbank, turned into the wind, sails flapping. Bronwyn's hair spins and twirls like Maypole streamers. Starlings swoop by in low noisy flocks, their wings slicing the air aggressively. It seems to Diane that everything is in rapid flux. Nothing wants to be nailed down.

So it is with Bronwyn, who appears to be open to answering Diane's questions, but cannot answer them to Diane's satisfaction. There is so much she claims not to know. How she does what she does. What else she might be capable of doing. She is able to enumerate the things she has done this past summer, but when Diane asks how she knows it's *she* who has done these things, how she can be sure it's not mere coincidence, Bronwyn turns to her, a little miffed. "You were there this morning—couldn't you tell?"

Diane has to concede—yes, she definitely could tell.

At the Weeks Footbridge they turn around. "You don't have to be so freaked out," Bronwyn says. "I'm not going to yell at you like I did last time." She grins in a kind of apology.

"Freaking out—is that what I'm doing?" Diane tries not to feel defensive. "It's not often I see something I can't begin to process."

"Maybe that's a good thing. I can't process it either. Not in the usual ways."

They table this discussion by mutual accord, and they end up at the Harvard Coop as they have so often in the past. Eschewing her usual routes to the periodical and science sections, Diane follows Bronwyn. They browse through coffee table books with full-page color photographs of apes and insects and photos of the Earth taken from space.

Only part of Diane's attention is on the photographs themselves, most of it is on Bronwyn. She has always known Bronwyn to be remarkable, but until today Diane has completely misunderstood her remarkable nature. Who would suspect, looking at her now, so small and retiring, what Bronwyn can do. There is nothing about her appearance that makes her stand out. She is pretty, yes, but pretty girls abound here in Cambridge. Her red hair is unusual enough to occasion second looks, but other than that she falls quickly from most people's radar. Diane always assumed it was the quality of Bronwyn's mind that set her apart, something few people, beyond she, were privileged to see. But now she thinks it's something else. It's another kind of acuity that has something to do with spirit, an awareness of the natural world that goes far beyond the norm. She can't help searching for some physical marker of this rare talent. Maybe Diane is imagining it and maybe not, but it suddenly seems, gazing at Bronwyn who is gazing at a photograph of a tiger's head, that there is something noticeably different about her. A force field. A subtle aura. She leans into Bronwyn and whispers. "You could do a lot, couldn't you?"

Bronwyn looks up, blinking, dazed.

"Maybe you could do something to significantly influence the climate?"

Bronwyn is about to laugh. She glances around the bookstore, which is packed as usual, then leans back toward Diane, whispering. "You really want to discuss this here?"

A text arrives from Joe. *When will you guys be home? Should we get stuff for dinner?* It's getting dark. Dinner needs to be made—Diane had forgotten dinner. It occurs to her they never had lunch. As they hurry out of the bookstore they run into Jim. They are all equally startled.

"Haven't seen you for a while," Jim says to Bronwyn, smirking a little. "How's the meteorology biz?"

Bronwyn shakes her head obtusely and smiles with closed lips, a masterfully guarded and dismissive smile, as if she's never seen him before and never will again. If he means anything to her, it certainly doesn't show. Diane is strangely distracted by Jim's active Adam's apple. She tells him they're in a hurry, she'll see him at school on Monday. If only he knew what they have been through today—but he never will, certainly not if Diane can help it.

Diane and Bronwyn push out into the harum-scarum, trafficky twilight of Harvard Square. They turn to each other simultaneously and screw up their faces, and with sudden and welcome abandon, they laugh.

PART THREE

The Arctic

51

Bronwyn stares out the window of the small plane to the lonely Siberian wilderness that stretches below them for miles, a subarctic peat bog patched with snow and freckled with strangely circular lakes, round as the art of a dutiful kindergartner. There hasn't been a sign of human habitation since they set out from Yakutsk over two hours ago. She's never laid eyes on such deep wilderness. She tries to open herself to its beauty, the colossal untamed emptiness, but there's something eerie down there, something almost demonic in the austere flatness.

From this distance the land's tipping point status—the huge quantities of methane it is about to release—is impossible to observe. She knows, as all devotees of climate science know, that this landscape is holding onto a grudge—bubbles of methane, seething for years, are creeping up through the lakes and the permafrost's fissures, and even offshore beneath the ocean. Methane emissions from Siberia have risen over thirty percent in the past four or five years, and the release is increasing geometrically, frightening news since methane is a greenhouse gas roughly thirty times more destructive than carbon dioxide. Recently scientists have been surprised to see pockets of spongy land all over Siberia bulging into methane-filled *bulgunyakh*, poised to explode at any moment. People aren't as scared as they should be.

Can she solidify the permafrost to seal in its methane stores as Diane wants her to do? If she were to pull that off, she could forestall the Earth's warming a little, and buy its human inhabitants more time to come to their senses. Could she do this without inflicting harm? She and Diane have been discussing this for days. Their conversations run like tangled tickertape through Bronwyn's mind. First

Diane wanted to know if Bronwyn could rebalance levels of carbon dioxide throughout the Earth's atmosphere, a grandiose plan. It's highly doubtful Bronwyn could do that. Her range is not global. *But have you tried?* Diane pressed. One minute Diane was skeptical, the next moment she was a fervent believer in Bronwyn's talent. Bronwyn has never witnessed this mercurial side of her mentor. Back and forth they went until one of them got testy. Diane desperately wanted Bronwyn to do more demonstrations like the one at Walden Pond, but Bronwyn refused, not wanting to exhaust herself or be scrutinized by Diane, and mindful of the potential hazards inherent in intervention, the dead woman in LA a case in point. *I promise you,* Diane said, *no one could possibly be harmed by refreezing the melting permafrost, or refreezing the Greenland ice sheet, for that matter.* Then Bronwyn became the skeptical one—how could Diane possibly know? Diane also suggested Bronwyn have a brain scan, but Bronwyn refused that too. What point would that serve? When Diane proposed this trip to Siberia, they came to détente and, eventually, a plan. Bronwyn has promised to size up the situation, and do what she can; Diane has promised not to pressure her.

What surprised Bronwyn most was that Diane invited Matt. *He'll be your chaperone,* Diane explained, but something tells Bronwyn that's not the whole story. She still has a hard time imagining their mysterious meeting in Cambridge. To think that Matt approached Diane sight unseen and they had lunch together! Initially, Bronwyn resisted having Matt join them, afraid he would be a distraction. But Diane insisted. He would be useful, she said, though she didn't specify how. Even now it's hard for Bronwyn to resist Diane's will entirely, and she can't pretend that memories of her interlude with Matt in New Hampshire don't still haunt her.

Diane pulled this expedition together quickly. She already had plans to come to the Arctic to grease her relationship with Dmitry Retivov, the newly appointed director of the Tiksi weather station where the Arctic Cloud Project gets a significant portion of its data (daily cloud cover, daily surface temperatures, measurements of the seasonal variability of the active layer above the cryotic soil, among other things). When Bronwyn agreed to come, Diane postponed her travel dates by a couple of weeks to allow them to get flights and visas, and for Bronwyn to get time off from her job. Matt, currently jobless, had no difficulty making himself available.

So here they are, Matt in the seat beside her and Diane across the row, about to land in Tiksi, Russia, above the Arctic Circle where the Lena River meets the Laptev Sea, one of the most northerly places on earth inhabited by humans. They spent the last two nights in Yakutsk, recovering from jet lag, making plans, and equipping themselves, Russian-style, for the cold. Dr. Fenwick insisted on purchasing for Bronwyn an ankle-length sable coat which the Russians say is the only foolproof way to truly armor oneself against the frigid temperatures. The coat now lies over Bronwyn's lap like a drowsy pet. It's the kind of garment that could get you killed on the streets of Cambridge by animal rights activists. Matt refused the offer of a fur coat, having equipped himself before leaving with expensive, high-tech Patagonia gear used by Himalayan climbers. Diane has an ankle-length goose down coat that has served her well. All three of them have fur-lined hats with ear flaps and fur-lined mittens. Yakutsk was nine degrees Fahrenheit when they set out, and Tiksi is likely to be colder.

The plane banks right as if they're coming in for a landing. Matt reaches over and squeezes Bronwyn's sweatered arm. She turns and gifts him with one of her dazzling smiles. She is like the Aurora Borealis. He has developed a whole new series of metaphors for her, all of which have to do with the natural forces with which she is so attuned. She has come into his life like the rising and setting sun, surprising him with an evanescent beauty, never the same from moment to moment and always eluding his grasp. She travels through rooms surreptitiously as mist, etching herself on the air so her presence lingers, her moon-white skin, her chute of resplendent hair, her jade eyes parsing and re-fracting the light like dewdrops. Since Walden Pond she has been out of her funk and sure of herself, and it makes him irrationally happy. To hell with the life stability he was supposed to be seeking. Coming here with her to the land of his lineage, the country where his father was born, is an unparalleled adventure, not one that Buzz or Metcalf or any of his old school buddies is likely to happen upon. He's always known he would have to come to Russia someday, but never expected it would be in a situation like this. His visa says he's a journalist writing an article about Diane Fenwick's research. There is no article in the works. Diane said that to assure his credibility. The Russians don't want him to be writing anything about them, but it's fine for him to be writing about her.

Every once in a while Dr. Fenwick and Bronwyn withdraw for a private talk, and he is acutely aware of being a third wheel. In the late afternoon of their first day in Yakutsk, which bills itself as the coldest city in the world, the two women went off for a walk together and to purchase Bronwyn a warm coat, leaving Matt in the hotel room to fend for himself. The hotel offered little in the way of distraction and it was depressingly dim, so he ended up going out for a walk of his own.

It was snowing, light flurries that ignored gravity. The city felt shrouded and exotic, more foreign than any of the foreign places he has visited, including Thailand and Zimbabwe. There was no feeling he'd arrived in his homeland. He studied the pedestrians, many of whom looked Chinese, with black hair and swarthy faces and almond eyes, not at all like his father, who is pale and brown-haired with a tendency to freckle. Russia is a big country, with many ethnic groups, and Matt felt stupid for having thought all Russians would resemble his father. He wished he'd made more of an effort to learn some Russian. All he knows are a few useless phrases his father taught him. *No flying from fate. Every man to his taste. One fire drives out another.* Not the most useful for daily conversation.

It was already getting dark, and he could see his breath swirling like smoke in the lamplight. His hooded orange mid-thigh parka, rated for extreme cold, was doing its job nicely so far. He'd had to ask his parents to front him the money—something he hadn't done for years and hated to do—but Ivan was thrilled that Matt was finally visiting Russia and was eager to fork over some cash. He gave Matt more than he needed. Now Matt must remember to express his gratitude with some gifts.

Back at the hotel Matt dozed a little under the covers of his single bed and woke when he heard commotion in the adjacent room where Bronwyn was staying. There was a knock on his door, and when he opened it Bronwyn and Diane were there, giggling like teenagers, wanting to come in. Bronwyn was wearing a grayish-silver fur coat that came down to her ankles and a fur-lined hat with earflaps like the hats of so many men in the streets. She held out her arms and spun for him, laughing. "Isn't it ridiculous? But it's so warm."

Later that evening they went out for dinner at a small café where they had beef and boiled potatoes and cabbage and sauerkraut which looked unappetizing but was surprisingly good. As they ate he could tell Bronwyn and Diane had had an intimate talk. He will have to accept the fact that, for the duration of this trip, he will be the odd man out.

"Oh my god, the Arctic Ocean," Bronwyn says. "Look." He leans over her and peers through the plane's small window and, though the opening is too small to see much, he sees black water and a shoreline and he pictures an elementary school globe and feels himself whirling to the top of it.

"Actually, more precisely, it's the Laptev Sea," Bronwyn says.

"Well, by all means, let's be precise," Matt says, which earns him another coveted smile.

For so long Diane has been dreading this trip which she suspects will be confrontational. Dmitry Retivov isn't the first difficult man she's had to face in her professional life, and no doubt he won't be the last. She'll do what is necessary to get the data released—a free flow of data from this station is important for dozens of international projects, not just hers—but that doesn't mean she *likes* being a hard-ass. The tone of the trip changed, however, when Bronwyn agreed to come. Now Diane feels almost giddy with the secret hope that maybe, just possibly, Bronwyn will do something to freeze the permafrost and impound its stores of methane. What happens in the next few days, may have a profound impact on retarding the Earth's catastrophic warming. She is trying to keep her hope sealed, as Bronwyn does not respond well to pressure, but within Diane the hope is robust. How much richer, albeit stranger, her life has become since Bronwyn returned to it.

Diane watches Matt leaning over Bronwyn's shoulder to peer out the window. It pleases her irrationally. Perhaps this trip will solidify Bronwyn and Matt's relationship. Diane has never played the role of matchmaker before, and she's not really a matchmaker now, as she had nothing to do with Bronwyn and Matt meeting one another, but she is definitely doing what she can to encourage the relationship. Matt is so much better suited to Bronwyn than that Reed character was. Diane honestly found Reed to be insufferable. He was perfectly friendly and nice, but you could see his unfettered ego from miles away. But Matt, he's an old soul, Diane could see that from the moment she met him. Maybe it's the Russian in him.

They are seconds from landing now, and the small plane registers every updraft and downdraft as they approach the runway. Matt looks poised to kiss the hair at the back of Bronwyn's head, but he doesn't. What nostalgia this sight invokes in Diane. The memory of young love—or at least younger love. She misses Joe and is remembering a certain trip they took to Big Sur early in their courtship. They went on a walk in a torrential rain storm that would have been hellacious under most circumstances, but their mutual infatuation tinged it with wonder and romance. She remembers picking several fragrant bay leaves and stashing them in the pocket of her rain jacket where they stayed, holding their scent for years.

The wheels smack the asphalt, and the pilot breaks hard, and they bump and swerve along the short runway. What a relief to be no longer airborne. For all the flying Diane has done, on specially equipped data-gathering planes that fly through clouds, she has never flown without anxiety. She knows too much about the unpredictability of pressure, temperature, wind shear. She can never credit a pilot with knowing as much as she does.

52

It is only two-thirty in the afternoon when they set out in a taxi from the tiny Tiksi airport, heading toward the town center. The sun is already low and the sky exerts the long dark pull of Arctic winter. There is little traffic and few signs of commercial enterprise, only a hodgepodge of unlabeled concrete buildings, flat-roofed and barracks-like. Some are emblazoned with fading red hammer and sickles; others appear abandoned; yet others are in various stages of collapse, buckling at their middles likes supplicants. A few idle bulldozers suggest interrupted demolition projects. The town's population has diminished since it was a thriving military base during the Cold War, and now it truly looks like an abandoned outpost, the edge of the known world. Bronwyn struggles to hold onto her excitement as they bounce along the empty rutted streets, passing not a single car. Beyond the town stretches the dark water of the Laptev Sea, shallower than most ocean water, but more mysterious. It's hard to imagine who would want to make a home in such an inhospitable place. It guts her spirit, makes her see all human enterprise as shockingly temporary.

Diane keeps up a steady patter, filling Matt in on the various efforts of the Arctic Cloud Project, how they have expanded into a study of the permafrost as well, and giving him a crash course in how clouds both cool and heat the Earth. Some clouds primarily reflect and scatter incoming sunlight, thereby cooling the Earth, while others absorb the infrared radiation and reradiate it back down to Earth, causing warming. They need satellite data and surface data to learn as much as they can. They need to know the heights of clouds, and whether they are composed of water or ice. Matt appears spellbound, but for Bronwyn this is Atmospheric Sciences 101 and she only half listens. She pictures them above the Arctic Circle, beyond reach of the usual comforts of the Western world. Disconnected. Sudden departure wouldn't be easy. Kansas and Oklahoma seemed vast and unfamiliar to her, built on a different scale from the New England landscapes she's used to, but this, this is vaster yet, a place unto itself, withholding its beauty from outsiders. Will she ever be able to know a landscape like this, merge and commune with it, overcome the feeling that it's simply cold and brutal?

They stop in front of one of the smaller buildings of blue concrete and unload their bags. The taxi driver, bearded and wearing a fur coat almost like Bronwyn's, speaks negligible English and Diane struggles with her rudimentary Russian to work out how much they owe.

Matt and Bronwyn stand in the frigid twilight looking north. It is early November, still six weeks shy of winter, but it feels like winter already, the calendar date a mere formality. Winter must almost be a permanent condition of life here, perhaps a perennial state of mind.

"Are you warm enough?" she asks Matt. His luggage, containing the high-tech gear he'd bought at great expense, did not show up at the Tiksi airport. Now all he has for warmth is an L.L. Bean parka he used for cool days in Florida.

"I'm okay." Hunching his shoulders and tapping his feet like a hyperactive child, he does not look okay.

"You should have gotten a coat like mine."

"It doesn't look as if there's much getting to be done here. I should have worn my gear on the plane. Stupid." He laughs and they both gaze north to the water. Two children run by, chasing one another, giggling with mischievous glee. She tries to borrow their energy.

Diane is done with her negotiations. "I have no idea if I've been scalped or not. Oh well, are you set? Poor Matt. Don't look so forlorn. We'll find you something warm."

They enter the blue building, four stories, the size of a small apartment building, and find themselves in an empty room with blue walls and a single chair. A long hallway leads off it. Diane has told them that this is the same place she stayed five years ago, run by a woman named

Lubov. It is part hotel, part B&B, part SRO. A little odd, she warned, but they will find Lubov to be wonderful.

"It's not the way I remember it somehow," Diane says. "Yoo-hoo? Lubov?"

Moments later Lubov hobbles in as if arriving from another century. She must weigh at least two hundred and fifty pounds, and she wears an uncountable number of colorful skirts over brown trousers and laced ankle boots. On her upper body she has layered a series of equally colorful wool sweaters. Her gray braids are fastened on top of her head as if to coronate her round red face. One of her hands is missing a pinkie. She regards them suspiciously for a moment before recognition sweeps over her and she lunges at Diane, enfolding her.

Lubov, spilling Russian with single words of English interspersed, escorts them up a flight of stairs to an apartment with two small bedrooms containing single beds, a modest living room with a foldout couch, and a bathroom with a clawfoot tub, sink, and toilet. The women are assigned to the bedrooms, Matt to the foldout couch. The décor is sparse and functional, with the exception of the beds which are equipped with luxurious goose down quilts.

"All right?" asks Lubov. "All right?"

Diane nods, and an enthusiastic half-mimed conversation about food ensues.

By 4:00 p.m. it's already pitch black. Lubov serves them cabbage soup and black bread in a small dining room on the ground floor. The three other tables in the room are all empty. Diane suspects they are the only people staying here; they certainly have Lubov's full attention. The last time she was here—five years ago when they were just initiating the Arctic Cloud Project—she came with colleagues from Indiana, Michigan, and Alaska, a French man and a Swede, and a very funny woman named Lorna from the National Science Foundation who became a good friend. The seven of them made for an unexpectedly raucous and fun-loving travel group, and Lubov encouraged their hilarity by sitting with them at the end of each meal to practice her English, and bringing tea and vodka and cake to their rooms after dinner when it was still light. It was July then and quite a bit warmer, and it never got dark, but for a slight surreal dimming at midnight as if the sky were on a rheostat. The woman from Alaska and the Swedish man were flirting unabashedly and finally slept together on the last night. If any climate could push people to coupling this was certainly it.

By contrast to that group Bronwyn and Matt are more subdued; along with the frigid temperature, and the scarce light, the mood of this expedition is entirely different. Still, Diane feels optimistic. Matt is proving to be a very amiable travel companion. Presently he is trying to get Lubov to identify the kind of meat that lies in an uncordial lump at the bottom of their bowls. Though it is obviously meat—boneless and minced and shaped into a columnar meatball resembling a small baseball bat—it is not recognizable. Lubov keeps repeating a word Diane doesn't understand. Matt is about to venture a taste. He pouches his lips and oinks for Lubov, who shakes her head, no not a pig. He quacks and flaps his arms, cheep-cheep. Lubov, laughing, shakes her head again.

"I'm doing the whole poultry and bird family here," he says. "Okay, not pig, not poultry." He moos imploringly at Lubov, and she continues to shake her head and laugh.

"Help me out here."

"Lamb?" Bronwyn offers.

"Baa, baa," Matt says.

No, no, asserts Lubov, perhaps only to encourage Matt's further performance.

"Now I'm running out of animals."

"Heavens," says Diane, "You're just beginning. What about deer, or reindeer, or goat?"

"What does a reindeer say?"

"Do the antlers," Bronwyn says, getting into the spirit of things.

Matt rises from his seat and uses his raised arms with splayed fingers to suggest antlers. He leaps across the room, bumping empty chairs as he goes. "I'm prancing here."

Lubov still shakes her head, still laughing.

"You haven't done bear," Diane suggests.

He descends to all fours on the floor and lumbers around them, growling and sniffing, clawing the table legs, endearingly unafraid of appearing the fool, the classic behavior of a youngest child. Lubov whips out a phone, a surprisingly modern-looking smart phone, and, still shaking with laughter, she photographs Matt who plays to the camera. What Diane would really like is a wide angle shot with all four of them in the frame, capturing them in this small room in Siberia on the verge of a major scientific breakthrough.

"Okay," says Matt, taking his place at the table again and reining in his body so as not to catch the floral tablecloth with his knee, "let's just call it the mystery meat. We really don't want to find out that it's horse or dog. I had horse once, by accident, in Italy. That's what you get for not knowing the language."

Lubov goes to the kitchen and returns with a tray of more food, tea and cookies, a hunk of cheese, a bottle of vodka, tea cups, and glasses. She pulls an additional chair up to the table and seats herself, as was her habit on Diane's last visit. There is no place for excessive formality here above the Arctic Circle. Here you are either friend or foe, and if you are friends, you stick together to help each other out in whatever way is necessary. Perhaps this is the uncomplicated reason why people choose to live here, or choose not to leave.

They are back in their "apartment" by 7:30 p.m., and at 8:00 Diane retires to let Matt and Bronwyn talk without feeling watched. Their bonding matters to her unexpectedly, as if some new calling has been opened up in her, tasking her with making sure these two young people do not let this opportunity pass, this chance at happiness that she herself has had with Joe. Perhaps it took coming to the Arctic to see this as her job, here where everything is pared down to bare essentials, food, warmth, sex and human companionship.

She dozes and wakes, worrying about her meeting with Retivov. An internet photograph of him swells in her vision, his broad face with mouth pinched to a short horizontal dash, an event horizon sucking everything into the black hole beyond. After years of working as a geologist for Rosneft, a state-owned oil giant, he was appointed to the directorship here, and he relocated from Moscow to Tiksi. Why would they appoint such a man, with ties to oil so out of sync with the weather station's mission? Why would he accept? Back in the States, when the data problem came to light in June, she assumed, as did her colleagues, that the problem was a mere technical glitch. But after a number of people made unsuccessful efforts to communicate with Retivov, Diane began to understand the problem might be more complicated.

Matt and Bronwyn's conversation makes for a soothing susurrus that lulls her to sleep, but when she rises to pee sometime in the night and passes through the living room to the bathroom, she is disappointed to see, on the fold-out couch, a single dark, bushy-haired head, emerging from under the heavy quilt.

Matt awakens to the sound of someone moving, it's unclear who. It is 7:30 a.m. and still dark out, not the loose gray-black of pre-dawn, but a glossy solid dark that seems entrenched. If it is supposed to be light by 8:00, as Diane has said, the sun better get busy soon.

His task for the day is clear—while Diane and Bronwyn visit the weather station, he must find a warm coat. Without a serious coat he won't be able to accompany Bronwyn tomorrow on her mission out to the tundra. Lubov has promised to help him out. He can't believe his luggage was lost on the final flight from Yakutsk to Tiksi. Maybe the bag never got on the plane in the first place—he's fairly certain someone stole it. All that new equipment was worth a lot, not just the Himalayan parka, but the wool pants and long underwear and socks and boots and space blankets and camp stove. When he lodged a complaint at the Tiksi airport everyone shrugged, blank-faced.

Bronwyn's door opens, and she makes her way to the bathroom, tiptoeing past the foldout couch without glancing down at him, her sable coat draping her shoulders like the cape of a reigning monarch. He doesn't move, feigns sleep. Minutes later Diane awakens him.

He hangs outside with Bronwyn and Diane while they wait for their cab. It is overcast and two degrees Fahrenheit. A light wind stirs the gelid air, dispersing it everywhere. Inescapable. Below a certain temperature does a human cease to feel gradations of cold? He hops up and down, listening to Diane and Bronwyn's playful banter.

A twinge of envy comes over him as he watches them drive off in the cab. He has never had anyone invest in him as Diane has invested in Bronwyn. Like a parent's investment, but possibly better, not clogged with the baggage of history and shared biology, still rife with the possibility they can surprise one another. If he were to accompany them today he would only be extraneous, trailing behind them and making wisecracks and yearning to be alone with Bronwyn, or the available version of her. He goes back inside to find Lubov.

53

Diane chats with the cabbie. Until this trip Bronwyn had no idea Diane was such a linguist. It has come to light that she speaks French, Italian, Spanish, and German, and even some limited Chinese. Who knew! She's obviously not entirely fluent in Russian, but she does a credible job of speaking with drivers and waiters, and with Lubov. What she lacks in vocabulary she fills in with gesture and facial expressions and, like Matt, she's uninhibited. As long as Bronwyn has known her, Diane has emphasized that scientists must also be good communicators. If they can't convey their ideas to the general public, much is likely to get lost. In this regard Bronwyn understands herself to be sadly lacking.

They've left behind the cluster of buildings that define the most inhabited part of town, and now they travel on a gravel road across the tundra where the stamp of humanity is less evident. A few small deserted structures made of concrete. A military tank from decades ago, hammer and sickle inscribed on its side. Blackened car parts and discarded wheels of a broken bicycle. Signs of surrender. Patchy snow dots certain areas, in others there is only dead grass and peat. She's impatient to get outside and feel this peat underfoot, begin to acquaint herself more intimately with the landscape.

Diane has fallen into silence, no doubt strategizing about the upcoming meeting. She wants Bronwyn to meet Retivov, though Bronwyn isn't sure why. Spending so much time with Diane again has made Bronwyn more acutely aware of their differences, how completely she, Bronwyn, has forsaken the norms of science. Today's expedition is of great importance to Diane and she wants Bronwyn to care as much as she does, and

Bronwyn has pretended to be interested, but she isn't really, not in the passionate way she might have been in the past. She remembers seeing data on her computer—numbers, tables, graphs—and a moment would arrive after she'd been studying them for a while, when clarity would suffuse her, meaning emerging in a sudden, almost magical, way. It was a wonderful rush, removing her from the ordinary hum-drum of daily living. But numerical calculations—the very ones Diane prizes—are useless to Bronwyn now. She depends on reports from her body, received through open pores, retinas, ears, and nostrils. A wave of defiance comes over her—she must assert the thing she's become.

The weather station is a low, white, rectangular building, reminiscent of a manufactured home, and set in a place as "nowhere" as any she's seen. "What does it say?" she asks of the sign on the front door lettered in red Russian letters.

Diane shrugs. "Beyond me."

The large room they step into is empty. The lights are on and there is the hum of human presence, but no sound. Diane is puzzled. On the last visit the place was a hub of activity with visiting scientists and reporters coming and going from all over the world, and there was a regular staff of at least ten. It's one of three Arctic monitoring stations that gather essential surface data and report to the world. Her own research team's projects on clouds and the permafrost are only a small part of all the scientific investigations that rely on this place. Others are doing black carbon sampling, aerosol sampling, ozone measurements. There are probably twenty separate projects, many international collaborations, that depend on the data gathered here.

"Hello? Anyone here?" Diane calls out. "That's odd. He was expecting us at ten and it's already ten-fifteen."

She ventures around the corner and finds two women sitting at computers wearing headsets and white masks over their noses and mouths. They look up, eyes above the masks bloodshot and wary. The closest of the two makes a shoving motion, *back off*. Diane retreats a few steps.

"We're here to see Dmitry Retivov."

The woman blinks, says nothing, continues the shoving motion. She wears a fleece with high white pile that makes her look like a sheep. Does she not speak English? On Diane's last visit everyone at the station was fluent in English.

"Is he here?" Diane persists, speaking Russian now. "He was expecting us around ten. I'm Diane Fenwick from the U.S.—MIT—and I'm here with my research associate."

The woman rises and retreats hurriedly down the hallway, entering one of the offices at the end. Something is clearly wrong. The woman returns with a man trailing her. She resumes her seat, nodding at Diane with lowered eyes. The man is gaunt and bespectacled, his back sporting the widow's hump of an academic.

"A terrible situation," he says. "You're Dr. Fenwick, am I correct?" His accent is British and he has the infamous disturbing gray teeth of that nation. "I am Tim Thom."

Diane offers her hand in greeting.

"I'm not going to shake your hand. We have an epidemic of the flu going around. Nasty strain. Almost everyone in the office has come down with it."

"How terrible."

"Yes, it has been. Dmitry didn't tell you?"

"No."

"He went home yesterday afternoon. He was so weak he could hardly stand."

Diane closes her eyes. She can't believe her bad luck. "How long does this flu last?"

"Two weeks. Three. Sometimes even more."

"I've come from the United States and we're only here for six days. It's imperative that I speak to someone about the data for the Arctic Cloud Project. Is Hannes Ekstrom here? Or Galina Konstantin?"

Tim Thom looks down the hallway as if a genie might appear to help him out. "I believe they're both out. I've only been here a month. We're pretty bare bones now. They're even thinking of closing down for a couple of weeks until everyone's better. I can't believe Dmitry didn't get in touch to explain."

"Frankly, I can't either." She sighs, but she's furious. She would like so badly to stage a scene, yell at someone for incompetence, but she can see the futility of that. Tim Thom is merely a transient researcher and unlikely to be able to help her much, and these masked staff women might report back to Retivov, blackening her name. For Christ's sake. She looks around for Bronwyn, but Bronwyn has stepped outside.

Tim Thom regards her apologetically, as if he's responsible. His skin is yellowish. He does not look hardy enough to survive in the Arctic.

"Have you been sick yourself?"

"Oh yes, I went through it." He shakes his head. "I'm still recovering."

"Do you have an address for Mr. Retivov? Maybe I could visit him?"

Tim Thom looks dubious. "Honestly, I don't believe you would want to risk a visit. This thing had me in bed for three weeks. Dreadful. I lost fifteen pounds. Very unpleasant." He swallows in such a pointed way that Diane has to work hard not to picture him vomiting.

"Well, give me his phone number and we'll see. His address too, while you're at it."

"Indeed." Tim Thom disappears.

Diane wanders to the window, rage simmering. They knew full well she was coming—why the hell didn't they get in touch with her? Outside Bronwyn is ambling in the peat several hundred feet from the building, immersed in her own world. She is almost comical in her sable coat, like some diminutive, bright-eyed, fictitious animal you might see in a Disney movie. It's good she's stepped out. They can't risk her getting sick; she, their most precious commodity.

54

The snow-crusted peat crunches underfoot as if it's alive, a quiet bleating, reminding her of walking over rocks at the beach, barnacles and mussels being crushed, a kind of murder.

The whir of wind. Not a single tree. White, brown, black. Along the horizon a curdling of gray indecision. Nothing blue except the feeling of blue with each intake of breath—a mentholated cleansing, cold constricting the nose, the trachea, the lungs. Who knew existence held so many new sensations?

She thinks of the Earth's curvature here, so different from New Hampshire's. Her vision splits equally between sky and Earth, soars into the distance, searching for animals she knows are out there, but are beyond her vision's range. Foxes. Wolves. Herds of reindeer. For now, they're concealed, but she can wait. She knows the rewards of patience, knows how the world reveals its wonders if you invest the time to watch, sniff, listen.

Though she walks, she seems to float, overcome with a new lightness, as if her body has lost its density, its molecules separating, about to disperse. She could travel forever over this flat landscape which now seems to beckon.

The top of the world, she tells herself, trying to understand, though *top, bottom, up, down,* are losing their meaning. The universe pays no attention to prepositions.

A patch of bare peat trampolines beneath her. She stops, taps a foot then releases it. The peat springs back, buoyant and spongy. Stepping back to firmer ground she crouches, reaching forward with mittened hand, pressing again. Again the surface ripples under her touch. A burgeoning *bulgunyakh*, she supposes, about to bulge into a larger mound, eventually to explode. How much pressure from beneath can this peat withstand? How long will it take for this particular one to build to the point of explosion? This poor land—does it feel as wounded as she feels it to be?

Bringing her nose down low to graze the peat she sniffs for methane. Nothing. Tendrils of moss—brown and green, black and yellow, tickling her cheeks—tangle into paisley filigrees. Beneath her sable coat she is her anemone-self again, opening, stretching, exposing the tentacles of all her surfaces to receive news.

55

Matt tugs the ear flaps of his hat lower and tries to keep pace with Lubov who, for all her excessive weight, is an impressively swift walker. It is only two degrees and there's a high cloud cover—are those the clouds that scatter the heat or reradiate it? How can you tell? Despite the cold, Matt appreciates the clarity of the air, its strange pinkish glow—it is quite possible he has never breathed such clean air in his entire life. A light clanging at the harbor draws his attention, but that will have to wait. Lubov turns in the other direction. He isn't sure where she's taking him to find the promised coat. He enjoys her company and they communicate like a pair of clowns, but all their miming and mugging has not been useful in clarifying exactly what she has in mind.

In a vacant lot two young boys, not older than five and unsupervised, pile rocks into a tumbling stack, shrieking as they collapse. A few feral dogs poke around a pile of trash. A young girl, not more than ten, emerges from a building and speeds toward Lubov, grabbing the older woman around the waist as if scaling a cliff. The two laugh, spouting Russian greetings. Has Lubov arranged this meeting? Matt can't be sure. The girl is a thin thread of happy energy, but she's as underdressed as Matt is. Hair, long and ratty, a stunning honey color, flies from the edges of her fur cap. Her eyes, he notices with surprise, are the same green as Bronwyn's, and the longer he looks the more he feels he's seeing a ghostly younger version of Bronwyn.

Lubov introduces them. Vera is the girl's name.

"You want coat?" Vera says, in heavily accented English.

"You speak English?" Matt says, stupidly delighted.

"Oh yes, I learn in school. Lubov says you want coat. I find you coat?"

"Yes. Thank you so much," Matt says, playing along, wondering what kind of coat this child can get him. She takes off down the street; he and Lubov follow.

The girl enters a small café with fogged windows and a handful of diners, all men. She proceeds to the back, oblivious to the men's stares. A dark stairway leads them to a second-floor apartment where they knock for a long time before anyone answers. Finally, an elderly woman, dressed in black, comes to the door. Her face is dusky, every inch drawn with wrinkles so fine they look like the work of a master calligrapher. She retreats slowly from the door with the aid of a cane and lets them in.

Daylight filters softly through the fogged windows and passes through several glass vases on the window sill, making prisms that dance lightly across all the surfaces. Bold primary colors issue from wall hangings, rugs, pillows, throws. It is cozy here and blessedly warm. Matt removes his jacket and mittens and hat. A muffled raucousness trundles up from the café below.

They sit at the table and the woman makes them tea, heating the water in an electric kettle, moving slowly but confidently around the kitchen which occupies a corner of the living room. The woman asks a few questions and Lubov and Vera trade off speaking. Matt drinks his tea and tries to enjoy his peripheral, invisible status, hoping they haven't forgotten his need for a coat.

"She has coat for you," Vera says suddenly.

"Great!" says Matt. "I'm so happy. Will you tell her thank you very much?"

Vera translates and the old woman smiles and nods. But where is this coat? Is it an excuse for a visit rather than a real end in itself? Matt is beginning to have a new understanding of Chekhov's plays—people sitting around, talking and talking, but never actually getting to Moscow. He waits, sips his tea, swaddling the cup with both hands and savoring its heat, thinking of Bronwyn and Diane and wondering how their day is going.

The old woman, whose name he has not received, tells a long story, and Lubov and Vera pay somber attention. Vera appears slightly frightened. When the story is done silence reigns. The old woman sighs and Lubov pats her hand.

"What did she say?" Matt asks Vera.

"Her husband die. He freeze."

"He froze to death?"

Vera nods. "His car break."

Great, thinks Matt, *just what I need to hear now*. The woman rises from the table and leaves the room.

"She get coat," Vera says, hopping up. "I help."

Back they come, Vera and the old woman, Vera lugging an unwieldy slab of dark brown fur, what looks to Matt more like a dead animal than a coat, almost too heavy for Vera to carry. Vera lays the thing on Matt's lap, and he stands and shakes it out, looking for an entrance. This is an exotic item, an old and well-used coat, worthy of museum display for its ancientness. He can't tell what animal it comes from, but it smells strongly of something primitive. Fermentation and body odor, perhaps lingering smells from the animal itself. Could a person get used to a coat that smells like this? Lubov, Vera, and the old woman watch him.

"You wear," Vera commands proudly.

He finds a hole and jabs his arm into it, slouching the coat over his back, then locating the other armhole. The coat is massive, much too large for him. Its fur is rough and slightly oily. It comes to his ankles, its collar rising over the back of his skull. He looks for a way to fasten the front and finds twine loops that hitch over pieces of bone. With each movement the coat off-gasses unsavory smells. He might almost be wearing chainmail for the weight of the thing. Surely a coat this heavy could give you back problems over time. But it's undeniably warm—he is already breaking a sweat. The old woman beams at him and he smiles back. Stretching his arms he spins.

"Ask her what animal this is," he tells Vera.

Vera translates and the answer comes back. Bear. Vera adds, unsolicited, "Her husband coat."

Matt does not need to ask if the husband died in this coat. He does not want to know. He removes it and lays it on his chair. "Ask her how much money I owe?"

Vera translates.

"No money. She want you wear it. She want you be happy. Like her husband be happy."

"Yes," Matt says. "I'm very happy."

56

Bronwyn has never seen Diane so outraged. In the cab on the way back to Lubov's she swears at Retivov for several minutes, without regard for what the driver might be thinking, or Bronwyn herself. "He's a monster!" she rages. "He didn't even have the courtesy—the human *decency*—to let me know about this epidemic. A quick email would have done it, for god's sake."

Bronwyn stares out the cab's side window, cleaving to silence, not wanting to speak, incapable of speaking. The tundra's lure is siren-like. Now their colloquy has begun, she cannot easily wrest her attention away. Diane's rage may be justified, but to Bronwyn it is irrelevant.

Matt is back at the apartment with his new coat, a behemoth bearskin, rancid and reeking. He puts it on for them to admire and narrates his tale of its acquisition, but Diane, unmoved by the story of a man freezing in the coat, cuts him off. Sitting at the table, she slaps down her palm, demanding Bronwyn sit too.

"We have to talk. Listen, I can't let you two go out to the tundra tomorrow. Any intervention is premature under the circumstances. We have to resolve the data problem first. I'm going to cancel the helicopter. We'll book it later. We still have some time."

Bronwyn says nothing, watches Matt removing his coat lovingly and laying it on the couch.

"Well? Bronwyn? Say something. Don't go all zombie on me."

Bronwyn angles her head to Diane, still unable to fasten herself in this moment and participate in an urgency and rage which is not hers.

"What were you doing out there while I was in the station?"

"Walking around. Getting a sense of things."

"Honestly, Bronwyn. I see your attitude and I don't like it. This gift of yours doesn't invalidate the science. You should be making use of all we've got. Your intuition should be working *in conjunction* with the data, not *against it.* Synthesize *everything.* If you don't, are you any better than some one-track-mind religious fanatic?"

Bronwyn blinks, bludgeoned. Her cheeks heat. Diane has never spoken to her so sharply before. A religious fanatic? Diane knows her better than that. There's no possible retort.

"Well," Diane says, rising from the table. "I'm going to make some calls, perhaps take a nap so I can see things freshly." She gathers her laptop. "I thought we were in this together, but apparently—" She heads to her bedroom, arm arcing over her head.

Matt stands frozen, gaze downturned as if willing invisibility. Behind the closed door Diane jets back and forth, talks briefly on the phone. The bedsprings snap then quiet descends, but the fumes of her anger ooze past all the barriers, circling Bronwyn as if to curb her. The steam heat rattles on though it is already cranked too high.

"I have to get out of here," Bronwyn whispers.

Matt nods. "Can I come?"

She nods and they bundle up in their furs and hats, faces muzzled by scarves as if they're bandits. Matt's coat lends him the resilience and might of a bear. They push out of the building into the town's silence, aware of leaving Diane behind. Not a betrayal, but almost. Her words buzz in Bronwyn's head, and her anger stalks behind them like an inescapable chaperone.

It is already sunset and high nacreous clouds striate the sky with threads of pink, orange, green. Its beauty is a sharp contrast to the ugliness of the streets, trash everywhere, food wrappers and slips of paper taking flight on gusts of wind then landing here and there, indiscriminate as gulls. Many of the buildings display fading images of Soviet glory, calling out from the brick like dying prideful pleas, exhaling a desolation that goes well beyond the frigid landscape. This is the home of renegades and loners, misfits and pioneers, people who have deliberately eschewed the comforts and conventions of more temperate climes.

"The harbor?" Matt suggests.

She nods, feeling a wave of appreciation for Matt, who knows little of the day's events, but isn't plugging her with questions. Instinctively, both their bodies angle north. They stay close to one another for ballast in the cold and fading light, their pelts grazing, sable and bear. She imagines them becoming animals, perusing this landscape, vigilant to all evidence of possible food and shelter.

The paved road becomes gravel. The wind subsides. The still air listens, waits. She takes up the waiting and it permeates her being.

They arrive at the water, the Port of Tiksi, the Laptev Sea. This was once an active harbor for fishing vessels and for Alaskan goods. Now it is a ship's cemetery for fleets that were brought up decades ago from Murmansk and Vladivostok. These boats have idled here for years; once majestic, they're now ravaged by weather and time, their hulls sagging, their masts split and rotting, their rigging whipped to fraying wisps. The pearlescence of the setting sun makes these abandoned ships even more poignant. A person with a particular vision might turn them into art, but they are long past reclamation as sea-worthy vessels. Ice floes the size of dinner plates stretch across the harbor, glowing pink, clattering against each other. The sea beneath them is not deep, she knows, but it appears darkly inscrutable. She feels the shadowy presence of the Soviet soldiers who were once stationed here, bored, stuck, drunk, looking for fun or distraction, staring out into near darkness as she and Matt are now. It wasn't so long ago, not in geological time.

Matt's respectful silence cloaks her, and she thinks of their time together in New Hampshire making love by the Squamscott River. The sun sets fast, taking every vestige of light as it goes, like a woman gathering harvested fruit in her full skirt. The safety of darkness gives rise to talk.

"I hope you didn't take her personally," Matt says. "I'm sure she didn't mean it."

How could it not feel personal? she wonders.

"How bad is the data situation?" he asks.

"She gets some data from other locations too. Satellite data and such. So I don't exactly know."

"If she doesn't get this data will her project fail?"

"She'll find a way to make things work. She always does. Failure isn't a word in her vocabulary."

"I guess there's no way to help her?"

The question is an obvious one, but Bronwyn is stunned to hear it. Why hasn't she thought to ask the same herself? Diane Fenwick has always been to Bronwyn like a human obelisk, solid and upright and self-supporting. Not someone in need of help. Bronwyn has always been the recipient of Diane's help, not the giver of help herself. But Bronwyn knows things weren't always easy for Diane. She was the youngest child in a rowdy family and different from her siblings, just like Matt. She had to fight to make herself into the esteemed Dr. Fenwick she is today. So much flux one fails to see—things on their way to becoming something else. Clouds moving, permafrost melting, a human body losing sweat. Stasis is an illusion, flux and entropy the rule.

The feeling she had outside the weather station descends again, the feeling of floating, her molecules separating, no longer exclusively hers, the call possessing her once more, each time more insistent. In planning this trip she repeatedly told Diane six days was not nearly enough time for her to understand a new landscape, but Diane had constraints that did not allow for more time away. What a surprise that the landscape has begun to communicate so quickly.

Her attention, so often focused upwards on sky and clouds, turns down to the Earth, in this liminal zone between land and sea. She pictures the harbor's manmade fixtures being stripped away, the rotting wharf, the chipped concrete pylons. She descends past layers of peat and soil, through rock—igneous, sedimentary, metamorphic—until she arrives, miles below, at the Earth's core where she resides for a while amidst fire and heat.

She reels, and Matt hooks her arm, luring her back to the moment.

"Do you think you can do something?" he says. "Change something with the methane and all?"

She hesitates, reclaiming her vocal apparatus, thoughts still elsewhere. "You're beginning to sound like Diane."

"I'm just curious."

"I don't know for sure. I'll see when we go out tomorrow."

"But I thought Diane doesn't want us to go out yet."

She turns to him, sees only his brooding, dolorous eyes above the scarf. He trusts Diane, believes in her prevailing wisdom as Bronwyn once did. She can't blame him for that—she knows how it feels.

Something moves out on the water. It could be a boat, a bird, a whale. Her vision, she thinks, is her least reliable sense. She would like to have the vision of a bird of prey, or the acute sense of smell of a bear or a shark.

"I'm scared for you," he says.

"Why?"

He pauses and when he speaks his voice wavers up and down, traveling a sine curve of assertion and hesitancy. "I just am."

By mutual accord they begin to move again, strolling back up the gravel road to the pavement, trailed by the ghosts of their different worries, past buildings whose lights have come on, reminding the world there are people inside, still alive.

57

Diane has withdrawn under the voluminous down quilt fully clothed, trying to escape the apparitions that have arrived with the day's dimming. The apartment's close air is much too hot and humid and a profuse tropical sweat has erupted on her scalp, armpits, and groin. There isn't a chance she can nap, not after such a horrendous day. The plan has always been to get the data released and then to send Bronwyn on her mission. But now, with the data situation uncertain, everything is open to question. They have only five more days here, not enough to get everything done, certainly nowhere near the time Bronwyn said she hoped to have to ready herself for an intervention. If Bronwyn were to be able to freeze the permafrost—a big *if* at this point—then future data would reflect the change without "before" data to indicate how bad things had gotten. Then what? People would assume the earth is mending itself. Then the urgency to make changes would fade, and burning fossil fuels would cease to be suspect, and people all over the world would continue to extract and consume and burn with abandon, and climate change deniers would lash out with impunity: *See, nothing's wrong. You scientists are all alarmists.* How she wishes Joe were here to use as a sounding board—they are so accustomed to solving problems together. She forces herself from under the covers, missing Joe intensely. A visit to Retivov can't wait.

Out in the living room she discovers Bronwyn and Matt have gone, taking their fur coats with them. No note. She stands in the emptiness not sure what to think. Of course they need to go off on their own— she is all about encouraging their bonding—but at this moment their absence feels like a desertion. She wishes they'd left a note.

She slogs through the dark streets. Cold fog has begun to roll in from the harbor in long plumes that reach through the streets and alleys and climb spectrally over the rooftops. Dmitry Retivov lives in one of the block apartment buildings that reminds her of a smaller version of Co-op City, which she sees so frequently on trains to New York.

The building's lobby has an untended reception desk and a few folding chairs; its walls are a dreary yellow. The quaking elevator transports her slowly to the seventh floor where she steps out into a bleak hallway, its walls whispering of fear, echoes of the totalitarian past. She knocks on Retivov's door and waits. This building, too, is overheated. She unzips her coat, loosens her scarf, removes her hat, and fluffs her hair, suddenly aware of wanting to create an unimpeachable professional impression.

She knocks again. Still nothing. She will not knock a third time, she decides. She can't stand the idea of dragging him out of bed, something he might hold against her for years to come. A terrible thought accosts her—he could be dead in there. It's not extremely unusual for people to die of the flu. As she turns over this dreadful thought, she hears footsteps. The door opens. A middle-aged woman with the affronted eyes of a raccoon opens the door and greets her in Russian.

"Good evening."

Diane introduces herself and asks to see Dmitry. He's sick, he cannot be seen, the woman tells her. Diane asks if she speaks English.

"A little," says the woman.

"You're Mr. Retivov's wife?"

The woman doesn't answer, as if to disclose her marital status would be too intimate a revelation. Diane explains that she has traveled from the U.S. to work something out, that she is only here for a few days, that she would like to see Mr. Retivov just briefly, it is of utmost importance. The woman impales Diane with a stare, before disappearing wordlessly, leaving the door open so Diane can see through the modest living room to a window whose curtains are drawn. It is unclear whether she should step inside or not. She hears a blather of Russian coming from a back room. She wonders where Bronwyn has gone, wishes things were not so strained between them, just when she could use a companion.

The woman returns and nods in such a curt way that Diane understands she's being allowed in, but isn't welcome. She'll make it quick. She only needs to communicate her commitment to resolving the problem as soon as possible. She hopes to be able to detect if the data roadblock is intentional or not.

The apartment smells of antiseptic and Clorox, with undercurrents of stewed meat and sauerkraut. The woman opens the door to a dim bedroom. The curtains here are drawn too. Dmitry lies on his back, slightly propped up by pillows, but still lying more than sitting. As soon as she sees him she wishes she hadn't come. He looks exactly as he looked on the internet, broad-faced and thin-lipped, but his eyes are more listless, his body limp, his chin stippled with the ragged start of a gray beard. She considers bolting, but indecision rivets her in place. She will state her case, then leave.

"I'm Diane Fenwick from MIT, here on behalf of the Arctic Cloud Project. I've emailed you—"

"Make it quick," he says.

"It's about the data sets. We haven't gotten them for a number of months now and they're crucial. I came to find out what the problem—"

"Look at me," he says, his voice a low whir, stripped of affect. "You bother a sick man with this?"

"Yes, I'm sorry you're feeling so badly. I know now isn't the time to resolve this fully, but when you're better I'd like to talk. This is why I came all this way, to see you and work this out. I'm only here for six days, so perhaps . . ."

He coughs extravagantly, as if to underscore the gravity of his illness. When he stops he sits up straighter. "You stop at nothing, do you? You come to a sick man's house. At night. Anything for publication, no? Pure ambition. No humanity. You are a missile."

He shakes his head and closes his eyes, and her insides curdle. A missile? The word itself, delivered with so much venom, is aggressive and penetrating. This is almost worse than finding him dead, finding him so weak and still so capable of rage. Surely this rage predates her arrival today and has to do with more than she?

"Thank you, Mr. Retivov, Dr. Retivov. I'll go. We'll talk when you're feeling better."

She turns and finds herself face to face with the glaring wife. Diane says nothing, ducks around her, and walks as speedily as she can to the front door. It is bolted shut and takes her a moment of fiddling to open.

She stands in the caterwauling elevator aghast, appalled at her own misjudgment. She should never have visited him, especially so late in the day—what possessed her? Not only has she ruined her reputation with him and her ability to negotiate further, she has also jeopardized her own health. She hopes her robust immune system can handle the assault. Will her colleagues on the project forgive her? She was selected to come here because she was deemed the best negotiator, blunt but gracious. But gracious she has not been.

You are a missile. Is she? As a woman in science she has always had to be bold, and she's lucky to have been born bold. She's always felt one of her greatest attributes is knowing where to draw the line between assertive and obnoxious. Now, she wonders.

She emerges from the elevator to the lobby and realizes she has misplaced her hat and gloves. They must have fallen from her grasp in her haste to escape. She can't stand going up there again, but it would be foolish to go outside with bare head and hands.

She steps back into the punishing elevator. Up to the seventh floor. Down the Kafkaesque hallway. There, outside the door to the Retivov apartment, lie her mittens and hat.

58

Lubov delivers a tray of food to the room and, though they did not expect this, the bowls of hot stew and bread and cheese, hot tea and a bottle of vodka are exactly what they need. Lubov deposits the tray on the table, lays out bowls and plates and utensils for three, and gestures around the apartment. "Diane?"

Matt and Bronwyn shrug. Diane has disappeared. "Gone," Matt says. "We don't know." He shrugs more theatrically. Lubov lingers for a few more minutes, chatting in unintelligible Russian, exclaiming again over Matt's coat, then she leaves them alone to eat.

Bronwyn, ravenous, spoons her stew quickly, as if to fortify herself for a long hibernation, her limbs coming alive with metabolizing stew and bread and cheese, even as she begins to crave sleep. They have off-loaded their coats and sweaters and sit side-by-side at the table, bare-armed, their bodies exchanging heat. She knows Matt wishes she would speak more, but he isn't pressing her to do so. She remembers how worked together at the second fire in LA, renting the ATV and traveling into the hills, his first experience watching her work. She could have done it without him, but she liked having him there. How excited he was, how amazed. He's a born collaborator, not a man who insists on his own will. Here on the tundra will it work the same way? What a strange position he's in, plunked squarely between her and Diane. She wishes she could explain herself to him more fully, this feeling of imminence that has overcome her of late, the sense of her atoms slowly reassembling themselves, on the verge of joining other entities, preparing her to do the work. It is too hard to put into words without sounding like a fool. She would if she could.

He lays down his spoon and finds her idle hand and squeezes it, as if he's heard her thoughts. "Tomorrow?" he says.

This is the question that has been hanging before them since they returned from the weather station. She is about to say something when they hear footsteps on the stairs. Seconds later Diane bursts in, huffing, stony-faced. "A disaster!" she says, disappearing into the bedroom without stopping.

They wait. Nothing.

"There's food out here," Matt calls. "Lubov brought us food."

Tension pops through the room like static. It rips Bronwyn's concentration. She retreats to the bedroom, closes the door, hoping Matt will understand. How foolish to think she can extricate herself from Diane so easily. She is too entangled. Diane has come out to the living room and is clearly furious, a fury erected on top of the morning's fury, compounded and elaborated into a veritable mountain of madness. Bronwyn would like to block her ears but, even when she crawls into bed and pulls the quilt over her head, she hears Diane's penetrating voice. She is talking about Retivov, how she saw him and he stonewalled her. So much worse than she expected. Now, Diane says, they need to figure out what to do next. "I can't let you two go out under these circumstances. I've canceled the helicopter. We have to be strategic. You agree with me, Matt, don't you? If we allow her to do an intervention now we won't have any proof . . ."

Bronwyn sails through the bedroom door, inflamed, made large with indignation. She can't let Diane solicit Matt as her ally—what a low thing to do. She charges up to the table where Matt sits, holding an inert piece of bread, and positions herself opposite Diane. Their eyes joust, their egos are butting bulls. This is a moment Bronwyn never imagined would come to pass. No, maybe more recently she did begin to imagine it, but she has done everything she could to avoid it, fearing Diane's force.

"You don't really believe I can do what I say I can, do you?"

"Of course I do. I wouldn't have brought you all this way if I didn't believe in you."

"But you're not a hundred percent sure. You still want this fucking data as proof."

"Not for me, for the scientific community. For the world. So I can show people exactly what you're capable of. You're one in a million, Bronwyn. We can't let your talent go to waste."

"They don't need to know whatever I do was done by me. Why can't it stay under the radar? I'm not out for glory. It's your style to go public, not mine. I'm not you, and I don't belong to you—I'm not—I'm . . ."

She hears herself yelling and stops, short of breath, reaching for more rational words. Diane is shaking her head dismissively, as if Bronwyn is an undergraduate imbecile again, a motherless girl from working class New Jersey never exposed to anything smart. Diane is still a superior force, still capable of out-arguing, outsmarting, outstaring Bronwyn, reducing her to timidity and ignorance. Bronwyn's head throbs. The ugly sound of her own voice, shouting in such desperation, still reverberates in her head. She has never raised her voice at Diane before, and now her voice is used up, her will to confront exhausted. How can her will be such a powerful force in the natural world, but be so negligible in influencing people. She turns away, shrinking, avoiding Matt's gaze, and returns to the bedroom. She slides under the covers again, closing eyes and ears, shoving the world away, trying to take hold of the other Bronwyn, the one who knows her own strength.

She is wide awake before dawn. She slides delicately out of bed, careful not to awaken Matt. Dressing quickly, she scrawls a note. *Out for a walk. B.*

She navigates her way to the harbor mostly by instinct, assisted by only a few streetlights, and she stands where she and Matt stood the previous evening. Tiny waves lap the gravel beach. A gull skims past, strangely silent, and disappears into the darkness—an act of faith. Or corporeal intelligence.

Something moves across the water, more felt than seen. Singing accompanies the movement, a tuneless soprano. A light comes into view, that gradually reveals itself as a headlamp. Emerging from the darkness is a girl, standing upright on a small wooden raft, paddling like a gondolier. She makes a graceful, nimble landing, and hops onto the gravel beach. Her raft is a few planks nailed together into a flat pallet, more found than made.

"Hey," says Bronwyn as the girl approaches her. She wears knee-high yellow rubber boots, a puffy pale blue jacket, a purple wool hat with ear flaps. She cannot be more than nine or ten, too young to be alone on the water in the dark and cold. And too lightly dressed. Her cheeks are flushed and a tangle of wheat-colored hair splays from the under her cap. Toting her paddle and humming, she makes her way up the beach to Bronwyn.

"You speak English?" she says.

"Yes. How did you know?"

"I see you yesterday. American?"

"Yes."

"Hollywood?"

"No."

"New York?"

"No."

"You see cowboys?"

Bronwyn laughs. What a forward little girl. "Not too many cowboys. You speak English well."

"We learn in school. You have childrens?"

"No."

"You have husband?"

"No."

"What do you have?"

Bronwyn laughs again. *What do I have?* she wonders. *Anger,* she thinks, *maybe some hope.* The girl reaches into her pocket and pulls out two wrapped candies that look as if they might have been in her pocket for a long time. She takes off a mitten and her tiny red fingers unwrap the cellophane. She pops one in her mouth and hands the other to Bronwyn who lays it hesitantly on her tongue. A strong lemon flavor, both sour and sweet. They suck in silence, the girl assessing Bronwyn.

"Why are you out here in the dark?" Bronwyn says. "It's so early."

"In dark I am king of town. All mine." She looks around. "Where your boyfriend? I see you yesterday with boyfriend."

"Oh, he's not my boyfriend. He's just a friend."

The girls laughs. "Itchy lips." She kisses the air and crunches the last of her candy.

"Do you like living here in Tiksi?"

"Oh yes. Tiksi is beautiful world. Most beautiful world." She points to her raft. "I have boat. I have friends. I talk with friends. Tiksi is good home." She pats the top of her hat. "Tiksi is world head. Best place."

Bronwyn nods. The shadowy masts sway in and out of darkness. The cold air releases sudden scents of mingled salt, wet wood, oil. The ice floes clink, chime-like. *Best place. Most beautiful world.* The girl's eyes are a pellucid glass-green. Bronwyn looks into them at herself.

"Oh," says the girl. "I tell you. You must know." She leans into Bronwyn as if to deliver a secret. "Your boyfriend has coat. I help him get coat. When you have evil eye on you, you do like this—take off coat, put other arm first. Okay? You tell boyfriend."

"Okay, I will." What makes the girl say this?

"Bye-bye America lady." She drags her raft higher onto the beach then heads up the gravel road, waving at Bronwyn before being absorbed into the still-dark streets of Tiksi.

Bronwyn finds Lubov in the kitchen, hands plunged in soapy dishwater.

"Taxi?" Bronwyn says. "Airport?"

"Taxi," Lubov echoes. Her attention turns back to the sink, soap bubbles taking flight as she re-submerges her hands. Has she understood?

"Taxi," Bronwyn says more firmly. "Now," elongating the word. She glances to the door, on the lookout for Matt and Diane. "Please," she adds, not wanting to be rude, but aware urgency is making her harsh.

Lubov wipes her hands on her apron and lumbers across the kitchen to a phone on the wall. She makes the call, watching Bronwyn with what feels like suspicion.

59

Matt finds Bronwyn's note on the living room table, saying she's gone out on a walk. He can't believe he didn't notice her leaving, but yesterday was a long, exhausting day, and he slept unusually soundly.

Steam billows from the bathroom's open door where he hears splashing.

"Is that you, Bronwyn?" Diane calls.

"It's me, Matt. Bronwyn went out for a walk."

"Can you come in here, please. I have to talk to you."

Go in? While she's in the tub?

"Come on in. I'm not going to attack you."

He feels strangely prudish. He has never even seen his own mother naked. The silence weighs on him. He clears his throat. "Are you still in there?" he calls.

"No, I'm taking a walk. Where else would I be. Come in already."

He marches in, glancing at her so quickly he sees nothing—nothing describable anyway, beyond a human being in a bathtub. The mirror over the sink is fogged. He wipes a patch clear and looks at himself.

Diane laughs. "You look terrified." She sighs. "I suppose I am scary." She readjusts herself, and he glimpses the top of her salt-and-pepper hair moving in the mirror. He perches on the side of the toilet, staring at the floor.

"Oh, come on, you can look. I don't mind. We're practically family now. Anyway, I'm mostly underwater. I just need to talk and it's awkward shouting through the door."

He lifts his eyes tentatively. She is, as promised, mostly submerged, her legs a shadowy presence under the gray water, a single knee breach-ing the surface. His gaze skims quickly past her breasts which bob like smooth pink, nipple-tipped buoys. He finds her face and raises his eyebrows sheepishly, feeling like a small boy.

"I'm not really that terrifying, am I? Well, the thing is, maybe I am. Dmitry Retivov called me a missile. I'm sure Bronwyn would agree." She shakes her head. "Is that really how I come across?"

"Heck no. I wouldn't say a missile." He laughs and runs his fingers through his hair which hasn't been combed for several days.

"But you'd say something like that, right? A bulldozer? A tank? A truncheon? What word would you use?"

"I only just met you a short time ago."

"I'm sure you have impressions. Go ahead. My feelings aren't easily hurt. Do you think I exploit people?"

"You're honest. You don't pull any punches. Some people don't like that I guess. But I'm not one of them."

"You're such a diplomat. Oh my god, he's a terrible man, Retivov. I don't trust him a bit." She raises herself higher, sloshing water over the tub's edge, exposing her breasts fully, suddenly formidable and rife with purpose. "Okay, I've made up my mind. We're going to the weather station now. I don't want to wait a minute longer." She stands, reaches for a towel.

"What about Bronwyn?"

"We can't wait. She can join us after her walk."

"I won't be much use to you."

"Moral support. Besides, we're in this together." She leans on his shoulder and steps out of the tub.

60

The taxi smells of smoke, but Bronwyn is so relieved to be off without having run into Diane and Matt she doesn't care. The driver speeds along the rutted road through the brightening dawn as if they're fugitives—in fact, she is a fugitive. A layer of new snow came down last night and it has white-washed everything. Tiny silvery ice crystals—diamond dust—glint and slide through the air so haloes spring up around signposts and abandoned shacks. The motion is electrifying, imparting the feeling she's at the center of a shaken snow globe. Tiksi's exotic ephemeral beauty has tiptoed to the surface. She holds her breath to prolong the sight, grasp it, remember. Best place. Most beautiful world.

At the airport she thrusts bills at the cabbie and ignores his reproachful grunts. The terminal is tiny, as is the helicopter outfit, and she's relieved to find that the woman behind the desk speaks English. Yes, they can take Bronwyn out, though she'll have to wait for the party that precedes her. Bronwyn takes a seat feeling accomplished, almost elated.

The terminal is mostly deserted, but for three men sitting opposite her, all wearing heavy olive green jackets and pants that make them look vaguely like members of the U.S. Army. They're speaking Russian and wearing fur-lined caps and sipping from flasks. Each has a duffel bag. Hunters, she thinks. She knows the helicopter service routinely transports people to the tundra to shoot wolves, bear, caribou.

One of the men calls out to her.

"I don't speak Russian," she calls back.

They laugh and make what she is quite sure are lewd comments. She looks away.

"Good. Men," shouts the same man, more loudly. "We—good—men."

She nods. They break out food and one of them holds up what looks to be some kind of meat pie, offering it to her. She demurs. "But thanks." Her suspicion of them ebbs, but there is no reason to get too chummy either.

After eating the men doze. In Bronwyn's current hopped-up state sleep is unimaginable. There is nothing to do but wait, trust. She closes her eyes and sees the girl's quizzical face, her green eyes and cat-like body. A bold girl. Transfixing. Bronwyn wonders if you always recognize the evil eye when you see it. She has never believed in superstitions, but sometimes she has honored them, just in case.

A racket jolts her, makes her realize she was falling asleep. A helicopter descends on the other side of the glass not far from where they sit. The men cheer, gather their things. Bronwyn stands to watch with them as the helicopter sways to a landing with the dubious grace of a portly man.

61

The weather station evinces a stoic silence. Diane pauses on the front step and inhales deeply of the brisk air to fortify herself. If she is a missile, so be it, she will behave like one.

"Go for it," Matt says. Hunkered in the rancid bear coat that expands his mass by a factor of at least three, he smiles at her, and she forces a cheerful smile back.

Inside Tim Thom is talking to one of the masked administrators. He turns his attention to them and strides over to greet them. "Dr. Fenwick, what a surprise." His mien is more forceful than it was yesterday, less obsequious. Diane makes the introductions.

"Matt is helping me out in various ways."

"You have a slew of helpers?" Thom observes.

Diane laughs. "I try."

"I didn't expect you'd be back," Thom says."At least not so soon. I see our illness hasn't deterred you."

What is it about the English that makes them seem so upright, so correct—it must be more than the accent, she thinks. "I spoke to Retivov," she says. "And he told me to come out here and have a look at the data myself."

Thom squints. "He said that?"

She elongates herself, making a rocket of her spine. "Yes." She doesn't retract her gaze.

"Really?" Pain clouds Thom's face. Physical or social discomfort, she can't tell. Matt is nodding, she's not sure why.

"Yes, really. He expects to be bedridden for quite a while, so it seemed to be the only solution given our limited time here."

Thom peers back at the masked woman who has not stopped staring at them since they walked in. The sight of her irritates Diane, and she wonders if this woman wields any power. She can't rule that out.

Thom sighs. "Alright then." He sighs again. "Come."

They follow him down a long corridor past a series of nondescript offices equipped with desks and computers, but nothing else. There isn't a soul in sight. "You're the only one here?" Diane asks.

"Me and the woman at the front desk, Svetlana."

"They're all sick?"

"Sadly, yes. It really isn't wise for you two to be here."

She looks at Matt. She shouldn't subject him to this. "If you'd rather not do this you can step outside and wait for me. You probably should. Or you could taxi back to Lubov's."

"Of course not." He pats his coat. "I'm tough."

She touches his arm and squeezes it. What a mensch.

At the end of the hall they enter a room with a large desk in one quadrant and, flanking two walls, six computers with large monitors. A few framed photos of children stand on the desk, but otherwise the office is devoid of personal effects.

"Retivov's office," Thom says. "Have at it."

He retreats back in the direction they came from, his footsteps echoing officiously throughout the building. He stops abruptly, then no other sound. She imagines him listening, and would like to close the door, but that would seem incriminating. She avoids looking at Matt who awaits her next move.

How can it be that she is here, on the verge of doing the very kind of thing that has always repulsed her in others? Well, she isn't altering data, but she is trespassing to get it. Though is it really trespassing if it is rightfully hers?

The computers are all off. Are they all connected to the same server? She assumes so, but maybe not. The first step is to turn them on. She presses the power button on one of the computers. Matt is poised over another.

"Shall I?" he says.

She nods, dousing another pang of guilt about bringing him here, making him her accomplice, not to mention exposing him to a serious flu.

Thom's footsteps mark the length of the hall again, and he enters an office across from them.

All the computers are on now, beeping and burping and whirring as they boot up. Diane takes a seat in front of one of them and Matt sits beside her. Would Joe approve of what she's doing? Maybe, maybe not. Certainly she could be censured professionally for this. Worse, she could be incarcerated, right here in Russia.

For now, she mustn't think of these things. She has come this far. The data has real merit and it's critical the world sees it. She may be being grandiose about its importance, but she doesn't think so. It shouldn't take too long for publication, and once the study results are published it will put the nail in the coffin of the lame, unsubstantiated arguments of the climate change deniers. And after that, there is Bronwyn.

The computers, done booting, are quiet now. She stares at a screen of Russian icons. She speaks Russian passably, but reading it is another matter entirely. This could be a long session of trial and error.

At the front of the building the phone rings, filling the empty hallways and offices with its lonely, loon-like sound. Svetlana answers in Russian and transfers the call to Thom, who picks up across the hall. Russian quickly cedes to English. What a jumbled composite communication is practiced here, humans making the best of things, using whatever words are within closest reach.

"The American woman?" Thom says. ". . . You don't . . . She isn't . . ."

Matt and Diane both freeze. Thom falls silent, but he hasn't hung up.

"Certainly . . . Certainly . . ."

Retivov has read her mind.

"No, I haven't seen her today . . . Yes, of course I'll let you know . . . Alrighty. I hope you feel better soon."

The receiver thunks back to its cradle and before Matt and Diane have even begun to move, Tim Thom is standing in the doorway, sentry-like, assessing them with a ghostly smile.

62

The clerk asks Bronwyn if she would like to go out with the hunters. It would be faster that way, she explains. Bronwyn wouldn't have to wait for the helicopter to return. Yes, Bronwyn agrees, that would be fine.

She and the hunters are ushered outside, and they stand in the helicopter's windy fracas. It is an ancient aircraft, not worrisome exactly, but not confidence-inspiring either. The men urge Bronwyn to take the front seat beside the pilot, and they load into the back with their gear.

"English?" Bronwyn asks the pilot.

"Oh yes! I am Pavel." He is ursine, with massive shoulders and massive enthusiasm and intense blue eyes that seem to suggest sharp vision.

"Bronwyn."

"I do not hear that name."

They rise quickly into the troposphere, Pavel shouting amiably over the helicopter's shuddering. "Hunter?" he asks her, laughing a little. "No, you are not hunter."

"Scientist," she says, surprising herself.

"You have cabin?"

"No, no cabin."

"You take tests?"

She nods. Tests of a sort, she supposes. He must wonder why she carries no equipment.

Pavel jerks his finger back at the hunters who are out of earshot. "The men, they want caribou," he says. "They think they find caribou. Caribou, ha." He finds this uproarious.

"There aren't many caribou?"

"You find caribou, I pay you. Ha, caribou."

Bronwyn stares down at the stretch of earth passing below them. Some areas are uniformly white with snow, others are mottled, peat and grass poking through. Not a single building or road, not a single human being. The sight fills her with yesteryear doubt, the doubt she thought she'd unloaded long ago.

After ten minutes the helicopter makes a rapid, nearly vertical descent and lands on a flat snowy area in front of a concrete cabin. The men leap out with their duffels and hurry away, waving and yelling, apparently thrilled to be where they are. Pavel and Bronwyn rise again and loneliness devours her. She shouldn't have come here alone, without Matt.

"You, where?" Pavel asks.

She peers down and sports a patch of peat without snow just ahead of them. "There," she says, the assertion bringing on a surge of bravery. Pavel again makes his move quickly, coming down on the grassy area with surprising finesse and reaching across her lap to unlatch the door.

"Two hours, right?" she says to Pavel. "How will you find me again?"

He rummages under his seat and comes up with a flashlight. "You hear me, you shine light. I navigate. GPS, I know."

She turns it on. The beam is assaultive. "Two hours," she insists. "No more than two hours."

"Two hours," Pavel says. "Okay."

"Okay." She stows the light in the deep pocket of her coat.

"You no freeze." Pavel removes his glove and holds out his hand. It is thick-knuckled and red and missing an entire pinkie finger just like Lubov's. "I freeze hand. I lose finger."

Pride prods her forth. She jumps out onto the spongy ice-crusted peat. The helicopter's madly spinning blades whap up a cyclone of tiny crystals and organic debris. The air is hibernal. With each breath it feels as if a razor blade is being lodged in her windpipe. Pavel waves, rises, and evaporates into the distance like an apparition.

The departing helicopter has stolen all sound. Even the light wind doesn't whisper, nor does the porous peat on which she stands. For a moment she has the sensation she has gone deaf. She takes a few steps and is relieved to hear sound kick in again, the rustling of the grass, the suck of moisture, a conversation beginning. She traverses the *talik*, an unfrozen section of the surface. Beneath there could be freezing to a depth of a thousand feet.

She shouldn't walk so far that Pavel can't locate her, but she has to move to stay warm, and walking is the best way to learn the land. Alone here, she is uncommonly aware of being alive. The sound of her footsteps, the rustle of her coat. To be alive is to be powerful like every other human and every animal, despite what Diane sometimes makes her feel. Living creatures wield energy and will. Under the shelter of her sable coat her blood courses quickly, a river with multiple currents, many rivers, undiscovered capabilities. Her spirits soar. The sun, prevailing over the clouds, is angled now, but there is still plenty of daylight.

A hundred feet in one direction, a hundred feet back. She traces the same path again and again. This bog, formed in the last ice age, is a large carbon sink storing billions of tons of methane. It needs more clathrates to retain a firmer grip on itself.

She closes her eyes, walking blind for several yards to augment her hearing, hoping for a stronger message from this earth. What is the language of a peat bog? Does it heave and sigh, clatter and crack? Does it emit some sound she cannot imagine, like the singing sands of certain deserts? Does it have a will of its own as fire does, as thunder and lightning do? The conversation she thought had begun has shut down. She hears only her own movement, no voices rising from the earth. She notes her impatience and tries to keep it in check.

She stops and opens her eyes. A small rodent is disappearing behind a grassy hillock. A vole perhaps. It's a surprise, but it shouldn't be. There is plenty of wildlife here, camouflaged though it is. She thinks of Pavel, *Caribou, ha.*

Twenty minutes have passed since she was dropped off. There is no pressure, she tells herself. No one but Pavel knows she is here. She wishes she had her backpack with food, water, space blankets; it was short-sighted to leave it back in the room, but she couldn't risk running into Matt and Diane.

The wind of low-swooping wings. A gruff call. A snowy owl has come in for a landing on a slight rise fifty feet away. It continues to call out, a throaty sound like the bark of a dog. It isn't mating season, but her presence is probably a good reason for distress. Does this owl know or care that the permafrost is melting? Has it adjusted to new norms? Would it be harmed by her abrupt intervention? They stare each other down. The owl hoots again. It isn't at all soothing, not like the long comforting call of her Great Horned Owl at home on the Squamscott River. This owl stands its ground and she stands hers. She is stilled by the owl's imperious gaze, that of a predator who will take what he wants without shame. The bird's eyes are yellow, almost amber, such an unusual color that she wonders if he has special gifts beyond the exceptional sight of his species. Can he see her terror? Could he be mistaking her for prey?

"Hello?" she calls, indulging a sudden need to hear her own voice. Her cheeks and tongue are numb so the word slurs and thuds dully into the air, repeating in her mind—*hello, hello, hello*—pathetically helpless.

Moments later, the owl takes off, flying low to the ground like a drone, his wing-span shockingly wide. She is no threat to him and he has voles to seek. As soon as he is out of sight she breathes more easily, but she misses him too. She misses the vole. She misses the heartbeat of another living creature.

63

"You're a bold woman taking on Dmitry Retivov." Tim Thom steps across the jamb and perches his narrow bottom against the edge of the desk. He puzzles over Diane. She says nothing.

"You overheard?" he says.

She nods. Beside her Matt's head is bowed, an expression of guilt she wishes he would resist.

"How did you expect to get into the files? They're all encrypted, you know."

Of course they would be encrypted. How did she fail to think of that? Her rage blocked her from thinking that far ahead. She shrugs and in the silence her body gives in to a terrible wilting. Could this be the first sign of the flu? No, it's worse. The wilting is a symptom of defeat. She isn't good at breaking rules. She never has been. But that doesn't make her any nobler than John Fiorini of UCLA who, slave to ambition, was a despicable liar and rule breaker and bluff artist, and had no qualms about deceiving colleagues and peers.

Thom moves to the door and closes it, then sits on the desk, legs dangling, pants riding up to reveal his spindly, yellow-socked ankles. "I'm in charge here, you know. While Retivov is out of commission."

"I understand. I'll go." Diane stands, determined to depart as quickly and proudly as she can, keep the damage to a minimum. She has never felt so depraved. It's nauseating to think of herself this way, as a dissembler, an impossible way to live in the long run. Could she ask Tim Thom to keep this between them? He has no real power over her, not really, despite being nominally in charge. Matt is already in the hallway, but she remains fixed in place, selecting judicious words.

"I hope you don't feel compelled to share this—incident," she says.

"Share it? Please sit." She doesn't sit; how can she sit? Thom continues. "I think you've misunderstood me. There is no love lost between me and Dr. Retivov. He's a difficult man, to say the least. I've only been put in charge because I'm the only one standing."

"Yes."

"I told him I haven't seen you. I thought you heard me."

"Yes, I heard. But I didn't presume—"

"Dr. Fenwick, I'm assuming you want the same thing I want—the unhindered practice of scientific research. Accuracy, efficiency, transparency?"

"Yes."

"Well then, how can I help you?"

Matt watches from the hallway. She wishes he'd come back in here and help her figure out if this is some kind of elaborate trap. Are Thom and Retivov in bed in ways she can't begin to imagine? Is this a test of her professional behavior, her moral fiber? But there's nothing immoral in wanting access to one's data, data that belongs not only to her, but to all the members of the Arctic Cloud Project, and to the larger scientific community, and ultimately to the entire world.

"What brings you here? What does your research involve?" she asks Thom, stalling, yes, but also truly wanting to know. What *are* his allegiances? Is he really just another scientist like her, doing his best to learn how the world works? Or is he working here for covert and dubious reasons?

He hesitates, and she recognizes the hesitation. When someone asks about her work she always questions how truly interested they are. So often the person is asking only to be polite. A moment passes. Then he begins to speak.

"I'm with the Climatic Research Unit at East Anglia University. We've been taking our inspiration from the remarkable work of Jason Box and his Dark Snow Project. We're looking at the composition of dark snow here in Siberia, taking surface samples monthly from various locations, analyzing them to see what kinds of algae are growing, what kinds of industrial pollutants are present, how much soot we see from wildfires, etcetera."

Her body centers itself a little, the nausea recedes. Tim Thom *is* a real scientist, he *does* care about the work. Matt has come to the doorway and also listens intently.

"Like Box we've used a portable spectrometer to determine how the snow's reflectivity has been affected. And we've been coordinating our results with what NASA is bringing back from its CALIPSO satellite. The results have been similar to Box's. Not surprising, of course. But very appalling."

Diane nods. "It *is* appalling. The last surface methane measurements we got from here showed a sudden dramatic spike. Very worrisome. Especially when you think about all those new *bulgunyakh* that have been discovered. It's only a matter of time before they'll explode."

They shake their heads with the disbelief of mourners.

"Well—" Thom pauses. "Shall we have a look?"

She barely nods. Of course she'd like to look, that's why she's here. And just because it's Tim Thom who is standing over the computer typing in passwords and opening files, just because she has not made the request outright, just because she is so overcome with the trepidation and doubt that she finally has to look away, does not make her any less culpable.

"I think you can probably take it from here," he says.

She looks at the screen, seeing at last files she recognizes in the form they've always been transmitted, labels in English. "Oh my god, I can't thank you enough."

He smiles down at her, clearly proud of himself. "You would do the same."

"Of course," she says, hoping she would.

"But work quickly. Retivov is unpredictable. He could get it in his head to show up."

"All these consoles connect to the same server?"

He nods.

"Would you mind opening the same files on this computer next to me so my assistant can help me? And is there a printer we could use?"

"I wouldn't risk printing. To do that we would have to get Svetlana involved. I don't think that's wise." He digs into his pocket and pulls out several USB flash drives. "I thought you might be able to use these."

She shakes her head in relief and disbelief—he's thought of everything. "I can't thank you enough."

He unlocks the files on the adjacent computer. "I'll be across the hall," he says. "Give me a shout if you need me."

She watches him leave with such a tidal swelling of gratitude it might almost be mistaken for love.

Matt sits beside her. "What are we looking for here?"

It doesn't matter that he isn't a scientist. He can help her download the most critical files to the flash drives. They work in silence in the windowless room, clicking and writing, Svetlana answering phones down the hallway, Thom puttering in his office across the hallway, the fluorescents whirring overhead reminding them of the passing time, the importance of speed. She tries not to think of Retivov, propelled by professional animosity, rising from his sick bed, feverish and irrational. Only once in a while does she feel an existential twitch at the fact that just beyond these walls the unknowable world is ready to swallow them.

Meanwhile, the tundra continues to melt.

64

Her eyes water with the cold. Her nose runs. The moisture of her breath freezes on her scarf. At some point she might have to pee, but she can't think of that now. This cold has teeth, sharp as incisors. The tundra's face has come into full focus now. A silent, passive, withholding force that seems to come from the refrigerator of deep space, a force easily as powerful as fire. But her task here is a new one. In LA she sought to eliminate the fires entirely, just as she had earlier vanquished tornadoes and storms, but now she wants to assist the tundra, help it thrive, restore it to the way it's been for millennia. The question is how, as it seems to resist her.

What a fool she was to come out here unprepared. Her coat no longer feels like adequate armor, and beneath her leather boots and smart wool socks her feet have begun to ache. She tries not to think of Pavel and Lubov's lost pinkies.

She paces more quickly to goose her dwindling metabolism and in her quickened footsteps she hears Earl pounding out his hymns. What was it about Earl she loved so much? His open mind? His selflessness? She could have learned so much from him. She thinks of her mother, Maggie, who died before Bronwyn could really see who she was beyond a mother. She never expressed the fullness of her love for Maggie. She should have been more expressive. Is anyone ever expressive enough? She regrets that she left Diane and Matt without explaining herself. What if she were to die out here—Diane and Matt would never know the depth of her feelings for them.

The water from her eyes has morphed into tears which freeze on her cheeks, despite their salt. She cannot locate the place she generates heat internally. It feels as if some connection has been severed. How can she possibly bring a deeper freeze to the landscape when she is so near to freezing herself. She thinks of fire, lusts for it, imagines invoking it here, the seductive flames bringing light and heat to this fading day. She imagines the reviving power of fire, sees herself sitting in front of it, coaxing hands and feet back to full function. She should not be thinking of fire.

The sun emerges from a cloud and pulsates in its descent like an exposed beating heart. Her own heart thunders in her chest as if bent on breaking out. She collapses to her knees, then to her belly. Her bare cheek hits the earth. Fire, ice. Fire, ice.

Her heart and brain fuse and thud in unison, a rhythm that pushes out past her skin, past the sable pelt. Before her eyes is a strand of copper moss, coiled like pubic hair. It whispers, joining the rhythm. A star bursts into existence, another dies. A snapped mast on a ship in the Tiksi harbor. Lubov's brown trousers. Someone's husky laugh. The amber eyes of the Snowy Owl. Everything oscillates, a harmonious symphony, one voice then hundreds, thousands, an intricate polyphony. The vole, the Snowy Owl, the Great Horned Owl from the Squamscott River. A congress around her, her mother, Lanny, Earl and Archie, Matt and Diane, Lubov and Pavel. The girl with the green eyes. Her heart is ruled by the heart of the Earth which heaves and cracks and teaches her its cadences. She isn't fighting the land, she has become part of it. The fire inside her begins to build.

She disperses herself, becomes another thing, unbound by derma, somewhere between the coming and going. Ice and fire, love and hate, prey and predator, owl and vole, the thing measured and the thing known instinctively. Sun, moon, rock, water, mountain, abyss.

All her atoms were once assembled from atoms that might have been part of Byzantine rats, or Medieval monks, or Egyptian slaves, or Himalayan chickens. They might have been drawn from Congolese chimps and Brazilian samba dancers, from mavericks and scribes, farmers and statesmen, hookers and truckers. Now those conjoined atoms explode and, sundered from one another, are sent off without certainty of return to the entity that has been Bronwyn.

A tone fills her ears, singular but layered with many notes like the invisible waves that compose white light. Her head seems to explode, her self vaporizes. The fiery burst of her intention sinks energy downward and works over the molecules of peat, the icy clathrates and cryotic soil. The energy is white hot, prodigious, glowing, all the energy a human being can possibly hold and more. It spreads beneath the tundra in mammoth rolling waves, mile after mile. At the risk of losing her toes, her life, of never returning to the self she's been, she bolsters and fortifies the subterranean freeze.

65

Sifting through these documents, Matt finally understands his purpose in being here. It isn't only to keep Bronwyn and Diane from eating each other alive, he's here because he is the only neutral party, the one person who can see things objectively. Here at the converging vortex of battling passions and points of view, he may be the only one who can say what is happening—or what has happened.

He isn't afraid anymore, he likes being here in this strange and different place, so sparsely inhabited and yet so central to the fate of the entire world. For over two hours he has been working alongside Diane, sifting through the files methodically and copying them onto flash drives. And now his watchful, wait-and-see patience may be paying off. He has just, by accident, opened a folder labeled in Russian. A short document, dated May 15th of the current year, six months ago. He reads in English. *FINAL REPORT: The Arctic Cloud Project (USA) has been terminated after collecting the last of its data. It will be closed down by the end of the month.*

He taps the monitor, corralling and directing Diane's attention. She reads to herself, hissing quietly. "Christ almighty," she says. "That bastard."

"I thought—?" he says. "Why would they—?" But he already knows, without knowing anything specific. The worst fear has proved to be true. This is the dreaded possibility that has been floating in the air all along, the thing that has been preoccupying Diane since before they left, the possibility that the data blackout was considerably more than a technical slip-up.

66

She returns in twilight, lying on her back. The light that remains is that of an Impressionist pastel, pink cirrus on pale blue. She blinks and the blue becomes gray. She lies like a mummy, arms cinched at her sides, unsure if she's alive, her brain lobes knocking against one another, the light a shimmying gauze curtain.

She sits up, panicked. Cold has dumbed her, fear is dumbing her further. She would call out if it meant anything, but no one can hear. She claps her blockish hands together. Frostbite, she thinks, trying to wiggle her reticent toes. She applies her mouth to one mitten opening and blows inside. The breath is hot, wet, but her hand does not respond. She needs hands that function. She needs to move and think clearly. She needs rescue. Shouldn't Pavel have come back by now? Has she missed him?

Something rustles behind her. She forces herself to stand, whirls, eyes shredding the twilight. Nothing. Only the shadowy silhouettes of the grassy hillocks. It could be a vole, but it could be something much bigger too. A caribou. A wolf.

She feels like a half-wit, incapable of thinking things through, seeing consequences. It will be dark soon. The tundra snickers around her, a cauldron of inchoate sounds and fuzzy apparitions.

She remembers Pavel's flashlight, still in her pocket, but she cannot coil her hand to grip it. She bends at the waist, wags her hips, nudges the base of the pocket. The flashlight falls to the ground. She kneels, jamming her mittened hand against the switch. It doesn't budge. She tries again. Nothing happens. Her hands are crude instruments, no more effective than stiff sticks. She stares at the flashlight with irra-

tional hatred. On sudden impulse, she yanks off her mitten. Her dig-
its are white and bloodless, immobile. She jams her thumb into the
switch, once, twice. No go. Her cracked skin bleeds. She struggles the
mitten on again, feeling her blood crawl at such a glacial pace she can
almost picture it stopping. Leaning down, she brings her teeth to the
switch. The flashlight's cold metal attaches to her upper lip and steals
a slab of skin. With the full force of her ire she bites and pulls and
pushes, until pain shoots through her gums, her lips and chin bleed,
the light goes on.

She recoils. The beam is nuclear in its brightness and it places her
center stage, alone and blinded to everything around her. Hands like
tongs, she clamps the light between them and begins to walk, gripped
in the calipers of night.

She lusts for sleep. Above all, she mustn't sleep.

*One foot the other continuous motion filmy night a single star the
moon's sharp tip pricking a cloud an arabesque voices hushed legato
lullaby the Earth's long aria she a single note blinking blinking*

The white fox smiles out of the darkness, taking her in. What does
the fox say? She regards him. He is not large, but he is commanding,
with magnificent fur, thick and pure white, his tail a plume in the air.
Such sentient stillness. What does the fox say? He speaks through prescient eyes in the plain-spoken way of animals. *Where are your people?
You shouldn't be alone.* His tail swishes back and forth, a semaphore.
What does he know? *Speak, please. Tell me what you know.* He blinks,
she blinks. The night percusses around them.

The fox is gone, vaporized.

No, please, don't go.

His shape lingers, an aura etched on the night, engraved in her
brain. She tries to see what he said—feel it. She waits, trembling, her
legs giving way, no longer capable of doing the supportive work of legs.
But Matt is beside her. *Oh thank you for coming.* She lets him take her
weight, lower her to safety. *Oh, Matt.* She isn't alone. *See, fox, I am not
alone.*

Sleep lumbers in noisily, an insistent mother.

67

In the cab on the way back to Lubov's Diane cannot stop shaking. What shocks her is not that people are doing underhanded things. She has always realized that criminal activity and all its more minor corollaries—lying and cheating—were commonly practiced by many human beings. She herself has just now done something that could be called illegal. It will certainly be considered illegal if Retivov finds out, and it is quite likely he will find out, though hopefully not until she's safely back in the U.S. No, what truly shocks her is that people like Retivov and all his ilk—profit-seeking oil moguls, coal producers, high-rolling car company CEOs, and so many others—appear not to care at all what happens to Earth.

Doesn't Retivov get it? He's a geologist for god's sake. Doesn't he understand how soon the Earth's surface will be a free-for-all, plagued by severe weather beyond the control or predictive skill of human beings? Parched beyond recognition, huge land masses will become playgrounds for fires and dust storms. The warmed atmosphere will be so oversaturated with moisture that the rainfalls will be voluminous and violent enough to kill. Frequent winds will reach stunning gale-force speeds and will agitate themselves into surface tornadoes. Glaciers will become a distant memory, and the ice caps on both poles will disappear, subjecting coastlines to such severe flooding they will no longer be habitable. No, she's wrong—there is no future tense here, it is happening already.

Death, Dmitry Retivov, will become a frequent visitor in most people's lives. Need I enumerate the ways you and your dear ones might die? If violent weather isn't your preferred avenue to death, perhaps

you'd choose to perish more slowly from famine. Crops become pee-
vish on a parched, too-warm Earth, forget livestock. Food supplies will
dwindle quickly and eventually become so scarce even the wealthy will
struggle. And need I remind you how badly human beings get along in
conditions of extreme scarcity? Opportunistic viruses will thrive under these conditions, replicating and mutating too quickly for humans
to develop vaccines. Ebola is just the beginning. Viruses always trump
humans—you should know that, Dmitry Retivov, you're a scientist. It
is a sad future out there, unless we act. Can't you see?

But of course he does see. This is what angers her so much. While
some people are simply ignorant, or victims of impoverished imagination, Dmitry Retivov is not one of those people. If he's any kind of a scientist at all he sees the data clearly, he understands its import, and he
wants to suppress it for that very reason. No, she is quite sure Dmitry
Retivov does not suffer from a failure of knowledge, or understanding,
or even imagination. His deficit is a failure of empathy. He doesn't *care*
that the human race is facing extinction. This is what galls her.

She must contain herself for the time being. She and Matt and Tim
Thom must not breathe a word of what they know. Except to Bronwyn,
of course. She hopes these new revelations will reconnect Bronwyn to
the world of science. It doesn't surprise her that Bronwyn, prickly as
she was last night, didn't join them today, but she will certainly share
Diane's shock. Now that they've secured the data it's time for an intervention from Bronwyn. As soon as possible. Diane will rebook the
helicopter immediately. This is all-out war and the time has come for
action.

After so much time in the windowless room, they've lost track of
time, and when they return to Lubov's it is past 3:15 p.m. The sun is
all but gone. The apartment feels hollow, empty, the windows smeared
useless with condensation. The radiator rattles as if it's on its last legs.
Matt checks the bedroom. No Bronwyn. No note beyond the one from
this morning. Diane collapses into a chair in the living room. Bronwyn's absence disappoints her and makes her feel bereft—she has so
much to say to Bronwyn she can barely contain herself. She takes off

her coat, suddenly hungry. Another day with no lunch. Maybe Bronwyn is downstairs having something to eat with Lubov.

"Let's ask Lubov where she is."

Matt stands by the table, strangely still. He still wears his coat and seems to have shrunk and blanched beneath it. "Shit," he says. "Shit, shit, shit. I should have known."

Downstairs in the kitchen he listens to Lubov and Diane hashing things out. Though he only understands the occasional word, they are confirming what he already knows. Of course she has gone out on her own. He should have realized she wasn't ever going to allow him to accompany her. She only agreed to that in order to appease him and Diane. But has she no sense of self-preservation? Having seen her at the fire he seriously doubts she does. She didn't die then, but she so easily could have. Now it's almost dark for fuck's sake, and who knows where she is. She could be anywhere out there. It could be night before they find her. She's gone to the airport, Lubov is saying.

He lets out an involuntary sound, the beginning of a wail, then cuts it short, embarrassed in front of these women. How the hell did he end up falling in love with such a determined loner?

They sit in the cab, bundled and stiff. Diane, incapable of small talk, doesn't bother to chat with the cabbie, or with Matt. She has a very bad feeling. This is the land of Murphy's Law. She is coming to hate these Russians. What can go wrong already has gone wrong, there is no future tense about it.

Matt is hyperkinetic, drumming his knee with his mitten, lightly but audibly clamping his teeth. She wishes he'd stop—the sounds are blades on her nerves—but she's not going to tell him to stop. He's probably blaming himself as much as she's blaming herself. They should have thought to wonder why Bronwyn didn't join them at the weather station.

The sun's battery is long dead when the cab drops them at the terminal and they make their way to the desk of the helicopter outfit. As she feared, there is not a soul in evidence. She knew this was a small operation, but it is also the only game in town. A double helix of desperation and rage twirls inside her, and she suppresses an urge to yell. Instead she pounds the desk uselessly. Matt is poking around, peering through the glass to the runway where a helicopter stands in darkness on its bird-like feet.

"I'm going outside to find someone," he says. He pushes through the door. God knows why he expects to find anyone out there.

Diane goes behind the desk to the closed door. It's locked. She pounds. "Open up! Open up!" Have they really closed up for the day? She puts her ear to the door, hoping to hear voices. She can't tell if she does or doesn't. She stands still for a moment without any idea of what to do. Has she ever not known what to do? A problem solver, she always has a notion of what should be done next, but now—no plan of action comes to mind at all.

She pounds again, calling out in a register that is inadvertently hysterical, an ululation. Desperation has banished all traces of embarrassment. She hasn't cried since she was seven years old, but now she cries.

As if the world was simply waiting for her breakdown, voices become audible behind the door. She pounds again, sobbing in a wet and helpless way that she will recall for years to come, sobs inflaming her nose and throat and chest, a weeping that infects her entire body so her circulatory system is amped and all her orifices exude moisture along with sorrow.

A woman opens the door so suddenly Diane almost falls against her. She wears a uniform and is shocked, or maybe disgusted, by the sight of Diane in this state. Diane tries to pull herself together. She begins to speak in Russian, but quickly reverts to English.

"We need a helicopter," Diane says. "Now."

Without a word the woman disappears.

It takes forever for the woman to reappear, but she finally emerges from behind the door accompanied by a towering man, burly and genial.

"Pavel will help you," says the woman.

Pavel explodes through the door, shoving a final bite into his mouth. His face is slick with sweat. How can anyone sweat so profusely in this climate? Still chewing and swallowing, he glances at his watch and lays his heavy arm around Diane's back in a gesture of reassurance. "It is time, yes," he says. She smells the alcohol on his breath. "We find your friend."

He lurches through the door to the runway, clearly drunk. Diane and Matt have no choice but to follow. It is truly dark now, but a light snaps on and its beam illuminates the helicopter which presides, beast-like, over the runway.

"Do you think he's going to fly us?" Diane asks Matt.

"It looks that way."

"But he's drunk."

"Do we have a choice? If she's out there. In the dark. In this cold."

Matt is keeping his cool so much better than she herself is, Diane thinks. Pavel guides them as if they are his flock, his arms wings. He unlocks the helicopter and they clamber aboard. Matt takes the front seat beside Pavel. Diane sits behind them, thinking this expedition in this ancient aircraft, piloted by a drunk, is yet another example of her increasingly poor judgment. Is Pavel going to plummet them to their demise on the tundra? All her life she has taken calculated risks, assessing cost and benefit, downplaying her own fear of flying as well as she could. But Matt is right. They have no choice now. If they hope to find Bronwyn, they must take this risk. Diane bows her head as the helicopter scrapes into action. She has been in plenty of small planes before to gather data, but never a craft that rattled and shook and roared as much as this thing does. Matt makes conversation with Pavel. Thank god the man speaks English. The engine is too loud for her to hear what they're saying. She pokes her head through the seats and taps Matt.

"What's going on?"

"He says he knows exactly where he left her. Not far."

Diane harrumphs. "I can't believe this. His license should be revoked. Tell him that."

Matt says something to Pavel, and Pavel guffaws and waves his hand. They sail through an absolute darkness. The helicopter might just as well be a space capsule, a place set apart, beyond the Earth's atmosphere, no longer subject to the sun's rising and setting. She re-members a Wellesley colleague of hers, Jack Finley, who was a heavy drinker and finally went into rehab. For months after he joined AA he would stop people on campus to apologize for this or that. At the time it was embarrassing, as he was apologizing for things no one had no-ticed or remembered, things they certainly didn't feel hurt by. But she feels that same urge now, to make amends. *I hope you know, Bronwyn, how much you mean to me, and how much I respect you.*

"There!" Matt calls. "I see something—a light, I'm sure."

Matt peers through the seats at Diane and offers a hopeful smile. The helicopter begins its descent.

68

She dreams of the white fox, the flag of his tail and his prescient eyes. Again he speaks without words so, though she knows he's saying something important, she can't make out what it is. Awake, she probes the image, looking for meaning that doesn't arrive.

Matt and Diane and Lubov come and go with hot water bottles, hot tea, more layers of blankets and quilts and fresh pillows. She hears their hushed voices, glimpses their worried eyes, feels their gentle ministrations, but cannot organize a response. The apparatus of speech— tongue, lips, cheeks—is not working, words are alien. She cannot even eke out a smile. She stares up at them dumbly, hoping her eyes can reassure them she's fine.

How she loves them. These people have believed in her so solidly, taken such risks to help her out. How she loves the whole world as never before. The Earth and all its creatures. She wiggles her fingers and toes, all seemingly intact. Miraculous really, as she remembers the intractability of that cold abrading her skin, gouging her insides, making her crack and bleed. Her face isn't right. It is huge, impounded as a root vegetable. Her lips are split. But her own heat saved her, she thinks, the energy she has learned to coalesce.

There was warning in the fox's gaze. Was he telling her she was wrong to do what she did? Was he accusing? Not exactly that, but something like that. *Where are your people?*

She did what she hoped she could do. She felt the earth responding, heaving, tightening, groaning as it froze. It can't be measured accurately, not completely, and it won't be repeated, that she is sure of. Not by her. She can't be a one-woman band traveling the earth to right the wrongs done to it. Refreezing glaciers, resurrecting depleted rivers, recovering lost islands, holding off rising oceans. It isn't work for a single individual. Was that what the fox was telling her? *Where are your people?*

If he didn't know better he'd think she'd been in a brawl. She lies on her belly, concealed under the quilts but for one side of her face, its cheek a mottled red and yellow, the lips swollen and cracked. He can hardly stand to think of her out there on the tundra, subjecting herself to the morbid cold, invoking her powers with arms outstretched like an eagle, as she did on that promontory in California. She looked to him otherworldly then, like a goddess almost, so much larger than the tiny woman he sees in the bed now. Did she accomplish what she wanted to accomplish? He doesn't care. She's here, alive.

She has been sleeping for hours, even as they soaked her hands and feet in warm water, laid warming rags on her chest and belly. Every once in a while she opens her eyes and smiles vaguely, and they have been able to coax her to take a few sips of hot tea. But she is not herself yet. Diane reports that Lubov says she will recover fully, Lubov claims to have seen this reaction to the cold many times, this extreme need to sleep. Lubov herself has survived extreme cold and lost her finger to frostbite. *Let her sleep,* Lubov urges. Matt remembers how long she slept after the fires. He feels like a gruff old man who, having almost lost everything, is broken open with gratitude, undone by love, ready at last to live a more authentic life for whatever time remains.

She stirs in the sheets, opens her eyes, turns onto her back and sees him. She doesn't say a word, but her eyes bulge, as if she is using them to speak. She opens and closes her lips. She nods slightly then succumbs again to the lure of sleep. He is suddenly aware of Diane standing behind him.

That poor battered face, Diane thinks. To think that they were working away in Retivov's office, oblivious, while she was out on the tundra ready to sacrifice herself. Of course Diane can't help herself from wanting to know what Bronwyn did out there, but she pushes that curiosity from her mind for now. What matters is that Bronwyn could have died and didn't.

How humbled Diane feels, how contrite. She was a fool to think that bringing Bronwyn here to do her work would be anything more than a stopgap measure. The melting permafrost is only a fraction of the overall carbon problem. Worse, why has it taken her so long to see Bronwyn clearly, not as another gifted scientist, but as the truly rare human being she is. What blindness in trying to mold and control a person who possesses something so remarkable, a knowledge that far surpasses Diane's own data-dependent understanding of the world. Bronwyn has moved beyond the usual limits of ordinary human capability, disregarded conventional notions of what is possible, acting on some occult knowledge inaccessible to most human beings. Long ago, when humans navigated by the stars, they might have known some of what Bronwyn knows. Diane is quite sure the repercussions of this experience will echo in her own life for a long time to come, personally and professionally, even if she can't now say exactly how. But things will change, she already feels it.

Hours later, on the cusp of dawn, she comes to him on the couch in a dream, lifting the heavy comforter and slipping effortlessly beneath as apparitions do. Eyes closed, he wills himself to stay asleep and continue dreaming. Warm feet stroke his shins. Hair tickles his cheek. He opens his eyes on her face, no dream face, the real thing, her green eyes singular and gleaming in the gray light, her body naked and throwing off shocking heat, a tiny furnace of a human being. Skeins of her warmth encircle him, as if she seeks to rearrange his insides as she does with the elements. He chuckles. His insides have long ago been rearranged. He holds her lightly, afraid of inflicting damage. She whispers in his ear, halting between words, as if she has only now discovered speech. "The fox," she says.

"What fox?" He searches her face, aroused, afraid, elated, trying to understand.

"You are my people." She presses a finger into his clavicle. "You," she insists.

"Of course." How fragile she is, yet not at all fragile. She has survived and is here beside him, pumping out heat.

They make love as if for the first time, both remembering the different people they were in New Hampshire, only half as alive, nothing like now, on fire in the Arctic.

69

The three walk slowly to the water, arms linked, Bronwyn in the center, flanked by Matt and Diane. The sky is ballerina pink and a light snow falls, filling the air like chimes. Around them, the collapsing buildings, dogs foraging in the trash, the silhouettes of the foundering ships. Through the desolation of it all, traces of beauty shimmer.

They breathe deeply, their outgoing breath visible and merging in the air then rising, majestic as murmurations of soaring starlings. There is a new fixity in their vision as they stand together and gaze out over the Port of Tiksi, picturing themselves at the top of the world.

Bronwyn listens and hears the Earth humming. Best home. Beautiful world.

ACKNOWLEDGMENTS

While it is true that the writing of a novel is mostly a solitary endeavor, it's the rare novel that comes to fruition without help from other people. When the idea for *Weather Woman* came to me, it was immediately apparent that I would have to educate myself about meteorology, scientific research in the academy, climate change, etc. I am hugely grateful to the many people who shared their expertise with me. Early brainstorming with biologist Don McElroy was very validating—he made me believe my idea might not be as crazy as I initially thought. Dr. Robert Rauber, Professor of Atmospheric Sciences at the University of Illinois, graciously addressed my long list of questions about science research, funding, and teaching at a university. Dr. Jason Box, climatologist, glaciologist, and professor at the Geological Survey of Denmark and Greenland (dubbed "The Ice Maverick" by *Rolling Stone*), is the first person I have come to know through Twitter. He encouraged me to come with him on a trip to Greenland where he was the resident scientist, and since then he has, in addition to being a friend, been an ongoing source of information and inspiration regarding climate change in the Arctic. Candace Campos, formerly a "Weather Woman" at KVAL in Eugene, Oregon, now at News 6 in Orlando, Florida, was open and enthusiastic about sharing day-to-day details of her job. She brought me onto the set, explained her training and duties at length, and shared her dramatic story about being inspired to be a weather woman while in Miami during Hurricane Andrew.

Many people I've never met were also extremely useful sources of information and inspiration. A series of excellent Great Courses lectures given by Dr. Robert Fovell, Professor of Atmospheric and Oceanic Sciences at UCLA—"Meteorology: An Introduction the Wonders of the Weather"—was an invaluable resource. Numerous books became touchstones: Elizabeth Kolbert's *The Sixth Extinction* and *Field Notes from a Catastrophe*, Bill McKibben's *Eaarth*, Naomi Klein's *This Changes Everything*, Craig Childs's *Apocalyptic Planet: Field Guide to the Future of the Earth*, Fred Pearce's *With Speed and Violence*, Lynne McTaggart's *The Intention Experiment*, and Gavin Pretor-Pinney's gem of a book about clouds, *The Cloud Collector's Handbook*. An early inspiration from my childhood was Oliver Butterworth's *The Trouble with Jenny's Ear*.

In the realm of cheerleading, moral support, early reading and critiquing, the ranks are strong. Thanks to Don McElroy and Charlene Decker, Dave and Becky Dusseau, Andrea Schwartz-Feit, Rebecca Nachison, Michele Hoffnung, Ellen Greenhouse, Katherine Guenther, Ruth Knafo-Setton, Brian Juenemann, Patty Emmons, and Ebe Emmons, all of whom read and responded to early drafts. I am deeply grateful. And special thanks to my hilarious and supportive writing group pals Miriam Gershow and Debra Gwartney.

Every book needs a team to shepherd it to print and into the marketplace. The people at Red Hen Press have been a delight to work with: Hannah Moye, Alisa Trager, Keaton Maddox, Deirdre Collins, Becky Hausdorff, Natasha McClellan, Rebeccah Sanhueza, Monica Fernandez, Tobi Harper, Mark Cull, and the inimitable Kate Gale. Without the tireless work and encouragement of my agent and friend Deborah Schneider I would still be languishing in the slush pile. No one could possibly be more appreciative, perceptive, and persistent than she. My gratitude is huge.

Then there is Paul Calandrino, my *hayati*, who supports me in so many ways it would take days to enumerate, and whose presence infuses everything I do with joy and meaning.

1. The novel explores issues related to mentorship. Bronwyn has
   benefitted from Diane Fenwick's interest and help, but as the
   novel begins their relationship begins to encounter problems.
   How do Bronwyn and Diane each play a role in the difficul-
   ties? Do mentorship relationships have a shelf life? How do you
   imagine Bronwyn and Diane's relationship continuing in the
   future?

2. Vince is another mentor for Bronwyn, though she has not met
   him and he knows nothing about her. How does her disappointment in him motivate her?

3. Each of the main characters in the book comes to believe in
   Bronwyn's power at a different rate. Some, like Earl, are quick
   to accept what she does. Others, like Diane, are very reluctant
   believers. If you had a friend like Bronwyn, who claimed to
   be able to change the weather, what would you need to see or
   know to believe her?

4. How do Bronwyn's early experiences as a child in New Jersey
   lead her to see the world differently from most people?

5. Why do Matt and Bronwyn fall for each other?

6. Bronwyn has two brief but important encounters near the end
   of the novel, one with the girl, Vera, and the other with the

white fox. What is the impact of each of these encounters? How do they change Bronwyn?

7. The novel portrays people who understand the world in different ways. Diane understands the world through the lens of science, Earl through the lens of religion, while Bronwyn understands things intuitively. What are the advantages and limitations of each of these modes of understanding?

8. Bronwyn's ability to affect the weather involves a process of summoning colossal internal energy. It is highly unlikely that most human beings could do what Bronwyn does. However, many people claim to be able to change aspects of themselves with the power of thought. Some athletes have used visualization techniques to improve their performance. Himalayan monks studied by Harvard researchers have been found to be able to raise their body temperatures and lower their metabolism all with the power of their thought. Do you believe that the human mind has untapped capabilities? Have you ever experimented with the power of your own thought?

9. Human beings have not been able to reverse global warming, but they have been able to affect local weather in limited ways, using techniques like cloud seeding to produce rain. Do you think it is advisable for human beings to attempt to control natural forces in this way? Do you think we should rely on technology to get global warming under control (with techniques of carbon capture still in development), or do you think human beings will change their behaviors enough to avert major global warming disasters?

10. If you had Bronwyn's power, what would you do with it? If you could have any superpower of your choosing, what would it be and why?

11. Diane has had a successful career as an atmospheric scientist, but Bronwyn feels, despite her smarts, inadequate in Diane's world. Do you think Bronwyn could have had a career in science if she had persisted? What does the novel show us about women in science?

Biographical Note

Cai Emmons is the author of the novels *His Mother's Son* and *The Stylist*. A graduate of Yale University, with MFAs from New York University and the University of Oregon, Cai is formerly a playwright and screenwriter. Her short work has appeared in such publications as *TriQuarterly*, *Narrative*, and *Arts & Letters*, among others. She teaches in the University of Oregon's Creative Writing Program.